# CRITICAL
# CONDITION

# OTHER BOOKS BY RICHARD L. MABRY, M.D.

*Stress Test*

*Heart Failure*

*Code Blue*

*Medical Error*

*Diagnosis Death*

*Lethal Remedy*

# ACCLAIM FOR RICHARD L. MABRY, M.D.

"A riveting medical suspense tale from an author at the top of his game. If you love thrillers then you must be reading Richard's books."

— Jordyn Redwood, author of the
Bloodline Trilogy

"Packed with thrills, *Stress Test* is a lightning-paced read that you'll read in one breath."

— Tess Gerritsen, *New York Times*
best-selling author of *Last to Die*

"Original and profound. I found the Christian message engaging and fascinating, and the story a thrill a minute."

— Michael Palmer, *New York Times*
best-selling author of *Oath of
Office*, regarding *Stress Test*

"Sirens, scalpels, and the business end of a revolver—*Stress Test* offers Code 3 action and a prescription for hope."

— Candace Calvert, best-selling
author of *Code Triage* and *Trauma
Plan*

"Vintage Mabry. *Heart Failure* weaves an intricate plot of mystery and suspense that will leave you guessing until the final page."

— Billy Coffey, author of *When
Mockingbirds Sing*

"*Stress Test* comes with a warning: Prepare to stop life until you finish the last page."

— Diann Mills, author of *The Chase*
and *The Survivor*

"Recurring legal, medical, and romantic thrills. Diagnosis: Pure entertainment."

— James Scott Bell, award-winning
suspense author

"Mabry's latest provides fast-paced, edge-of-your-seat action and suspense. His medical knowledge is evident in the realistic and detailed characters and scenes."

— *RT Book Reviews*, 4 1/2 star review
of *Stress Test*

"The plot moves along with plenty of action and empathy, and there's suspense and suspicion enough to keep readers zipping to the last pages."

— *Publishers Weekly* review of
*Stress Test*

# CRITICAL CONDITION

## RICHARD L. MABRY, M.D.

THOMAS NELSON
*Since 1798*

NASHVILLE   DALLAS   MEXICO CITY   RIO DE JANEIRO

Published in Nashville, Tennessee, by Thomas Nelson. Thomas Nelson is a registered trademark of HarperCollins Christian Publishing, Inc.

Published in association with the literary agency of WordServe Literary Group, Ltd., 10152 S. Knoll Circle, Highlands Ranch, CO 80130. www.wordserveliterary.com.

Thomas Nelson titles may be purchased in bulk for educational, business, fund-raising, or sales promotional use. For information, please e-mail SpecialMarkets@ThomasNelson.com.

Publisher's Note: This novel is a work of fiction. Names, characters, places, and incidents are either products of the author's imagination or are used fictitiously. All characters are fictional, and any similarity to people living or dead is purely coincidental.

Scripture quotations are from the NEW AMERICAN STANDARD BIBLE®, Copyright © 1960, 1962, 1963, 1968, 1971, 1972, 1973, 1975, 1977, 1995 by The Lockman Foundation. Used by permission.

**Library of Congress Cataloging-in-Publication Data**

Mabry, Richard L.
 Critical condition / Richard L. Mabry, M.D.
  pages cm
 Summary: "Dr. Frasier couldn't save the gunshot victim on her front lawn. Now she's fighting for her own life. It began as a quiet dinner party honoring Dr. Shannon Frasier's colleague, but became a nightmare when a man was shot on her lawn, reviving emotions from a similar episode a decade ago. Then a midnight call from her sister, Megan, causes Shannon to fear that her sister is on drugs again. Her "almost-fiancé" Dr. Mark Gilbert's support only adds to Shannon's feelings of guilt, since she can't bring herself to fully commit to him. She turns for help to her pastor-father, only to learn that he's just been diagnosed with leukemia. Shannon thought it couldn't get any worse. Then the late-night, threatening phone calls begin, the rough voice asking, "What did he say before he died?" With everything around her in a critical state, simply staying alive will require all the resources and focus Shannon has"— Provided by publisher.
 ISBN 978-1-4016-8740-3 (pbk.)
 1. Women physicians—Fiction. I. Title.
 PS3613.A2C75 2014
 813'.6—dc23                                                                                                    2013041288

*Printed in the United States of America*

14 15 16 17 18 19 RRD 6 5 4 3 2 1

*For the folks who got me started on my road to writing: Al, Jim, Gayle, Rachelle, Barbara, and Kay (to name only a few)*

# PROLOGUE

THE VALET PARKING ATTENDANT ASSISTED SHANNON FRASIER from the car, and she pulled her sweater tighter around her against the gusty autumn wind. "Todd, this place looks expensive."

Todd Richardson made his way around the car and took Shannon's hand. "Yes, but I hear the food's wonderful."

As they walked down the canopied sidewalk toward the leaded glass doors, Shannon said, "But if it's too expensive . . ."

Todd grinned down at her. He shook his head and a few strands of dark hair dropped onto his forehead. "Don't worry. I can handle it." The grin became a smile, and Shannon's heart rate sped up, as it always did. "I just got a nice promotion, with a significant boost in salary. On the other hand, you're not going to be earning anything until you get out of medical school. You deserve something nice every once in a while."

"I'm proud of you for getting the promotion," Shannon said. "And the bigger salary would be nice if . . ." She let the words trail off. When Todd was ready to ask the question that was on both their minds, he would. Meanwhile, she'd just enjoy tonight.

Todd seemed to read her mind. "I know what you're thinking," Todd said. "We can talk about it—"

Shannon felt the tug on her arm a split second after she heard the gunshot. She felt, more than saw, Todd crumple to the ground beside her. When she looked down, he lay on his side, eyes wide, a stunned expression on his face. His lips barely parted as he whispered, "Help me."

Shannon knelt, making no attempt to avoid the blood pooling beneath Todd. She screamed at the top of her lungs. "Help! My boyfriend's been shot! Call 911! Someone please help!" She yanked off her sweater, hoping somehow to stanch the bleeding, but she couldn't see the source.

A man, well dressed and with a smattering of gray at his temples, hurried over. "Someone's calling 911 right now." He knelt on one knee beside Todd. "I'm a doctor. Let me see what I can do."

When Shannon later tried to reconstruct the events that followed, she couldn't. She was certain the paramedics arrived. She must have talked with the police. But her next clear memory was of two men in dark coveralls zipping Todd's lifeless form into a body bag and lifting it onto a wheeled stretcher.

The doctor, his bloody hands hanging at his sides, stepped between her and the gruesome scene. "Don't look."

Shannon nodded dumbly.

"I'm sorry," the doctor said. "Sometimes there's just nothing you can do. I tried." Then, as much to himself as to her, he said in a low voice, "That was all I could do. All any doctor could do."

Gradually, the reality dawned on Shannon. In an instant her future with Todd, a future they'd planned together since high school, had vanished. Todd's life had ended and hers had forever changed, all in the space of a second, all because of a single gunshot.

It wasn't that she'd never seen death before. Just today she and three other students had stood in the gross anatomy lab on either side of a cadaver, dissecting, probing, examining, in preparation for lives spent as doctors. But this wasn't a cadaver. This was the man she loved. This was death, up close and personal, and she'd been unable to do anything to stop it.

Shannon looked down at her blood-covered hands. Tonight she'd been powerless to respond to Todd's dying words. She hadn't been able to help him. But she vowed that would change. She would no longer stand idly by. She'd fight against death. And she'd win.

She lifted her head and stared into the heavens, a star-studded sky that Todd would never see again. This would be her commitment . . . to herself and to Todd.

# ONE

DR. SHANNON FRASIER LOOKED AROUND HER AND SMILED. SHE was surrounded by some of her favorite people, she wasn't on call, and she had a long holiday weekend ahead of her. Things couldn't be better.

Three people sat with Shannon at her dining room table tonight. On her right was the man who referred to himself as her "almost-fiancé," pathologist Dr. Mark Gilbert. She knew that given the opportunity, Mark would remove the "almost" from that designation. Shannon didn't fully understand the barriers that held her back from that decision, but tonight wasn't the time to examine them.

Across the table from Shannon sat Dr. Le Duan (Lee) Kai. Yesterday was June 30, the last day of the academic year and the final day of Lee's residency. He was about to enter private practice, and although she knew he would do well in that environment, Shannon hoped one day Lee would join her on the faculty of the Department of Surgery at Southwestern Medical

School, working, as she did, to prepare other doctors for the specialty of surgery.

Beside Lee sat his diminutive wife, Ann. An audiologist, Ann worked at the medical center, but that could change, since the couple made no secret of their desire to start a family once Lee's practice was well established. Shannon envied them that.

Shannon raised her glass. "I think we should toast—"

A noise from outside—three flat cracks—made her pause. "Did you hear that?" Shannon asked. "Is someone getting an early start on the July Fourth weekend?"

"I guess it could have been firecrackers," Lee said.

"Maybe it was a car backfiring," Mark offered.

"Not three in a row. Besides," Lee said, "that's rare now that fuel-injected engines have largely replaced carburetors."

Shannon pushed back her chair and dropped her napkin on the table. "While you guys discuss advances in the internal combustion engine, I'm going to look outside and see what's going on."

She turned on the porch light and opened her front door. Warm July air rushed in, but nothing caught Shannon's eye. The porch was empty. No cars moved in the street outside her house. Then she saw something on the lawn—a crumpled mass, like a pile of old clothes. She jumped, startled, when the clothes moved, and she could discern a hand clawing at the dirt. A faint cry, like that of a wounded animal, reached her ears.

"Someone's out there, and they're hurt," Shannon said to Lee, who'd edged up behind her.

The man lay sprawled facedown on the lawn. Lee reached him first, with Shannon right behind. The faint light spilling from the open door was enough to show a dark stain in the center of the victim's back, spreading rapidly outward. Shannon felt her heart race as she was seized by déjà vu.

She touched the man's neck. "He's got a pulse—faint and thready, though."

"Call 911," Lee yelled over his shoulder. Mark, now standing in the doorway, disappeared into the house.

Lee and Shannon exchanged looks. Help was unlikely to get here in time. The man had been shot three times in the back and was bleeding out fast, probably from injury to a major vessel. The two doctors knelt at his side, powerless to intervene. Without equipment there was nothing they could do, and they both knew it. Shannon's stomach knotted at her helplessness. She began to sweat. Her heart threatened to jump out of her chest.

The man stirred. His eyes fell on Shannon, and she almost felt as though there was recognition there. He mumbled something before a gush of blood issued from his mouth. The man sighed, seemed to sink into himself like a balloon deflating, and lay totally still.

Shannon bowed her head and felt defeat wash over her. She'd lost one more fight with death, a fight she'd been forced to wage with no weapons. Once more a gun had taken a life while she watched helplessly. Memories came rushing back like a flood.

"Police and EMTs are on the way," Mark called from the doorway.

Lee rose and shook his head. "Too late." He edged around the body until he was next to Shannon. "Get into the house. I'll stay out here until they arrive."

Shannon nodded and rose slowly. As she moved toward the lighted doorway where Mark waited, she clenched her fists and felt the stickiness of the blood clotting there. The racing pulse and sweating palms were already subsiding, but she knew they'd be back. They always came back.

She brushed by Mark and walked purposefully to the downstairs half bath. Carefully, like a robot moving in slow motion, she turned on the taps. Then she started to scrub the blood from her hands. In the mirror over the sink, her blond hair was perfectly in place. Her makeup was understated and unspoiled. Her blue eyes displayed not a touch of red. There was no evidence of the turmoil within her. But it was there.

She was still at the sink when Mark spoke from behind her. "The police are here. They're interviewing Lee now and want to talk with you after that."

Shannon nodded but kept her hands under the running water. It was several more minutes before she reached down to turn off the faucets. As she dried her hands, a line ran through her head—not one from the Bible, although she wished she could remember an appropriate verse. No, this one was from Shakespeare.

*Here's the smell of the blood still. All the perfumes of Arabia will not sweeten this little hand.*

# TWO

THE DINNER SAT FORGOTTEN ON THE DINING ROOM TABLE. PLATES and glasses were pushed aside, napkins crumpled next to them. A little more than an hour ago, as Shannon sat at this table, everything was serene—but no longer. Now she slumped in her chair, trying to concentrate on the questions coming her way.

"Doctor, can you think of anything that might help us?" If the badge hanging in a holder from the breast pocket of Detective Jesse Callaway's wrinkled suit didn't identify his profession, the bulge under his left arm and his thick-soled shoes did. Without the identifying characteristics, though, he bore a striking resemblance to a former Chicago Bears linebacker whose name danced tantalizingly at the edge of Shannon's memory.

The detective's voice was calm, but his dark eyes burned with an intensity Shannon found almost hypnotic. He glanced down at his notes, then nodded as though he'd found what he wanted. "You're sure you never saw this man before? Think about it. Please?" The last word was almost an afterthought, but it was clear there was no choice involved.

Shannon shook her head. "Think about it? That's all I've done since this happened." She squeezed her eyes shut, but opened them when images intruded unbidden.

The gesture apparently wasn't lost on Callaway. "This seems to have hit you extremely hard. As a doctor, surely you've encountered death before. What's different about this one?"

Shannon bit back the retort that came to her. She opened her eyes. "They're all bad, Detective. Surely you feel that way, too."

Callaway's partner, Detective Steve Alston, leaned casually against the doorframe. His voice was soft, almost soothing. "We all do. I guess we're just more used to violent deaths than you."

"I've told you everything I remember. Do we have to keep going?" Shannon clenched her fists, glad that, like all female surgeons, she kept her nails trimmed short. It was all that prevented bleeding wounds in her palms. When she looked at Callaway again, it came to her. *Brian Urlacher. That's the football player he resembles. His build, his shaved head . . . his intensity.*

Alston said, "Let's take a breather. Can I get you some water?"

"Yes, please." She gestured to the door connecting the dining room where she sat with the kitchen. "In there."

Callaway remained across the table from her, alternately scanning his notes and looking at the ceiling as though piecing together what he'd read. The burly detective's tie was at half-mast. His head glinted with sweat in the overhead light.

Detective Alston was back quickly. He placed a glass of ice water on the table in front of her, and Shannon was surprised and pleased to see that he'd found a coaster in her kitchen and used it.

Alston was about her age, which put him in his mid-thirties. His light brown—almost blond—hair was cut short.

His hazel eyes seemed to convey a message that he'd seen too many of life's bad things and regretted the experience. He was trim but muscular, neat and well dressed, all in marked contrast to his partner. And, although Shannon felt somehow ashamed for noticing it, Alston didn't wear a wedding ring.

A stocky blond woman in a police uniform stuck her head through the door from the living room. The nameplate above her right breast pocket read "Daley." She looked from Callaway to Alston and back. "The medical examiner's finished. Okay to remove the body?"

Callaway answered with a brusque nod and an indifferent wave of his hand. Daley ducked back through the door as quickly as she had appeared.

At first Shannon fixed her gaze on the table, refusing to add to the images she was sure would fill her dreams for weeks ahead. But finally, in response to the same reflex that makes people slow and gawk at the carnage after a car crash, she stood. "Excuse me. I think I need to see this. Maybe it will help me get some closure." She walked slowly from the dining room, through the living room, to the open front door.

Mark stood waiting in the living room. He edged up beside her and put his arm around her waist. Shannon gave him a wry smile and focused on the scene in front of her. There, in the glare of portable floodlights, two men lifted a black body bag onto a gurney. They covered it with a deep-maroon-colored cloth and wheeled their burden to a van parked at the curb. Shannon shuddered as she saw the wheels bump with the drop to street level. Her mind knew it made no difference to the passenger on the litter, but her heart cringed at the thought.

Shannon looked for a moment longer before turning away. She took Mark's hand and squeezed it, then dropped it and walked slowly back to the dining room. She stopped behind her chair but didn't sit. Maybe the detectives would get the hint. "Aren't we about through?"

Callaway hadn't bothered to look at the work of the coroner's crew. Shannon decided he'd seen enough of that to last a lifetime. With one last scan of his notes, he said, "Yeah, I guess that does it for now."

Alston moved away from the doorframe to stand next to his partner. He looked at Shannon with eyes that were more sympathetic than she expected. "Why don't you come down to the station tomorrow? We'll get your statement typed up, and you can sign it. If you've thought of something else by then, we can add it at that time."

"But this is the start of the July Fourth weekend," Shannon said.

Callaway stood and shrugged. "If you think about it, I don't imagine you believe crime will stop so the police can take the day off. That would be like you guys closing all the emergency rooms on a holiday."

"The homicide bureau will be operational tomorrow," Alston said. "How about ten in the morning?"

Callaway tossed a card on the table in front of Shannon like a Las Vegas dealer at the blackjack table. "And if you think of anything important before then, give me a call."

Alston moved closer to Shannon. He took a card from his shirt pocket with two fingers, then lifted her left hand and gently pressed the card into her palm. "Or call me, if you'd prefer. My cell number is on the back."

Shannon continued to stand at the dining room table, leaning on the back of a chair, her eyes closed. For a fleeting instant she wondered if she should usher the detectives out. *Don't be ridiculous. This isn't a party.* Soon she heard the slamming of doors, the sound of a car driving away.

In a moment, the house was quiet. *Quiet as a tomb*. Shannon shuddered as the phrase brought back images she knew would fill her nightmares for days to come. She tried to brush away the pictures as she might deal with a pesky fly.

"They're gone." Mark stood in the doorway and gestured to the empty living room. "Lee and Ann left as soon as the police finished interviewing them. I'm pretty wrung out by all this, and I suspect you feel the same."

Normally the very epitome of the phrase *put together*, Mark now showed evidence of the ordeal. His sports coat was off, his tie was askew, and the cuffs of his blue oxford dress shirt were turned back. His dark, wavy hair lay tousled over his forehead, threatening to cover his brown eyes. A sheen of perspiration shone on his face. Shannon decided that he looked the way she felt.

Shannon pulled out the chair and dropped into it. Mark moved to a spot behind her and gently kneaded her shoulders. "What can I do?"

"Nothing," she said. "I'll be okay. This just hit me hard."

"Of course it did." He stopped the massage for a moment. "Let me make you a cup of tea."

Shannon wasn't sure tea would help, but she knew Mark well enough to realize he needed to do something, so she nodded. "Who do you think the man was?" she asked.

Mark filled a cup with water and put it in the microwave. "No idea," he said. "I never got a good look at him. Did you recognize him?"

"Never saw him before. Why do you think he was shot in my yard?"

Mark leaned on the counter, his arms folded. "Again, I have no idea. I'd guess it was some kind of gang-related drive-by shooting, but not in this neighborhood."

The microwave beeped. Mark busied himself at the counter for a moment, then eased into a chair beside Shannon and set a steaming cup in front of her. "Here you go—green tea with honey. Just the way you like it." He slid his arm around her shoulders and squeezed. "Shannon, I want to help. You know I love you."

"And I . . ." She took a deep breath. "I know you do, but I need to be alone." She looked down at the mug, trying to avoid the hurt look she knew would be on Mark's face.

Shannon and Mark had been together for over a year, but their relationship was stuck just short of an engagement. She recognized that it wasn't Mark's fault. He loved her. He'd said it often enough. And she'd used the *L* word as well. When she did, it seemed natural. Yet she'd generally managed to deflect the conversation away from marriage. Mark, although at times seemingly frustrated by her indecision, had respected her feelings. So here they were—in a sort of relationship limbo.

Mark rose and pushed back his chair. "If you're sure there's nothing I can do, I'll head for home. Call if you need me. Otherwise, we'll talk tomorrow." He kissed her lightly and left the room. At the door, he called, "Lock up after me."

"Push the button. I'll throw the dead bolt after I finish my tea."

After she heard the door close behind him, Shannon took one sip of the tea, then left the cup on the table. She went through the house, assuring herself all the doors and windows were secure before shuffling off to shower. Maybe the hot water would relax her. She was certain that no amount of soap and water could wash away what she felt.

MARK, FRESH FROM HIS SHOWER AND NOW WEARING THE SCRUBS he preferred over pajamas, climbed into bed, retrieved the

Bible from the table beside his bed, opened it to the place he'd marked the night before, and began to read.

Right now he was in Psalms, and the one to be read next, Psalm 50, seemed appropriate, given the events of the evening. He stopped when he reached one particular sentence and repeated it aloud. "Call upon Me in the day of trouble; I shall rescue you, and you will honor Me."

Mark reached for his phone, wondering if those words might help Shannon. Then he drew back his arm. No, Shannon wasn't there yet. He doubted that she'd take much comfort from God's Word right now. Outwardly, she might talk the talk, but she still didn't walk the walk . . . not consistently, not yet.

Since their first meeting, when they shared a table in the medical center's food court, he'd fallen more deeply in love with Shannon each day. He wasn't sure why, couldn't put his finger on the reason, but there it was. She was an intelligent, talented professional, and they shared many common interests. She was attractive, although he'd met other women who were as beautiful. Whatever the attraction, he was ready to move forward, but for some reason Shannon seemed unwilling to take the final step of commitment.

Mark didn't think religion was a roadblock. Although her faith seemed more superficial than his, he was certain that their beliefs coincided. They even attended the same church, the one where her father served as pastor.

Did she love Mark? She'd said so many times, and he thought she was sincere. Maybe Shannon was still hung up on the shooting death of her boyfriend. Was she clinging to what might have been with Todd to the degree that she couldn't yet fully accept Mark's love?

How long ago had that been? Almost ten years? If she

hadn't yet gotten past her loss, would she ever be able to move forward with him?

Well, for now he'd continue to do what he'd always done—walk beside her and love her. He marked his place, replaced the Bible on the bedside table, and closed his eyes to pray. When Mark turned out the light, he wondered how Shannon would sleep that night. He doubted that it would be soundly, if at all.

SHANNON STOOD UNDER THE SHOWER UNTIL THE WATER RAN cold. Yet when she stepped out and swathed herself in a robe, she didn't feel clean. She looked at her hands, scrubbed until they were almost raw—not a trace of blood there, not even under the nails, yet in her mind's eye they were clothed in scarlet gloves.

She stopped in front of her dresser and opened her jewelry box. Mark had been wonderful tonight: kind, supportive, always there. She knew his love was unconditional. Why couldn't she accept it and move forward?

Shannon knew one reason why. She took the tray from the top of the jewelry box and removed a small velvet-covered box. With trembling fingers, she opened it and looked once more at the brilliant emerald-cut diamond solitaire set in the center of a white gold ring. It had come to her a month after Todd's funeral. The accompanying note said, "We found this in his room. He was going to give it to you. We think you should have it."

She squeezed her eyes to hold back the tears. Would the specter of Todd and what might have been always haunt her? Was it because no one could compare with the image she'd built up of him . . . an image that time had probably polished beyond reality? Or did she somehow think she was unworthy of happiness? Shannon knew all about survivor's guilt. She'd directed dozens of families for counseling after the death of a loved one. Why couldn't she get past her own?

She slipped into pajamas and eased beneath the covers. She tried to read, but the evening's events played in a continuous loop on the screen of her mind. Shannon laid the book aside and stared at the ceiling.

Maybe she should pray aloud. Perhaps the act of venting her frustration would help. Shannon recalled someone saying, "Tell God everything, even if you're angry with Him. He's big enough to take it."

She tried to voice her thoughts but found the words sticking in her throat. If God was just and kind and loving, as she'd heard her dad preach time and again, why did deaths like Todd's happen? She knew it was foolish to continue to blame God, but she couldn't help it. Maybe someday she could get past it—but not tonight.

She turned out the light, buried her head in her pillow, and tried to find sleep.

The ring of the phone at her bedside brought Shannon awake with a start. She didn't bother to look at the caller ID. Whoever the caller was, they provided a welcome interruption from her nightmarish dreams. "Hello."

"Shannon, this is Megan."

Shannon tried to analyze the voice speaking those few words. Were they slurred? Was there panic in them? Were tears forming behind the six syllables? As best Shannon could tell, and she'd gotten very good at it over the years, Megan sounded sober, subdued but in control. A glance at the bedside clock told Shannon it was well after midnight. Calls at this hour rarely, if ever, brought good news . . . especially if they came from her sister.

"Megan, you're up awfully late. What's going on?" Shannon

tried to keep her voice neutral, her tone bright. There was no need to introduce tonight's shooting into the conversation. Generally, Megan had enough problems in her life. Shannon didn't want to give her more—not now, at least.

Megan's voice sounded as though she was struggling for calm. "I . . . I need a place to stay."

Shannon's first inclination was to ask questions like why and when. But she knew she'd get the answers soon enough. And she'd been down this road before. She realized she had only one option, and she exercised it. "You're welcome to stay here." She took a deep breath. "Do you want to come over now?"

A sniffle came across the line. Then Megan, in a tiny voice that told Shannon her sister was hanging on by a thread, said, "I'm okay for tonight. I'll be there in the morning. And thank you so much."

"Are you sure—"

"No, I'll make it tonight. I'll see you in the morning."

"I'll be at . . . I have to go out in the morning. Do you still have your key?"

"Yes. I'll see you then. And thanks."

Shannon hung up the phone. She'd hear what was going on soon enough, and whatever the problem, she'd be the one to fix it. She always had.

SHANNON HADN'T KNOWN WHAT TO EXPECT WHEN SHE ARRIVED AT THE police station the next morning. As it turned out, she talked only with Steve Alston. He asked a few questions, showed her several printed pages restating what she'd told the detectives the night before, and asked her to read them and make any needed corrections or additions before signing. In less than an hour, she was out the door, relieved to have this part of her ordeal over.

As soon as she stepped out of the police station, Shannon felt heat wash over her like a fiery wave. Downtown Dallas was a furnace during the summer, and on this second day of July the sidewalks and streets radiated the stored heat from a half-dozen consecutive 100-degree days. Shannon thought about ducking into one of the hole-in-the-wall cafes and delis in the area for a cold Coke, but she checked her watch and decided she really didn't have time. There was somewhere she needed to be. It wasn't really an appointment—more of an obligation.

Yesterday had been July first, a date she'd heard called the most dangerous day of the year for patients in a medical center hospital where resident physicians provided much of the care. These doctors, although certified MDs, were now learning the ins and outs of their specialty, performing surgery, and ordering treatments under the watchful eye of staff physicians. July first was the day when residents moved up a notch—first year to second, second to third, and so on. And that meant the first-year residents were fresh out of medical school.

This wasn't the new graduates' first experience with patient care. They'd received instruction during their clinical rotations, with staff and senior residents supervising them, but now they had more responsibility, more independence. Shannon was certain that most of the first-years would do well. A few would need help beyond what the senior residents could offer, though. And that was why Shannon was headed for the medical center's primary teaching hospital, Parkland.

Shannon wasn't on call, but she knew most faculty members in the Department of Surgery would drop by Parkland Hospital during the weekend to help and to observe. Despite the circumstances in which she found herself, Shannon felt compelled to do her part.

As she walked into the emergency room, Shannon saw

Dr. Will Foster. Now advancing to his second year of specialty training in surgery, the ER was his first rotation. She waited to approach him until he finished with one patient and was moving to the next. "Will, how's it going?"

He pushed a tangled lock of blond hair away from his eyes and gave her a smile. Even in the controlled chaos of the ER, he seemed calm. Will not only had the dexterity that marked a good surgeon, but he possessed a sharp analytical mind that rivaled that of the recently graduated Lee Kai. There'd be no problems here in the ER with Will in charge.

"Pretty routine so far," Will said. "But you might want to look in over there." He pointed to one curtained cubicle. "I called the team down to see the victim of a motorcycle accident. Both the senior and second-year residents on trauma call were scrubbed in on an emergency. They sent Andy Zisk, a first-year, to check the patient."

Shannon recalled Andy's interview when he applied for residency training here. He came from a mid-level medical school, graduating with adequate grades and decent recommendations. Ordinarily he wouldn't have had a chance at this prestigious surgery residency, but because of a confluence of events—the sudden withdrawal of one of the accepted candidates, a glowing letter of recommendation from a former Parkland resident, and a few other pieces falling into place— here he was.

She pulled aside the curtain and entered the cubicle where Andy stood over a middle-aged man wearing motorcycle leathers. The patient's face was contorted in a rictus of pain. "What do we have, Andy?" Shannon said.

Andy turned so sharply he almost hit Shannon with the clipboard he held. "Uh, this is . . ." He looked down. "This is Mr. Davidson. Thirty-four-year-old white male. He was involved . . ."

If Andy needed to hone his skills at doing a quick evaluation and reporting it, there was no better time or place than the present. She held out her hand, and he passed her the clipboard with obvious relief. Five minutes later, Shannon gave concise orders to the nurse standing on the other side of the patient's gurney. She and Andy stepped outside the curtain, where she gently explained a few steps that would help him handle emergencies such as this quickly and efficiently, without missing something obvious . . . something like the probable fractured fibula Davidson had sustained. "Get the big picture. If you focus on ruling out a ruptured spleen, you could miss a broken leg. Be thorough, be fast, and have confidence in your diagnosis," she said.

"Thanks, Dr. Frasier," Andy said. "I appreciate your help."

"No problem. If you have questions, ask your senior resident. Or you can check with Will, here in the ER. You'll learn. It takes time."

Shannon wondered if she'd ever be as competent in handling her personal life as she had become professionally. She guessed what she told Andy could apply to her own situation—it takes time.

Satisfied that she'd done enough at the hospital, Shannon headed for her car, first stopping for the cold Coke she'd passed up earlier. She drove on automatic pilot, while her mind wrestled with something that was always there but that she managed to ignore most of the time. Where were things going with Mark?

She wondered about the problem of their faith—Mark's was deep, and hers was . . . well, it wasn't what it used to be. She wasn't sure she could live up to Mark's expectations.

In contrast with her upbringing in the home of a pastor, Mark had grown up in a home where God was never mentioned. Shannon had become a Christian in her preteen years.

When many medical students, including Shannon, were letting their busy lives separate them from God, Mark had found Him and embraced a daily walk with the Lord. So now they were two sides of a coin—Mark quietly living out his faith, and Shannon struggling to regain hers.

If she'd admit it, Todd's death had changed a lot of things in her life. As she knelt at his side, raging at her own impotence in the face of the emergency, she'd prayed for Todd, prayed harder than she'd ever done in her life. But he died.

She'd suffered the usual survivor guilt. She'd tried to pray. She read books on why bad things happen to good people. And deep down she realized she had never forgiven God for what happened. Maybe Mark could help her there. But that was for another time. Right now she had other problems.

Shannon took the last sip of her Coke as she parked her car in the driveway of her home. Megan's car was already at the curb. Shannon entered quietly, thinking her sister might be asleep. Should she have a late lunch of peanut butter and crackers, or try to make up for her sleepless night with a nap? She was about to move to the kitchen when a sharp command brought her up short.

"Stop right there. I've got a gun."

# THREE

SHANNON'S HEART HAMMERED IN HER CHEST. *WHOEVER IT IS,* *they have a gun, but they haven't pulled the trigger.* She closed her eyes, took several deep breaths, and fought for calm.

The first thing Shannon saw when she opened her eyes was a gun aimed at her midsection. Then she realized who was holding it—Megan, her expression reflecting equal parts of fear and anger. Was her sister on something? Megan sober was unpredictable enough. Megan high could be dangerous . . . maybe even lethal.

Megan stood in the doorway leading from the hall into the living room. Ordinarily a younger, stockier version of Shannon, at this moment the resemblance was less discernible. Her blond hair was tousled and tangled, her face devoid of makeup, and her blue eyes seemed unfocused.

Shannon stopped dead in her tracks and held up her arms, palms out and open to show she was unarmed. "Megan, it's me—your sister, Shannon. Put the gun down. Everything's okay."

The gun in her sister's trembling hand was a revolver, and Shannon's blood ran cold as she focused on the brass-colored noses of bullets in the chambers. Megan wasn't bluffing. The gun was loaded, her sister's finger was on the trigger, and it was pointed at her. It was time to take action.

"Megan, settle down. You're in my home. You're safe here." Shannon took a tentative step forward, then another. She lowered one hand and held it out, palm up. "Let me have the gun before someone gets hurt." *Especially me.*

Megan gave her head a little shake, as though by doing so she could clear her thoughts. Then she lowered the gun. "I'm sorry. I stretched out in the guest room, and when you came in you woke me. Guess I was a little disoriented."

As she moved closer, Shannon noticed her sister's pupils were normal size. Sleep wrinkles from the bedclothes marked her cheek. Then Shannon realized that Megan wasn't wearing the glasses she needed but hated, and the last puzzle piece fell into place. Megan wasn't high. She awoke in a strange place, heard a noise, and came to investigate. And she probably hadn't fully identified the person she held at bay until Shannon spoke and moved nearer.

The sisters met in the middle of the room and hugged, but not before Shannon gently took the gun from Megan's hand. The gun was heavier than she'd imagined . . . or was it just that this was the first time she'd held one? Shannon fought to keep her hand steady as she laid the gun gingerly on the end table near her. She'd put it in a more secure location later. Right now, her attention was on her sister.

"Where did the gun come from?" Shannon asked.

"I got it right after I started my job. A woman alone in some of those areas—well, I needed some security."

"So you have a permit and everything?" Shannon was pretty sure of the answer, but she had to ask anyway.

Megan looked at the floor. "One of the contacts I made when I was rehabbing at First Step got me the gun. I've mostly kept it in my car. I didn't want to bother taking the classes to get a carry permit and all that stuff."

"I think you're safe enough here," Shannon said. "I'll take care of the gun for now."

Megan's lower lip trembled. "Oh, Shannon, when am I going to get it all together?" A tear ran down her cheek. "I've messed up my life again, so here I am, running to my big sister."

This was exactly what Shannon didn't need. She bit back a retort. She had problems of her own, but this wasn't the time to mention them. That could wait. Megan needed her, so she'd do what she'd done before. She'd help her sister. "We'll take it a day at a time. Why don't we go into the kitchen? I want something to eat. How about you?"

Over peanut butter sandwiches and glasses of cold milk, Shannon coaxed Megan's story from her. She not only needed a place to stay, she'd just lost her position as a pharmaceutical representative—one Shannon had helped her get.

"What reason did they give for letting you go?" Shannon asked.

Megan ducked her head. "Samples were disappearing."

Shannon knew that some drug reps were given large boxes of samples, medications they dropped off at physician offices. This was a good way for doctors to get patients started until they filled a prescription, while encouraging the use of those particular medications. Lately Shannon had seen the sample stream in her clinic slow to a trickle, undoubtedly an economic thing. Maybe pharmaceutical companies were also tightening inventory control of these samples. "Did you keep a record of where and with whom you left the drugs?"

"Of course. When I left samples at a doctor's office, I wrote everything down in my logbook. That's standard procedure. I stored the boxes in Tony's garage—"

"Tony? Is he the guy you were living with? I thought that was Mike."

"No, I broke up with Mike when I went into rehab. I've been crashing at Tony Lester's place since I got out."

Shannon sighed, wondering if she'd ever be able to keep track of the men in Megan's life. "Go ahead. You kept the boxes of medicine in Tony's garage."

"Right. I stored them there and restocked the trunk of my car every two or three days. But when it was time to inventory my drugs, I always came up short."

Shannon had a bad feeling. "What kind of medicines were these?"

"We're not talking about narcotics," Megan said around a mouthful of sandwich. She drank some milk and continued. "These were antibiotics, allergy medicines, muscle relaxants, stuff like that. It wasn't as though I was stealing them for my own use."

"I imagine the company thought you were selling them. There's a pretty good market for high-priced medications, and samples can be sold if you know the right way to go about it." Shannon looked Megan in the eye. "Is that what you did?"

"What? No. No! I don't know what happened to them." She ducked her head.

Shannon thought she did. "And you have no idea where they went?"

"Well . . ." Megan wiped at the corner of her eye. "I think maybe Tony took them. But when I asked him if he knew anything about the samples, he flew into a rage. He said if I didn't trust him any more than that, I should move out." She sniffled. "We fought about it. Things got pretty bad. That's when I called you."

Shannon wanted to ask more questions, but experience had taught her to approach her sister as carefully as a hunter stalks a particularly skittish deer. She'd save most of the questions for later, but there was one answer she needed before Megan unpacked. "And you're still clean? No narcotics? No booze?"

Megan pulled a tattered tissue from the pocket of her jeans and blew her nose. She nodded. "I haven't touched any of that stuff for almost six months. Not since I came out of rehab. Honest."

Shannon had learned that addicts could be charming, convincing, plausible . . . and total liars, but she was willing to give her sister another chance. How many was this? She'd lost count.

Megan finished her milk and wiped her lips with a paper napkin. "I appreciate you taking me in, Shannon. I'll start looking for a job soon. Really."

Shannon recalled the favors she'd called in to get Megan her last job. She wondered who was going to hire a pharmaceutical rep with a history of addiction, one who'd been fired when drug samples disappeared. "We'll deal with that later." She yawned. "I was up most of the night, and what I need right now is an afternoon nap."

Megan gathered the dirty dishes and put them in the sink. "Up with a case? Did the patient make it?"

Shannon decided this wasn't the time to spring the story of the shooting on her sister. She shook her head. "No. He didn't make it."

"Sorry. But I guess you can't save them all." Megan turned and left the kitchen. In a moment, her light tread on the stairs marked her climb to the guest bedroom.

Still at the kitchen table, Shannon placed her fingertips on her temples and pressed. *No, you can't save them all. Right now I'm wondering how I'm going to save you . . . again.*

SHANNON HAD FINALLY SETTLED INTO DEEP SLEEP WHEN NOISES in the kitchen startled her to wakefulness. It took a few seconds for her to identify the source before she remembered that Megan was in her house now.

Shannon had stretched out for her nap fully clothed. She slipped out of bed, shoved her feet into loafers, and eased into the living room. Two suitcases stood by the outside door, something Shannon hadn't noticed when she first entered the house. The noise from the kitchen was clearer now—the periodic *thunk* of a closing cabinet door, the muted rattle of dishes. Shannon moved through the dining room and stood in the kitchen doorway. Megan was at the dishwasher, unloading it. Occasionally she held a glass to the light, sometimes polishing it with a dishtowel before putting it away.

"What are you doing?"

Megan didn't appear to be startled. She turned and favored Shannon with a smile. "Just trying to make myself useful. I mean, when you dump yourself on someone, it's supposed to be good form to help out."

Her sister was no longer the frightened, disheveled woman Shannon had seen earlier. Megan had brushed her hair, applied makeup, and changed into fresh clothing. She was even wearing her glasses. And her attitude was different as well—more chipper.

Shannon couldn't help wondering if her sister had taken something. Or was it just relief at being away from a bad situation? She pulled out a kitchen chair and sat. "I never asked you where you slept last night after you called. You said you'd be okay until morning, but I should have insisted."

"No problem. It was just nice to know I had somewhere to go after Tony threw me out."

Shannon took a moment to think that through. "So you left the house after you called me?"

"I was already out of there. I wasn't about to spend another minute in that house with Tony. I used my cell phone and called from my car."

"You slept—"

"In my car? Sure. I pulled into a parking garage, found a nice corner, locked the doors, and slept. I've done it before." Megan's face threatened to crumble. "You'd be surprised at some of the things I've done."

Shannon didn't want to go there. Not now, at least. "So where do you stand with Tony?"

"That's over. I'll need to get the rest of my things from his house, but after that I'm not going back." She turned and pointed toward the front door and her suitcases. "And don't get the idea that I'm here to stay. In a week or so—ten days tops—I hope to have found a job and an apartment of my own."

Shannon figured her sister was being optimistic, but she decided not to argue the point. "So, what—" The ring of her cell phone stopped her. She pulled it from the pocket of her slacks. Mark was calling.

"Have you been to police headquarters yet?" he asked.

"I went this morning."

"How did it go?"

"About like you'd expect," she said. "Read through my statement, signed it. Have you been down there yet?"

"Earlier this morning. I guess I just missed you. Basically I did the same as you. I signed my statement and left." He cleared his throat. "I'm not sure how you feel after what happened, but I was wondering if you'd like to have dinner with me tonight."

"Mark, I'm not sure. Megan is staying with me now."

"Oh?"

Shannon wondered how Mark could put so much meaning into one syllable. He knew about Megan, including her two trips to rehab and the other times Shannon had come to the rescue of her sister. Although Mark never came out and said, "Why do you keep putting up with this?" Shannon figured he'd thought it more than once. Maybe his Christianity prevented him from being overtly critical, but she knew it was a struggle for him.

"Is that Mark?" Megan asked.

Shannon looked around and found that her sister had moved closer. "Yes."

"Could I . . . could I ask him for a favor?"

Shannon didn't want to be caught in the middle here. She decided to let her sister handle this herself. She gave Megan the phone.

"Mark, this is Megan. Listen, I need a man for this. I've left Tony, but some things of mine are still in his house. I'm afraid to go there by myself. Would you . . ." She let the words trail off, apparently hoping Mark would jump in and offer his services.

There was an uncomfortable silence. When Mark finally replied, Shannon could tell he was talking but couldn't make out the words. Then Megan said, "Thanks. We'll look for you in a few minutes."

She handed the phone back to Shannon. "Mark said he'd go with me."

"Great," Shannon said. *Couldn't he think of an excuse?*

"I'm glad Mark's going," Megan said. "I don't think Tony would do anything foolish, but just in case . . ."

Shannon wished she could be so confident. Wasn't the superstition that bad things came in threes? There was the shooting, then Megan's sudden arrival. What was number three?

SHANNON CHECKED THE CLOCK ONCE MORE: 6:00 P.M. MARK AND Megan had been gone for more than two hours. They should be back by now. She'd called Mark's cell phone once already, but it went to voice mail. Maybe he had it turned off. Perhaps he'd left the phone in his car.

She told herself to stop worrying. They were two responsible adults—well, one of them was responsible. Mark would call if something came up.

Shannon was sitting in the living room, turning the pages of a magazine but unable to concentrate, when she heard the front door open. She looked up in time to see Megan come in, followed by Mark. He was holding a wet handkerchief to his head with his left hand, and he seemed to be in obvious pain. Mark moved to the sofa where he eased down beside Shannon, then leaned forward, his head cradled in his hands.

"What happened?" Shannon asked.

Mark held up a hand. "Could I have some ice?"

"I'll get it." Megan hurried through the door, returning with ice wrapped in a dish towel. Mark switched it for the handkerchief he had been holding to his head, saying, "Thanks."

"What happened?" Shannon asked once more. *This must be number three.*

"I guess I was wrong about Tony not presenting a problem," Megan said. "He was at the house when I arrived, and he'd been drinking."

The look on Mark's face said he knew something like this would happen, but it was gone almost as soon as it appeared. He took away the towel, and Shannon saw his left temple was already swelling. "I told him we didn't want any trouble," Mark said. "All we wanted was to get Megan's stuff and be on our way."

"Apparently he didn't react well to that," Shannon said.

"For a while he just stood there and swore—at Megan, at me, at life in general. I decided to take it, because while he was spouting curses we were gathering her things and taking them out to my car."

"But—" Megan began.

"I'll tell her," Mark said. "We'd finished and were about to walk out when he picked up an empty beer bottle from the end table. He started cursing louder, mainly at me, saying I was responsible for Megan's leaving. Then he took a swing at me. I ducked, but he still managed to clip my head with the bottle." Mark reapplied the towel.

Shannon turned to Megan. "So you and Mark ran?"

"Not exactly. When I saw what Tony was doing, I picked up another bottle and crowned him with it. He went down like a felled ox. At first I was afraid I'd killed him."

"Probably took something like that to put him out of commission," Mark muttered. "He'll be okay."

Shannon turned toward Mark. "Let me look at your head."

He resisted at first, but finally Shannon was able to check the injury. The skin over the swollen area was intact. She didn't feel any depression or crepitus, the crunching sensation of two edges of bone rubbing against each other that was the hallmark of a severe fracture. A quick neurologic exam seemed normal. "You're probably okay, but you really should have X-rays and a thorough exam to make sure," she said.

Mark shook his head, although she noticed he did it gingerly. "I'll be fine. I just need to get home and put more ice on it."

"At least let one of us drive you," Shannon said.

"I can make it on my own. I don't live that far away."

Arguments proved useless. *Typical doctor, especially a male doctor,* Shannon thought. Injuries and illnesses happened to everyone else, not to them. "Call after you get home," she said. "I'll phone you later, and if you don't answer, I'm going to come over and take you to the ER, even if I have to hog-tie you."

Mark managed a sheepish grin. "Yes, Doctor."

Shannon saw him out the door, exchanging a kiss with him after reinforcing her warnings. It was only as he pulled away that she realized Megan's stuff was still in Mark's car. Oh well. They'd get it tomorrow.

Megan was still on the couch, her face screwed up, tears drying on her cheeks. "I guess I've done it again. Bad things seem to happen when I'm around."

Shannon patted Megan on the shoulder. "I'm sure Mark will be okay."

Megan looked up at her sister. "I'm sorry I've caused you and Mark so much trouble," she said. "Maybe I should load up my things and go."

"Where?" Shannon asked. She realized how cold her response had been, so she hurried to say, "Megan, you're welcome to stay here as long as you want. Now, why don't you freshen up. I'm going to treat you to dinner, and then maybe we can take in a movie." *Perhaps a comedy or a musical. Goodness knows I've had enough drama recently to last a lifetime.*


THE RING FROM SHANNON'S PURSE CAME JUST AS THE WAITER delivered chips and salsa to the table. She nodded her thanks, then retrieved her phone. "Hello."

"Reporting in," Mark said. "A couple of Tylenol have suppressed my headache to a dull pounding. No double vision. No problem speaking or moving all extremities. The swelling's going down after I used ice. In other words, once more my hard head saved me."

Shannon smiled in spite of herself. "That's good. So I guess you want me to promise not to check on you every hour."

"Would you like me to drive back there so you can check me out in person? We could even order in something to eat."

"We're already at dinner," Shannon said. "Afterward we're headed to the theater for a movie. And I think you'd better stay right where you are."

"But I'm—" There was a pause. "Remind me not to shake my head. It woke the little men with hammers. Anyway, I guess you're right. I'll fix myself a light supper and get a good night's rest."

Shannon felt a degree of relief. She almost wished Megan had stayed home as well. What Shannon would enjoy most was sitting alone in a dark movie theater, putting the events of the past twenty-four hours aside. "That's fine. I'll call you tomorrow."

She ended the call at the same time the waiter approached with their food. He placed it before them with the warning of waiters in Tex-Mex restaurants everywhere: "Hot plate." Shannon suppressed the desire she had every time she heard that, the temptation to touch the plate to check its temperature. Instead, she nodded her thanks and took up her fork.

Shannon looked at Megan and the two hesitated. When they were growing up, their dad had always prayed before a meal, even in public, and it embarrassed them both. But he wasn't here. Megan gave her head a small shake and dug into her enchiladas. Shannon hesitated and formed a single sentence in her head. *God, I need some help here.* As she chewed the first bite of her chile relleno, she wondered if that counted as saying grace.

THE KNOCKING CAME ABOUT 2:00 A.M. AT FIRST, SHANNON SIMPLY folded the noise into her dream, a scene in which she was standing in the midst of a home that was still under construction. No matter how she urged the carpenters to be quiet, despite her earnest entreaties, the workmen continued to ply their hammers. Finally, she struggled up from her dream to find that the noise represented someone pounding on her front door—someone who apparently had no intention of giving up or going away.

Shannon shoved her feet into slippers, wrapped her robe around her, and stumbled down the stairs. She flipped on the porch light and looked through the peephole, where she saw two uniformed policemen, one male and one female, taking turns banging on her door.

"Just a minute," she said. She fumbled at the lock and security chain, and eventually swung the door wide. She made no attempt to hide her irritation as she asked, "What is it?"

The woman took a step forward, stopping at the threshold. "May we come in?"

Shannon's brain kicked into high gear. Whatever this was, it couldn't be good. The police wouldn't come knocking on her door at this hour for something routine. Then again she could think of no valid reason to deny them entry. She stepped back and motioned both officers into the living room.

"Sorry to bother you," the woman said. She looked familiar, but the reason danced just outside Shannon's memory. "I'm Corporal Daley, and this is my partner, Officer Mikowski." The male officer nodded. He was almost a head taller than Shannon's five eight, and his blond hair, what there was of it, was in a buzz cut.

"What's this about?" Shannon asked again.

"We're looking for a Megan Frasier," Daley said. "We were hoping you could help us find her."

"Megan's my sister. What do you want with her?"

"We need to ask her some questions about the man she's been living with—Tony Lester."

*Has something happened to Tony? Did Megan hit him too hard with that bottle?* Mark's words came back to her—*"He'll be okay."* But despite that assurance, she had visions of a late complication, maybe a subdural hematoma or other bleeding into the brain. Was that what this was about?

"Why did you come here to look?" Shannon asked. She didn't think Megan had told Tony where she was going when she left him. Had Mark let it slip while they were there?

"When we were in Mr. Lester's house, we found your sister's address book. Most of the addresses had been crossed out, but yours hadn't. Same last name as hers, so we thought you could help us. Do you know where we can find her?"

Shannon thought for an instant about pleading ignorance, but she knew the lie would come back to haunt her. "She's staying here—moved in less than twenty-four hours ago."

Mikowski spoke for the first time. "We need to speak with her, ask her a few questions. Can you get her?"

"Does she need an attorney?"

Daley shook her head. "This is a field investigation, just a few questions. We can take your sister down to the station and let her call an attorney from there, but it would be simpler if she talked to us here."

Shannon left the officers on the couch in her living room. Halfway to Megan's room she remembered where she'd seen Daley before—at the scene of the shooting in her front yard. Was this about that incident? Surely not at 2:00 a.m.

"Do you think Tony would press charges for my hitting him with that bottle?" Megan slipped into a T-shirt and jeans as she talked.

"We'll know more when we see what kind of questions they're going to ask."

When they were settled in the living room, Daley pulled a leather-covered notebook from her hip pocket. She opened it, and Megan said, "Are you going to read me my rights or something?"

"Not for this. Right now we just have a few questions."

"I guess that's okay," Megan said.

"I understand you'd been living with Tony Lester for a while," Daley said.

"Less than six months," Megan said. "And I should have gotten out long before I did."

"When did you last see him?"

Megan looked at her sister, and Shannon could almost read her thoughts. Should she reveal what happened at that last encounter? Megan was an accomplished liar—Shannon knew this from bitter experience—but, in the end, something always happened to trip her up. Better to be truthful. She gave a brief nod. *Tell them.*

"My sister's boyfriend took me to the house yesterday

afternoon. I'd moved out earlier, but I wanted to get the rest of my things."

"And what was Mr. Lester's state of mind at that time?" Daley's expression revealed nothing. Her tone of voice was neutral. She might have been asking about the weather.

"He'd been drinking. He was really belligerent. Then, as we were leaving, he hit Mark. So I . . ."

Shannon gritted her teeth. *Shut up. Don't volunteer.* Apparently Shannon's extrasensory connection with her sister failed this time.

"I . . . I hit him in the head with a bottle—knocked him out." Megan dabbed at her eyes. "Has he filed a complaint? Because Mark and I will testify that he attacked first."

Mikowski shook his head. "No, Mr. Lester hasn't filed a complaint. He can't. He's dead."

# FOUR

THE QUESTIONING LASTED ALMOST AN HOUR. FINALLY, DALEY pulled two cards from her pocket and handed one to each of the women. "Call me if you think of anything else. My cell number's on the back. A detective should be in touch with you soon."

After the door closed, Megan slumped back in her chair and squeezed her eyes shut. "This is a nightmare. What am I going to do?"

Shannon sighed. She'd been through a number of crises with her sister, but this one was the worst by far. "We'll get through this. Right now we need some rest. We can talk about what to do in the morning."

"Should we call Mom and Dad?"

Shannon was already shaking her head. "No. Dad needs his rest. Tomorrow—I guess it's today now—he'll be preaching. There's nothing he or Mom can do tonight. We'll let them know later."

"What about calling a lawyer?"

"Think it through, Megan," Shannon said, working to keep her voice calm. "It's almost three in the morning. You haven't been charged with anything. If Tony died from a blow to the head, the police would have taken you in for questioning, maybe charged you. They didn't—matter of fact, they wouldn't say much when I asked how he died."

"Maybe you're right."

"I know I am," Shannon said. "This probably has nothing to do with you except that you were one of the last people to see him alive. We'll talk with the detectives when they contact us. If it looks like you need a lawyer, I know a criminal defense attorney who's married to one of the doctors in the surgery department. We'll call her when the time comes."

In her bed, Shannon stared at the ceiling. Megan's question about their parents made her think. It must be embarrassing for them to have a daughter who was in and out of trouble on a regular basis. Shannon didn't want to shame them even more. She guessed that was the reason she went to church even when she didn't feel like it, why she tried to be seen doing the right thing even when she didn't really mean it. Did she want people to think well of her so they'd think well of her parents? And in the final analysis, was she really nothing more than a card-carrying hypocrite?

Shannon knew that the Bible told her not to worry about tomorrow, that it would take care of itself. But she couldn't let it go, so until the first rays of sun struck her bedroom blinds, she worried about the man who'd been shot on her lawn, she worried about the tangled web of her sister's life, and—try as she might to avoid it—she worried about what was going to come next in her own life. Where would her relationship with Mark ultimately go? Would he propose to her? And, most bothersome of all, would she say yes if and when he did?

*God, I need some help here.* That was the second time in less than eight hours she'd had that thought. Or was it a prayer? She felt totally at sea. Dr. Shannon Frasier, the confident professional, the cool-as-ice surgeon, didn't know what to do next. She just wanted to curl up in her dad's arms and feel safe and secure again.

SHANNON WAS AT THE KITCHEN TABLE, A CUP OF COFFEE COOLING in front of her, when she heard Megan come down the stairs.

Wordlessly, Megan shuffled to the coffeemaker, poured a cup, and eased into the chair beside her sister.

The two women sat in silence for a moment. Then Shannon raised her cup in a salute. "Here's looking at you, kid." Her Bogart imitation was far from good, yet it had never failed to bring a smile to Megan's face. This morning, despite everything, was no exception.

"Of all the sisters in all the world, I had to get one who fancies herself a mimic," Megan said. Her expression turned serious as she said, "Shannon, I'm so sorry to get you involved in this mess."

"Let's don't go there," Shannon said. "What we have to do is see where we are and figure out what we need to do next." She finished her coffee and shoved the cup away. "And while we're at it, you should know what happened here before you called Friday night."

Megan's eyes widened as Shannon related the story of the shooting on her front lawn. "Why—"

"I have no idea why he was shot, why it was on my lawn, who he was, or anything else," Shannon said. "Maybe when the detectives find out something, they'll let me know. But in the meantime, I think our first priority is to clear up your status with the police in Tony's death."

"Well, the policewoman said we should hear from some detectives. Do we need to stick around, maybe try to call them?"

Shannon shook her head. "We don't know who to call. They'll find us when they're ready. No, I've given it some thought. I think the best thing we could do this morning is go to church."

As soon as the words were out of Shannon's mouth, Megan's expression changed from one of confusion to one that bordered on terror. "You mean Dad's church?"

"Yes, Dad's church. The one you and I attended when we were kids. The one I *still* attend." She regretted coming down so hard on Megan with the last sentence, but Shannon had to admit she harbored some resentment. There were lots of Sundays she wanted to stay in bed, but she always showed up. It was hard work, being the "good sister." But she didn't want to embarrass her parents.

"Should we call to warn them or anything?"

"There's not going to be a bolt of lightning or an outpouring of fire and brimstone when you walk in," Shannon said. "We can sit in the back if you want to. But after the service, we need to talk with Mom and Dad, tell them what's going on."

"But I—"

"Megan, we're going. They may not kill the fatted calf when they see you, but Mom and Dad aren't going to turn their backs either. Whatever you may have done in the past, they're still your parents . . . and mine."

WITH THE FIRST NOTES OF THE ORGAN POSTLUDE, THE OLDER woman sitting next to Shannon and Megan gathered her Bible and purse, stood, extended her hand, and said, "We're so glad to have you here today. I'm Elsie. Remind me of your names again, would you?"

"I'm Shannon. This is my sister, Megan."

"Now isn't that a coincidence? Pastor Frasier has two daughters by those names."

"Elsie, I see you've met my daughters."

Shannon knew the voice before she turned and saw her mom standing in the aisle. Sarah Frasier had the trim figure of a woman thirty years her junior. Her reddish-blond hair showed an unashamed touch of gray at the temples. Her blue eyes gleamed behind gold-rimmed glasses. She was, and had been for all of Shannon's life, the perfect pastor's wife. Only after Shannon was grown and living away from home did she realize how difficult it must have been at times for her mother to fill that role.

Her mom did what Shannon figured she must have done hundreds of times, easing Elsie away while avoiding any appearance of doing it. When they were finally alone, their mother hugged first Shannon, then Megan. There were tears in her eyes. "It's good to see you both. You'll come over to the house for lunch, won't you? I know your dad wants to visit, and there's no way we can do it here."

A deer-in-the-headlights expression flitted across Megan's face. She opened her mouth, but Shannon managed to speak first. "Of course. We'll let you and Dad talk to everyone here, and we'll see you at the house."

"Do you have your key?" her mother asked.

"Of course." Shannon saw the look Megan gave her, and a small thrill of satisfaction ran through her. *Sure, I still have my key. I'm the good daughter, the responsible one. Remember?*

As their mom walked away, Megan tugged at Shannon's sleeve. "You didn't tell me we'd have to have lunch with them."

Shannon's voice was firm. "I think you owe them a visit, don't you? How long has it been since you saw Mom and Dad? Have you talked with them at all since you got out of rehab this last time? A hospitalization, I'd remind you, that they paid for."

"I'm not sure. I guess I've been putting it off."

"And speaking of rehab, are you still going to meetings? Didn't they talk with you about that when you left First Step?"

Megan was spared replying by a masculine voice behind them. "Dr. Frasier, I thought it was you. I don't think I've seen you here before."

Shannon turned to see Detective Steve Alston. "Nor have I seen you," she said. "Are you a member here?"

"Yes. Since it's a fairly good-sized congregation, and we have two morning services, I guess it's understandable that I've missed you."

Shannon could tell Megan was dying for an introduction, but she ignored the look her sister gave her. "Is this an official visit or just a coincidence?"

"Nothing official, so relax." He turned to Megan and stuck out his hand. "I'm Steve Alston. And you are . . ."

"Shannon's sister, Megan," she said. "I'm staying with her right now."

"Pleasure meeting you."

"Me, too," Megan said. "So how do you know Shannon? Are you a doctor, too?"

"No, I'm a detective. We met . . . Well, I think I'll let Shannon tell you about that."

Shannon decided she'd observed enough of the social niceties. Now it was time to get her sister out of here before she made a pass at the detective. "I'm sorry, but we really need to run. We're meeting someone." She took Megan's elbow and guided her to the opposite end of the pew, into the aisle, and toward the door.

"Who was he?" Megan asked as they edged through the thinning crowd toward the parking lot.

"Steve . . . Detective Alston is one of the detectives investigating the shooting at my house on Friday night." Shannon beeped her car unlocked and they both climbed in.

"Well, even though you're in a relationship, I'm not. Why did we have to run off that quickly?"

Shannon kept her eyes on the car in front of her as she guided her blue Toyota out of the church parking lot. She guessed she should be used to her sister's love life, if you could call it that. But this was too much. "Megan, your former live-in boyfriend is newly dead. The police were at my house to question you just hours ago. I don't think you should begin the search for a replacement quite yet." Shannon forced herself to smile and wave courteously at the elderly lady in a Buick who turned in front of her. "And definitely don't start with a detective—especially that one."

ROBERT FRASIER AND HIS WIFE, SARAH, HAD LIVED IN THE SAME house in the Oak Cliff section of Dallas since he first assumed the pastorate of the Mount Hermon Bible Church more than two decades earlier. Shannon sensed Megan stiffen as their car pulled into the driveway. She wondered when Megan had last been back home. Funny, Shannon had lived in a college dorm, then an apartment near the Southwestern Medical Center campus, and finally a house of her own, but this was— and probably always would be—home for her.

They were about to exit the car when Shannon's cell phone rang and Mark's name flashed across the screen. She looked at Megan, who made a "Be my guest" gesture. Apparently, anything that delayed her reunion with her parents was fine with her.

"Hey, you," Shannon said.

"How are you today?"

"Not too bad, considering. How's your head?"

"Pretty sore, and I'm going to have a doozy of a bruise. Otherwise, no lasting effects. I skipped church, but I'm feeling a little cabin fever." Mark cleared his throat. "Would you and Megan like to have lunch with me?"

"Sorry, Mark. We're going to have lunch with my folks," Shannon said.

"*Both* of you?" Mark's tone told Shannon he had a hard time believing what he'd just heard.

"Mark, I need to cut this short—my folks will be home from church any minute. We had a visit from the police last night about Tony."

"What about him?"

"He's dead."

Mark's shock registered in his voice. "Tony's dead? Did Megan hit him too hard? Did he develop a subdural hematoma or something?"

"We don't know. The police wouldn't tell us. Said they were simply doing field interviews, getting stories from everyone they could."

"How did they know Megan was living with Tony?"

"They said they found her address book in his apartment. I suppose after that they just put two and two together."

"We searched all over for that address book," Mark said. "Guess we needed the police to help us hunt." He cleared his throat. "Did you tell them I was there?"

"We didn't mention you by name, just said that my boyfriend

was with Megan. But if they ask, we'll have to identify you, so you might hear from them."

Shannon turned her head as a black Chrysler turned into the drive and stopped beside her car. "My folks are here. I'll call you later."

As Shannon dropped the phone into her purse, Megan looked at her sister. "How long have you and Mark been dating?"

"About a year. Why?"

Megan shook her head. "I was wondering how long it would be before he asks you to marry him."

"Don't worry. You're in line to be the maid of honor." *I'm just not sure when that will happen . . . if ever.*

WHETHER IT WAS COINCIDENCE OR GOD'S PROVIDENCE, HER father's sermon that morning had been based on Luke 15—the parable of the prodigal son. Shannon's feelings made her squirm then, and they continued to make her uncomfortable now. Maybe it was because she identified too closely with the son who stayed home, the good son—the one who resented the attention the prodigal received.

Before the front door closed behind them, the girls both got enthusiastic hugs and kisses from their parents.

"Mom, we don't want to be any trouble," Shannon said. "Can we take you out to lunch?"

Her mother was already tying on an apron. "Not on your life. I have a roast in the oven, with potatoes and vegetables. I'll just pop in some rolls and put together a salad." She looked at her younger daughter. "Do you still like creamed corn?"

"Sure," Megan said, "but I haven't had it in a while."

"Well, you'll have it today. And I'll fix some green beans for you, Shannon."

After their dad excused himself to get out of his coat and tie, and their mom hurried off to the kitchen, Megan whispered to her sister, "Dad looks like he's lost some weight. Is anything wrong?"

"I don't really know. I guess I see him often enough that if there was a gradual change, I might not notice it." *But I should have. Ah, guilt . . . the gift that keeps on giving.*

When her dad took his accustomed place at the head of the table, Shannon decided Megan might be right. He had lost weight. But everything else was the same. His neatly trimmed mustache matched his full head of steel-gray hair. His blue eyes were bright as ever behind horn-rimmed glasses. In a changing world, her dad was a constant, an anchor. Shannon took a deep breath and relaxed. It was good to be with family.

After a blessing that included thanks for the reuniting of the family, everyone devoted themselves to passing and consuming roast beef with gravy, potatoes, carrots, creamed corn, green beans, salad, and homemade rolls.

Toward the end of the meal, Shannon's dad put down his fork and said, "Shannon, would you like to tell us what's bothering you?"

"What makes you think something's bothering me?" she said.

He smiled. "Before I went to seminary, I earned a good bit of my college spending money playing poker. That's when I learned about tells. You have a tell, you know. Sarah and I noticed it when you were a teenager."

"You what?" Shannon asked.

"It helped us a lot when you were younger," her mom added.

"When you're hiding something, you fiddle with your right ear—play with the earring, finger the lobe," her dad said. "You've been doing that for the past five minutes. Want to share?"

Shannon put her napkin beside her plate. "Well, I guess you need to know some things."

"You mean that Megan has moved in with you," her dad said.

"There's a lot more to it than that," Shannon said. "Megan, do you want to tell this?"

Megan shook her head, then looked down and rearranged the napkin in her lap.

"Okay, I guess it's up to me." Shannon related how Megan had lost her job, her breakup with Tony, the trip back to the house, and finally the police visit during the night.

"Is Mark okay?" her dad asked.

"He called me after church. He still has a headache, but he'll be all right."

"So where do we go from here?"

"We don't know yet. The police obviously think Megan was the last person to see Tony alive, so I imagine they'll have more questions for her."

The Frasiers looked at each other. "If she needs a good attorney, we'll help," her mom said.

"I should be able to handle it, but thank you," Shannon said. "The wife of a colleague is an excellent defense lawyer. If the time comes, I'll call her." She finished the iced tea in her glass. Her hand went to her ear, then dropped as she realized what she was doing. "I guess you need to know this, too. There was a shooting outside my house on Friday night."

Shannon related those events as concisely as she could, careful to hide the emotion that the retelling generated. Her mind kept replaying scenes burned into her memory—the body bag being wheeled off her lawn and into the coroner's van, alternating with the scene ten years ago as Todd's body was taken away. As her narrative wound down, she said, "Steve

Alston is one of the detectives investigating that shooting. I almost jumped out of my skin when he approached me at church this morning. I thought he'd come to arrest me or something."

"Steve's a nice fellow. He moved here about six months ago," her dad said. "I'm not sure where he came from—Oklahoma or Arkansas, I think. His wife was killed in an auto accident. He took a position with the police department in Dallas, hoping to get a fresh start, get away from the memories."

"So he wasn't at church just to see me," Shannon said.

"No, he comes every Sunday when he's not working." Her dad pushed back from the table. "Why? Is there any reason for you two girls to be afraid of the police?"

Shannon looked at Megan, who kept her eyes on her plate. Then she shook her head. "No, Dad. No reason at all."


AFTER SHANNON PARKED HER CAR IN THE DRIVEWAY OF HER HOME, Megan broke her silence. "Mom and Dad seemed pretty calm when you told them about everything that's happening."

"Did you expect anything different?" Shannon said. "No matter what life throws at them, they seem to take it pretty well. How many times have we heard Dad say, 'God's in control'?"

"Well, I wish I could be that certain everything's going to come out all right. I keep waiting to be arrested."

"Hold on," Shannon said. "Remember, you're innocent until proven guilty."

"Did you have a chance to ask Mom about Dad's weight loss?" Megan said.

"No, but I will." *I'll just add that to the million other things I'm juggling right now.*

Once inside the house, Megan said, "Tomorrow I'll start looking for a job. Okay if I use your iron and ironing board? I don't want to go job hunting wearing wrinkled clothes."

"No problem."

"I'll take them to my room. I think that will be easier."

"Fine," Shannon said. "I'm going to lie down for a while."

In her bedroom, Shannon kicked off her shoes and flopped onto the bed. She lay there, staring at the molding in the far corner of the room, and tried to get her thoughts together. *Take things in order. Decide what you can do something about and what you can't.*

The shooting on her lawn remained a mystery. She'd talked with detectives. If something more came up that involved her, they'd call. There was nothing she could do right now—although it was a real surprise to see Detective Alston at church this morning. Was that really a coincidence?

As if one murder weren't enough, there was Tony's death. From the little Megan had said about her boyfriend, he appeared to have moved on the shady side of things. Her sister might be a suspect, but she undoubtedly had company in that respect. There were probably a lot of people who had it in for Tony Lester. Until she knew more about the situation, all Shannon could do was sit tight.

Other things? What about her relationship with Mark? The ball was sort of in his court. Frankly, she was comfortable with their current relationship. If he didn't move forward, she'd eventually have to decide what to do—but not today. Not right now.

The ring of her cell phone brought her up short. She pulled the phone from her pocket. Caller ID didn't help—private number. Shannon rolled over to sit on the side of the bed as she answered the call. "Dr. Frasier."

"Is this Shannon Frasier?"

"Yes." Shannon thought she recognized the voice, and her heart rate sped up.

"This is Steve Alston. We need to talk."

# FIVE

A DOZEN THOUGHTS RACED THROUGH SHANNON'S MIND, NONE OF them good. She cleared her throat. She had no idea how to respond, so she simply waited for Alston to continue.

"First, let me say that I'm glad I ran into you at church this morning. Maybe we'll see each other there again."

Shannon remained silent. She had no idea where this was going, but she had a terribly uneasy feeling about it. Alston's next words confirmed that feeling.

"Now for the official part. After church, I went back to the office. Jesse had more information about the man who was killed outside your house."

"Isn't this your partner's day off, too?"

"Jesse's divorced. Happens to a lot of cops. Since he doesn't have anyone at home to keep him there, he spends a lot of time working."

Shannon tried to get the conversation back on track. "You said you know who was killed on my lawn."

"Yes, but I don't want to discuss it on the phone."

"Do . . . do you want me to come down to police headquarters?" she asked.

"Not at all," Alston said. "I don't have anything scheduled. I thought perhaps I could come by your house later this afternoon. Would that work?"

Shannon's head was reeling. Didn't detectives do questioning in pairs, so there'd be a witness to what was said? Was this truly official, or did Alston want to see her outside the presence of his partner? Should she call Mark and ask him to be here during the interview?

"I guess that would be okay," she finally said. "When can I expect you?"

"I need to wrap up some things down here at the office. Say, in an hour?"

She started to ask if he knew where she lived, then bit back the words. He knew where she lived—he'd been here less than forty-eight hours ago. By now he'd probably run her name through all sorts of databases and knew more about her than she could imagine. She settled on saying, "Fine. I'll see you then."

After she ended the call, Shannon lay back on her bed and squeezed her eyes shut. What was coming next? And how could she prepare for it?

She was still trying to decide whether to call Mark and ask him to come over when the doorbell rang. She glanced at the clock on her bedside table. Less than thirty minutes had elapsed since Alston's call. Was he early?

Shannon opened the door and found Mark on her tiny porch. He was holding a slightly grease-stained white paper sack. "I was in the grocery store down the street from me when I smelled this wonderful fragrance coming from their bakery. They had just turned out a fresh batch of chocolate chip cookies. I know how much you like them, so I decided to bring some by."

"Mark, you always seem to know the right thing to do," Shannon said. "I need something to cheer me up, and nothing does it like chocolate." She ushered him inside, gave him a hug and a kiss, and gestured toward one of the chairs in the living room.

"Would you like some milk? Coffee?"

"Milk would be great with the cookies," he said.

In a few minutes they were seated at the kitchen table, each with a glass of milk, the sack of cookies between them. They munched silently for a moment. "Is Megan around? I need to unload her things that are in my car."

"In her room, ironing," Shannon said. "How's your head?"

"I'll be okay." He touched his temple where the swelling had almost subsided but the bruising was fully developed. "Any further word from the police about Tony?"

"No, but I'm glad you're here. Detective Alston called. He has more information about the man who was shot in my front yard Friday night, and he's on his way over."

Mark frowned. "Do you want some privacy? Should I go?"

"No," Shannon said, and realized she meant it. "Please stay. This concerns you as much as it does me."

Megan came through the doorway. "I thought I heard voices." She walked over to the sack and helped herself to a cookie. "What's up?"

Shannon decided there was no need for Megan to be involved in her conversation with Alston. The less visible her sister was, especially to the police, the better things would be. "Mark brought over some cookies. The police will be here in a few minutes to talk about the man who was shot in my front yard Friday night." Before Megan could say anything, Shannon moved on. "Would you mind staying in your room while they're here? Take some cookies with you."

Megan raised her eyebrows. "Any particular reason you want me out of sight?"

"Frankly, this is about the Friday-night shooting, so it doesn't concern you. Given the situation of Tony's death, the less involvement you have with the police right now, the better off you'll be," Shannon said. "I'll fill you in later."

"Okay. Let me know when they've gone." Megan took the carton of milk from the refrigerator, poured a glass, picked up three more cookies, and flounced out of the room.

Mark shook his head. "Trying to make sure she keeps a low profile?"

"Among other things. We saw Detective Alston when we were leaving church this morning. She was anxious to meet him, but I got her out of there before she could try to work her wiles on him."

"I noticed that you told her the police would be here, not Detective Alston," Mark said.

"As I said, she was batting her eyes at him this morning after church."

"Isn't it a little soon after Tony's death for Megan to be getting back into the game?"

"Exactly," Shannon said. "But, in case you haven't figured it out, that's Megan. She doesn't feel complete without a man in her life, and she's already looking for a replacement."

"Shannon, I've tried not to say anything, but Megan's—"

Mark stopped when the doorbell rang. Shannon looked at her watch. "That should be the detective now."

Mark stood and followed Shannon to the front door.

If Alston was surprised by Mark's presence, he hid it well. He shook Mark's hand, thanked Shannon for seeing him on a

Sunday, and took the seat to which she directed him, facing the sofa where she sat down beside Mark.

She wasn't sure if Alston intended for this to be a social call, but if that was the case, Shannon decided to short-circuit it right now. "What have you learned about the man who was shot in my yard?"

Alston reached into the inside pocket of his suit coat and extracted a thin sheaf of papers, which he unfolded. "We ran the man's prints. His name was Barry Radick. He was sentenced in 2007 to ten years at Huntsville for aggravated robbery. Paroled after four. We're still piecing together his movements from that time until he turned up dead on your lawn."

Shannon asked the question that had been bothering her since the shooting. "What was he doing in my neighborhood?"

"We're still working on that. He was there on purpose, though. The keys in his pocket matched a Ford Focus that was parked a half block away, on the other side of the street."

"What else do you know about Radick?" Mark asked.

"Nothing yet," Alston said, refolding the paper and putting it away. "I mainly wanted to see if the name meant anything to you."

Mark and Shannon looked at each other, then both shook their heads.

Alston rose. "Well, I should let you folks get back to your Sunday afternoon." He turned toward the door. "You needn't show me out." He turned his eyes on Shannon. "I'll be in touch."

In that look, Shannon felt that a message had been passed. *Don't be afraid of me because I'm a policeman. I'm interested in you as a person, not as a person of interest.*

After the door closed, Mark said, "That was odd. You'd think that he could have waited until tomorrow to tell you that. Or maybe even done it over the phone."

Shannon shrugged. "I think the new information was just an excuse to come over." *And I'm betting that's not the last I see of Detective Steve Alston, even if the crime were solved tomorrow.*

Before the conversation could go further, Megan peeked around the doorway. "I heard a car drive away. Police gone?" she asked. "I hope so, because I've run out of cookies."

"Megan, how can you eat all those and still keep your figure?" Shannon asked.

"If you notice, I'm not as slim as you. I like to think of myself as full figured. But believe me, these are the first cookies I've had in weeks. Right now, I crave comfort food."

"I think we all do," said Mark. "That's why I brought them."

Megan took the chair recently vacated by Steve Alston. "So what did the police have to say about your shooting?"

"Not *my* shooting," Shannon almost snapped. "The shooting that happened in my front yard." She took a deep breath. No need to come down on Megan. She had problems of her own. "They found out the name of the man who was shot, but I'm not sure it brought us any closer to figuring out why it happened."

Megan finished her cookie and dusted her hands together. She licked a few crumbs off the corner of her mouth. "What was his name?"

Shannon looked at Mark. "I'm not sure I got it right. Do you remember it?"

Mark nodded. "It was an unusual name, and it stuck in my mind because I used to know someone with the same last name. It was Radick. Barry Radick."

If Shannon hadn't chosen that moment to turn back toward her sister, she might have missed the wide-eyed look that flashed across Megan's face. Then, as though a shade had been drawn, a neutral expression replaced it. No need to ask Megan if she recognized the name. She'd deny it . . . but Shannon was sure she did. *Now what does that mean?*



BEEP, BEEP, BEEP. WITH HER EYES STILL CLOSED, SHANNON SLAMMED HER hand down in the general area of the snooze bar of her alarm clock, stilling the annoying electronic sentinel. She started to roll over for five minutes, then realized that it was Monday. Mondays were always more demanding, with patients who'd been admitted over the weekend, cases requiring consultation, problems of various sorts. And this would be an especially busy Monday because the new resident year had just begun.

New resident year? With her eyes still tightly closed, she counted back. Friday had been July first, marked by the cele-bratory dinner that had such a tragic ending. Friday, Saturday, Sunday, Monday. One, two, three, four. Today was July Fourth! It was a holiday. True, she'd still need to go to the medical cen-ter, make hospital rounds, check with the residents, address any problems. But there was no need for her to be up this early. She could sleep a bit longer.

But, of course, by now she couldn't sleep. All the mental gymnastics had her wide-awake. Shannon opened her right eye far enough to squint at the LED figures of her clock: 6:08.

Oh well. She'd get an early start on the day. By a quarter to eight Shannon had showered, dressed, applied makeup, eaten breakfast, read the paper over a second cup of coffee, and was ready to head to the medical center. Should she wake Megan? No, she'd let her sleep. Shannon left a note next to the coffeepot. "Megan, gone to work. Call my cell phone if you need anything."

She was about to walk out the door when the phone in the living room rang. She hurried back to pick up, hoping to let Megan sleep a bit longer. "Dr. Frasier."

"What did he say?" The voice was masculine, muffled and rough, making the words hard to understand.

"Pardon me?"

"What did Barry say?"

"I don't know what you mean."

Whatever the caller was using to mask his voice essentially robbed his speech of emotion, but there was no mistaking the irritation and menace in the words. "I want to know what Barry Radick said before he died."

Shannon hugged herself, despite the comfortable temperature of her house. She looked all around, scanning the room as though the speaker might be there. She'd left the front door standing open to answer the call. Shannon carried the cordless phone with her as she hurried to close and double lock it.

"Look, I don't know what you mean. If this is about the man who died in my arms, I wasn't paying attention to what he might have mumbled. I was trying to save his life." She took a deep breath. "Now I'm going to hang up and call the police. Don't call here again."

She ended the call, only faintly aware that her caller was saying something more. Shannon rummaged in the pile of papers on her desk until she found the cards of the two detectives. She shuffled them, one in front of the other, considering which man to call. In the end, the decision was easy. She read the front of the card she'd chosen, then flipped it over, consulted the number written on the back, and dialed.


DETECTIVE STEVE ALSTON SAT IN SHANNON'S LIVING ROOM, HIS LEGS crossed, a leather-covered notebook open on his lap, a Bic pen in his hand. Today he wore a light gray sports coat with a faint maroon stripe. His shirt was white, the tie a paisley of gray on a maroon background. His cordovan oxfords appeared freshly shined.

When she called his cell number, Alston told her he could stop by on his way to work. For reasons she either didn't understand or wasn't prepared to accept, Shannon had checked her makeup in the mirror and put on a fresh pot of coffee while she waited.

"You say the man's voice was muffled. Like he was talking through a handkerchief, maybe?"

Shannon thought back to the conversation, trying to be analytical, her initial fright at the call fading a bit. "I'm no expert on disguising a voice, but he was doing something. The only person I've ever heard talk like that was a man with cancer of the throat."

"And tell me once more what he said." Alston held his pen at the ready.

Shannon related the conversation as accurately as she could recall it.

"Did Radick say something to you before he died?"

"Who . . . Oh, the man who was shot." She closed her eyes, trying to go back to the scene she'd attempted to wipe from her memory. "He mumbled something right before he died, but I couldn't really make out what he was saying."

Alston closed the notebook and stowed it in the side pocket of his coat. "If it became necessary, would you submit to hypnosis to see if we can clarify your recollection?"

Shannon shook her head.

Alston smiled. "Surely, as a doctor, you realize that hypnosis, in the hands of a trained professional, isn't a parlor trick. It can be a useful tool."

"I . . . I'm not sure I want to be hypnotized."

"Well, keep it in mind." Alston crossed his legs and leaned back.

"What do I do if he calls again?" Shannon asked. "Is there some way you can trace the call?"

"I'll see about getting an order for that. But it generally doesn't help. Criminals used to use different phone booths. Now they've gone to throwaway cell phones, totally disposable and untraceable."

"So what will you do next?"

"Right now, I'm sure Jesse is running Barry Radick through our computers. We'll see who his known associates are, interview them." He made a dismissive gesture. "Police work is largely a matter of routine. We keep digging, keep asking questions—lots of them—until eventually we find out what we need to know."

Shannon felt a cold chill creep down her spine. The police wouldn't just look into the background of the man who'd been shot. What would the detectives find when they dug into Megan's past? Or Mark's? Or Lee's? Or hers? Had they already unearthed secrets best kept hidden? She dreaded finding out.

# SIX

MARK WAS AT A TABLE IN THE HOSPITAL CAFETERIA WHEN HE SAW Shannon come in. He watched her as she went through the line, and as she turned away from the cashier with her tray, he caught her eye and beckoned her over.

They exchanged a quick hug. "How's the head?" she asked.

Mark touched his temple and flinched slightly. "It's going to be sore for a few days, but I'll live."

"Are you working today?" she asked as she unloaded a tuna sandwich and milk from her tray. "It's a holiday."

"Got some things to finish, and it's always nice to be here when it's relatively quiet." He took a bite of his grilled cheese sandwich, washing it down with a drink of Diet Coke. "How about you?"

"I'll see a couple of post-ops, check with the residents to see if there are any problems. But mainly I wanted to get away from the house for a while." She lifted her sandwich from the plate, thought for a moment, and put it down. "Glad I ran into you, though. I need to talk."

Mark wiped his lips with a paper napkin. "That's me, 'listeners 'r' us.' What's on your mind?"

Shannon told him about the phone call and Detective Alston's visit. "Could you hear the man who was shot—Radick, I guess his name was—did you hear him say something?"

"I was in the doorway, too far away to hear much of anything. Lee was right there with you. Maybe he knows."

"Of course. I should check with him." Shannon shoved her plate away. "Alston said the police would run Radick's name through their computers. Do you suppose they'll do the same with us—you or me or Lee? Even Megan?"

Mark shrugged. "Maybe. But what difference does it make? They may turn up a few traffic tickets, although it's been years since I got one. Are you worried they'll find something in your past?"

Shannon was silent, looking out the windows with what Mark had heard called a thousand-yard stare. He gave her a minute or two before he said, "Shannon, are you there?"

"I'm sorry," she said. "My mind wandered. What was it?"

"Were you thinking about Todd's shooting?" She'd shared that experience with Mark, but only superficially. He guessed that she wasn't about to discuss it today either.

Shannon nodded. "I was going over it in my mind again." She reached over and took a sip of his Diet Coke. He shoved the rest of it toward her.

"And . . ."

"I've had two men die in my arms, and I couldn't save either one of them." She crumpled a napkin in her fist. "How do you think that made me feel?"

Mark leaned forward and covered her hand with his. "When Todd was shot, you'd barely started medical school. You weren't into your clinical courses, weren't treating patients. You didn't—"

"I know. But it was such a helpless feeling. I'd never seen anyone die, much less have their blood on my hands."

"Shannon, that was then. This is now. Nothing you or Lee could have done would have saved Radick. You couldn't start an IV to give fluids or replace blood loss, you couldn't open his chest to clamp off the bleeders, you couldn't . . ." He leaned forward. "There was nothing you could do. It was a miracle he stayed alive that long."

He watched her fight back tears. Mark knew Shannon well enough to be certain she wasn't going to cry, not right here in the hospital cafeteria, not in front of everyone. That was another part of the doctor persona she'd worked so hard to put in place. Patients and families didn't want to see their doctor cry . . . or show fear . . . or uncertainty.

*Oh, Shannon. If I could just get inside your head for a bit and help you get some things straight.* Mark took her hand and spoke just loudly enough to be certain it carried over the low din of the cafeteria. "Listen carefully. Ten years ago, there was nothing you could do to save Todd. Three days ago, there was nothing you could do to save Radick."

"But I'm a doctor."

Mark nodded. "True, now you're a doctor. But you're not God."

ALL DURING THE TIME SHE WAS MAKING ROUNDS WITH THE SURGIcal resident on call, while she was at her desk reading lab and X-ray reports, even on her walk to the parking lot, Mark's words ran through Shannon's mind. *You're a doctor. But you're not God.*

Finally, she could no longer postpone the visit she dreaded. Shannon climbed into her car and pulled out of the medical center's physicians' parking lot. It would probably be quicker to walk the few blocks to her destination, but unfortunately that would mean crossing a busy freeway, and she'd seen the results when others tried, only to end up critically injured or DOA in the emergency room. No, she'd drive.

She wasn't sure whether her UT Southwestern parking sticker would work at the Southwestern Institute of Forensic Sciences, but she was unlikely to need it anyway. Most people never spared a thought for the office of the Dallas County Medical Examiner, much less had a desire to visit the offices. The examiner and his deputies, like baseball umpires, worked in obscurity unless they made a mistake, at which time everyone noticed them.

Once in the building, she sought out the person she hoped could give her the answers she needed. It took her fifteen minutes, but soon she was seated in the office of Dr. Gordon Taylor, Deputy Medical Examiner. She and Gordon had gone through medical school together. Now they saw each other occasionally in the faculty club at lunch. But she'd never visited him where he worked.

Gordon had changed since Shannon worked across from him in the gross anatomy lab. His hairline had retreated, his waistline expanded, and it seemed to her that the horn-rimmed glasses he always wore were a bit thicker. But despite all that, he was the same Gordon—cheery, unflappable. She hoped his disposition would be the same after she asked her favor.

He shrugged his shoulders to settle his crisply starched white lab coat, leaned back in his desk chair, and smiled. "So what brings you to our humble abode?"

"I need a favor, Gordon."

His cherubic face never changed expression, but his eyes reflected caution. "You know I'll do anything I can, but I work within some pretty stringent rules. What do you need?"

"Did you do the autopsy on Tony . . ." What was Tony's last name? Had Megan even mentioned it? Then it came to her. "Lester. Did you do the post on Tony Lester?"

"Name's not familiar, but sometimes the old memory slips," Gordon said. He turned to the computer on his desk, tapped a few keys, and said, "Dr. Rao did that autopsy earlier this morning. Nothing in the system yet about the results."

"If I asked him, would he tell me the cause of death?"

Gordon frowned. "Why would you want to know that? Are you involved in some way?"

Shannon hesitated, then decided that if she wanted the information, she'd have to tell Gordon why. "He was my sister's boyfriend. She was one of the last people to see him before he died, and I think the police consider her a suspect, or at least a person of interest."

"Shannon, you know this as well as I do. Although the results of that autopsy may eventually become public record, at present they're not. They'll go first to the detective in charge of the case. I'm not sure your personal interest justifies my asking Dr. Rao to give you what, at this time, amounts to privileged information."

Shannon leaned forward in her chair, as though by her posture she could convey the importance of her request. "I know it may take awhile for Rao's report to be typed up, proofread, and signed. And the toxicology might not be available for six to eight weeks. But it's important that I know the gist of the report now." She decided she had to trust Gordon with the information. "Tony was drunk when my sister last saw him. He was combative, tried to hit my boyfriend, who had accompanied her. She had to defend herself. She . . . she hit him on the head with a bottle."

"Spunky girl."

"Spunky, but misguided sometimes. Anyway, I was worried that Tony might have developed intracranial bleeding afterward, and that was what killed him. All I need to know is whether Rao found a subdural hematoma, anything like that."

Gordon turned back to the computer and scanned a few lines. "I think your sister can relax," he said. He swiveled around to face Shannon. "The notes that accompanied the body say he came in with a gunshot wound to the head."


SHANNON WASN'T ON CALL. SHE'D TAKEN CARE OF A FEW THINGS at the medical center. There was nothing pending that seemed more important than the two deaths that had suddenly taken over her life. She decided to head home.

When Shannon had left that morning, Megan's car was at the curb in front of the house. Now it was gone. Once inside, Shannon went from room to room, not sure what she was looking for, but thinking she should see what her sister might have been up to in her absence. Some might call it snooping. Given Megan's history, Shannon thought it made sense for her to look around.

Megan's room was surprisingly neat. Shannon guessed her sister had finally developed the habit of cleaning up after herself, rather than waiting for someone else to do it. In their teen years, that someone was often Shannon.

*Here I am again, cleaning up after her, but this time it's not picking up clothes or washing dishes.* How long before Megan became a responsible adult? How many more messes, both figurative and literal, would Shannon have to clean up for her sister?

In the living room, Shannon noticed that she'd left her address book by the phone. It was open to the page with the name of the attorney she was going to call if the police appeared to be coming after Megan. She closed the book and stowed it in a desk drawer.

As she was about to close the drawer, something nibbled at the edge of her memory, something that didn't seem right. She stood there for a moment before it came to her. And when it did, she had a sinking feeling in the pit of her stomach.

When Shannon had come home and encountered Megan holding a gun, she'd taken the weapon and laid it on an end table in the living room. After Megan left the room, Shannon moved it to the top drawer of her desk, wanting to get it out of sight, away from her, to be dealt with later. She hadn't thought of it since.

Now Shannon scrabbled through the contents of the drawer, shoving aside papers, pens, all the material that collects in a desk. When she failed to find what she was hunting, she opened the other drawers and repeated the actions. At last she took a deep breath and held it for several long seconds before letting it out slowly. Her shoulders sagged. She sank into the desk chair and put her head in her hands.

The gun was gone.

# SEVEN

THE FIRST THING SHANNON DID, AFTER TAKING A MOMENT TO gather herself, was go through the house from top to bottom, looking for the gun. There was no doubt in her mind about where she'd left it. But if the gun wasn't in that drawer, maybe Megan had reclaimed it and put it somewhere. She hoped that was the case. Because if it wasn't . . . No, she didn't want to think about that right now.

When her search proved fruitless, Shannon clung grimly to the hope that Megan knew what had happened to the gun. She imagined a conversation in which her sister said, "Oh, yes. I decided it wasn't a good idea to have the gun around, so I gave it to . . ." To whom? That wasn't a great scenario either, to have a weapon covered with her sister's fingerprints (as well as her own) floating around the city. Suppose it was used in the commission of a crime? Maybe it had already been used for that purpose.

When Megan finally came through the door, it was ten o'clock. Shannon bit back the question she wanted to ask. You don't confront a grown woman and ask her to explain her movements, however much you want to do just that. Instead, she forced a smile to her face. "How was your evening?"

"Pretty good. I hooked up with some people I knew and got some leads on a job. There's a small pharmaceutical company looking for field reps. I'm going to call them tomorrow."

Shannon wasn't sure that being fired from her last job would serve as a great employment recommendation, but that was a conversation for another time. "I guess you've already eaten."

"Yeah, we had hot wings and mini-tacos at the bar."

*Bar? This just gets worse and worse.* "Oh?"

"Don't worry," Megan said. "I stuck to Diet Cokes. I wasn't going to come back to your house smelling of margaritas." She spread her hands. "Honest. I'm clean, and I intend to stay that way."

Shannon decided it was time to ask the big question. "I looked for the gun you had on Saturday, but I can't find it. Have you seen it?" Shannon mentally crossed fingers and toes, hoping for the right answer. She didn't get it.

Megan hesitated for a moment, apparently thinking about the question. "No, I didn't touch it. But when you find it, go ahead and get rid of it. I don't think it's such a good idea for me to have a gun. Do you?"

"No, I agree." *But we may be too late.*

AS MARK SHAVED ON TUESDAY MORNING, HE STARED PAST THE IMAGE IN THE mirror and considered the two crimes in which he'd been involved, either directly or indirectly, within the past few days.

In the shooting of the man outside Shannon's house, he was pretty much a bystander, staying in the house to comfort Lee's wife, Ann, while Lee and Shannon knelt over the victim.

When Detective Alston mentioned the man's name—Barry Radick—it had meant nothing to him. Of course, Radick might have undergone a biopsy or even a surgical procedure at one of the University Medical Center hospitals, and if so, there was a chance Mark had rendered a diagnosis from the tissue slides. He made a mental note to check that out, although he was pretty sure it would be a dead end. Other than that, the whole thing seemed to involve him only by happenstance.

As for the death of Megan's live-in boyfriend, Tony, he'd been more intimately connected with that one. He gingerly touched his temple, pleased that the soreness and swelling were much less, although the resulting bruise decorated his temple with varied hues of green and yellow. Mark thought back to the encounter with Tony. He wished he'd followed his first instinct and drummed up an excuse not to accompany Megan. Try as he might, even though she was Shannon's sister, he couldn't get past the way Megan always seemed to be a problem waiting to happen.

When Megan asked for his help, despite his underlying feelings he responded as he felt a Christian should. If a man asks for your coat, give him your shirt as well, to paraphrase the scripture. Of course, it had been obvious from the moment they walked into the house that Megan's fear of Tony was well grounded. Could Megan have set up the whole thing in order to get back at Tony, maybe even get rid of him? That was ridiculous . . . or at least Mark hoped so.

SHANNON FACED THE WORLD ON TUESDAY OUT OF NECESSITY, NOT desire. She dragged herself from her bed, stumbled to the kitchen for a first cup of coffee, and somehow got through everything necessary before walking out the door.

She slowed as her car neared her favorite donut shop. After everything that had happened over the long weekend, her stomach was producing acid at a rapid clip. Common sense told her to steer clear of coffee and breakfast pastries. The rest of her, though, said, "Gimme." She ended up getting a large coffee and a bear claw. Shannon nibbled and sipped her way to the medical center, licking the last bit of glaze off her lips as she pulled into a parking space.

This morning she was scheduled to staff the new senior surgery resident on a gallbladder. The time wasn't too far past when that would involve an incision of six inches or longer and the use of retractors and force to give wide exposure of the area of the liver where the gallbladder was located. The surgery would take several hours, and the patient would be hospitalized for days.

Now surgeons used endoscopes—small fiber-optic instruments that allowed visualization through a virtual buttonhole, guiding other instruments inserted through another similar small incision. In skilled hands, the operating time had been cut in half, sometimes even less. Patients ended up with four tiny incisions covered by Band-Aids, and some left the hospital on the same day.

When she finished medical school, Shannon figured there'd be no more major advances in her specialty for a while. But things were constantly changing and, other than the regulations and paperwork that seemed to be multiplying, changing for the better. She wished she could say the same for her life, which seemed to be going in the opposite direction.

The new chief resident did a nice job with the surgery. He hadn't yet reached the level of competence Lee Kai demonstrated, but then, Shannon couldn't recall when she'd last had the privilege of training a resident like Lee. And she would enjoy telling him that today, because he was to be her guest for lunch at the medical center's faculty club, celebrating his first official day in private practice.

Shannon went by her office to check messages before lunch. Most of the notes on her desk dealt with routine matters, but one made the hairs on the back of her neck stand at attention. "Call Detective Alston," followed by a number she recognized as his cell phone.

She knew she wouldn't taste any of her lunch so long as she was worrying about the call. She had to return it now. Lee would understand. She closed the door to her office, took a deep breath, and dialed Alston's number.

He answered on the first ring. "Alston."

"This is Shannon Frasier. You called?"

"Yes. Hated to call your office, but there was no answer at home or on your cell."

"Sorry. I was in surgery." She didn't know why the apology slipped out. He was the one bothering her, not the other way around.

"I have some more information about the man who was shot in your yard, and it brings up a few more questions. Would you be available sometime today to talk?"

"Just a second." Shannon scanned the daily schedule her secretary, Janice, had centered on her desk blotter. "I can fit you in about four. Would that work?"

"Fine. I'll come by your office."

Shannon hung up the phone and wondered where this was going. What new information could possibly involve her? And Alston had said, "I'll come by," not, "We'll come by." Was he coming alone again? Shannon wondered if Alston's interest in her was more than professional. *Don't be ridiculous. You're almost engaged.* Then again, maybe she hadn't acted like it around Alston. She'd need to make sure her relationship with Mark was more evident the next time she met with the detective.

She wondered momentarily about calling Mark to ask him to be in her office at four. Shannon decided to think about it. Right now, she had to meet Lee.

"DR. FRASIER, GOOD TO SEE YOU. THIS WAY, PLEASE." HANS, THE maître d' of the faculty club, showed Shannon and Lee to their table. Before he left, he nodded to Lee. "Dr. Kai, congratulations on entering private practice."

"How did he know that?" Lee asked when Hans had walked away.

"Hans knows everything that goes on around here." Shannon unfolded her napkin.

Lee looked over at the dessert buffet. "That always looks great."

"If you'd let me recommend you for a faculty position, you could eat here regularly."

"Sorry, I guess I've got to try my wings flying solo. But I appreciate you bringing me here today." There was genuine regret in his voice when he said, "I'd better just have a sandwich, though."

After they ordered, Lee stirred his iced tea, then asked, "What's the latest on the shooting in your front yard? The detectives interviewed me, but I couldn't really tell them anything. When they called me yesterday to give me the victim's name, I had to tell them it wasn't familiar." He took a sip.

"Me, too. I'd never heard of Barry Radick," Shannon said. She told Lee what Alston had passed on to her, pausing frequently to sip water. "And apparently they've uncovered something more. Alston will be here around four to talk with me again."

"Let me know if there's anything I can do."

"You can answer a question for me," Shannon said. "I got an anonymous phone call Monday morning. The man kept asking what Radick said before he died. I know he mumbled something, but I couldn't catch it. Did you?"

They paused and leaned back as a waiter placed their sandwiches on the table, added a bottle of catsup, and departed. Lee picked up his Reuben on pretzel bread and took a big bite. He chewed, swallowed, and washed it down with iced tea. "I love these," he said.

"I'm glad," Shannon said, "but wait a minute before you take another bite. Did you hear what Radick said before he died?"

"Yes. He recited a string of numbers. They didn't make any sense to me, though."

Shannon felt herself deflating like a party balloon when the string was untied. "And of course you aren't able to remember the numbers."

Lee feigned a hurt look. "Dr. Frasier, I'm ashamed of you for forgetting so quickly. I have an eidetic memory. Certainly I remember."

SHANNON SAT AT HER DESK, SCROLLING THROUGH LAB RESULTS and biopsy reports on her computer. She looked up when she heard a knock on the frame of her open door.

"May we come in?" Detectives Alston and Callaway didn't wait for a response. They entered and took the two chairs across the desk from Shannon.

*So much for this being a social visit.* Shannon wasn't sure whether she was relieved or disappointed. No matter. She looked at the men with what she hoped was a neutral expression. This visit was their idea. Let them talk first.

The two detectives looked at each other and apparently some sort of silent communication passed between them. Alston nodded and said, "We need to locate your sister."

"Megan?"

"I believe that's the only sister you have," Callaway said.

"Where can we find her?" Alston asked. "We have some questions for her."

"She's supposed to be job-hunting today," Shannon said. "She should be back at my house this evening."

Alston nodded while Callaway jotted something in his notebook. The two men started to rise, but Shannon stopped them.

"Wait! At least tell me why you want to talk with Megan." She turned toward Alston. "You said you'd discovered more about the shooting in my yard. What does that have to do with her?"

Callaway shrugged. "Barry Radick, the man who was shot, did a stint in drug rehab at a place called First Step not long after he got out of prison. Your sister was in that facility at the same time as Radick." He rose and shoved his notebook into his pocket. "When you see her, have her call us. We have some questions for her."


MARK WAS READY FOR THE DAY TO END. IT WAS THE TUESDAY after a long holiday weekend. He'd faced the problems associated with the influx of new first-year residents. And now there was this new discovery. His heart ached as he thought of the implications, and his stomach knotted with the realization he'd need to tell Shannon, and the sooner, the better.

He picked up his phone and dialed Shannon's private line, figuring the odds were at least even that she'd be in the operating room with one of the new residents. Mark was surprised when she picked up on the first ring.

"You're in your office and it's only a quarter to five. Will wonders never cease?" he said.

"I'm ready for this day to be over." Shannon's tone told him what he needed to know before she finished her sentence.

"Can you come by my office when you're ready to leave?" Mark almost wished Shannon would say no. He dreaded telling her his news.

"I suppose. Why?"

"I need to talk with you, and I think we should do it in private."

Shannon's puzzlement was reflected in her voice. "Okay. I'll see you in half an hour."

That gave Mark time to prepare. He gathered some things and made a couple of phone calls, all the while grieving over what he had to do. Shannon tapped on his office door as he hung up from the last call.

"Come in." He gestured to the chair he'd pulled to a position beside his desk.

Shannon collapsed more than sat. "It's been a tough day. I hope you have something good to tell me."

Mark leaned down and kissed her. "No, I'm afraid not. But I've already got the wheels in motion to handle it."

"Mark, you're scaring me. What's the matter?"

"I kept wondering if maybe Barry Radick had come through the system here at the medical center. I did a computer search through all the tissue samples in our database for the past decade or so—biopsies, surgery, all that kind of thing—and it was negative. Then I thought to check lab reports." He picked up a sheet of paper off the desk. "Just before Radick went into drug rehab, he showed up in the ER with a near overdose. In addition to the usual tox screens, the doc ordered an HIV test." He saw the look on her face and hurried on. "Yes. Radick was HIV-positive."

"And I had his blood all over my hands," she said. "And so did Lee."

"Afraid so." He pointed to the equipment laid out on his desk. "I'll call Lee first thing tomorrow, but right now let's deal with you. I need to draw some blood for baseline studies. One of the doctors from the infectious disease group is on his way over with your first doses of medication. You have to start on AIDS prophylaxis."

# EIGHT

SHANNON GUESSED SHE SHOULD BE FLATTERED THAT THE CHIEF OF THE infectious disease service at the medical center would come in person to get her treatment started. But at that moment, she'd give anything for the whole thing to be a bad dream. She wanted to wake up in her own bed, with no thought of AIDS added to the fears that already dominated her life. But it wasn't a dream.

Even though Radick's blood hadn't contacted her mucous membranes, even though she'd had no break in the skin to allow the blood (and therefore, the virus) free access to her circulation, Dr. Jay Sanders felt it was prudent to place her on what he termed "post-exposure prophylaxis," or PEP. "Maybe I'm being overly cautious, but these things are never black and white."

"So what's next?" Shannon asked.

"We'll do baseline labs, including liver and kidney functions. Then we'll need follow-up studies while you're on the meds."

"What meds?" she asked. "And how long will you want me to take them?"

He removed his wire-rimmed glasses and polished them with the end of his tie. "I'm following the CDC's recommendations here. If the risk of exposure were high, we'd put you on three antiretroviral drugs, but most patients can't tolerate the side effects and never finish the full four-week course. You'll be better off on two drugs, and fortunately they're available in a single tablet you take twice a day."

"I guess you'll want serial HIV tests," she said, her eyes fixed on the carpet.

"We'll do one now, of course, and expect it to be negative. Then you'll need one at six weeks, twelve weeks, and six months after exposure." Sanders forced a smile. "If that one's negative, you're safe."

So she'd have six months to worry. Why hadn't she taken the time to don gloves? She had a dozen pair in her home, gloves she'd taken from the operating room to use in chores ranging from cleaning floors to painting a cupboard. But she'd ignored the need for caution and followed her gut instinct, rushing to the aid of the fallen man.

It was almost seven o'clock when Mark walked Shannon to her car, opened the door, and kissed her. "I'll call you later tonight," he said. Was it her imagination, or was his kiss a bit hesitant? Was this going to sound the death knell for a relationship that had been stuck in one place for months? *Don't be silly. Mark's not that kind of guy.*

In her heart, Shannon knew she could depend on Mark to be with her every step of the journey that lay ahead of her. She wondered how she'd break the news to her parents. And that, in turn, reminded her that she needed to find out about her dad's weight loss. Maybe his doctor had told him to lose a few pounds. Perhaps his blood sugar had crept up, and he'd been warned to change his diet or risk developing diabetes. Then, as a doctor generally did in situations of this sort, she leaped to the worst possible diagnosis. Her heart thudded against her chest wall when the word crossed her mind—did he have a cancer of some sort?

She made the drive home on autopilot while she considered the practical implications of tonight's discovery. The first thing Shannon had to do in the morning was talk with her chairman to see how this would affect her clinical responsibilities. Since the department chair was lecturing and teaching at a symposium in Greece, that meant another session in the office of Tom Waites, the vice chairman. Even though she'd kept him in the loop about what was going on in her life, this latest development was going to be a bombshell to him.

Tom had always seemed to Shannon to be more collegial than the department chair. She hoped he'd understand and be supportive. She planned to double glove before surgical procedures—a common preventive measure for the operative team when a patient was HIV-positive, but this time she'd be doing it to protect her patient—and be extra careful about hand washing. Maybe Tom would agree that was more than enough to let her continue her clinical duties.

Thoughts of Tom made Shannon think of Tom's wife. Beneath the beautiful visage of Elena Garcia Waites was one of the sharpest legal minds in Dallas County, if not the state of Texas. With each new development in the murder of Megan's boyfriend, Shannon moved closer to calling Elena, laying out the facts as she knew them, and engaging her services to defend her sister. Maybe now was the time to do that.

As Shannon pulled into the driveway, she saw Megan's car at the curb. Well, they had plenty to talk about tonight.

AFTER SEEING SHANNON OFF, INSTEAD OF GOING TO HIS OWN CAR Mark went back to his office. He was a pathologist, well versed in the diagnosis of human immunodeficiency virus states, but he had only a basic knowledge of post-exposure prophylaxis, the regimen to follow when health professionals suffered occupational exposure to the virus. He'd tried to pay attention to what the infectious disease specialist said, but he wanted to make sure he had a firm grasp of the subject, now that the problem was more personal.

Almost an hour later, he closed down his computer. Mark was grateful that the Internet allowed him to read the latest information almost as quickly as it was released, in contrast with articles in print journals that were sometimes as much as a year old by the time they reached his desk.

He leaned back in his chair and tried to make sense of what he'd learned. He was relieved to learn that Shannon's likelihood of contracting the disease was extremely small. Even had she been stuck with an infected needle, the chances of active HIV infection resulting would be less than one percent. These odds dropped another tenfold when HIV-positive blood contacted only a mucous membrane such as the eyes or nose. Since Shannon's exposure was through blood on intact skin, and she scrubbed her hands thoroughly afterward, the risk was infinitesimal—but it was there. They couldn't ignore it.

Mark pondered how he should act—how Shannon would *want* him to act—in view of these new circumstances. He knew her well enough to realize she wouldn't want sympathy. But he also recognized that the ghost of Barry Radick would haunt them both, at least for the next six months, hovering in the background, poised to strike the woman Mark loved, inflicting a potentially lethal disease.

He turned from his computer and pulled a worn leather

Bible from the shelf behind his desk. The guidance he sought wouldn't come from the Internet. Mark wasn't sure what the end result would be, but he had no doubt he'd find the direction he needed in the Book.

MEGAN WAS SITTING IN FRONT OF THE TV SET, ENGROSSED IN some sort of game show, when Shannon came in the door. Megan muted the sound and said, "You worked late tonight. Trouble at the hospital?"

Shannon dropped her purse in a chair by the front door and eased onto the sofa beside her sister. "Lots of trouble today, but not the kind you're thinking about." She slipped off her shoes and tucked her feet under her. "We need to talk."

Megan punched another button on the remote, and the image on the TV died. "Sure. What's up?"

"Two detectives came to my office today. They're investigating the man who got shot in front of this house on Friday night."

"Have they found out something more?"

"Yes," Shannon said. "Do you recall Mark mentioning the man's name?"

"Uh, I think so."

"And I saw recognition flash across your face. I didn't say anything at the time, but would you like to tell me about your connection to Barry Radick?"

Megan screwed up her face as though trying hard to remember. After a few seconds, she said, "Now that I think about it, there was a guy by that name in First Step with me. Do you think it could be the same one?"

"It not only could be. It is," Shannon said. "And I expect the detectives will want to question you."

"Why?"

Was her sister being purposely dense? "Connect the dots. An ex-con whom you know is shot outside your sister's house. Could he have been trying to make contact with you? Were you and he together in some sort of deal?"

Megan shook her head. "I haven't seen Barry, haven't even thought about him, since the day I left First Step. I'll be glad to tell them that, but it's all I know."

"How did someone like Radick get into First Step anyway? It took a lot of money to pay for your treatment there."

"Barry explained it to me once—some kind of support from the county, or the state, or . . . I don't know. I wasn't thinking too clearly at the time," Megan said.

Shannon wasn't sure how to broach the next subject, but it had to be said—especially given her sister's history of promiscuity. "While you were both at First Step, was there ever a time . . . a time when you were . . . when you and he were romantically—"

"Don't even finish that sentence," Megan said. "No way."

"You're certain? This is important."

"I don't know why it is, but, yes, I'm certain. We saw each other in the halls. We sat at the same table for some meals. I talked with him from time to time—most of the other people there shunned him, and I felt sorry for him. But that's as far as it went." She hitched herself straighter on the couch. "Unlike some of the people in the facility, I was serious about getting my life straight. And hooking up with a guy who was both a criminal and a drug addict wasn't going to get it done."

"Good."

Megan frowned. "Why did you ask that?"

Shannon had thought about this on the drive home. If Megan was going to live with her, she deserved to know what was going on. "I just found out tonight that Radick was HIV-positive."

"So you wanted to make sure I hadn't been exposed?"

"That, but there's more." She went on to explain her own exposure through the blood of the murdered man, and the treatment she'd be on for the next month. "Let me assure you that you're in no danger. I'll be tested several times, I'm on medication, and there's no chance that HIV can be passed on via saliva or touching or—"

Megan reached over and hugged her sister. "I'm not worried about me," she said. "I'm worried about you. Do you think you're going to be okay?"

Shannon was touched by Megan's concern. With more confidence than she felt, she said, "I'm going to be just fine, Megan. And so are you."

The words had hardly left her mouth when the doorbell rang. Shannon moved to the door and looked through the peephole. Then she turned to Megan with a look that she hoped reflected encouragement. "The detectives are here."

SHANNON LOOKED AROUND AT THE GROUP ASSEMBLED IN HER LIVING room. She and Megan were on the sofa. Callaway sat at a right angle to them in an overstuffed chair. Steve Alston declined a chair with thanks, saying he preferred to stand, so he leaned against the doorframe. Outwardly, everyone seemed calm, but Shannon knew that a storm could burst forth at any moment.

As before, Callaway took the lead in the interview. If they were playing good cop–bad cop, Callaway was doing a great job as the unpleasant half of the team, with Steve Alston providing a sympathetic contrast. But Megan's answers were consistent, her demeanor calm and cool, despite the occasional accusatory tone of Callaway's questions.

Finally, Alston straightened from his position and said, "To summarize, then, you were in rehab with Barry Radick, but your contact with him was limited to occasional chats, and you haven't seen him since your release. Right?"

"That's right."

"Are we about done here?" Shannon asked.

"Just a few more questions," Callaway said. "Let's talk a little about Tony Lester."

Shannon felt her stomach roil. She'd almost forgotten the death of Megan's latest boyfriend for a moment. The police had said detectives would be contacting Megan. It never dawned on her the case might be assigned to the same men who were investigating the shooting outside her house Friday night.

"How did you hook up with Tony in the first place?" Callaway asked.

Megan averted her eyes. "I met him when he visited a friend of his in rehab. When I got out, my former boyfriend had moved on. I called Tony and asked if I could crash at his place. We . . . it just kept going from there."

"Tell us about the circumstances of your moving out," Callaway said. "Why did you do it? Was it acrimonious? What about the last time you saw Lester?" He paused, and almost as an afterthought, said, "Why did you shoot him?"

Shannon held up a hand. "Hold on. Does Megan need an attorney?"

Once more, Steve Alston stepped in. "If your sister wants to answer questions for us here and now, we can do it without an attorney. You'll notice we haven't even warned her of her rights. If you want to get an attorney into the mix, we'll go down to headquarters. Your choice."

"That's okay, Shannon," Megan said. "I don't have anything to hide." She turned to Callaway, who sat with his notebook open on his knee. "I left Tony because I think he stole some pharmaceutical samples from me and got me fired. I accused him, and he lost his temper. He did that a lot. I decided I'd had enough, so I moved out."

"And that was the last time you saw him?" Callaway said.

"No, I went back the next day to clear my stuff out of the house. Tony was drunk. At first he was verbally abusive. I was used to that. Then he attacked the man who accompanied me. There was a struggle. I hit Tony on the head with a bottle. He was alive when I left. I didn't shoot him, and I resent your asking if I did."

"That's pretty much the story you gave the police who interviewed you, but is there anything you'd like to change?" Callaway said. "You're not under oath . . . at least, not yet. If you want to give us something different, now's the time."

"No. That's the truth." Megan clenched her jaw, and Shannon knew what that meant. She'd seen it a lot when the girls were growing up. Megan had decided to dig in her heels. "I believe I'll take you up on that offer now. If you want to ask me the same questions over and over, maybe I'd better have an attorney. Otherwise, I think it's time for you to leave."

Callaway opened his mouth but closed it without saying anything. He rose and shoved his notebook into his pocket. Meanwhile, Alston was already moving toward the front door.

With the door half open, Callaway turned and said, "You might like to know that the medical examiner recovered the bullet that killed Tony Lester. Right now we're searching for the gun that fired it. When we find it, we may be back." He touched his forehead with two fingers in a sort of salute. "Ladies, good night."

SHANNON ROSE FROM THE KITCHEN TABLE CARRYING HER GLASS and a bowl. "Was that enough for you?"

"Plenty," Megan said, mirroring her sister's actions.

Shannon took her sister's dishes and loaded them into the dishwasher, along with her own. Neither had much of an appetite, so dinner had been soup, crackers, and milk. Idly, Shannon wondered if she might shed a few pounds during this ordeal. Perhaps she could market it, call it the "stress diet."

"I'm going to take a hot shower, then try to relax. I might even take advantage of that TV set in the guest bedroom," Megan said.

Alone in the living room, Shannon considered the two phone calls she needed to make. She decided to leave the hard one for last. Having made the decision, she lifted the receiver and dialed.

Mark answered on the first ring. "I was thinking about calling you, but wasn't sure you'd want to talk tonight."

"When I left the medical center, I wasn't sure I'd ever want to talk with anyone again. I felt like digging a hole and pulling the dirt in over me."

"How are you doing now?" Mark asked.

"If you mean do I have any ill effects from my first dose of medicine, no. If you want to know how I'm doing in general, I feel as though I've been dropped into a mixer set to high speed. The detectives just left." She told him about their visit. "So I really haven't had much time to feel sorry for myself about the exposure to Radick's HIV-positive blood."

"I've been researching that. The chances of your becoming infected are extremely slim."

"Unless they're zero, I'm afraid I'm going to worry. I suspect that for the next six months, I'll be running to the infectious disease specialist with every sniffle and cough."

"And you shouldn't hesitate to do that." Mark paused. "Is there something I can do for you?"

"I'm not sure there's anything that anyone can do for me," she said.

"There's one thing," Mark said. "I'll pray."

SHANNON WAS STILL SITTING IN THE LIVING ROOM, STARING INTO space, when she heard Megan come into the room. Her sister was wearing a set of scrubs Shannon had given her a couple of years ago. She was barefoot. Her hair was still wet from the shower. Scrubbed clean of makeup, Megan's face was that of an innocent eighteen-year-old. Shannon wished she could turn back the clock to that time in both their lives.

"Everything okay with Mark?" Megan asked.

Shannon nodded. "I'm glad you're in here. I was about to phone Mom. Let me get her, then I'll put the call on speakerphone."

She wanted to call her mom when her dad wasn't home, and the window of opportunity was closing. It was the first Tuesday of the month, time for the regularly scheduled church elders meeting. It would be ending about now, but customarily the pastor went out for coffee with the chair and vice chair after the meeting. He'd be home soon, though, so Shannon couldn't put off the call any longer.

Her mother answered after a couple of rings. "Hello?"

"Mom, this is Shannon."

"Is anything wrong, dear?"

How bad was it that Shannon's call were so infrequent that her mom's first thought would be that something was wrong? She made up her mind to remedy that in the future. "No, we're doing fine." Not really, but there was no need to burden her parents with the details of all her problems. "It's just that Megan said she thought Dad had lost some weight. I guess I hadn't noticed, but I thought I should call and check it out."

The silence on the other end of the line went on much too long for Shannon's comfort. She was hoping for a quick answer, something like, "His doctor put him on a diet," or "No, his weight hasn't changed." Finally, she heard a sigh. "He insisted that we not bother you girls with this—that was his word, 'bother'—so we decided not to mention it until we had to."

Shannon felt as though she couldn't get enough air. Her throat seemed to be closing. She swallowed twice before she could say, "So what is it?"

"It appears that your dad has cancer."

# NINE

IN AN INSTANT, SHANNON SWITCHED FROM A CASUAL CONVERSA-
tion with her mom to full-on doctor mode. "Cancer? What
kind? When was it diagnosed? What do they plan to do?"

"Take it easy, dear. By the way, is Megan on the line, too?"

Shannon looked across the room at her sister, who was
frowning, obviously wondering what was going on. "No, I
intended to put this on speakerphone, but I haven't done it
yet." She punched a button and laid the receiver on the desk.
"Okay, now you have us both."

"Mom, what's wrong? Is something going on with Dad?"
Megan's brow was furrowed, and her voice quivered a bit.

"We don't know all the details yet. It started when Robert
found himself tiring easily. He noticed his clothes fitting more
loosely, which at first pleased him, but later it became worri-
some enough for him to respond to my urging to see his doctor."

"And what did they find?" Shannon asked.

"When Ralph . . . Dr. Gutekind did a complete physical, he

found some prominent lymph nodes. Robert's spleen was also enlarged. The blood test showed a high white cell count. Ralph sat down with us and said it was probably a form of leukemia."

"Let me call and set up an appointment for him to see a specialist," Shannon said.

"We already have an appointment at the medical school for the end of next week," her mom said. "After we see the specialist, when we know more, I'm sure your father will want to call you both and tell you. Until then, though, I don't think he wants to worry you. If—" In the background, a car door slammed. "That will be Robert now. I have to hang up."

"Isn't there something we can do?" Megan asked.

"You can do the same thing we're doing—trust God."


SHANNON SAT IN THE SURGEON'S LOUNGE AND BLEW ACROSS THE surface of her third cup of coffee of the morning. She yawned and wondered if she'd ever again get a good night's sleep. The conversation with the detectives hadn't been conducive to pleasant dreams. Instead, it left her feeling unsettled, waiting for the police to find the gun that killed Tony Lester and wondering if it was the same one she'd taken from Megan. That weapon would have her sister's fingerprints on it—it would have Shannon's as well.

As if that weren't enough, the news about her dad had taken away any chance at peaceful sleep. In a way, she admired his desire not to worry his daughters about his health problem, at least not until the details were settled. Although every fiber of her being wanted to pick up the phone, find out which hematologist-oncologist her dad was going to see, and make a call to grease the wheels, Shannon knew she shouldn't get involved in his case, certainly not without his knowledge and permission. Nevertheless, the waiting made her feel helpless. After all, she was a doctor. Surely she could do something to help her dad.

Shannon finished her coffee and tossed away the paper cup. That thought had triggered another. She'd been so engrossed in the interview with the detectives that she'd forgotten to pass on the information Lee Kai had given her about what Radick said before he died. Shannon figured she could be forgiven, since after learning that Lee remembered the information, she'd had to face being told she was exposed to HIV-positive blood, following which she learned that her dad had leukemia. It was a wonder she'd been able to get out of bed and dress herself this morning.

"Dr. Frasier?" The tinny voice reverberated through the intercom speaker.

"Yes." Shannon rose, figuring the nurse was calling to say they were ready in the operating room.

"I'm afraid we're going to have to delay your case. There's a patient in the ER with a ruptured ectopic pregnancy, and this is the only free OR either here or in OB. It'll be about an hour, maybe a bit more. Shall I page you when we're ready?"

"Please. And would you have someone explain the delay to the patient and his family?" Shannon had been sitting on the most comfortable sofa in the surgeon's lounge, the one whose springs hadn't yet surrendered to pressure from thousands of surgeons doing the same thing she was—waiting. She rose, drew another cup of coffee, sat back down, and pulled the phone toward her.

Although she probably should know the number by heart, she dug into her pocket and pulled out the card she'd transferred from her wallet as she dressed in scrubs. Shannon stabbed in the numbers and waited through four rings. What if he had his cell phone turned off? What if it was still in his car, while he— "Alston." Shannon almost jumped when the word interrupted her thoughts.

"Detective, this is Shannon Frasier. Can you talk right now?"

Now she could make out the noise in the background, the murmur of several voices, the random ringing of phones, an occasional shout. "Sure. I'm at my desk. Did you think of something you forgot to tell us last night? Or are you calling to ask me out?"

Either Alston was joking, or she'd been right about the vibe she thought she'd picked up. No matter. Shannon decided to ignore the remark. She needed to get this information out and go on with her life. "I have some information about Barry Radick and what he said before he died."

"Did you get another call from our harsh-voiced friend? I think the paperwork to record your incoming phone calls is hung up somewhere."

"No, there hasn't been another call, but my former resident, Dr. Lee Kai, was with me when Radick was shot, and he tells me he remembers what was said."

"Do I need to record this? If so, I need you to call back on my landline."

"No, all you'll need is a pen and paper to write down what I'm going to give you." She went on to explain about Lee's eidetic memory, and to apologize for not mentioning the material last night, saying that she was preoccupied with other things.

"I'm ready. What did he say?"

Surgical staff and residents alike always seemed to have blank three-by-five cards in their pockets for jotting down notes and recording patient information. Apparently Lee had continued the practice. In the faculty club, he had pulled such a card from his pocket and written down Radick's last words.

Now Shannon extracted the card from the pocket of her scrub pants and read, "324 8160 964 7900."

The puzzlement in Alston's voice was obvious. "Numbers? A string of numbers?"

"That's right."

"And there's no chance that Dr. Kai could be mistaken?"

"Lee can read a page in a textbook and recite it back, word for word, a month later. No, I'm pretty sure that's what Radick said."

There was silence on the line. Even the background noise seemed to have abated. At last Alston heaved a sigh that made it sound like the phone had been placed in a wind tunnel. "Well, thanks for giving us this information. Now we have to figure out what it means."

MARK FLEXED HIS SHOULDERS AND ROLLED HIS HEAD FROM SIDE to side. He'd just finished his review of the tissue slides from the previous day's surgery. Although he loved his work as a pathologist, he often felt chained to his desk. Some of that time was spent looking into a binocular microscope, and that was what he'd done for much of the morning. He made it a habit to take frequent breaks, walking around the room, stretching, but today that hadn't been enough. He yearned to get out of the office and into the open air. Despite the July heat, he decided to go for a noontime walk.

He was moving toward the door when Shannon stuck her head into his office. She was wearing scrubs covered by a white coat, and he could see the imprint made by the pressure of her surgical head cover and mask on her forehead and cheeks.

"Got a minute?" she asked.

"Always."

She stepped inside the office, looked behind her, and closed the door. As soon as the door was shut, Mark hugged and kissed her. "I hope you closed that to keep prying eyes from seeing us kiss, but something tells me you want to have a private conversation."

"The hug and kiss were great, and I needed them, but—yes—I need to talk with you."

Mark gestured toward one of the side chairs across from his desk. He took the other chair and turned it to face her. "Give," he said.

"First, I heard last night that my dad might have leukemia."

As he was sure Shannon had done when she heard the news, Mark's "doctor brain" kicked into high gear. He wanted to ask who made the diagnosis, which doctor would be treating Pastor Frasier, and a thousand other questions. Instead, he simply asked, "How can I help?"

He listened patiently as Shannon related what she'd learned the night before. "He has an appointment for next week here at the medical center, so he'll get good care. And, before you ask, Mom tells me I'm not to get involved. Dad doesn't want special consideration just because he's part of a doctor's family."

Mark turned that over in his mind. "And once he's in the system, HIPAA will clamp down on access to his information." The law, designed to protect privacy, prohibited physicians from revealing any information about patients without specific authorization. "Knowing your dad, he'd be pretty stingy with allowing such access, even to his own family." He shook his head. "I guess we have to leave it in God's hands."

Shannon looked down at her feet. "Mark, I've been at odds with God for a decade or more, ever since I knelt beside my boyfriend and watched him die. I prayed then, prayed hard, and it didn't help. I guess that's when I decided it wasn't worthwhile to try it again."

"I'm sorry for your experience," Mark said. "I'd like to help you get back on speaking terms with Him, though."

"That's so like you," Shannon said. "Sometimes I think there's no way I could be a good wife for you, because I don't have your unwavering faith." She looked up at him, and tears made her blue eyes sparkle even more. "But I want it. Would you help me?"

Mark wasn't sure what to say. Sure, he knew the platitudes he could mouth, but he sensed that Shannon needed more. He took a moment before he replied. "Of course. Why don't we start by praying together for your dad?"

SHANNON LOOKED AT THE MAN IN THE HOSPITAL BED. "WE'LL GET a repeat CAT scan tomorrow. If it looks good and your blood count is stable, I think you can go home."

"Good. And how about going back to work?"

In her mind, Shannon had named the man "the gentle giant." He was probably six four or five, over 250 pounds, with muscles that bulged against the abbreviated sleeves of his hospital gown. His light brown hair was almost bleached to blond by what Shannon figured was sun exposure. His cheeks were ruddy in a complexion already tanned. She could picture him doing some type of outdoor work, lifting heavy loads, sweating in the Texas heat. "You probably shouldn't be exerting yourself until we're sure that lacerated spleen has fully healed."

"How long?" He was a man of few words, spoken quietly, but the intensity behind his question was obvious.

Shannon thought about it. The man had been admitted to the hospital two days ago after blunt trauma to his abdomen in an industrial accident. A CAT scan confirmed a splenic laceration, but his blood count and follow-up X-rays remained unchanged during his hospital course. He apparently wouldn't need surgery right now, but there was always a risk of recurrent bleeding. "We'll get you back on an outpatient basis for repeat CAT scans and blood counts. If you're stable, you can resume light activity in three weeks, but no heavy lifting or significant pressure on the abdomen for three months or more."

"But that Dallas Cowboy—"

"I know," Shannon said. She'd followed the story, the same as every sports fan in the community, and held her breath when a player on the local team had gone back to playing football just a few weeks after an injury similar to this. He'd been lucky. This man might not be. "No, I'm sorry. It's too risky."

She left the man's room, knowing he'd been fortunate to avoid surgery, but recognizing that he was disappointed. Like so many patients, this one wanted to be well retroactively, preferably with no pain or downtime. It would be nice if it worked that way, but it didn't. All she and her fellow surgeons could do was their best. After that . . . The words rattled around in her mind, and finally she allowed them out. After that it was in God's hands.

That was what Mark was trying to tell her when he'd said, "You're a doctor. But you're not God." Once more her thoughts flashed back to that September night a decade ago. That doctor had done everything he could. He'd been frustrated, but he seemed to recognize that there were times when it wouldn't be enough. That was what Shannon was having so much trouble accepting. All she had to give was her best effort, in every situation, for every patient. After that, the result was out of her hands.

Shannon had thought more than once about seeking counseling. Try as she might, she had trouble coming to grips with her human limitations. She always gave her best. But when she lost, it still left her feeling empty and impotent. Maybe this time she'd follow through and see a therapist. Maybe.

STEVE ALSTON SAT AT HIS DESK, A CARDBOARD CUP OF COLD COF-fee at his elbow, a stack of reports in front of him. Two homicides, and the only factor tying them together was Megan Frasier. She'd been in rehab with the man shot Friday night in front of her sister's house. She'd lived with the man shot Saturday, and she had admitted striking him with a bottle earlier in the day.

As with any suspect, Alston thought about the triad of means, motive, and opportunity. That would take some more detective work, but he probably could pin down those factors in both cases. He needed to dig deeper, maybe interview some more people. But right now, Megan Frasier seemed a decent suspect in both killings. Alston wasn't sure what that might mean for his relationship with her sister, but he supposed he'd cross that bridge when he came to it.

He moved his computer mouse, clicked and scrolled, and reviewed what he already knew about Megan. She came from a stable home background, graduated from college with less than spectacular grades, and had a couple of arrests during that time for public intoxication, though the charges were dropped through a bit of manipulation by her attorneys. She'd had two different jobs, interspersed with two stints in rehab for addiction to alcohol and prescription painkillers. She'd lost her latest position after medication samples repeatedly disappeared from her care.

Alston swiveled around to face Jesse Callaway, sitting at the desk behind him. Although he and his partner played the good cop–bad cop duo effortlessly, for some reason Jesse always took the bad cop role. Not only that, he delighted in it. And it seemed to Alston that his partner had come down particularly hard on the two Frasier women. "Jesse, in these two homicides, what's your take on Megan Frasier?"

Callaway didn't hesitate. "I think she's dirty. Some way or another, she's tied into both those murders we caught. I don't know yet how we're going to do it, but I'm pretty sure we'll be able to nail her for something pretty soon." He clicked his mouse. "Meanwhile, I guess we keep hunting."

Callaway stopped and looked up as a patrolman eased up to his desk. Alston couldn't make out all the conversation, but whatever it was, it brought a smile to his partner's face.

As the policeman walked away, Callaway stood and retrieved his coat from the back of his chair. He shrugged it on and readjusted his shoulder holster. "We're getting closer. They recovered a gun from a storm drain two blocks from Tony Lester's house. Ballistics is checking it against the bullets they took out of Lester's skull at autopsy. Meanwhile, Forensics ran the prints they pulled up on the gun. And guess whose they found?"

SHANNON WAS GLAD TO SEE THE DAY END. IN HER CAR ON THE way out of the faculty parking lot, she retrieved her cell phone from her purse and dialed Mark's office. When the office number rang several times with no answer, Shannon punched the button to end the call. She hesitated a moment, then called his cell.

"Hi, Shannon." Mark's voice was upbeat, in contrast with the way Shannon felt.

"I see you managed to get away, too."

"Yep. I was in early, so after slaving all day over a hot

microscope I decided enough was enough. Want me to pick you and Megan up for that dinner we had to postpone the other night?"

"Let me see what's going on when I get home," she said. "I mainly called to thank you for the time we spent together today. What you said, what you did, helped."

"Shannon, I'm here for you, anytime, in any circumstance. Scripture says . . . Never mind. You don't need me to quote Bible verses to you. Just know that I'll always be around."

"That's what I love about you, Mark." She hesitated, wondering if this was the time to extend the dialogue, and decided it wasn't. Not quite yet. "I do love you. And after all this has blown over, I think we need to talk about our future."

"Sounds wonderful to me. I love you, too."

As she thumbed the remote to open her garage door, Shannon noticed that Megan's dusty Ford Focus wasn't parked in front of the house. She wondered why her sister would be late getting home today. Sure, she was going to be job hunting, but most of the people to whom she'd talk would have left their offices an hour or more ago. Shannon hoped Megan hadn't stopped at a bar. She could picture her, laughing and drinking, throwing away months of sobriety.

Shannon picked up her cell phone and checked to make sure there wasn't a missed call or text. Nothing. She exited the car and hurried inside the house. Maybe Megan had left her a note.

Ten minutes later, she was certain there was no note, no indication of where her sister had gone. *I should have called her cell.* Shannon quickly punched in Megan's number. After five rings, the call rolled over to voice mail.

Shannon chastised herself for being this worried. After all, she wasn't really her sister's keeper. But the more she thought of it, the more she realized she really was. When Megan fouled up, it had been Shannon who came to her rescue. Sure, Mom and Dad paid for her last stint in rehab, but it was Shannon who'd driven her there, who'd visited her.

If Megan slipped again, might it be more than their parents could take, especially now with her dad about to begin a fight with cancer? Or could Shannon be worried because she didn't want to have to bail her sister out of yet another jam? She'd thought more than once that she'd reached the end of her patience with her sister, but with each scrape, whether minor or major, Shannon had gathered her resolve and stepped up to help once more. *Stop worrying. Megan's a grown-up. If she weren't living here, you'd never even wonder where she was.*

The front doorbell rang. Maybe Megan had forgotten her key. Shannon hurried to the door, but when she opened it, it wasn't the face of her sister she saw, but rather the slightly off-putting countenance of Detective Jesse Callaway. Steve Alston was beside him, but Shannon's gaze fixed on Callaway's dark, almost black, eyes. Were they here to bring her bad news about Megan?

"May we come in?" Alston said, his hat already in his hand.

"Certainly," she said.

Alston came through the door first, followed by Callaway. In the living room, Alston took up his usual station, leaning against the doorframe. Shannon gestured Callaway to a chair, but before he sat, he chilled her with his words. "Dr. Frasier, we came about your sister, Megan."

# TEN

STEVE ALSTON STUDIED SHANNON'S REACTION TO THE STATE-
ment, and what he saw wasn't what he expected. He was sure
Jesse had chosen his words carefully. "We came about your
sister, Megan." But instead of responding with "Why?" or perhaps "She's not here," or even "I'll call her," Shannon remained
silent and turned so pale that Steve moved a step closer, preparing to catch her if she fainted.

The moment passed, though, and after Shannon regained
her composure she said, "Please, sit down." She lowered herself into an overstuffed chair and waited until Callaway was
seated before proceeding. "What's wrong? Has she been in an
accident? Something worse?" Shannon was obviously fighting
for self-control. "What did you come to tell me?"

Steve decided it was time to step in. He moved from his
post in the doorway to take a seat on the couch next to Jesse.
"Nothing bad has happened to Megan, at least not so far as we
know. We need to ask her some questions, that's all."

Steve caught Jesse's look, one that told him this wasn't the way he'd planned to play this. But Jesse's way might send Shannon over the edge. Better to tiptoe into the questions they wanted answered. He'd straighten things out with his partner later.

"So you don't know where Megan is either?" Shannon said.

"No, but when you hear from her, let her know we want to talk with her." Steve reached toward his pocket, but Shannon stopped him.

"I have your cards, both of them. And I'll have Megan call. But why?"

"I'm afraid that's something we'll have to discuss with her," Jesse said.

Steve leaned closer to Shannon. "But while we're here, there's something we need to ask you. We found a gun in a storm drain near Tony Lester's house, and ballistics tests show it was the weapon used to kill him."

A strange expression passed across Shannon's face, and Steve wondered what it meant. "So you're closer to finding out who killed him?" she said.

"Maybe," he said. "Do you own a gun?"

"No," she said. "I never wanted one. Some of the doctors at the hospital have them for protection, but I . . . I don't like guns. I won't have one in the house."

Jesse apparently decided to unleash the bad cop. He rose from his seat beside Steve, standing so that he towered over Shannon, and said, "Then perhaps you can explain why your fingerprints were on the gun that killed Megan's boyfriend."

SHANNON'S HEART SEEMED TO STOP. FROM THE FIRST MOMENT she'd seen the gun in her sister's hand, she knew it would ultimately cause trouble. Now it had. Megan had been printed during her earlier arrests, and Shannon's fingerprints were on file from her staff application at the VA Hospital. If the gun with their prints was the one used, and if it was used to kill Tony, it wouldn't take the police long to connect the dots. Matter of fact, that's what they were doing now.

The time Shannon had hoped would never arrive was here. "You know, I think I'd better wait and talk with my sister. I'm pretty sure the questions you want to ask her are the same ones you're starting to ask me. And I'd prefer to have that questioning take place with our attorney present."

Alston held up a calming hand. "Shannon—"

"No, I'm sorry, but unless you want to arrest me, I think I'll leave it at that. As soon as I hear from Megan, we'll discuss this with our attorney. Then she and I will come in and answer your questions for you." She rose. "Until then . . ."

Callaway looked at his partner, then at Shannon. "Doctor, you're acting awfully suspicious. If you'd answer a few questions—"

"On the contrary, Detective. I'm acting like a citizen taking advantage of the rights guaranteed me by the Constitution."

Alston shrugged and said, "If that's the way you feel. But I must say, I'm disappointed."

"No more than I am," Shannon said, fixing him with a glare that could have cut glass.

In a few moments, the detectives were gone. Shannon slumped on the sofa, waiting for her heart to resume its normal rhythm. She had her address book in her hand, searching for the phone number of Tom and Elena Waites, when the front door opened and Megan walked in. Shannon took a deep breath and fought the urge to either kill her sister for making her worry about her whereabouts or enfold her in a bear hug because she was safely home. Instead of either option, she simply said, "Have a seat. We need to talk."


MEGAN THOUGHT SHANNON LOOKED ANGRY, BUT SHE COULDN'T imagine why. Even if she were, it wouldn't last long. She gave her sister a hug and sat beside her on the sofa. "Before you start, I have wonderful news."

Shannon looked doubtful but said, "Okay, you go first."

"I have a job," Megan said.

"That was fast. Unemployment is a problem in the entire country, and you get a job the second day you look for one. You want to explain that?"

"When I was in First Step, I met this guy—"

Megan could almost see the fire in Shannon's eyes. "You need a job, so the first thing you do is turn to someone you met in rehab? Perfect! I mean, it makes sense—"

"Will you let me finish?" Megan took a deep breath. "There were all kinds of people at First Step. This guy was a real straight arrow. He got hooked on prescription painkillers after surgery, just like I did the first time, and he was there to kick the habit. He was the CEO of a profitable company, a responsible family man, and because I was educated and had been in a profession related to his, we became friends. He told me that if I ever needed anything after I got out to give him a call."

Shannon nodded, her jaw muscles clenched with the effort to keep silent.

"I called him yesterday. We set up a lunch for today with him and a couple of people from his firm." Megan couldn't help beaming. "He hired me. I'll need to spend some time going through orientation, but I can start hunting for an apartment of my own."

"What kind of job?" Shannon asked.

"Selling durable medical equipment. The man is Jeff Robiteaux, and the company is R&R Medical Supply."

The look on Shannon's face told Megan that she recognized both the name of the company and the owner. "That's right," Megan said. "Not everyone in rehab is a hopeless misfit and outcast. Some of the patients are decent people trying to overcome their addictions." She tried to ignore the tightness growing in her throat. "I'm still fighting mine, and I thought you'd be proud of me for trying."

Shannon's features softened. "I'm so sorry. It was just that I—"

"I know. You were worried that I wouldn't be able to find a job, and you'd be stuck with me."

"Not at all. I was worried because you weren't home. With all that's going on, including murders and threatening phone calls, I hoped you hadn't . . ." She let the words trail off as she leaned back and spread her hands wide.

"As a matter of fact, I went by to tell Mom the news. Dad was in his study at home, too, so we had the chance to sit down and talk some. They . . . they prayed with me. Mom wanted me to stay for dinner, but I told them I needed to get home and tell you about the job." She squeezed her eyes shut. She absolutely would not cry in front of her sister. Not anymore. "Shannon, I want you to believe me. I'm trying."

THERE WAS NO OTHER WAY TO DESCRIBE IT. SHANNON WAS ASHAMED. Ashamed that she'd immediately interpreted her sister's prolonged absence in the worst possible way. Ashamed that Megan had gone to visit their parents for the second time in a week, while, although she lived just twenty minutes away from their home, Shannon hadn't done that much in the past month.

But that didn't change the situation. There was the matter of the gun that demanded their attention. "I don't want you to think I'm not happy for you, but we have some things to talk about—important things."

Megan nodded. "Okay. Shoot."

"Poor choice of words," Shannon said. "The police have found the gun that killed Tony. It had my fingerprints on it, and that means yours were there, too, because there's no doubt in my mind it's the same gun you had when you confronted me right here."

"I didn't kill Tony," Megan said through clenched teeth.

Shannon wanted to ask more questions, but she decided to accept her sister's word. "We're supposed to be at police head-quarters tomorrow to answer some questions." She held up the address book. "I'm going to call an attorney and ask her to represent us. But before I do, I need to know about that gun, including whether you have any idea who might have taken it from here." Shannon gestured to the drawer of the desk where she'd put the gun.

"A number of people I met in rehab told me I should have a way to protect myself as I made my calls, driving from office to office, going through some pretty sketchy neighborhoods. One of the guys told me how I could get a gun, and when I got out, I bought one."

"But you didn't get a permit for it."

"Hey, I doubt that the guy who sold it to me had one either. I looked for the serial numbers, and they'd been burned off some way—acid, I'd guess. I shoved the gun in the glove compartment of my car, kept it in my purse when I felt the need for it, and let it go at that."

Shannon shook her head. "So it could have been used in the commission of any number of crimes before you got it."

She picked up the phone. "Megan, sometimes I wish you'd think these things through before you do them. Let me call Elena and see if she can help get us out of this mess."


ELENA GARCIA WAITES FOLDED HER NAPKIN AND DROPPED IT beside her plate. "I'll get the phone," she said as she rose from the dining room table. "Are you on call?"

Dr. Tom Waites shook his head. "Nope, although that doesn't always mean much."

Their daughters, now teenagers, had their own cell phones, as did both parents. But those numbers were closely guarded. When the landline rang, it might be anything from a telephone solicitor to a colleague of hers or his, asking for advice or help. But there was never any thought of simply letting the answering machine take the call. In both Tom's and Elena's professions, there was too much chance that the call might literally be a matter of life and death.

In a habit of long-standing, Elena pushed her hair back off her ear before picking up the phone. "Waites residence."

"Mrs. Waites, this is Dr. Shannon Frasier. I'm a colleague of Tom's, and we've met at various faculty gatherings."

"Of course," Elena said. "Do you need to speak with Tom?"

"No." The woman on the other end of the line cleared her throat, and Elena could detect an element of nervousness in her voice. "No, I'm afraid it's you I need. I apologize for calling tonight, but in your profession, like mine, situations arise outside normal hours that require help."

"No need to say anything more. And please call me Elena. What can I do for you?"

Elena eased into the chair by the phone, pulled a pad and pen toward her, and began to take notes. She listened intently, allowing Shannon to tell her story uninterrupted. The narrative didn't so much end as run down.

"I have a few questions for you, but those can wait," Elena said. "Let me assure you that I'll represent you. I'll call in the morning to set up a time for you to be at the police station for an interview with the detectives. We'll talk before the interview, and I'll be at your side the whole time. Right now I think I can counter any theory they put forth. So don't worry."

"Thank you. But let me be clear about one thing. My sister, Megan, and I both need representation. Can you . . . would you do that?"

"Actually, I can do that only until or unless your interests diverge. If that happens, I'll represent you. Is that satisfactory?"

There was hardly any hesitation before the reply. "I think so. And as for the fee . . ."

"I'm flattered that one of Tom's colleagues would engage my services, but I need to remind you of something. I suppose you know about the professional courtesy discount psychiatrists give to other doctors."

"They don't give a discount. They charge their full fee."

"That's right—because if you're not paying full price, you're more likely to ignore the recommendations you get. Do you understand what I'm saying?"

"I think so." Another throat clearing. The woman still was obviously very nervous. "So, what you mean is . . ."

"I'll represent you for my usual fee," Elena said. "We can work out a payment schedule if necessary. I won't discount my fees, but I'll plan to represent your sister at no additional charge so long as her interests and yours coincide. Is that acceptable?"

"Yes. Thank you."

They exchanged cell phone numbers, and Elena told Shannon she'd call her the next day to set up the appointment for the session with the detectives. When she returned to the dining room table, her husband said, "Obviously that was for you. Anything wrong?"

"No, just someone who needs my services." She wouldn't mention Shannon's name unless it became necessary, even though her client was a woman with whom Tom worked every day. After all, she thought, doctors weren't the only ones who kept professional secrets.

ONCE MORE SHANNON AND MEGAN COBBLED TOGETHER AN EVENING meal, this one consisting primarily of leftovers from the refrigerator. The quality of the food didn't really matter, since neither of them had much of an appetite. Then, after some time spent watching mindless sitcoms, Megan yawned. "I think that does it for me. I'm going to wash my hair, then read until I fall asleep."

"I'll call you tomorrow after Elena lets me know when we need to be at the police station."

"Thanks for taking care of hiring an attorney. Once I've gotten a couple of paychecks, I'll pay my fair share."

Shannon hadn't mentioned Elena's warning that she could represent Megan only as long as it didn't interfere with her defense of her primary client. No need to worry her sister with that now. "We can talk about it later. Right now let's be glad we have a good lawyer on our side."

After a shower, Shannon phoned Mark. "I started to call and see if you wanted to get together tonight," he said, "but I figured you'd probably want to just relax."

"I don't know if you could call it relaxing," she said. "The detectives were here earlier. They found the gun that killed Tony Lester, and my fingerprints were on it." She went on to explain about the disappearance of Megan's gun from the drawer where she'd stowed it.

"What can I do?" Mark asked.

"Nothing for now," Shannon said. "I've engaged a defense attorney to represent me . . . actually, to represent both Megan and me. We meet with the detectives tomorrow for questioning. I'll know more after that."

"Well—"

Shannon heard a sound on the line. "Mark, there's another call coming in. Let's talk tomorrow."

"Fine. I love you."

"And I love you," Shannon said. She ended Mark's call and said, "Hello?"

It was the same voice, rough and unrecognizable. "I'm getting tired of asking. Tell me what he said before he died."

"I don't—"

"What did he say? If you don't tell me now, you're not going to like what I do to get the information out of you later."

Shannon gripped the receiver so tightly her fist ached. Should she give this man the string of numbers Radick gasped out before he died? Why not? She saw no need to hold on to them. The police already had the information, and if it would put an end to these phone calls, she'd give the man what he wanted. She'd explain to Steve or Detective Callaway later. But first, she needed to dig out the slip on which Lee wrote the numbers. "Can you hold on?"

"I'll bet the police put some of their fancy equipment on your phone, and you want to keep me on the line so they can trace this call. Well, forget it. You had your chance."

Shannon heard a click, and her heart dropped to her shoes.

# ELEVEN

MARK MUTED THE TV SET AND REACHED FOR THE PHONE ON THE table beside him. He sat, relaxed, in his easy chair, his shoeless feet propped on a footstool. He glanced at the caller ID and smiled. After he talked with Shannon earlier, he'd decided to stay in his living room and channel surf for a while before turning in. Now he was glad he did. Otherwise her call might have caught him in the shower.

"Mark, I'm afraid! I'll call the police in a minute, but I wanted to—" Her voice carried pure fear.

"Hold on." Mark was already on his feet. He wriggled his feet into shoes and looked around for his keys. "I'll head for your place as soon as we hang up, but first, tell me what's going on."

"I've just had another call from the man who wants to know what Radick said before he died." Shannon's words seemed to pour out as though by voicing them she could dispel her fear. "I tried to get him to hold while I found the slip of paper with that information, but he hung up." She took a deep breath, which came out as almost a gulp. "He . . . he threatened me. Said I wouldn't like what he was going to do to me if I didn't tell him what Radick said."

Mark was almost walking in place, anxious to be out the door, but he forced himself to stay calm. He had to be to help Shannon. "Are you alone in the house?"

"No, Megan's in her room."

"Are all your doors and windows locked?"

There was a pause while she apparently thought about it. "Yes, we're buttoned up tight."

"So you're safe for now. When we hang up, call the police, then don't open the door except for them or me." Mark took another deep breath and forced himself to think. "You said you were going to get the slip of paper with the information on it. I thought you didn't know what Radick said."

Shannon's breathing sounded like a hurricane in the receiver. "I'm sorry I didn't tell you, but things have been—"

"Never mind. Tell me now."

"Lee heard Radick's dying words, and because he's got an eidetic memory, he recalled them. It's a string of numbers. If you want to hear them, let me dig out the card Lee wrote them on."

Mark opened a drawer in the table by his chair and pulled out a scratch pad and pencil. "Okay."

"Here they are: 324 8160 964 7900."

The numbers made no sense to Mark, but he wrote them down anyway. "Do you have any idea what these numbers represent?"

"I don't know. I thought maybe they were phone numbers. Or maybe it's some kind of code."

"Well, go ahead and contact the police and tell them about the phone call. I'm amazed they haven't wired your phone to record these calls so they can try to trace them. You make that call, and I'll be there as quickly as I can."

After Mark hung up, he grabbed his keys and headed for the door. As he drove, he occasionally held the memo pad with the mysterious numbers in the glow cast by the instrument panel. Try as he might, he couldn't decipher the message they conveyed.

That wasn't as important as Shannon's safety. He hoped she was calling the police right now. In the meantime, he leaned forward behind the wheel of his car, as though by his posture he could arrive more quickly at her door.

SHANNON ENDED THE CALL WITH MARK, FEELING ONLY MARGIN-ally better. She should call the police now and tell them about the anonymous call, and the threat that accompanied it. But how should she do it? She could call 911, but that would mean spending a half hour trying to explain to a couple of police officers the events leading up to tonight's call. On the other hand, she could phone one of the detectives. At least the two men knew the story. She wasn't looking forward to making that call, especially considering the suspicion in the eyes and voices of the men when they'd told her about finding her fingerprints on Tony's murder weapon. Then she thought about that distorted voice, and a frisson of fear ran up her spine. No, she needed protection from this man, and the police could give it. She'd depend on Elena Waites to protect her from the police.

She rummaged in the stack of papers on her desk until her fingers pulled out the cards the two detectives had given her. Picking one to call was an easy decision for Shannon by now. She checked her watch—ten o'clock. She wasn't sure what shift the men worked, but she recalled her dad saying that Alston was a widower, and Steve himself had hinted that he spent a lot of his hours at his desk or in the field. She dialed his cell phone, and sure enough, he answered on the first ring.

"Alston."

"Detective, this is Shannon Frasier."

The pleasure in his voice was obvious. "I'm assuming that a call coming this late isn't necessarily a professional one."

"And your assumption is wrong," she said, with a bit more acid than necessary. Was this man really flirting with her? Weren't there rules about that sort of thing? "I got another call tonight from the man who wanted to know what Radick said before he died. He threatened me."

Alston's voice was all business when he replied. "Are you at home?"

"Yes."

"Are all the doors and windows locked?"

"Yes. I'm sure."

"Do you have a weapon in the house?"

"Other than the bat I used in intramural softball? No."

"Well, stay put. I'm on my way to your house. Check the peephole before you open the door."

Megan padded into the living room, a robe covering her pajamas, as Shannon ended the call. "What's going on? I keep hearing voices. Either you're getting lots of phone calls, or you've begun talking to yourself."

Shannon decided it was probably a good idea for Megan to sit in on this conversation with Alston. "I've had a phone call—the second one like it—from a man disguising his voice and wanting to know what Radick said before he died. He threatened me. I called Detective Alston and he's on his way over. Mark, too."

Megan frowned. "Why am I just hearing about all this?"

"Because I've been playing big sister and trying to shield you, I guess. I'm sorry. I'll change that, starting now. I'd like you to be with me when I talk with Alston. Just remember that if he asks anything about the gun that killed Tony, we don't answer any of those questions until tomorrow when our attorney is present. This is only about the threatening phone calls. Got that?"

"Yes, Mother," Megan said.

"Megan, this isn't the time for that. You need to—" Shannon's retort died on her lips when the doorbell rang. She turned on the porch light, looked through the peephole, and saw Mark and Detective Alston standing side by side on the porch, trying unsuccessfully to avoid looking at each other.

STEVE ALSTON WASN'T TERRIBLY HAPPY TO HAVE SUCH A LARGE gathering for the session. He'd envisioned a one-on-one with Shannon. Instead, he had Shannon's sister and her boyfriend, Dr. Gilbert, added to the group. Alston took a deep breath and slipped into professional mode. After everyone was seated in the living room, he pulled a leather-covered notebook and ballpoint pen from the inside pocket of his sports coat. "Dr. Frasier, tell me about the call."

He listened, took a few notes, and when he was certain Shannon was finished, said, "I'm sorry we didn't have a recorder on your line. I put in that request after the first phone call, but I can assure you that I'll check on it as soon as I get to my office in the morning."

"Could you have traced the call if you had the right equipment installed?" Dr. Gilbert asked.

"Probably not. At first it was only the drug dealers who used anonymous cell phones, but now they're common. We might be able to triangulate the location from the cell towers used, but if I had to guess, I'd imagine he was in his car, driving around."

"I may have heard some traffic noise in the background,"

Shannon said. "If tracing the call is unlikely, do you still need to put equipment here?"

"We'll put in everything, but mainly I want a recording of this guy's voice—what he sounds like, exactly what he's saying. That might help us."

"What do you make of the string of numbers Radick gave before he died?" Gilbert asked.

Steve frowned. He couldn't very well silence Dr. Gilbert, since he was also involved in the Friday shooting, but neither did he want him monopolizing the conversation. This was supposed to be an interview with Shannon. Steve chose to give a short, truthful answer. "I have no idea, but I'm going to get some help tomorrow from a guy who's a pretty good cryptographer."

"So—" Gilbert began.

The detective rose and put away his notebook and pen. "I think that's enough for tonight. Shannon, someone will be contacting you tomorrow about putting in equipment to record further conversations. Will anyone be home?"

"I will," Megan said. "They can call here, and I'll let them in."

Steve started to say something to Shannon's sister about her involvement in the second shooting, but he decided he'd probably get the standard answer—"I'll answer that tomorrow with my attorney present." Instead, he shrugged and said, "Okay, you should get a call before noon."

"What about Shannon's safety?" Gilbert asked.

Steve took a deep breath, fighting the urge to ask the man to butt out. "I'll ask the precinct to have a patrol car come by periodically tonight." He turned toward Shannon. "When you go out, be very careful—"

"I know how to take care of myself," Shannon said. "Just do your best to find out who this guy is and get him off the streets."

"We're looking at all of Barry Radick's associates. Jesse . . .

that is, Detective Callaway thinks Radick might have been involved in something that had a payoff, and now his partner is trying to find out where the money is hidden." Steve turned to go. "For now, just let us do our job."

At the door, he nodded to Megan and Shannon. "I'll see you ladies tomorrow. I presume your attorney will be checking with Detective Callaway or me to set up a time."

"Yes," Shannon said. "I've engaged Elena Waites to represent us. She'll be in touch."

As Alston walked to his car, he thought about Shannon's last statement. *Elena Waites is one of the big guns. That could mean Shannon or Megan—maybe both—have something to hide. We may have to dig deeper than I thought.* Despite that, he was surprised to find that his feelings about the two women hadn't changed. He'd have to watch his step.

"I APPRECIATE YOUR OFFERING TO BE HERE WHEN THE POLICE install the equipment on our phone," Shannon said over breakfast the next morning.

Megan looked across the kitchen table. She was having black coffee, orange juice, and a piece of unbuttered toast. "No problem. I'll call Mr. Robiteaux and explain the situation. He said I'd only need a day for orientation, and I should be able to do it tomorrow."

"When Elena calls me, I'll tell her what's going on. Maybe we can postpone the interview until after the equipment is installed." She was anxious for the police to catch the man making these mysterious phone calls, but Shannon wasn't looking forward to answering questions about Megan's gun, especially now that she knew it was the weapon used to kill Tony Lester.

Her fingerprints and those of her sister on the gun would

undoubtedly shine the spotlight of suspicion on both of them. When you thought about it, in addition to their connection to the murder weapon, although the evidence was circumstantial, Megan certainly had a motive to get rid of Tony. And a case could be made that after Shannon discovered how Tony had treated her sister, she might try to exact revenge on the ex-boyfriend as well. As for opportunity . . . well, that would depend on what the autopsy indicated was the time frame for Tony's death. She hoped Elena could guide them safely through the shoals of police suspicion.

"Do you need anything?" Shannon asked.

"I do have some clothes that need to go to the cleaners," Megan said. "Would you mind dropping them off?"

Shannon glanced at the clock on the kitchen wall. "No problem, but I need to get going. Show me where they are and tell me which cleaners you use."

Ten minutes later, Shannon backed her car out of the garage, a stack of Megan's clothes on the front seat beside her. She'd drop them off, then head for the medical center. Fortunately, she didn't have surgery this morning, just patients to see in the clinic. She might even have a chance for a leisurely—well, that was a relative term—an unhurried lunch.

At the first stoplight, she glanced left, right, and in the rearview mirror. She'd made it a habit since her first driver's education class. Other than the dark compact car sitting on her rear bumper, traffic seemed pretty much normal. She didn't like it when cars crowded her, so when the light turned green she got across the intersection and changed lanes, moving to the inside one. The dark car—now she saw it was a black Hyundai—moved with her, staying pretty much on her tail.

Shannon pulled her cell phone from her purse and dropped it into her lap. This might only be someone with bad driving manners, but she wanted to be ready in case it was more than that. Had everything that happened made her paranoid? Or was she just being careful? In either case, she determined to be cautious.

She was two blocks from Megan's dry cleaners when Shannon looked in her rearview mirror and saw that the Hyundai had dropped back. Not only that, but at the next intersection it turned off. *Get a grip, Shannon. Stop seeing bad guys behind every tree.*

She wheeled into the strip mall and found a parking place almost directly in front of the sign advertising Young's Cleaning and Laundry. She exited her car, then leaned over and scooped up Megan's clothes. Inside, a very nice lady smiled broadly when Shannon said the cleaning was for Megan Frasier.

"I hope nothing's wrong with Megan," the woman said. "She's a nice lady. Sometimes when she comes in to pick up cleaning she brings me a donut from the shop next door."

"She's okay," Shannon said. "I'm her sister, and she's living with me until she can find a new apartment. And I'm sorry, I didn't know to bring you a donut."

"Oh, that's not necessary. I just wanted to tell you how nice I think she is." The woman busied herself at the computer, and in a moment it spit out a dry-cleaning ticket. "I know it's none of my business, but I'm glad she's moved away from that boyfriend of hers." The lady made a sour face, and for a second Shannon was afraid she'd spit on the floor.

"Why do you say that?" Shannon asked.

"He came in with her once. He was . . . what's the word I want? Shifty. I wouldn't have trusted him alone for a minute, afraid he'd grab an armload of clothes and run."

So Megan wasn't the only one who thought Tony wasn't trustworthy. That made Shannon wonder who else didn't care for Tony. Maybe one of them had disliked him enough to use a gun to end his life. But why use Megan's gun? And how did the murderer get his or her hands on it?

Shannon was still thinking about this when she returned to her car. A dark sedan now sat in the parking space next to Shannon's. She hit the Unlock button, but no sooner had the beep sounded than she realized she hadn't locked the car when she left it. Shannon climbed behind the wheel and was reaching for the button on her armrest to lock all the doors when the front passenger door opened and a man slid in beside her.

His face was partially hidden by mirrored sunglasses. His wild black hair was two weeks past needing a trim. But what caught Shannon's eye was the gun he pointed toward her.

In contrast with the small, shiny revolver she'd taken from Megan, this was a large, black, boxy gun. The man held the gun low enough to keep it from being visible from outside the car. The barrel was pointed where her blouse and skirt joined. She'd seen enough gunshot wounds to realize that a bullet there would do major damage—she might not die right away, but without medical help the wound would soon be fatal.

The man's lips barely moved when he said, "What did Radick say before he died?"

# TWELVE

SHANNON'S BREATH CAUGHT IN HER THROAT. SHE SAT, PARALYZED by fear, fighting for calm. She'd lived for more than thirty years without seeing the business end of a gun up close, much less having one pointed at her. Now she'd had that experience twice in one week. And as if the sight of the gun weren't enough, the hand that held it was shaking a bit. If there was a twitch of the trigger finger . . . She recalled what happened when someone aimed a gun at Todd, and again at Barry Radick. A little too much pressure on the trigger and . . .

"What did Radick say?" the man said. "I'm not going to ask again."

Shannon realized that the voice over the phone and the one she heard now were the same. The man hadn't used anything to disguise his voice. It really was the muffled, raspy one she'd heard in the calls. What had she told the police? The only other time she'd heard such a voice was from a patient with a cancer of the throat. Could this man have the same problem?

"I . . . I have that information now. It's in my purse." She reached toward the space between the seats where her purse lay. "I need to reach in—"

The man held out his other hand. "Never mind. I'll just take the purse." He grunted a laugh. "You're not going to need it."

Shannon noticed that the gun seemed steadier now, and the gunman's aim was higher. The barrel was pointed at her heart. He wasn't going to let her go free. After all, she'd seen his face, the part that wasn't covered by sunglasses. Shannon saw his plan as clearly as if it had been drawn out for her. The man would take the purse, shoot her, and drive off. Her brain whirled, looking for and discarding solutions with the speed of a computer.

Maybe if she—

"Excuse me." The voice outside the driver's-side window startled Shannon. It was the lady from the dry cleaners. She waved a small piece of paper. "I forgot to give you the ticket for your sister's cleaning."

Shannon saw her chance, and she took it. She turned away from the gunman, who'd dropped his hand to his side so the weapon was hidden by his body. In a flash Shannon had snatched up her purse and was out of the car. She grabbed the woman and hurried with her toward the open front door of the dry cleaners. "Don't ask questions. Just run."

"What was that about?" the woman asked.

"Lock the door."

The woman gave Shannon a quizzical look but complied.

"Now we need to get away from the front window." Shannon pulled the cell phone from her purse and quickly dialed 911, shepherding the clerk toward the back of the store as she talked.

Before Shannon could complete the call, she heard a car burn rubber away from the storefront. She edged around the clothing behind which she'd hidden and saw that her car was still there, but the sedan that had sat next to it was gone. In all the excitement, she hadn't noted the license plate. But she could identify the gunman's face. She'd see it in her dreams . . . or, more accurately, her nightmares.

DETECTIVE STEVE ALSTON PULLED UP IN FRONT OF YOUNG'S Cleaners, taking note of the Dallas Police Department white-and-black SUV, its strobe lights still flashing, idling at the curb behind an unoccupied blue Toyota Corolla. One patrol-man was inside the police vehicle, talking on the radio. The other stood beside the Toyota, notebook in hand, conversing with an obviously frightened Shannon Frasier.

Steve turned to his partner. "Jesse, I think Dr. Frasier's just about on her last nerve. Why don't you let me take the lead on this one?"

Callaway sniffed. "You know what department regulations say about personal relationships with citizens, especially sub-jects in an active investigation. Are you sure you want to take that chance?"

"There's nothing between Shannon and me. I attend the church her father pastors, so I sort of feel a connection."

"Be sure that's the only connection you feel," Callaway said as he climbed out and ambled toward the group on the sidewalk.

Steve held up his badge wallet and asked the policeman who stood with Shannon, "What happened?"

The patrolman, a tall, slightly built black man whose nameplate read "Robinson," said, "This woman says a man climbed out of a dark sedan, got into her car, and held her at gunpoint. He apparently was ready to shoot and grab her purse when the woman from the dry cleaners interrupted them. That's when she jumped out and ran. My partner's calling in an APB on the car." He grimaced. "Of course she didn't get a license number."

Steve stowed his badge and nodded at the patrolman. "This is connected to a case we're working. We'll write up the report and take it from here. You guys can get back on patrol. Thanks."

Robinson touched the bill of his cap and gave a wry smile. "Good enough, Detective." He climbed into the police vehicle, said something to his partner, and the two laughed.

"Patrol officers always hate it when detectives take a case away from them," Steve said to Shannon. "Now, do you have anything to add to what I've already heard?"

"No, that's pretty much the whole story," Shannon said as the police pulled away. "The man was the same one who's been calling. I recognized that muffled, raspy voice. It must be his natural one."

"What did he look like?"

"Not too tall. Sort of slightly built. Pale complexion. Long, dark hair that looked overdue for a cut."

"What about his face?" Steve asked.

"He wore sunglasses, but I got a good look at the rest of his face. I'll work with a sketch artist if you want me to."

"We've advanced past that," Callaway said. "We do it on a computer now. The expert guides you through the process, and we usually turn up with a pretty good likeness."

"What about the man's voice?" Shannon said. "Could you input 'raspy voice' or something like that into the computer and get some names?"

Steve knew he had to walk a fine line so as not to spook Shannon. They needed to get information from her about her attacker, but they also had questions for her and Megan about their fingerprints on a murder weapon. "It's not quite that simple, but we'll see what we can get from the information you've given us." Steve looked at his watch. "The technician should be at your house soon to install the equipment on the phone."

"I've asked Megan to call my cell when that's done," Shannon said.

"After that you can coordinate with your attorney. No matter how late it is, we want you and Megan down at headquarters."

Shannon looked at her watch. "I need to get to work. Am I free to go now?"

"Yes, but be careful. Keep your car doors locked. If someone threatens you, run them over," Callaway said.

"Don't worry," Shannon said. "I won't take any chances."

"Is there a guard in the medical center parking garage?" Steve asked.

"We have security officers all over campus," Shannon said.

"Call the security office. Have someone meet you in the parking garage and walk you inside. When you get ready to leave, get an escort."

The detectives sat in their car until Shannon pulled away. Steve turned to his partner and asked, "What do you make of this?"

"I'm not sure how the two cases tie together, but somehow I think there's a connection. It makes no sense . . . yet. But when we find the right end of the string and pull on it, I have a hunch it's going to unravel."

Steve agreed. He just hoped that when things unraveled, Shannon Frasier wouldn't find herself holding the short end of the string.

ELENA WAITES TAPPED A PEN AGAINST HER FRONT TEETH AS SHE LEANED BACK in her desk chair. She wiggled the toes of her stockinged feet beneath the desk, happy to have them free from her very stylish but uncomfortable shoes. She wished she could go back to her law school days, when being stylish meant that the bare places in your jeans didn't show too much skin and the soles of your Reeboks weren't held together by rubber cement. Now, as one of the partners in the firm of Gilmore, Chrisman, and Waites, she followed a stricter, although self-imposed, dress code.

She closed her eyes and thought back over the phone conversation she'd just completed. Detective Jesse Callaway told her quite simply that the fingerprints of her two clients had been found on the gun that was the weapon used to murder Tony Lester. How those prints came to be on that particular Smith & Wesson .38-caliber Airweight revolver was the focus of the questions Callaway and his partner wanted to ask Shannon and Megan Frasier. The two women were considered "persons of interest" in the investigation. The detective wasn't prepared to say more.

Although Callaway had been cool, she didn't find that unusual. The police often had little use for lawyers. She'd heard one veteran detective complain, "The lawyers get them out faster than we can put them in." Elena knew what she was getting into when she chose a criminal defense practice. The right to due process of law antedated the Constitution, going back to English common law, and she was proud to be part of the system, especially when she was able to prevent an innocent client from going to jail.

Elena dialed the number of Shannon Frasier's cell phone, which rang six times and then went to voice mail. She wasn't surprised. Her husband had told her that he generally turned off his cell phone before going into surgery, and she suspected that was the case with Shannon as well. However, in less than five minutes she received a return call.

"Sorry," Shannon said. "I was with a patient. I'm in clinic this morning."

"No problem. Have the police installed their equipment on your landline yet? Once that's done and Megan's free to leave your house, I need to arrange to meet the detectives and get this questioning out of the way."

"Oh," Shannon said. "You . . . you don't know what happened this morning, do you?"

"Apparently not. Why don't you tell me?"

As Shannon related her story, Elena reached into her desk drawer and pulled out a fresh legal pad. By the time Shannon finished, Elena had filled a new page with notes and questions. "Are you safe now?" she asked when the recital ran down.

"I think so. I don't think the man would try to attack me while I'm here at the medical center. I was going to ask one of the security guards to walk me to my car when I leave, but as soon as I told Mark what happened, he said he'd do it. Matter of fact, he sort of insisted."

"Well, take him up on it. The main thing is to keep you safe," Elena said. "Can you arrange to get away this afternoon? I'd like to meet with you and Megan before the questioning, and I'm guessing you'll also need to spend some time with the composite system to help the police identify the gunman you encountered this morning."

"I'm pretty sure I can free up my afternoon. As soon as I hear from Megan, I'll get back to you and we can arrange the time for all this." She cleared her throat. "I'll be so glad when this is over."

"Me, too." *And my job is to keep you free until then. I hope we can keep you alive as well.*

SHANNON RECOGNIZED THE ROOM WHERE SHE SAT. SHE'D SEEN IT or variations of it dozens of times on TV. The scarred table obviously predated the current no-smoking regulations in the police station, and bore multiple scars from cigarettes laid down and ignored. The straight chairs she and Megan occupied were lightly padded but not really comfortable. She and her sister were seated facing what she figured was a two-way mirror.

*All that's missing is a bright light in my eyes and a rubber hose.* Shannon stifled a grin at her jailhouse humor. This was no time to smile—this was dead serious. She dried her wet palms on a tissue she took from the pocket of her slacks and tried to slow her breathing.

Shannon had no illusions that, despite Steve Alston's attentive manner when he'd directed them to this room, she and Megan were both suspects in Tony Lester's murder. She wondered how hard the police were trying to find out who shot Barry Radick in her front yard. Although there were three solid witnesses who could attest that she was inside the house when that shooting took place, Megan had no such alibi.

She'd passed on lunch, and although even the thought of food made her nauseous, Shannon wondered if hunger was the cause of the queasiness she felt in her stomach, the weakness and cold sweats. No, she knew the reason for those feelings. And food wouldn't cure them.

Jesse Callaway preceded Steve into the room. The two detectives sat facing Shannon and Megan. Elena Waites was at the head of the table, almost like a referee with the two factions to her right and left. "If you don't mind," Callaway said, "I'll record this interview."

Shannon looked at Elena, who nodded. She and Megan exchanged glances. "Okay," Shannon said.

Callaway turned on a recorder sitting in the middle of the table. He checked the recording level, said the words that made everything official, then leaned back and cleared his throat. The corners of his mouth turned up for a fraction of a second, but it was more a look of anticipation than a true smile. His eyes were like two cold, black marbles as they flickered between the two women across the table from him.

"Dr. Frasier, Miss Frasier, we've identified the weapon used to kill Tony Lester as a .38-caliber Smith & Wesson Airweight revolver." Callaway reached into the briefcase at his feet and pulled out a plastic bag holding a gun. "Do either of you recognize this?"

They'd discussed this with Elena, who'd advised Megan and Shannon to tell the truth about the gun—how Megan came to have it, how Shannon took it from her, and its subsequent disappearance. So that's exactly what they did, not waiting for Callaway to ask the expected questions—"How did your fingerprints get on the gun?" or "Did you use this gun to kill Tony Lester?"

The two sisters tag-teamed their story, with Megan telling how she got the gun. "I probably should have had a license or permit or whatever for the weapon, but I only kept it in my car for self-defense."

"I trust the detectives won't pursue that, given how cooperative Miss Frasier is being," Elena said.

Callaway brushed past that. "So, Dr. Frasier, after you took the gun from your sister, what happened?"

Shannon told about putting the gun in a drawer and forgetting about it. When she found it was gone, did she report its disappearance to the police? No. Did she know who might have taken it? No. Was there evidence of a burglary? No. Did anyone else have keys to her house? Yes, several people:

herself, Mark, Megan. Had others been in the house? Yes, the police.

Callaway frowned at that last statement, but Steve Alston touched his arm. "So you deny any knowledge of the shooting of Tony Lester."

"My clients deny it categorically," Elena said. Both women nodded their assent. "Now, what other questions do you have for them?"

There were other questions, but none that made Shannon feel uncomfortable.

"So, to summarize," Elena said, "we've explained how the fingerprints of both my clients came to be on the gun. Obviously someone took it from Dr. Frasier's home and, while wearing gloves so as not to leave his or her own prints on the gun, used it to kill Tony Lester." She paused, as though to emphasize her next question. "Do you intend to charge my clients with a crime?"

Neither detective said anything, so the attorney continued, "Although Shannon has some unfinished business here, Megan, I believe you're free to go."

"I think I'll head to my new job." Megan shot a defiant look at the detectives. "Assuming I can get in a few hours without being interrupted by the police."

Elena turned to Shannon. "Do you want me to stay with you while you try to help these gentlemen identify the man who attacked you—the man who's been terrorizing you with phone calls and threats despite whatever efforts they may have—"

"Counselor, that's enough," Callaway said. "We're working the homicides involving these women as hard as we can. Patrolmen have been knocking on doors in both neighborhoods, canvassing the occupants to see if anyone saw anything at the time of either murder. If Dr. Frasier can help us make a positive identification, I'm hopeful that we'll have the man who threatened her in custody by the weekend." He paused to gather himself. "And if you're asking if you need to babysit your client while we piece together an ID of her attacker, I promise we'll behave ourselves and not ask her to incriminate herself."

"If you do, she's been instructed to call me immediately, then not say another word until I get here." Elena gathered her purse and briefcase. "Shannon, will you be okay?"

"I'll be fine," Shannon said. "Megan, take the car. I'll call you to come back for me when I'm finished."

"No need. I'll see that you get home safely," Alston said.

Shannon wasn't sure whether the detective was protecting her or using the opportunity for some alone time with her. But she certainly wasn't about to turn down his offer.

STEVE ALSTON STRETCHED AND HEARD A SATISFYING *POP* FROM his back and shoulders. He'd been hunched over a computer monitor for what seemed like a year. The specialist in use of the facial reconstruction software had been very patient with Shannon, and she assured him that the picture that now filled the screen was an accurate likeness of the man who'd held her at gunpoint.

While this was going on, Callaway had been poring through the files of "known dirtbags," as he put it, looking for any notes pertaining to the unusual voice that Shannon described. Now he made his way through the warren of desks and filing cabinets to where his partner sat. "I've gone through the files twice. There's no one with the abnormal voice the doctor describes."

Steve pointed at the computer screen. "Does this bring anyone to mind?"

Callaway looked, then did a double take. "It certainly looks like him. Take away the dark glasses, make the eyes like two lasers, and that's him. But that's impossible."

"I know," Steve said. "Unless he's got a twin—or had one . . ."

"What? Don't talk over me. Tell me what you mean," Shannon said.

The two detectives looked at each other. Callaway shrugged. Steve turned so that he was facing Shannon. "Are you sure this is the man?"

"Positive," Shannon said.

"Then we have a miracle on our hands." Callaway hit a few keys on the computer and the display changed to a picture matching the composite the computer artist produced from Shannon's description. At the top of the page was the name Walt Crosley, followed by several aliases. Beneath that were the words "Presumed dead."

# THIRTEEN

MARK WAS GLAD TO GET AWAY FROM HIS MICROSCOPE, EVEN IF IT meant attending a department faculty meeting at the end of the workday. He came out the door of his office and almost collided with Shannon. "Hey, nice running into you," he said with a smile.

"Sorry. My mind was elsewhere." She touched his arm. "I've been at the police station most of the afternoon. There's been a new development in the case, but I can't stop now. I'm due in the OR."

Mark didn't have to ask which case Shannon meant. "Sure, anytime. You can't take a second right now?" He inclined his head toward his office, just behind them.

"Sorry. Got to run," she said. "Come over tonight about seven." She mimed a kiss with pursed lips. "See you then." And with that Shannon was off, the tail of her white coat billowing behind her, rubber soles squeaking on the waxed floor.

Mark stood for a moment pondering what this "new

development" could be. Oh well. He'd know in a few hours. Meanwhile, he had a faculty meeting to attend.

He managed to get through the balance of the afternoon, and at exactly seven, Mark stood on the porch of Shannon's home and pressed the doorbell.

Megan answered the door wearing a tailored navy skirt, topped by a pale blue sleeveless blouse. "Hey, Mark. How's the head?"

Mark touched his temple. "Pretty much back to normal." He moved through the door. "You look nice."

"Thanks." She ushered him into the living room. "Make yourself comfortable. I'm going to change. I'll let Shannon know you're here."

He'd hardly had time to sit before Shannon came into the room. Mark rose, kissed her, and enfolded her in a hug. "Sorry we couldn't talk earlier today," he said. "Did your time with the police throw you behind?"

She eased onto the sofa and gestured for him to follow suit. "It both threw me behind and threw me for a loop."

Mark listened as she told him about her identification of the man who was so intent on learning Barry Radick's last words. "So if you identified him, won't that make it easier for the police to find him?"

Shannon shook her head. "Ordinarily, I guess it would. But in this case, maybe not. You see, according to their records, he's dead."

Before Mark could comment, Megan came into the room and sank into an easy chair. She now wore jeans and a T-shirt, and her face had been scrubbed free of makeup. "I guess she's been telling you about the ghost who held her at gunpoint."

"Megan, it's not funny," Shannon said. "You weren't the one looking down the barrel of a gun."

"Sorry. I'm sure it was bad enough to sit there with a gun aimed at you, much less to be held at gunpoint by a supposedly dead man. Did you tell him the rest of the story?"

"I was getting to that." Shannon turned back to Mark. "The last information our police had was that this guy, Walt Crosley, was involved in drug smuggling down at the Texas-Mexico border. The *policia* caught Crosley and his partner in a sting in Matamoros. In the shoot-out that followed, he was hit. The authorities were sure the wound was fatal, but since his accomplice managed to drive away with Crosley's body in the car, there was no confirmation."

Mark shook his head. "In forensic pathology, if there's no body, it's very difficult to be certain a person is dead. You see stories all the time of people faking their own death. True, some of those are probably just concoctions, but it can be done. Who's to say that Crosley didn't spread some pesos around to get the authorities to swear to his death? If he was wanted in the US, that makes sense."

"Or what if he was shot, say, in the throat," Shannon said. "There'd be blood gushing everywhere. An observer would swear the wound was fatal, but suppose Crosley's buddy got him to a doctor who managed to save him."

"And if the gunshot wound fractured his larynx—" Mark began.

"He'd have a rough, weak voice," Shannon finished. She rose. "Just a second. I had the police print out a copy of the computer sketch we came up with."

Megan shook her head. "This is getting weird."

"More than weird," Mark said. "If this is the guy who's after Shannon, she's in real danger. I'm going to advise her—"

Shannon hurried back into the room holding a folded sheet of paper. "Here he is," she said.

Mark took the computer-generated drawing from her, unfolded it, and studied the face. The artist had added the eyes hidden from Shannon by sunglasses, and they seemed to match the rest of the man's expression. The word that came to mind was *evil*. This was a man who didn't care who he hurt so long as he got what he wanted.

Megan rose and walked over to stand behind Mark. "Let's see."

When Mark turned to look back at Megan, her face was pale. "What's the matter?"

Megan shook her head. She braced herself with both hands on the back of the sofa. "I recognize this man."

"Who . . . What . . . ," Shannon stuttered.

"I only saw him once, but that's a face you don't forget. It was visiting day at First Step. He was there to see Barry Radick."


SHANNON TURNED TO LOOK AT HER SISTER, WHO CONTINUED TO lean heavily against the back of the sofa. "Are you certain?"

Megan swallowed twice before she could speak. "No doubt in my mind. That's him." She moved slowly back to her chair, keeping one hand on the sofa as though to maintain her balance. Once she was seated, Megan said, "So do I share this information with the police?"

"My first reaction would be 'of course,'" Shannon said. "But . . ."

She could tell from the progression of emotions across his face that Mark was struggling with the same thoughts that ran through her mind. He took a deep breath, blew it out through nearly closed lips, and said, "Megan, I'm sure you realize this may focus the attention of the detectives on you more than ever. Are you ready for that?"

Megan's face contorted, and Shannon thought her sister might be ready to cry. Instead, her voice was firm and her tone defiant as she said, "Do you mean, are you innocent? For what seems like the hundredth time, yes." Her voice rose steadily in volume. "I had nothing to do with the shooting of Radick. I don't know this guy, Crosley. I didn't shoot Tony Lester. What else do you want to know?"

Shannon opened her mouth to speak, but closed it when the phone rang. Was this Crosley calling again? Should she answer it? Did she need to record it? The police had installed the equipment earlier that day, but she hadn't asked Megan how to operate it.

Never mind. She'd find out later. If this was Crosley, she wanted to tell him he could have the string of numbers that constituted Radick's dying words—anything to get him out of her life. Megan reached for the phone, but Shannon beat her to it. "Dr. Frasier."

"Shannon, this is Elena Waites. How did things go today at the police station? I expected to hear from you when you were finished, but since you didn't call, I supposed there were no problems."

"Actually, we found out a couple of pretty important things since you and I talked." Shannon looked back at Megan, who sat with her head down. "Can we meet at noon tomorrow? I think we need your advice about where to go from here."


MEGAN TURNED TO HER SISTER AS THE ELEVATOR CARRIED THEM up to the office of Elena Waites. "I don't know why I have to be here. Couldn't you do this for me?"

Shannon struggled to keep her temper under control. The events of the past week had played havoc, not only with her personal life, but with her professional schedule, too. If Megan hadn't been a part of the equation . . . Never mind. That was water under the bridge. "It's necessary for both of us. Let's leave it at that."

Elena came out of her office to escort them, and soon the two women were seated across the desk from her, having declined coffee, tea, or water. The attorney leaned forward and addressed Shannon. "So tell me what happened at the police station after I left."

Shannon related her story of identifying Walt Crosley through a computer-generated sketch and his unique voice, conscious as she spoke of Megan fidgeting beside her.

"And in their database, he's shown as presumed dead?"

Shannon nodded. "But I think I've convinced them he's very much alive."

Elena tapped the legal pad on her desk with her pen. "This gives the police some other avenues of investigation to pursue. I should think this would be good news for you," Elena said.

"Yes and no," Shannon said. She nodded toward Megan, who had the grace to look up, if only briefly. "When she was in rehab, Megan saw Crosley visiting Radick. We realize she needs to pass this information to the police, but she's afraid it will only make them redouble their efforts to connect her with Radick's murder as well as Tony Lester's."

Elena shook her head. "This could be awkward for me. As your attorney, whatever you tell me comes under the heading of client privilege unless it involves intent to commit a crime. But technically, I represent you, not your sister." She flashed an apologetic look at Megan. "Fortunately, I think I can make sure the police don't do anything more than thank you for bringing this new information to them. But we need to do it now, so there's no question of our trying to keep this under wraps." She reached for the phone but paused with it halfway to her face. "Do I have your permission? Both of you?"

"Yes," Shannon said. She looked at Megan, who seemed to consider the question far longer than was necessary. Finally, she dropped her chin a fraction of an inch in what was apparently a nod of assent.

A couple of minutes later, Elena said to Shannon and Megan, "I have Detective Callaway on the phone. He understands that you're providing this information of your own free will, that you attest to its accuracy, and that it in no way indicates knowledge or participation by either of you in the two murders you've been unfortunate enough to be associated with recently." She punched a button and laid the receiver on the desk. "Is that correct, Detective?"

Callaway's voice rumbled through the speakerphone. "Yeah. And I presume you're recording this."

"Of course," Elena said, unruffled. "Aren't you?"

The detective chose to ignore that remark. "Ladies, what's your information?"

At first Megan failed to respond, but eventually she spoke. "Shannon showed me the sketch of Walt Crosley. I recognized him as a man who came to First Step to visit Barry Radick when I was a resident there."

"When was this?"

"I don't remember. One day's pretty much like another there."

"Are you sure it was Crosley? Did you hear his name?"

"I'm sure he's the man in the picture Shannon showed me. I don't think I ever heard his name."

"Did you hear what was said?"

"No. I just saw them together that one time."

The questions went on like that for another five minutes

before Elena said, "Detective, I believe my client has given you all the information she has. If you have any other questions for her, feel free to pass them on to me. If she has answers, I'll be certain you get them. Now, I'm sure you need to get on with your work, and so do I." She returned the receiver to the phone base and opened her hands wide. "That's it. You've done your duty. If the detectives give you any grief, let me know."

In the elevator headed back to the parking garage, Shannon looked at Megan. "Glad that's over?"

Megan shook her head. "I'm glad this part is, but I'm pretty sure it's not all over. Not yet."


SHANNON LOOKED THE MAN IN THE EYE AND SAID, "TOM, I'M really sorry."

The conversation was taking place in the hall outside the vice chairman's office at Southwestern Medical Center, and the man Shannon was addressing was the spouse of the attorney she'd left less than an hour ago. Dr. Tom Waites shrugged. "I understand, Shannon, but I hope you're about finished with these last-minute 'emergencies' that require you to be off campus."

"I hope so, too." If she told Tom what was going on, even simply asked him to get the details from his wife, she knew he'd be more understanding. But Shannon was determined not to play the sympathy card. "I wish I could promise this was the last, but things keep coming up."

Tom ran his hand through his crew-cut blond hair. In his scrubs and white coat, he could have passed for a senior resident, not the department vice chairman. "Well, I hope you have this straightened out by the time Bill gets back."

Shannon didn't need a detailed explanation. Dr. Bill Meyer,

chair of the Department of Surgery, might not be as sympathetic and understanding as Tom. "I'll do my best. And thanks."

Shannon had thought she'd have no trouble getting away in time to meet with Elena at noon, but the surgical case she was staffing ran long. She had to ask one of the other faculty surgeons to step in for her, and Tom Waites was the only one available. Tom had been gracious enough to help, but Shannon knew she couldn't neglect her job much more without jeopardizing her position. She hoped the situation might improve, but, like Megan, she had a feeling that wasn't going to be the case.

Shannon glanced at her watch and decided she had time to swing by her office and check messages before she was due in the clinic to see her first patient. She came through the door to find her secretary, Janice, with the phone to her ear.

"She just came in." Janice moved the phone away from her mouth and covered the end with her hand. "This is Dr. Kim. She needs to speak with you."

Shannon searched her memory for a Dr. Kim but came up empty. "What's it about?"

"She said it was about a patient, and that she was sure you'd want to talk with her. Shall I ask for more details?"

"No. I'll take it in here." Shannon moved into her office, dropped into her desk chair, picked up the receiver, and punched the blinking button. "Dr. Frasier."

The voice on the other end was slightly accented, belonged to a female, and was totally unfamiliar to Shannon. "Dr. Frasier, this is Dr. Liu Kim in hematology-oncology."

"Yes? How can I help you?"

"I've just seen your father. He asked me to call you and discuss my findings with you." There was a hint of laughter behind the next sentence. "His exact words, I believe, were, 'I won't be able to remember those fancy terms, and I know I'll have no rest until my daughter finds out all the details.'"

But this was Friday. Her dad's appointment was next week. She'd made a note on her calendar so she wouldn't forget. "I . . . I don't—"

As though reading Shannon's mind, Dr. Kim said, "We had a cancellation first thing this morning. Since the doctor who referred him indicated that Reverend Frasier would probably appreciate being seen earlier, we called him. Fortunately, he was able to come right over."

Shannon tried to swallow, but there was only dust in her throat. "What did you find?" she finally managed to choke out.

"I'm afraid I have good news and bad news."

Shannon's heart fell.

# FOURTEEN

SHANNON FOUGHT TO STAY CALM. SHE WANTED TO PACE. SHE wanted to close the door of her office. She wanted to throw something against the wall. Instead, she forced herself to sit quietly and listen to the specialist. "Please tell me about it." Shannon pulled a blank three-by-five card from the breast pocket of her white coat and took the pen from her desk set.

"First, the bad news," Dr. Kim said. "As you may surmise, not every patient referred to us actually has a hematologic malignancy. Some have an overwhelming infection that is responsible for their abnormally high white blood cell count. Some are discovered to have enlargement of the spleen or liver from relatively innocuous causes such as infectious mononucleosis." She sighed, and Shannon knew what was coming next. "Unfortunately, in this case we confirmed the diagnosis made by the family physician. Your father has chronic lymphocytic leukemia."

Although she'd been anticipating this, Shannon still felt

disappointment wash over her. She scribbled CLL on the card. "I can't say this is unexpected. And you're right. It is bad news."

"Yes. As you may know, the prognosis for CLL is highly variable. Patients may succumb to complications such as hemorrhage or overwhelming infection. Of course, they are at risk of developing other malignancies. It is not a benign disease."

Shannon nodded to herself. *What's the good news?*

The doctor seemed to anticipate Shannon's unspoken question—or perhaps it was because she'd had this conversation hundreds of times before with anxious patients and families. "But as I said, there's good news," Dr. Kim said. "We have several treatment regimens that can provide prolonged periods of remission—some even long enough that a layperson might call the situation a cure."

"What about a bone marrow transplant?" Shannon knew of the procedure, although her knowledge of it was limited. If she wasn't mistaken, such a procedure might effect a true cure of CLL. "Would he be a candidate?"

"Of course we'll consider him for one, but that process may take several weeks. We want to assess his general health, the state of his disease, and so forth. Then we need to find a donor. But let's not get ahead of ourselves."

"So what's next?"

"I plan to put your father on what we call the FCR regimen: fludarabine, cyclophosphamide, and rituximab."

Shannon jotted down notes about how often each drug would be given, determined that before the sun set she'd be well versed on the regimen. She was still writing when Dr. Kim asked if she had additional questions. *I have a dozen, but I don't know enough to ask them right now.* "Not at this time. Maybe later." She took a deep breath. "Thank you for seeing Dad, and thanks for calling me."

"Not at all," Dr. Kim said. "Let me give you my number." She reeled off the phone numbers for her office, her pager, and her cell phone. "Don't hesitate to call."

Shannon hung up, leaned back, and closed her eyes. Her head—her doctor brain—realized all along that her dad probably had a potentially fatal disease. But now it was sinking into her heart as well. What would her mom do if the leukemia took the life of her husband? What about Megan? For that matter, what about herself? Shannon couldn't imagine a world without her dad in it. *Please, God . . .*

She felt tears trying to force their way out. She brushed moisture from the corners of her eyes and tried to summon the strength to move on and finish the clinic for which she was already late.

When she was younger, bad news always sent Shannon running to her dad. He'd hold her, reassure her, pray with her. Now it was her turn to do the same thing for other members of her family. She'd start with a call to Mark, though. That would help.

She recalled a sermon her dad had preached once about a situation such as this. The message she took away was that it wasn't a matter of God removing the burdens so much as giving the strength to bear them. If that was the case, she could look forward to receiving a lot more strength as the future unrolled, because her burdens right now were almost unbearable.

*Lord, how much more can I take?*


MARK'S EVENING ROUTINE WAS TO WATCH THE NEWS, THEN TAKE a shower. Tonight he had just turned off the water when his phone rang. He wrapped himself in a towel and hurried to answer the call. The display showed it was from Shannon.

"How did it go?"

"About like I expected." Shannon's words were flat, her voice soft, as though the very act of speaking required more energy than she possessed. "Megan was upset, of course. I finally managed to convince her that leukemia isn't a death sentence anymore. I told her Dad would go on chemo, and the hematology-oncology team would investigate to see if he's a candidate for a bone marrow transplant."

"From what I've heard, I think Dr. Kim is pretty much the person I would pick if I were the patient," Mark said. He pulled a robe from the closet and managed to slip into it without missing any of the conversation.

"So Dad seems to be okay with Dr. Kim and the treatment program," Shannon said.

"Will he tell the congregation about his diagnosis?"

"I didn't ask, but knowing Dad, I suspect he'll announce it from the pulpit on Sunday, then put it in the church newsletter next week."

Mark dropped onto the bed. "And how are you holding up?"

Shannon's sigh said it all. "I've had better days . . . better weeks. Let's see. Two murders, threatened by a known killer via phone and in person, found out my dad has leukemia, exposed to HIV-positive blood, and put on notice by one of my bosses that I can't let all this interfere with my work. Yes, definitely not one of my best weeks."

At first Mark wondered if he should encourage Shannon to ask God for strength and direction. If he caught her just right, it could be a great opportunity. Then again, if his suggestion hit her wrong, it might undo any progress she'd made in that area. He settled for "What can I do?"

Apparently where Mark had been afraid to speak, God had stepped in. Shannon's voice was a bit stronger. "Mark, if all this has done one good thing, it's made me realize that I can't get through it by myself. After you prayed with me today, I actually felt more at peace."

"You know, you don't need to wait for me—"

"I know," Shannon said. "I've tried to pray on my own—probably not enough, and maybe not even the right way, but I'm trying."

"That's a great start," Mark said.

Before Mark could say more, Shannon changed the subject. "Tonight I got Megan to show me how to operate the recorder on my home phone, so I'm set if Crosley calls again. And if he does, I'm going to give him those numbers. Maybe if I do, he'll leave me alone. The police already have them, so it can be a race to see who can figure them out first." Shannon's words almost faded away. "Either way, I want out."

"Are you sure you want to give Crosley what he wants? Have you discussed this with the detectives?"

"No! I'm tired of asking everyone what I can and can't do—my lawyer, the detectives, my sister, you." There was a brief silence. "I'm sorry. I didn't mean to lash out at you like that. You've been nothing but supportive, even when I've acted like a child . . . like now."

"That's okay. But I'd think it over before giving in to Crosley. I was wondering . . ."

"What? Go ahead."

Mark ran through the idea once more in his head. "Do you have that card handy? The one with the numbers on it?" It made a slight degree of sense, and might accomplish what Shannon wanted without actually betraying critical information.

"Just a sec." He heard Shannon moving around, papers shuffling. "Here it is."

"Give the information to Crosley when he calls, but reverse the first couple of numbers in each sequence. If he comes back on you for some reason, you can say he copied them down wrong, or you were nervous and reversed them by mistake. That may get him away from you, at least until the police can track him down." He gave her a few seconds to consider the option. "What do you think?"

"It might work. Just reverse the first two numbers of each seven-number sequence. Maybe I'll do that."

Mark checked his bedside clock. "It's getting late. Shall we try to get some sleep? I'll call you tomorrow morning. It's Saturday. Maybe we can do something to take your mind off your troubles."

"It would take something extra special to do that. But I look forward to the call."

THE RINGING OF THE PHONE AT HER BEDSIDE ROUSED SHANNON, and like a person struggling free of quicksand, she emerged grudgingly from sleep. The clock on her bedside table showed 6:12 a.m. Surely Mark wouldn't be calling this early. She wasn't on call, so this shouldn't be from the medical center. And if this turned out to be a telephone solicitor, she might crawl through the wires and strangle them.

She lifted the receiver and croaked, "Hello?"

"How did it feel to be looking down the barrel of a gun?"

The voice was rough and raspy and unmistakable. She'd heard it on the phone and in person, and each time it brought more and more fear into her heart. And the recollection of sitting next to that man, fearing for her life, made Shannon literally shake.

The harsh voice continued, "I thought I'd give you one more chance before coming after you. And this time, there won't be anyone to distract me. I want—"

"I know what you want. And I'll give it to you. I have the information written down, but you'll have to hold on long enough for me to get it. Will you do that?"

There was a pause as he apparently thought about it. "No. But I'll call back in five minutes. Have it ready for me then."

"I'll—" Shannon heard the click and realized he'd hung up. Should she give him the numbers? Why not? They meant nothing to her. The police already had them. Maybe if she gave this man what he wanted, he'd go away.

She hurried from her bedroom to the desk in the living room. The card was where she'd left it. And as she picked it up, she saw the black box on the desk next to the phone. All she had to do was push a button when the man—why didn't she call him by his name? When Crosley called back, she would record the conversation. Surely that would be helpful to the detectives.

Then another thought hit her. After the police found him, what then? What would they charge him with? Did something like making menacing phone calls and holding a gun on her carry a stiff enough sentence to keep him out of circulation? She was enough of a realist to figure a good lawyer might get him off with the proverbial slap on the wrist.

Should she— The phone rang, and Shannon almost jumped out of her skin. She pushed the button and lifted the receiver. "Yes?"

"Give me the information." The four words, delivered in guttural tones, sent chills down her spine.

"You'll need to write this down," Shannon said.

"Do you think I'm stupid? I'm ready. Give."

Last chance. Was she willing to risk making him angry? "234 8160 694 7900."

The silence on the other end of the line lasted long enough

for Shannon to think she'd lost the connection. She took the phone away from her ear, but before she could hang up, Crosley said, "You're sure?"

That did it. "I'm not sure of anything. You—" Her voice broke. She cleared her throat. "You've scared me half to death. But this is what Radick said. The man who heard it has an eidetic memory."

"What's . . . Never mind. This better be right."

She was still gripping the receiver when she heard a click. When she replaced the phone and pushed the Stop button on the recorder, her hand shook. She hoped she'd done the right thing.

MARK PLACED THE CUP OF HOT COFFEE NEXT TO THE OPEN BIBLE on his kitchen table and sat down. The scripture for this morning's quiet time was Psalm 139. He paused when he came to the words, "I will give thanks to You, for I am fearfully and wonderfully made." As a pathologist, Mark normally had occasion to see the human body after its spirit had flown, but he never failed to marvel at the intricacies of that piece of machinery and the genius of its Creator.

He was about to start his prayer when the phone rang. This had to be either a wrong number or something important. He rose and hurried into the living room, catching the call just before it went to voice mail. "Dr. Gilbert."

Shannon's words were tentative. "Is it too early?"

*Something's wrong.* "Not at all. I'm up. What's going on?" Mark was ashamed that one of his thoughts was that Megan had made another mess that Shannon would have to clean up.

"I've had another call from Crosley, and I wanted to talk with you before I reported it to the detectives."

Mark carried the cordless phone back to the kitchen and sat down at the table. "Tell me about it."

"He said he'd give me one more chance to give him Radick's dying message. I . . . I did what you suggested. I switched some of the numbers. When he asked me if that was correct, I sort of stammered and said he was making me nervous."

"Good. That would explain it if the numbers aren't the ones he needs." Mark sipped from his cup. "You did the right thing. Did you think to record the call?"

"Yes. I had to go into the living room to get the card where Lee wrote down the string of numbers, so when I picked up the phone in there I turned on the recorder."

"So are you going to report this to Callaway and Alston?" Mark took another healthy swig of coffee. Something told him he was going to need the caffeine today.

"I wanted to talk with you first, make sure I did the right thing. I'll call one of them as soon as we hang up."

*And I know which one you'll call.* "Yes, you did the right thing. Don't worry about it." He cleared his throat. "Uh, do you think you'll have to go down to police headquarters this morning? I can come with you."

"Steve . . . Detective Alston has seemed to prefer coming by my house so far. I imagine he'll do the same this time."

That cinched it for Mark. "Tell you what. Call me back when you know the details. Either place, I'll be beside you."

Mark drained the last of his now-cold coffee and went to get dressed. Shannon was certainly right to fear Walt Crosley, and her next call should be to the police. But Mark was concerned. He didn't think it was by any means a certainty that Steve Alston's interest in her was purely professional. If Alston was going to be there, Mark wanted to be there as well.

SHANNON WAS POURING A CUP OF COFFEE WHEN SHE HEARD Megan enter the kitchen. "Smells good."

"Here, let me pour you a cup."

Megan was barefoot, her pajamas partially covered by an open robe. Her hair was tousled, her face still creased by wrinkles from sleep. She yawned, nodded her thanks, and took the cup Shannon held out. "About two of these and I may wake up." She blew gently on the coffee, then sipped. "What are you doing up so early on a Saturday?"

"Walt Crosley called this morning."

"Who . . . Wait. Is that the guy whose picture I identified, the one who's after Barry Radick's last words?" Megan stifled another yawn and addressed herself to her coffee once more.

"Yep. Mark and Detective Alston are coming over. If you plan to sit in on the meeting, you may want—" Shannon found herself talking to an empty room. "Where are you going?"

From the hall, Megan yelled, "Got to get dressed."

Shannon had just finished her own coffee when the doorbell rang. Who was here first? Mark? The detectives? Or had Crosley decided to make a house call—hold a gun to her head until she gave him the correct sequence of numbers? *Stop jumping at shadows. Crosley wouldn't ring the bell.*

She hoped it would be Mark. He'd been nothing but supportive and protective during this whole trying series of episodes. She found it comforting in a way she couldn't explain. Maybe by the time this was over—

The bell rang again. Shannon squared her shoulders and marched to the front door. She looked through the peephole, something she had to admit she'd rarely done before the shooting. The expression on Steve Alston's face was somewhere between anticipation and annoyance. When Shannon opened the door, she saw why. Jesse Callaway stood off to the side, and there was no doubt about his expression. It was his usual scowl.

"Dr. Frasier," Alston said, "I understand you have more information for us. And we have some for you, so either way we were going to meet today."

"Yeah, but not this early," Callaway growled. He walked past Shannon and into the house. Alston threw Shannon an apologetic look and followed the larger detective through the door.

As Shannon was about to close the door, she saw Mark's car pull into the driveway. She ignored the detectives and waited to greet him.

"Are you okay?" he asked.

"A little shaken, I guess."

It seemed to Shannon that Mark's hug was a bit tighter, his kiss a little longer than usual. "I came as soon as I could," he said. "Looks like I haven't missed anything, though."

"No. And I'm glad you're here."

In the living room, the group took seats. Once more, Shannon and Mark were on the sofa. Callaway sat at a right angle to them in an overstuffed chair, a notebook open in front of him. Steve Alston, as usual, chose to lean against the doorframe.

Callaway started. "According to what you told Detective Alston," he said, "you had a call this morning from Crosley. Did you record it?"

"Yes," Shannon said. She went on to explain how she'd originally answered in her bedroom, but when she came into the living room she'd started the recorder.

Alston moved to the equipment, hit a couple of buttons, and in a moment the conversation issued from the small speaker. Shannon shivered as she heard that rough voice again. The mental picture of Crosley sitting next to her, leveling a wicked-looking gun at her, flashed unbidden into her mind. She shook her head, as though by doing so she could erase the image.

When the recording ended, Alston removed his own notebook and flipped a couple of pages. "Let's hear that again."

Shannon saw a frown cross his face as she heard her voice speak the numbers. "If you're wondering about it, yes, what I gave him was wrong," she said. "To me it was a no-brainer to give him what he wanted. By changing the sequence, I thought I could keep Crosley from finding whatever he's after until you people can catch him. I presume you're checking out the numbers."

"Sorry to be late." Megan entered the room and took the other chair, opposite Callaway. She pointed to the recorder. "Was what I just heard the conversation with . . . what was the man's name?"

"Crosley," Alston said. "Walt Crosley."

"And what you gave him were Radick's last words? That string of numbers?"

"Not really," Shannon said. She rose and crossed to the desk, picked up a three-by-five card, and handed it to Megan. "I switched a couple of numbers. This is the correct information."

"We're checking out what you gave us," Alston said, "but so far, no luck. We thought it might represent a couple of phone numbers, but the US has almost three hundred area codes, so that's going to take a little time to investigate."

"We thought the sequence might be a safe combination," Callaway said, "but there are too many numbers. Same thing with any kind of combination lock." He spread his hands. "But we're still working on it."

Megan frowned. "I presume you're grouping these like I see them written here, but is that the way Radick said them?"

Shannon frowned. Radick's dying words had been all but unintelligible to her. But this was the way Lee wrote them. "I don't know. I suppose so."

"I was wondering . . . ," Megan said. "Oh, maybe not."

"Why don't you call this doctor with the whatever-you-call-it memory?" Alston said. "Maybe the way he gave them to you wasn't right."

Shannon pulled out her cell phone and scrolled until she found Lee's number in the directory. She punched it in and waited. "Lee, Shannon Frasier. Sorry to call so early."

Everyone leaned forward, as though by doing so they'd be able to hear the conversation. It didn't last long, and when Shannon hung up, she frowned. "Lee said he grouped the string of numbers that way—you know, three digits, four digits, three digits, four digits—because it was easier for him to give them to me like that. But Radick actually spoke them a different way." She took the card from Megan. "The way he said them was 32 48160 96 47900."

"Still makes no sense to me," Callaway said.

Shannon was about to say something when she noticed a strange expression on Megan's face. "Is there something you want to tell us?"

"Maybe," Megan mumbled.

"Let's hear it," Callaway said.

"I . . . I may know what those numbers represent."

# FIFTEEN

MEGAN HAD THE SENSE THAT EVERY EYE IN THE ROOM WAS turned in her direction. This was exactly what she didn't need . . . didn't want. *When will I learn to keep my mouth shut?* Well, there was nothing to do now but plunge on. "I think I know what they are," she repeated. "I could be wrong, of course, but—"

"If you're wrong, we're not going to shoot you," Callaway growled. "What's your idea?"

She looked around the room. "When I was in rehab, I did a lot of reading, and one of the books was about an activity I thought might be fun—geocaching. I tried it after I got out, and although I didn't have much free time, anyone who does geocaching will tell you it gets under your skin. So when I saw the way the numbers were grouped, it reminded me."

"What's geocaching?" Callaway asked.

"People hide things, called caches, and others look for them using GPS coordinates," Megan said. "Maybe those numbers are coordinates of a location where something is hidden, something that was important to Barry Radick. And apparently to this guy as well."

Megan looked at the detectives. She felt like a third grader who'd just answered a teacher's question and was waiting to see if she'd get approval or correction. "So does that help?" she asked.

"It may," Steve Alston replied. "I want to get back to the station and check out these coordinates. If they're somewhere near here, that could explain a lot."

"Exactly what would they explain?" Mark asked. He looked first at Callaway, then Alston. "I get the distinct impression that you're not telling us everything—about Radick and Crosley, for starters. What are you holding back?"

"It's none of your—" Callaway started.

"Jesse, they deserve to know," Alston said. "When we found out that Crosley was the man trying to find out what Radick's last words were, it linked up with some things we heard from an informer. Last month two men held up a bank in the Park Cities area. They got away with three-quarters of a million dollars."

Megan watched the exchange like a spectator at a tennis match, looking first at Mark, then at the detectives. Attention seemed to have turned away from her, and she edged toward the wall, as though by doing so she could make herself invisible.

"We heard Crosley was one of the bank robbers, but we didn't believe it because we thought he was dead."

"And you think Radick was the other bank robber," Mark said. "Crosley wants the share his partner hid, and maybe Radick's dying words were a clue. Right?"

"Why would Radick come here? And why would he whisper those numbers to us as he died?" Shannon asked.

"He met Megan in rehab, and for some reason he was looking for her," Mark said. "He found your name in the phone book and figured he could locate Megan through you. After he was shot, in the weak light he mistook you for her. That's why he whispered the numbers."

Megan shivered. As events unfolded, she felt herself being drawn deeper into the situation. How could she distance herself once more?

Alston's cell phone vibrated. He pulled it from his pocket and frowned at the display. "I've got to take this." He rose and walked into a corner, turning his back to the group. The conversation was short, and mainly one-sided. Finally, Alston said, "Right," then stowed his phone and said, "We have to run."

Callaway rose to join his partner, and they had a quick whispered conversation. Megan breathed a sigh of relief. Maybe they'd drop the question of her involvement for now.

The detectives had the door open when Mark asked, "Is this about Shannon and Megan's case?"

Alston paused with one hand on the doorknob and uttered a noncommittal, "I guess you could say that."

Mark spread his hands. "If it involves them . . ."

Alston slid one foot forward, ready for a quick getaway. "A patrol officer just called in a report that he'd located one of Crosley's associates, Frankie Brown. We need to head for that location right now."

"What's the hurry? Why don't you ask the officer to bring him to police headquarters and hold him until you can question him?" Mark asked.

"Ordinarily we would, but not in this case," Callaway said. "The officer found Frankie lying in a doorway with two bullets in his head." He turned to his partner. "C'mon. I want to get there before someone steps all over the evidence."

MARK STOOD AT THE FRONT WINDOW AND WATCHED THE DETEC-
tives leave. He doubted that they'd stand outside the door and
eavesdrop, but it never hurt to be certain. Once he was sure
they'd gone, he turned back to Shannon and pulled her close.
"How are you doing? Sounds like this is escalating."

He felt her arms tighten around him for a moment. Then
she pulled back and looked up at him, and he saw determina-
tion in her eyes. "I'll be okay."

"Then I think we should do a little investigating of our
own," Mark said.

"What are you talking about? You want to try crashing a
murder scene?" Shannon said. "I'm not sure how that would
help. Besides, I watch enough TV shows to know we'll never get
past that yellow crime scene tape they put up."

"That's not it at all." Mark turned to Megan. "If you've tried
geocaching, do you have one of those apps on your smartphone
that shows the location of coordinates?"

Megan gave a tentative nod.

Mark held out his hand to Shannon. "Let me see that
card." He showed it to Megan. "So, where do these coordinates
point us?"

"I don't—"

"Megan, we really need your help. Please. For once in your
life, do something for somebody else," Mark said.

Megan sighed. She punched in some numbers on the
phone, studied the display, then said, "Near downtown Dallas.
Greenwood Cemetery."

Mark looked at Shannon. "I say we go there. The detectives can only be in one place at a time, and I'm guessing they'll
be tied up at that murder scene for an hour or longer—plenty
of time for us to do our own reconnaissance."

Shannon stared at him as though he'd gone mad. "Why

would we do that? Why not let the police do their job? And what if we run into Crosley there?"

"Remember, the coordinates you gave him were wrong. I'm not sure where they lead, but for all we know they're in the middle of the Indian Ocean. So he's not going to be where we're going."

Both women looked unconvinced.

"Let's head there while we can," Mark said. He pulled his keys from his pocket. "I'll drive."

Shannon sighed. "Okay, I'll go along with you." She turned to her sister. "Megan, you sit in front and direct Mark. I'll be in the back, regretting our decision."

STEVE ALSTON STOOD IN THE DEPTHS OF THE ALLEY AND LOOKED down at the body huddled next to the Dumpster. He rocked back and forth on his heels, both hands in his pockets, a posture he'd learned years ago. Don't risk contaminating a crime scene. Look it all over, take a mental picture, file it away so you can pull it out later and use it. That's what he was doing. "What have you got, Sergeant?"

The policeman took off his hat and rubbed his balding head. "Two shots behind the ear. ME will tell us the caliber of the gun, but I'm betting a .22. No exit wound, so the slugs are still in there."

"Sort of a surprise," Jesse Callaway said. "Most of the bad guys use Glocks now. Pretty soon the crooks will have mortars and flamethrowers."

"Except the ones who take pride in their work. They still like .22 target pistols," Steve said. "This looks like an execution." The posture of the body, the bullet wounds in the back of the head—all the signs pointed to it. He could picture the scene. The victim forced to kneel, probably begging for his life until two shots ended it.

"I'm betting it's drug related," Callaway said. "Most likely Frankie was dealing and cut the merchandise too much or did it one time too many. Someone down the chain didn't like the quality of the stuff he delivered and decided to express their displeasure in a tangible way—like two in the back of the head."

The sergeant looked expectantly at the detectives. "So this isn't tied to your cases?"

"It could be," Steve said. "There's another homicide we're working, and I'm pretty sure that guy was dealing. But that's not the case we're chasing right now." He turned on his heel and started away.

Jesse stayed put long enough to say, "You know the drill, Sergeant. Canvass the area, see if anyone heard or saw anything, write a report and file it. We may catch the killer. We may not. Personally, I think whoever did this performed a favor for society."

MARK STEERED HIS CHEVY MALIBU THROUGH THE STREETS OF downtown Dallas, responding to occasional directions from Megan. Shannon, in the backseat, had been silent since they left her house.

Mark wondered if Shannon was having second thoughts about going on this—whatever it was—quest, expedition, a way of being something other than a passive bystander. Maybe he'd been foolish to make this suggestion.

"Turn onto Oak Grove. The entrance is on your right," Megan said.

Greenwood Cemetery. The name suggested to Mark that this was a logical hiding place to choose. Freshly turned ground wouldn't arouse suspicion. Radick could have found a recently closed grave and buried the loot a few feet beneath the surface. He wondered how big a bundle that much cash would make. Did the bank robbers take only large bills? Mark had a vague recollection of something called bearer bonds. One of those might be worth ten thousand, even fifty thousand dollars.

As he entered the cemetery, Mark revised his thinking. This wasn't an active cemetery. Greenwood Cemetery was located in downtown Dallas right under the flight path for Love Field, but once through the iron gates, everything changed. Under a myriad of shade trees were monuments and gravestones for individuals buried here well over a hundred years ago.

The car moved slowly down the main road, which a street sign designated as Peace. From the passenger seat, Megan said, "Turn left on Glory. Turn right on Friendship." Finally, she pointed ahead and said, "Pull over there. That's the spot."

Mark pulled his car to the side of the road and everyone exited. He looked around. The headstones showed dates long past. "I'd thought we could look for fresh graves, but I don't think there will be any here."

Shannon stood at the side of the narrow paved road and said, "Do we even know what we're looking for?"

"Anything that could point to where the bank loot is hidden," Mark said.

For the next fifteen minutes, they wandered in ever-widening circles. Mark marveled at the old tombstones and monuments. He was especially taken with the granite statue of a Confederate soldier, raised on a plinth, standing with his rifle resting butt-first on the ground, the other hand shading his eyes as he gazed into the distance. Maybe this was the pointer. Perhaps the money was hidden somewhere in the statue's field of view. Mark stood beside the monument and looked in that direction—nothing caught his eye.

"This looks sort of out of place here, but I like it," Shannon called. Mark and Megan wandered over to where she stood, pointing at a series of bell-shaped chimes hanging one above the other from the curved end of a metal rod stuck in the ground near one of the tombstones. She ran her hand over the bells, setting them chiming. "I think it would be nice to have this next to a grave."

"Maybe we can get one for Mom's and Dad's graves," Megan said, then immediately clapped her hand over her mouth. "I'm sorry. I don't know why I said that."

"Because ever since we found out about Dad's illness, it's been in the back of our minds," Shannon said. "But I hope we won't be worrying about something like tombstones and cemetery decorations for a long time."

At last, the group gathered around Mark's car. "I didn't find a thing that suggested a hiding place," Shannon said.

"Me either," Megan echoed.

Mark held his hands out at his sides, palms up. "I'm stumped. I'm not sure where we go from here," he said.

"Where do you go? You go home!" Detective Callaway emerged from his car and walked toward them, one hand on his gun as though ready to draw it at any moment. "That is, right after you explain why you're here."

# SIXTEEN

SHANNON HAD A SINKING FEELING IN THE PIT OF HER STOMACH, akin to the sensation she experienced when riding the glass elevators of a high-rise. In the space of a few seconds, she found herself wondering why she'd let herself be talked into this expedition, scrambling for an excuse that might satisfy Detective Callaway, and looking around for a handy escape route.

Before Shannon could say anything, though, Mark spoke up. "We decided to have a look at the scene that's caused Dr. Frasier so much trouble. So far we don't see the attraction of this place, but if there's anything to be found, I'm sure you folks will find it."

"Do you know the penalty for impeding a police investigation?" Callaway said, stepping nose-to-nose with Mark.

"So far as I can see, we're not impeding anything," Mark said.

Shannon edged over next to Mark and put her hand on his arm. She hoped he wouldn't end up making the detective angry. The last thing she wanted to do was spend the rest of her Saturday getting Mark out of jail on bond for whatever charge Callaway might decide to throw at him.

The detectives' car was parked perhaps fifty feet away on the nearest cross street, and now Steve Alston exited the passenger door and ambled over. "My partner's being his usual, hard-nosed self. I presume you folks didn't disturb anything."

"Nothing to disturb," Mark said. "It's an old cemetery. We didn't find any evidence of fresh digging, no hiding places, nothing."

Shannon increased her pressure on Mark's arm. "I think it's time we left."

Before Callaway could say anything more, she steered Mark away, motioning for Megan to follow. As the car moved away, Shannon turned to look out the back window to see Callaway and Alston with their heads close together in earnest conversation.

STEVE ALSTON MOPPED HIS FOREHEAD AND LOOSENED HIS TIE. "IF those numbers really were directing us here, I wish they'd give us a clue about where to look."

"I'm not so sure about this GPS, geocache thing," Jesse said. "Maybe Megan was trying to throw us off the scent."

"Why would she do that?" Steve asked.

Jesse shook his head. "I know she's a nice-looking woman, and everyone seems to feel sorry for her because her boyfriend was murdered, but I think something smells fishy about the whole thing. My instinct tells me that Megan Frasier is part of this whole deal."

"You're just being contrary, Jesse."

"Think about it. Do you believe in coincidence? She and Radick were in drug rehab at the same time. Crosley comes to visit. I think the three of them put their heads together to plan a nice little bank job for when Radick got out. We don't know how many were involved, but there were at least two in the bank—Radick and Crosley—and one driving the getaway car. Why couldn't that be Megan Frasier? I mean, driving is an equal opportunity occupation."

"What about her boyfriend? Where did Tony Lester fit into this?"

"We know he was dealing drugs. Why couldn't he have found where she stashed her share of the bank money? That would really help him increase his inventory, let him move up to the next level."

"And if she found out . . ."

"She killed him to get the money back. Then she got rid of the gun, talked her sister into hiring a good lawyer for the two of them, and sat back while we all felt sorry for her," Jesse said.

Steve shook his head. "Nice little fantasy you've constructed, partner, but unfortunately we don't have any evidence to support it." He inclined his head toward their car. "Those numbers may or may not be GPS coordinates, but we've got to follow up. Let's get some police academy cadets out here to comb this place. Dollars to donuts, they're not going to find anything."

Jesse climbed behind the wheel. "Speaking of donuts, I didn't get breakfast yet this morning. I think some coffee and a couple of chocolate-coated ones are next on the agenda."

AS SOON AS SHE WAS INSIDE HER FRONT DOOR, SHANNON LEANED INTO Mark's arms and rested her head on his shoulder. "I was afraid you were going to go too far with Detective Callaway. I had visions of him arresting you for interfering with a policeman in his duties, or some such, and my having to get you out of jail."

"I'm going to make some fresh coffee," Megan said and disappeared into the kitchen.

Mark nuzzled Shannon's hair. "I shouldn't have mouthed off. But I'm tired of all the information flowing one way in this thing. I know they're the detectives and we're not, but you're the one getting phone calls from a man who, by all accounts, is a stone-cold killer. You're the one who had to stare down the barrel of his gun. I'd like to be more confident they have your best interests at heart."

Shannon motioned him into the living room where they settled onto the sofa. From the kitchen, the aroma of brewing coffee tickled her nostrils. "I think they're doing their job, Mark."

"Maybe," Mark said. "But there's something that bothers me about the way they're going about it. I'm not sure Steve Alston's interest in you is purely professional."

Shannon realized she should have seen this coming. "Okay, I'll admit I've had the same impression. But there's no need for you to be jealous. I love you. You're the only one I care for."

Mark had his arm around her shoulders, and now he pulled her closer. "And I love you. So don't you think it's time . . ."

Shannon felt her throat tighten. "When this is settled. I promise. But not right now. I have too much on my mind." When would she get over this aversion to a commitment? She thought she knew where it was coming from, and she could probably work through it. But not right now.

Shannon was pressed against Mark's chest, but she didn't have to see his expression to know his reaction. His sigh said it all. He was silent for almost a full minute before he said, "Okay, back to our problem. Assuming Crosley figures out or already knows the numbers represent GPS coordinates, it's not going to take him long to discover you gave him the wrong ones. And he won't be a happy camper when that happens."

"I know. But I'm not going to run away. I have too many reasons to stay."

"Which brings me to my next point," Mark said. "I think you should have a gun to protect yourself."

Shannon felt a trip-hammer start in her chest. A trickle of sweat coursed down between her shoulder blades. She forced herself to breathe slowly and deeply. The thought of a gun in her hands, much less of aiming it and pulling the trigger, was beyond her. "Mark, you know I hate . . . I hate guns. Please. Let's don't talk about them right now."

"I realize you have this aversion to guns, and with good reason," Mark said. "But we're not playing games here. There's a killer who's threatened you. I'd feel better if you had a way to protect yourself."

Shannon shook her head. "If I change my mind I'll call on you for help. But I don't see that happening."

"Ready for coffee?" Megan stood in the doorway bearing a tray with three mugs, sweetener, and milk.

Shannon was relieved to change the subject. As she stirred Sweet 'N Low into her coffee, she tried to imagine what Walt Crosley would do next . . . and how it might impact her life. She was already second-guessing her decision to turn down Mark's suggestion that she get a gun. Would it make her feel safer? Or stir up the past even more?


MEGAN WAS SITTING ON THE EDGE OF HER BED, FILING HER NAILS, when the ring of her cell phone startled her. She picked it up from the bedside table and checked the display—her parents' number. Had something happened to Dad?

She tried to keep her voice steady. "Hello?"

"Megan?" Her mom's voice was calm. "I was hoping you and Shannon could come to dinner tonight."

"Um, I sort of figured we'd be coming over for lunch after church tomorrow, but I guess tonight would be okay. Why don't I check with Shannon and call you back?"

"Oh, is Shannon there at the house? I'm glad you two are getting to spend some time together."

Yes, she and Shannon were spending time together—time at the lawyer's office, time at the police station, time chasing down clues that didn't make sense while trying to avoid a killer. Oh yeah. Quality time. Megan decided to let her mother's remark pass.

"How's Dad?" she asked.

"I think he's all right. But we can talk more about that tonight. Call me back after you've spoken with your sister."

SHANNON WOULD NEVER ADMIT IT, BUT IT HURT HER FEELINGS when her mom phoned the dinner invitation to her younger sister. Truly, the story of the prodigal son (or in this case, daughter) was playing out here. For longer than she cared to admit, Shannon had been the good daughter—checking on her parents, shielding them from some of Megan's scrapes, doing all the "right" things. She'd even gone to church regularly, although she didn't particularly feel like it much of the time.

But tonight the menu featured Megan's favorite dishes. Even the invitation had come through Megan. Shannon fought hard to suppress the resentment within her, and so far she wasn't sure she was winning the fight.

As the family took their places around the dining table, her mother brought in the last dish from the kitchen. "I called

Mark to invite him, but he couldn't make it," she said as she placed a ham in the middle of the table.

When Shannon was living at home, Saturday night dinner at the Frasiers often consisted of hurriedly consumed sandwiches. Shannon, with one eye on the door, was usually anxious to leave on a date. Her dad had his mind on putting the finishing touches on his sermon. And Megan . . . well, Megan was probably already gone for the evening. Not tonight, though. This was a full-fledged, civilized, cloth napkins on the table, use the good silverware, sit-down meal with ham, sweet potatoes, creamed corn, green beans, salad, and a pan of corn bread.

Shannon's dad took his place at the head of the table, the four of them joined hands, and he said grace. She had to admit that in the past she'd been guilty of letting her mind wander as her dad prayed. But that wasn't the case tonight. She wanted to know the reason for this family get-together, and she suspected there'd be a clue in the prayer.

"Dear Lord," her dad said in his soft yet authoritative voice, "we're grateful for the chance to sit down as a family. We thank You for the food, for all Your blessings, including the gift of health. As changes take place that send us looking for answers, we pray for wisdom in our decisions. We ask these things in Your name. Amen."

The conversation during the meal skipped from subject to subject, everyone avoiding the eight-hundred-pound gorilla in the room. Why had the family gathered? When her mom put an apple pie on the table, Shannon heard tension in her voice despite the smile on her face. "I have ice cream if anyone wants it." There were no takers.

Finally, with coffee cups and empty dessert plates before the four of them, Shannon's dad carefully folded his napkin and looked around the table. "I'm glad you girls could be here tonight. I want to get your opinion on something." He sipped his coffee, then gently put the cup back in the saucer. "I'm meeting with the elders tomorrow morning before church. And I need to decide what to do after that."

Shannon listened intently as her dad explained his situation: the diagnosis, the treatment Dr. Kim had outlined, and the outlook for the future. When he finished, he clasped his hands on the table before him and said, "So what do you think?"

The question remained unasked, but Shannon had no doubt what her father wanted to know from his family. She figured that, as a physician, she was best qualified to render an opinion. "Dad, I don't think you have to resign your position. From what Dr. Kim told me, you have an excellent chance of responding well to chemotherapy. And you may even be a candidate for a bone marrow transplant, which could lead to a cure, not just a remission. Leukemia is no longer an automatic death sentence. You have to remember that."

"I understand," he said. "And I plan to go through with chemotherapy. But that will most likely mean periods of weakness, lack of energy, side effects like vomiting." He forced a smile. "What if I lose my hair? What church wants a bald pastor? Of course, I can think of a few that already have a pastor who's bald . . . from natural causes."

"Dad, I'm sure Dr. Kim told you this already, but let me remind you that hair loss isn't a problem with the FCR regimen. You can put that out of your mind. One thing you will have to consider, though, is that chemotherapy makes you more vulnerable to infections."

"So no hugging the ladies of the congregation?" her dad said.

"Not even handshakes," Shannon said. "But you can still preach, and that's important."

Megan said, "Dad, your congregation loves you. What makes you think they'd love you any less because of this diagnosis?"

"Leukemia, or any other illness for that matter, doesn't come because God has visited the disease on you due to your sins," Shannon said. "You know that. You've preached about it. Now practice what you preach."

Her father looked at his wife. "What do you think?"

Shannon had heard the reply so many times she could have given it for her mother. "Whatever you do, I'll support you."

Both Megan and Shannon nodded silently. Their father rose from the table. "If you'll excuse me for a few minutes, I want to be alone in my study. God already knows my decision. Now I need to find out from Him what it will be."

"YOU'RE SURE OF THAT?" WALT CROSLEY'S RASP WAS AS LOUD AS he could make it. The bullet in his throat might have made his voice rougher, and he could no longer yell, but he was still capable of putting enough menace into his words to instill fright in the listener.

The man seated in front of the computer cowered as much as his frail frame would allow. He didn't turn to look back at Walt, who stood with a hand on each of his shoulders, gripping them with enough pressure to bring pain. "I'm certain. First, I agree that these numbers could be GPS coordinates. But if we assume that, the ones you gave me are smack in the middle of the North Atlantic Ocean. The numbers must be wrong. Somebody made a mistake."

"Yeah, and I know who made it." Crosley took one hand from the little man's right shoulder long enough to rub his chin. "How about switching around some of the numbers? Can you do that?"

"S-s-sure, Walt. Just gimme a minute." He tapped a few keys. "How do you want me to do this? Are you looking for someplace in particular?"

Once more, Crosley rubbed his chin, this time with his other hand. He felt the muscles of the man sitting at the keyboard relax, so he quickly resumed his grip. The little man needed some encouragement, and when administered by Crosley, that usually took the form of pain. "I'm looking for someplace local." He hesitated, then decided there was no harm in giving the man more information. "I'm looking for someplace near here where you could hide . . . something."

It took thirty minutes, during which time Crosley kept up his painful grip on the shoulders of the computer operator. At last, the little man said, "Look here. Does this sound right?"

Crosley leaned forward and squinted at the screen. The map showed a teardrop-shaped pointer off Hall Street in downtown Dallas. The marker was within an area shaded in gray. "What is it?"

"Greenwood Cemetery. It hasn't been active for years, but it's still sort of a tourist attraction. Lots of graves and monuments going back to the time of the Civil War."

"Yeah," Crosley said. "That would probably be the kind of place he'd choose." He squeezed the man's shoulders even harder. "Thanks, you did well."

"And you know I'm not going to tell anyone," the man squeaked. "My lips are sealed."

"I know they are," Crosley said. He cupped the computer operator's head with one hand on top, one beneath the chin. A quick twisting motion, and the man slumped over his keyboard. Crosley nodded in satisfaction. "I know they are."

# SEVENTEEN

WHEN THE ELDERS OF THE MOUNT HERMON BIBLE CHURCH CONvened, there was generally a certain amount of talking among them before the meeting came to order. But whether it was because of the early Sunday morning hour or the unusual circumstances of a called meeting, the twelve men gathered on folding chairs in the pastor's study that morning were quiet.

Promptly at 8:00 a.m., the chairman, Herb Freeman, stood and turned to face the group. Herb was middle-aged, tall and lean, and dressed like a funeral director, which wasn't surprising since that was his profession. He called the group to order and led an opening prayer. Then he inclined his head toward the pastor, who was seated in one of the chairs in the front row. "Pastor Frasier, I believe you have some things you want to say."

Robert Frasier stood and faced the group. *This is it. Lord, give me the words.* "I have some news to share with you. After you've heard it, I will answer any questions you may have. Finally, I need your prayers and support for what follows."

In a quiet voice, he told them how he'd been diagnosed with leukemia. He laid out the treatment plan his doctor had proposed. Then he came to the heart of his presentation. "Obviously, I will accept the program the doctor has suggested. That will involve chemotherapy, with all the potential side effects and possible complications that go with it. Unfortunately, there's no way to predict how it will affect my ability to function."

He scanned the faces before him, but they gave no clue of the men's thoughts. Robert swallowed twice. "I will announce this news to the congregation this morning, but I wanted you to hear it first." Several men started to speak, but he silenced them with an upraised hand. "This change in my status raises a question. I've spent a great deal of time in prayer over this decision." He took a deep breath. "I hope to continue my role as pastor of this church so long as I am able. If I reach the point where I can no longer function, I will offer my resignation."

Dr. Ralph Gutekind rose and moved to stand beside Robert. He looked directly at him and said, "You have been my pastor and my friend, and I have been your physician, for over twenty years. I was devastated by news of this diagnosis, yet encouraged by the possibility of a prolonged remission, perhaps even a cure." He turned to face the assembled elders. "I hope you will join me in pledging our unanimous support of and prayers for Pastor Frasier, affirming his decision to continue as pastor, preaching as his condition allows, with the church staff and the elders shouldering as much of the load as necessary."

One by one, the elders joined in with similar words. Robert touched the corners of his eyes, hoping to wipe away the tears forming there before anyone noticed.

NORMALLY, SHANNON PREFERRED THE BACK OF THE CHURCH. SHE figured Megan's preference was to be at home, asleep. But today they both sat on the second row, flanking their mother, as Pastor Robert Frasier delivered his sermon to the congregation of the Mount Hermon Bible Church.

To her right, Shannon saw her mom's head bowed in silent prayer, her hands clasped together so tightly the knuckles were white. Megan sat impassive on the other side of her mother, her emotions impossible to read. Shannon turned her eyes back to the pulpit, recognizing that the sermon was coming to a close.

"I challenge those of you who have not yet made Jesus Lord of your life to do so now. Those who have already placed your trust in Him, I ask you a question. Do you believe God can do anything? If so, will you trust Him to choose what that anything is . . . even if it's something you don't want?"

As the congregation bowed for a closing prayer, Mark, sitting on Shannon's left, slid his hand over hers and squeezed. "I'm glad you're here with me," she whispered.

"I'm here every Sunday," he whispered back.

"I mean today especially," Shannon murmured. Actually, she wasn't sure she could have made it through the past few days without him. There was no doubt in her mind. She loved Mark. But she still couldn't fully accept the thought of marrying him. Soon, she hoped. Soon.

After the amen, there were no swelling chords from the organ in the usual postlude. When the congregation looked up, they saw Pastor Frasier still standing beside the pulpit. Herb Freeman slowly rose from his seat and made his way to the platform, adjusted the microphone, and made a patting gesture. "Please be seated. I'd like to call the church into a special business meeting." A gentle murmur went up. "I don't think this will take long." He turned to the pastor. "Pastor, I believe you have an announcement to make."

A buzz went through the crowd. Behind her, Shannon heard a woman whisper, "He's going to another church." Her husband whispered back, "I doubt that. Maybe he's retiring."

The pastor cleared his throat. "I shared with the elders this morning some news I've recently received. I've been diagnosed with leukemia." A ripple of whispers swept across the room but quieted quickly. "I'm due to begin chemotherapy soon. The outlook is good, but I wanted to advise you of this occurrence as soon as the diagnosis was confirmed. At this time, after a great deal of prayer, it is my desire to remain as your pastor, unless you ask me to do otherwise." In the stunned silence that followed, he picked up his Bible from the pulpit and walked slowly down the stairs to a vacant seat in the front row.

Freeman moved to the microphone again. "I'd like one of our elders, Dr. Ralph Gutekind, to report to you our reaction when we heard the news this morning, and our unanimous recommendation to the church."

The doctor climbed slowly to the platform, leaned on the pulpit, and looked out at the congregation. "To put it simply," Gutekind said, "the elders pledged our prayers and support to Pastor Frasier and affirmed his decision to remain as our pastor. I trust you will do the same."

It took perhaps ten minutes for those assembled to overwhelmingly voice their support for Pastor Frasier, most of that time given over to glowing tributes from various members. When the business meeting came to an end, the organ struck up a triumphant tune, and the congregation rose as one and applause thundered through the sanctuary.

Shannon hugged her mom, then moved forward with

the rest of the family to enfold her dad in a bear hug. "I never doubted how the church would react," she said.

"I prepared for the worst, hoped for the best, and left it to God," he said.

"I'll call later this afternoon," Shannon said. "Mark is taking Megan and me to lunch." She turned to look for her sister and found her deep in conversation with Steve Alston. *Oh, I don't need this.* She moved until she was in Megan's line of sight. "We need to go now."

Megan smiled. "You go ahead. Steve invited me to lunch."

"Actually, I'd hoped you both would join me," Alston said.

"Sorry, my sister must have forgotten. My boyfriend is taking us to lunch," she said, bearing down perhaps a little too hard on the word *boyfriend*.

Alston held up his hands, palms out. "Didn't mean to start a family fight. I'm happy your father is staying on as pastor here. If I can do anything to help . . ." He left the words dangling, smiled, and turned away.

As Alston was walking away, Mark came up to Shannon and asked, "What was that?"

She shrugged. *I wish I knew.* Actually, Shannon was pretty sure she did know—but it wasn't something she wanted to discuss with Mark right now. Right now, all she wanted was a chance to relax.

Her cell phone vibrated, and when she pulled it from her purse, her face fell. "It's the hospital. I'm on call. I have to go."

A SURGERY RESIDENT AND THE ER DOCTOR FLANKED THE GURNEY on which the man lay. IVs ran into both his arms, one delivering blood, the other a clear fluid. Oxygen flowed into a mask placed loosely over his face.

"What do we have?" Shannon asked, slipping on a pair of exam gloves.

The resident held out his stethoscope. "Gary Hermanson was the driver in a head-on crash. The other driver was going the wrong way on Central Expressway. He and his passenger were dead at the scene."

Shannon took the proffered instrument and listened to the man's chest and abdomen. She ran her hands over the injured man's extremities. She shined a light into his eyes. Without looking up, she asked, "What do you think?"

"Fractured right femur, minimally displaced. No suggestion of significant head or neck trauma. He has marked ecchymoses along his torso, about where the seat belt would restrain him. That bruising plus significant hypotension made me think of a ruptured viscus—probably stomach."

"Think he's got enough blood sequestered around his leg fracture to explain the drop in blood pressure?"

"Not really," the resident said.

Shannon nodded in agreement. She, too, had noticed the evidence of severe pressure from the seat belt. The distention of the man's abdomen and absence of bowel sounds further pointed to the rupture of a hollow internal organ. "X-rays?"

"Confirmed free air in the abdominal cavity. I think we need to do an exploratory lap right now."

"Agreed," Shannon said. She flipped off the gloves and washed her hands. "Is the family here?"

"We're working on notifying next of kin," the ER doctor said. "I'll sign off with you on an op permit for abdominal exploration as an emergency."

Thirty minutes later, Shannon stepped away from the scrub sink and asked her chief surgical resident, "Tim, ready to do this one?"

"Sure," he said.

In a matter of minutes, the two surgeons stood under the bright operating lights, looking down at the rectangle of skin tinted orange by antiseptic solution and outlined by sterile green sheets. Tim looked to the head of the table. "Everything okay up there?"

The anesthesiologist reported, "Pressure's continuing to drop. He's asleep enough for you to make the incision, but it's going to take a few more minutes to get good muscle relaxation."

"Can't wait for it," Tim said. "We'll have to pull harder on the retractors for now. Let's go."

It took the operating team twelve minutes of intense activity to enter the abdomen and explore the contents. Just as they suspected, there was a small rent in the man's stomach, spilling its contents into the peritoneal cavity. In addition, they found tears through the outer capsule of the spleen and liver, with bleeding into the abdomen from both organs.

"What's your game plan?" Shannon asked. So far Tim's performance was good, and she had no doubt he'd have the right answers.

"Stomach contents in the peritoneal cavity, so make sure prophylactic antibiotics are running in his IV." He looked at the anesthesiologist.

"Started in the ER."

"Close the hole in the stomach with a purse-string suture, then wash out the abdominal cavity thoroughly. Sew up the lacerations of the liver and spleen."

"Consider a splenectomy?" Shannon asked.

Tim kept his gaze on the abdomen but shook his head. "The laceration isn't bad enough to warrant that."

"Closure?"

"Close the incision with staples, leave drains in for a few days."

"And . . ."

"Get orthopedics to check on that femur."

"Good," Shannon said.

In the recovery room, a nurse approached Shannon. "The patient's wife is in the waiting room now."

"We'll talk with her," Shannon said. She turned to Tim. "Want to do that before you dictate the operative note?"

"Sure."

In the waiting room, it wasn't hard to pick out the patient's wife from the few people sitting there. The others were talking among themselves, some watching TV, some reading. These were family members waiting to enter the surgical ICU for their allowed visitation time. This woman sat alone, staring into space, her lips moving in silent prayer.

Shannon and Tim walked to where the woman sat. "Mrs. Hermanson?" Shannon asked.

"Yes?" The woman looked up at them. "Is Gary . . . is he . . ."

"He's okay," Shannon said. She took the chair next to Mrs. Hermanson. "He sustained quite a few injuries—a hole in his stomach, some other internal injuries. He may need another operation for a broken leg, but he came through this one just fine."

The woman's face relaxed a bit. "Oh, thank you. I've been praying for him . . . and for you all."

Shannon felt her throat closing. She knew a bit about what this woman felt right now.

Tim had taken the chair on the other side of Mrs. Hermanson, and he spoke now. "Thank you. The nurses will let you know when you can see your husband. I'll be by tonight to check on him, and I'll talk with you then."

The two surgeons started to leave but stopped when Mrs.

Hermanson said, "What about the other driver? The one who was going the wrong way and hit Tim? What about him?"

Shannon turned back and crouched in front of Mrs. Hermanson's chair. How would she take the news? Would she exult that the driver had paid the ultimate price for his mistake? Shannon put one hand on Mrs. Hermanson's and said, "I'm sorry. He and his passenger were both dead before help could get to them."

Mrs. Hermanson looked down at her lap and shook her head. "I'm sorry to hear that. I'll pray for their families, too."

As she walked away, Shannon thought back to the time when she knelt at Todd's side, watching him die. How would she have felt if the police had told her the person who shot him had been killed in a car crash just after the shooting? Could she have prayed for their families? Or would she have thought what had crossed her mind this evening when she learned the fate of the wrong-way driver? *Serves them right!*

As she started to change out of scrub clothes, the phone in the dressing room rang. Shannon looked around and saw that she was the only person there. She picked up the receiver. "Dr. Frasier."

"Doctor, glad we caught you before you left. Dr. Fell called from the ER. They're bringing up a patient with a gunshot wound of the abdomen for emergency surgery. He asked if you'd scrub in with him on the case."

As Shannon hung up, she felt the familiar queasiness. Elective surgery posed no problem for her. Operating on victims of motor vehicle accidents, such as the one she'd just completed, was something she could take in stride. But gunshot wounds still brought a reaction that Shannon couldn't ignore. True, the symptoms weren't as bad as they used to be. She wondered if they'd ever disappear completely.

"READY WHEN YOU ARE," THE ANESTHESIOLOGIST SAID.

Shannon fought against the dimming of her vision. She was light-headed. A growing sense of nausea made her gag. She felt her heart pounding in her chest, heard her pulse roaring in her ears. Under her surgical gown, rivulets of perspiration trickled slowly down her back. She looked at her gloved hands and saw a fine tremor, which she attempted to hide by resting them on the draping sheet that covered the patient.

She looked at Will, who nodded that he was ready. Shannon was glad he was the resident physician on this case. If something happened to her, Will was quite capable of finishing. *No! Don't think about that. You can do it. You've done it before, and you can do it again. This will pass.*

She took several deep breaths, then strained, tensing her abdominal muscles to force blood toward her brain, a trick she'd learned early in her battle with these attacks. Shannon swallowed the bile that had crept into the back of her throat and held out her hand. The scrub nurse slapped a scalpel into her palm.

"I'll make a midline abdominal incision. Clamp the bleeders as we go. We'll stop and Bovie the small ones," she said, looking to make certain the electrocoagulation unit was set up. "We'll tie off the larger bleeding points later, but for now, just leave the hemostats in place. What's important is to get good abdominal exposure, locate the damaged areas, and repair them."

Will nodded.

Shannon was sure he wondered why she was telling him what he already knew. But she knew from experience that her symptoms would subside in a matter of minutes, and the longer she could safely delay, the better.

For the first time since she'd begun battling her attacks,

Shannon added one more action. *God, please help me get through this one.* And with that, she made a clean stroke with the scalpel, dropped it onto the instrument tray, and held out her hand for a hemostat.

# EIGHTEEN

SHANNON WAS SCHEDULED FOR OFFICE TIME ON MONDAY MORN-
ing, a welcome break from her surgical practice. She stopped
by the hospital to check on the two patients from the day
before and found that, although Mr. Hermanson had done
fairly well through the night, the course of the gunshot victim had been much rockier, requiring medications to keep his
blood pressure up.

She talked with the resident, suggested a couple of changes,
and asked him to call her with the results of that morning's lab
tests. "You can get me on my cell," she said.

Back in her office, Shannon closed the outer door before
calling up the faculty directory on her computer. She noted
a number and picked up the phone. Should she do this?
She was a female working in what had at one time been the
male-dominated domain of surgery, so she remained constantly aware that to show vulnerability might undermine
her status as a faculty member at a high-profile institution

such as this. But to keep putting off this move might do even more damage—not only to her professional status, but also personally.

Resolutely, she tapped out the numbers. "This is Dr. Shannon Frasier, in the Department of Surgery. Is Dr. Kershaw available?"

In a few moments she heard a soft, warm contralto saying, "Shannon? So good to hear from you."

Shannon's first encounter with Dr. Ann Kershaw had taken place shortly after she joined the faculty. Surgery for breast cancer had thrown a patient into deep depression. Shannon requested a consultation by one of the faculty psychiatrists, and it was then that she discovered in Ann Kershaw a psychiatrist who counseled with compassion and common sense. Their paths had crossed only rarely since then, but Shannon knew there was only one person she'd ask to help with the problem that had plagued her for so long.

"Ann, I need help. I wonder if I could see you."

Shannon heard paper rustling, undoubtedly Ann checking her schedule. "I'm afraid the best I can do is at the end of the day. Could you come by my office about five?"

"I'll be there. Thanks so much."

As she hung up, Shannon wondered if she'd done the right thing. No, she'd had this monkey on her back far too long. It was time to get rid of it, one way or another.

IN THE PARKLAND HOSPITAL PATHOLOGY LAB, MARK LEANED BACK from the microscope and felt the bones in his back crackle like Rice Krispies. He stared up at the ceiling, changing the focus of eyes that had spent too long scanning blue-and-red-stained slides prepared from surgical specimens. It was time to move around a bit. "I'm going to my academic office for about a half hour," he told the lab tech.

His route took him past one of the medical school lecture halls, where he encountered Jay Sanders coming out the door. They nodded and stepped to the side of the corridor to avoid the group of students pouring out of the room.

"Just lectured to the sophomores," Sanders said. "Sharp group. Every year the admission standards keep going up, and I find myself wondering if I could get into this med school."

"I have the same thoughts when I interview applicants for a pathology residency," Mark said.

"How's Dr. Frasier doing on her antiviral meds?" Sanders asked.

"I suppose she's doing okay," Mark replied. "She hasn't mentioned any problems, but thanks for reminding me. I'll ask her specifically. Otherwise, knowing Shannon, she'd probably just ignore them."

"Well," Sanders said, "if she has any side effects, tell her to call me. I may be overly cautious in treating her, but even if there's only one chance in a thousand that she'd become infected with HIV, I don't want to ignore the possibility."

Mark nodded, reflecting that so much had gone on since then he'd almost forgotten Shannon's exposure to Radick's virus-laden blood. He'd have to remember to ask her if she was having any ill effects from the medication. And although his primary connection with Lee Kai was through Shannon, Mark decided he should call him to see how he was feeling as well. True, Sanders was the treating physician in both cases, but Mark felt a degree of responsibility, both as the doctor who'd discovered Radick's positive HIV status and as Shannon's significant other.

As he made his way to his office, Mark decided that he

hated that term, *significant other.* It was a sort of shorthand, a convenient set of words often used to designate partners living together without benefit of marriage, something neither he nor Shannon would ever contemplate. But what was he right now? He was much more than a boyfriend. But he wasn't her fiancé either.

Had all they'd been through in the past ten days brought them close enough to each other that Shannon would finally say yes to a proposal of marriage? His gut instinct told him to hold off a little longer. Maybe after Crosley no longer posed a danger, perhaps after Shannon's father's health status was clearer, possibly after Megan was settled into her new job and there was no charge of murder hanging over her head— maybe then he could talk with Shannon about marriage. Until then, he'd continue to play the role he currently occupied: the "almost fiancé."

DR. ANN KERSHAW USHERED SHANNON INTO HER OFFICE, CLOSED the door, and gestured her to a seat on the sofa against the wall to the right of her desk. The shelves on the opposite wall were loaded with books and journals, some in piles that threatened to spill over, others neatly stacked or shelved. By contrast, Kershaw's desk was a model of neatness. Apparently the psychiatrist thought some things were worth taking care over, others were not.

Kershaw had short brunette hair with just a hint of silver beginning to show. Horn-rimmed reading glasses hung from a chain around her neck. She took a seat on the sofa beside Shannon and smoothed her navy skirt over her knees. Half turning to face Shannon, Kershaw asked, "So what's going on?"

Shannon had spent much of her free moments today trying

to decide how to approach this. Part of her wanted to simply say, "Nothing, it was a mistake," and flee. But she was here, and she might as well proceed. "I'm having panic attacks."

If Kershaw was surprised, she didn't show it. "Tell me about it."

"They're not as bad as they once were, but I've been having them since my first experience with surgery as a medical student. The symptoms are always the same—queasiness, cold sweats, a feeling that I might pass out. They're tolerable, more so now than when these first started, but I still get them."

"And yet you went into the field of surgery. Why do you suppose that's the case?"

Shannon had wondered the same thing dozens, if not hundreds of times. "I'm not sure. Some sense of 'I'll beat this,' I guess. And once I finished my residency, I didn't want to change my specialty."

"Is there a trigger?"

Shannon nodded. "Yes. They're pretty specific. I only get the attacks when I'm caring for a patient with a gunshot wound. I can still function, but it takes effort."

"And this isn't simply the reaction anyone might have to blood and trauma?"

"Just yesterday I scrubbed in on the case of a man injured in a car crash, tearing a hole in his stomach. The abdominal cavity was almost filled with blood and gastric contents, and I did fine." She took a deep breath. "The next case was a gunshot wound, and I had a minor panic attack while I was helping the resident with it."

Kershaw leaned forward, her chin resting on her hand. "When's the first time you recall having one of these attacks?"

"I've been trying to pin it down, and I'm pretty sure they started in med school when I took some elective time on general surgery. I scrubbed in on the case of a man who'd been shot multiple times. He didn't make it, and all during the case I thought I was going to throw up. I wondered if it was the old 'can't stand the sight of blood' thing, but I had no problem with similar cases. Just gunshot wounds."

Kershaw stood and began to pace in front of her desk. "And ever since, you've had these attacks when caring for a patient in such a situation?"

Shannon nodded. "They were slowly getting better. Then a man was shot in my front yard. Lee Kai was at dinner with us that night, and he and I tried to help the man, but there was nothing we could do. Since then the attacks have been worse again."

"You're smart enough to know what I'm going to ask next. Was there some incident with a gunshot wound earlier in your life?"

That was what Shannon was afraid she'd hear. She'd hoped Ann would give her a magic bullet, maybe prescribe a beta-blocker or something similar to prevent these spells. Instead, she'd gone right to the episode Shannon still saw unreeling behind her closed eyelids some nights.

"Yes. It was at the start of my freshman year in medical school. Things were getting serious between my boyfriend and me. We were out for a nice dinner . . ."

MARK PULLED TO THE CURB OUTSIDE SHANNON'S HOUSE. NO LIGHT showed through the partially open blinds. At half past seven in the evening, even with daylight saving time, sunlight was fading and some people had turned on one or two lights. The closed garage door gave him no clue as to whether Shannon was at home. To his eye, the house looked deserted. Where was Shannon? Was she okay?

He'd tried to call her, both at her office and on her cell, with no response. His call was triggered by concern for her safety, and now that concern increased.

*You're worrying about nothing, Mark.* On an intellectual level, he realized there was probably a logical explanation for Shannon's absence from her home and her failure to respond to his call. But his heart kept telling him that something bad had happened to her.

Maybe she met up with Crosley again, and this time there was nothing to intervene and let her escape. He wished she'd taken him up on his offer of a gun.

Megan's car wasn't in its usual place at the curb. Perhaps the two sisters were having dinner out. Then again, maybe Crosley had them both. Mark's fears multiplied moment by moment.

He climbed out of his car, strode up the walk, and rang the bell. No response. He rang it again, with the same results. He was about to pull out his cell phone and try calling Shannon one more time when he heard the rumble of the garage door opening. In a moment, a blue Toyota Corolla pulled into the driveway and parked in the garage.

Mark felt himself let out a breath he didn't know he was holding. He relaxed a bit and started toward her.

Shannon waved to him, then emerged with two grocery sacks in her arms. "You're just in time to help me carry these in," she said. "There are two more sacks in the car."

Once inside, he hurriedly set his burdens on the kitchen counter before drawing Shannon close to him and kissing her. Then he said, "I was worried about you."

"Sorry," Shannon said. "I'm fine." She gestured to a chair at the kitchen table. "Have a seat."

Shannon moved about, putting away groceries. "I was

going to cook for Megan and me tonight, but she called to tell me she was eating out with some of her colleagues from work. So it's just the two of us." She opened a cabinet door, set several cans of food on a shelf, and said, "How about spaghetti?"

"Fine," Mark said, but he refused to be sidetracked. "Surely you know why I was worried about you. As I was ready to leave the campus, I tried calling you. I thought I could walk you to your car. You know, as long as Walt Crosley is loose, you're not safe."

"I appreciate your worrying about me, although I certainly didn't mean to do that to you," Shannon said as she filled a pot with water and put it on to boil. "Honestly, I had an appointment at five, and I've been a bit preoccupied since then." She started toward the living room, calling back to say, "I turned off my cell phone when I got to the appointment, and I must have forgotten to turn it back on." She picked up her purse and extracted the phone. "Yep, still turned off. Thanks for the reminder."

Back in the kitchen, she opened a jar of spaghetti sauce, dumped it into a saucepan, and put it on to simmer. Then she reached into the refrigerator for a Diet Dr Pepper. "Want one?"

"No thanks."

Shannon took the chair next to Mark. "Are you curious about my five o'clock appointment?"

"I figured if you wanted me to know . . ."

"I saw Ann Kershaw." She waited, but when she saw he wasn't going to react, she went on. "I've been having panic attacks, anything from full-blown ones to minor episodes, every time I'm called on to deal with a gunshot wound. I finally decided it was time to get to the root of them. That's why I saw Ann today."

Mark searched his memory. He didn't think Shannon had

ever told him about panic attacks. He knew they were more common than the general public thought, and that it was possible to get through them. Many actors had episodes, ranging from nervousness to vomiting, before every performance. Some surgeons, when they would admit it, told of similar reactions when faced with major surgery or extremely stressful situations. But he had no idea Shannon was afflicted with them. "So what did Ann say?"

Shannon walked to the stove, stirred the sauce, dumped a handful of pasta into the boiling water, and returned to her chair. "Panic attacks usually stem from a feeling of helplessness, either at the time or in the past. In my case, they probably arose from Todd's shooting."

Mark had heard the story, although he was certain there were some details he'd never been told. "And ever since your boyfriend was shot, you've been blaming yourself because you couldn't save his life?"

Shannon turned down the burner under the sauce, then took a wooden spoon and lifted out a strand of spaghetti. She looked at it, then dropped it back into the boiling water. "I guess that's part of it." She pulled down a bowl and started making a salad. "But I think it was more than that—the loss of a man I thought I could marry, the shock of the way it happened, my feeling of total helplessness as I crouched over his body, his blood on my hands."

"So from then on, blood has been a trigger?" He shook his head. "No, that's not true. You see blood every time you operate. These episodes are tied to gunshot wounds." Mark took a deep breath and paused to organize his thoughts. "That's pretty specific."

She looked up from her work. "There should be a package of crispy bread sticks in the cupboard. Would you get those?"

Mark shuffled through the contents of the cupboard, found the package of bread sticks, and put them on the table. "So what did Ann think was the catalyst? What specifically happened when Todd was shot that sets you off with every gunshot wound victim?"

Shannon paused with a knife in her hand. "I'd shoved a lot of those memories into a corner of my mind. Ann helped me get them back."

"She hypnotized you?"

"Actually, she taught me what amounts to self-hypnosis. It's not difficult. And with that I was able to go back to the shooting scene, picture it in detail, reproduce every action, every word."

"Every word? You never mentioned Todd saying anything after he was shot."

"I'd repressed it, but today I saw and heard it again. The bullets struck him, and he sprawled on the walk with his head turned toward me. As I knelt beside him, he whispered something to me. They were the last words I heard him speak."

Mark started to reply, but decided he'd keep his mouth shut. She'd tell him in her own good time.

Shannon shuddered a bit. "He whispered, 'Help me.' And I couldn't."

SHANNON CLOSED HER EYES AS THE PHRASE ECHOED IN HER MIND. *"Help me."* She'd managed to push the voice and the words deep into her subconscious for ten years.

She looked up at Mark. "I know. You probably think that one incident so long ago shouldn't be affecting me right now, and maybe you're right. I thought I'd begun to get past it, and then the shooting on my lawn brought it all back."

Shannon didn't remember putting the salad together, but

she looked down and the bowl before her was filled. She checked the spaghetti, found it acceptable now, and poured the contents of the pot into a colander. From there she dumped the spaghetti into a bowl, added the sauce, and set it all on the table beside the salad and breadsticks. "Would you get the dressing? And get yourself something to drink."

Mark complied. When they were seated, she asked Mark to say grace. He probably did a good job, but while he prayed her mind continued to stray. She'd given him only half the story. He deserved to hear the rest.

She realized Mark was silent. He was finished, and she hadn't even noticed the amen. Shannon looked up at him and said, "There's more, if you want to hear it."

Mark paused with his hand halfway to the bowl of spaghetti. He relaxed back into his chair. "I want to hear all of it. I love you, and you're important to me." He sipped from the Diet Coke he'd retrieved from the refrigerator. "Tell me."

"Ann helped me see that those words—*help me*—from Todd were the reflexive expression of a dying man. But my mind interpreted them as being a command to use my medical training in the future to help every victim of a gunshot wound. And that's why I've felt so nervous, had panic attacks, when confronted with such a scenario. It was as though God had spoken to me, making it clear that my duty was to save every one of those people. And if I should fail, I would have failed Him."

Mark frowned. She could tell he was trying to choose his words carefully. "And this was the reason for your panic attacks? Every time you were faced with that situation, you had that unconscious feeling you were being tested?"

"More or less," Shannon said. "But there's more." She started to reach for the salad, then pulled back her hand. Her appetite, if she'd ever had one, was gone now. "Barry Radick's shooting reinforced the feelings I'd almost managed to put behind me."

"You mean bending over a man who'd been shot, getting his blood on your hands, not being able to help?"

"All that and one more thing." She took a long swallow from her Diet Dr Pepper. "When I used self-hypnosis to go back to Radick's shooting, I could remember the string of numbers he said, just as well as Lee did."

"And were they the same ones he recalled?"

"Yes. I checked afterward. But there was something else."

Mark frowned. "What?"

"Right before the numbers, Radick whispered two more words. He said, 'Help me.'"

# NINETEEN

DETECTIVE STEVE ALSTON SAT AT HIS DESK IN THE SQUAD ROOM ON TUESDAY morning, surrounded by files and notes, oblivious to the activity around him. He tapped keys on his computer, shook his head, made another entry, uttered a few uncomplimentary words, and was trying again when he heard his partner's voice behind him.

"What in the world are you doing?" Jesse Callaway said.

Steve swiveled around. "I'm presuming the GPS coordinates the doctor with the perfect memory gave Dr. Frasier are accurate. They pointed to Greenwood Cemetery, but we didn't find anything there. So I'm wondering what we missed."

Jesse perched one haunch on the desk behind him. He started to pull a cigarette from the pack in his shirt pocket, thought better of it, and dropped his hands to his sides. "I hate this no smoking in public buildings policy."

Steve had learned to ignore these asides from his partner.

He held up his hand and began ticking off points. "If we assume Greenwood's where Radick hid the money, where did he put it? And what form would it be in? His share of the money would be about a quarter of a million dollars. If the robbers got away with a mixture of bills—hundreds, fifties, twenties—then a third of it, two rows of bills stacked beside each other, would be a foot high and weigh about twelve pounds. That's easy enough for one man to carry and hide."

"Great. So you've done some research. But what does that mean?"

"We had men search the cemetery, not just the location the coordinates pointed to, but all around there. There was no evidence of fresh digging anywhere. No convenient hollow trees or hiding places. We've even looked in the mausoleums. There's absolutely no place where a bundle that size could be hidden. Except . . ."

Jesse leaned forward, obviously interested. "Except what?"

"A bundle like that would fit in a coffin."

"So . . ."

"We know Greenwood isn't an active cemetery, but suppose there was evidence of vandalism—fresh digging around a grave, a mausoleum left open—in the time period between the bank robbery and when Radick was shot. We should check with the cemetery authorities. If there were any incidents like that, we can get a court order to exhume the bodies involved."

"Man, I don't like the sound of that," Jesse said.

"Neither do I, and I'll admit it's a long shot, but that's exactly the kind of thing a reasonably smart crook like Radick might do." Alston swiveled back to his desk. "I'll get hold of the people at Greenwood and start asking questions."

Jesse pushed off from the desk. "And I'm going out in the parking lot for a smoke."

SHANNON FELT MORE ALIVE THAN SHE HAD IN MONTHS, MAYBE even years. She had an appointment to see Ann Kershaw again next week. She had no idea how fast or slow her recovery would be, or whether it would eventually be complete. But at least she was headed in the right direction.

Her first surgical case was delayed, giving her the opportunity to check messages and return calls. Before she could completely sort through the call slips, her secretary buzzed. "Dr. Jay Sanders is on the line for you."

Shannon lifted the receiver and punched the blinking button. "Jay, what can I do for you?"

"Actually, it's the other way around. Did Mark ask you about side effects from your antiretroviral therapy?"

"No," Shannon said. If Mark was supposed to explore that subject, it obviously had fled his mind when they began talking about her session with Ann Kershaw. "I saw him last night, but we were busy with something else. I'm not having any side effects as far as I can tell, if that's what you're after." She paused to think. "No nausea or GI symptoms, no unusual weakness. Are there other things I should watch for?"

"Not really. Most of the problems with side effects from antiretrovirals come with longer courses of treatment. You only have three more weeks—and I'll be checking on you frequently."

As she hung up, Shannon pulled her calendar toward her. She'd marked a red asterisk on the date she started treatment, with smaller ones noting the next twenty-eight days. At six weeks, there was a note, "Follow-up lab." She'd have her first HIV test then, with more tests at three and six months. If they were all negative, she could relax. Of course, it was possible that at that moment the virus was multiplying in her bloodstream. And she wouldn't know about it for more than a month.

She lowered her head until it rested on her desk. If this were happening to Mark, he'd undoubtedly draw on his faith for strength, turning the problem over to God. She wished she could do the same, but there remained a tiny bit of her that refused to accept that, even though she was a physician, she was powerless to affect the course of this particular disease. Shannon had heard this referred to by colleagues in the health-care professions as the Jehovah complex. It was often said in jest, but she was coming to realize that it was all too real—and she was infected with it, just as certainly as she might be with the retrovirus from Barry Radick's blood.

MEGAN HAD ONE FINAL LOOK AROUND THE APARTMENT. "IT'S perfect." She leaned over the table, scribbled her signature on the lease, and dropped the pen into her purse. "I'll start moving in tonight. I should be sleeping here by tomorrow night."

"I think we're going to get along well together."

"I think so, too," Megan said. "It's funny. Ten days ago, in the middle of the night, I essentially fled the place where I lived. I had no job, no place to go. I wound up living with my sister. Now I have a new job and a fantastic apartment with a great roommate. Who'd have thought things could turn around so fast?"

"Well, it helps that we're working together, so one thing sort of led to the other."

"I guess I'll see you tonight," Megan said. "I'll be here about seven with some of my stuff.

"Sounds great."

They hugged, and Megan left the apartment. She could hardly wait to tell Shannon. Her sister would be so surprised.

MARK DROPPED HIS GLOVES AND HIS SURGICAL MASK INTO THE trash container. "I'm going to shower and change, then head for my office. Call if there's another autopsy for me."

This was the first postmortem exam Mark had performed in a couple of years, maybe longer. But when a violent bout of food poisoning had incapacitated the pathologist scheduled for autopsy duty today, Mark volunteered to step in. After all, it was something he knew how to do. And the whole idea didn't particularly gross him out—if it did, he wouldn't have chosen pathology as his specialty in the first place. Nevertheless, he'd be glad when today was over and he could get back to his regular activities.

The clock in the locker room showed noon. He wondered if Shannon was free for lunch. He dialed her office. No answer. His next call was to her secretary, who told him Dr. Frasier would be in surgery for most of the day. Would he like to get a message to her? He would not—lunch wasn't an urgent matter. "No, thanks. I'll call her at home this evening."

He was almost dressed when the intercom called, "Dr. Gilbert? Are you still in there?"

"Yes," Mark answered, resisting the temptation he always had to raise his voice when replying to the metallic voice issuing from the wall right behind him. "What is it? Another autopsy already?"

"No, sir. Looks like we're going to be quiet for a while. But would you call your office? They said it's urgent."

Mark frowned at this news. He picked up the phone and punched in his office number.

"Ellie, it's me. What's going on?"

"You had a call from a . . ." Mark heard the sound of rustling paper. Ellie could never find the message slip she wanted, and this time was apparently no exception. "From Mrs. Sarah

Frasier. She and her husband are at the Simmons Cancer Center. He received his first chemotherapy today, and he had a problem. They're observing him right now, but she wondered—"

"Call her back and tell her I'm on my way."

Mark wondered if he should call the center where Robert Frasier was receiving treatment, but he decided against it. The staff there was good. Undoubtedly they'd handled hundreds of patients who had reactions during chemotherapy. Mark suspected that what the Frasiers needed most of all was someone to lean on. Since Shannon was in surgery, he was elected. *Glad they called. Makes me feel more like one of the family.*

In a few moments, Sarah Frasier hugged Mark and pointed to her husband, who was as pale as the white curtains that had been closed around his cubicle. "Thank you for coming. They were about to disconnect his IV, when—"

"I fainted. That's all," Pastor Frasier said. Despite his pallor, his voice was strong.

"It's not uncommon for patients to almost pass out when they're getting their first chemo treatment." The female voice behind him was unfamiliar to Mark. He turned to see a petite woman whose white lab coat bore the embroidered name "Liu Kim, MD." Her complexion was fair. Her black hair framed delicate features with high cheekbones and sparkling dark eyes.

Mark extended his hand. "Dr. Kim, I don't believe we've met. I'm Dr. Mark Gilbert. The Frasiers' daughter and I . . . I'm a close family friend."

Dr. Kim took the proffered hand. "Liu Kim." She pronounced the first name almost like Leo, with the emphasis on the last syllable. "Reverend Frasier seems to be fine right now. We just wanted to keep him around for a bit to make sure he's stable. I don't think it's anything to worry about, and it probably won't affect his next treatment."

"What is his treatment schedule?" Mark asked.

"He's getting the FCR regimen." Dr. Kim looked at Mark to see if he needed further explanation. When he remained silent, she said, "He'll get another dose by IV tomorrow and the final one the day after that. Then there's a twenty-eight-day rest period before we repeat the cycle." She looked down at her patient. "We'll watch you closely with the next two, but I think you'll do fine."

"I feel okay now. Think I can go home?"

"Pretty soon," Dr. Kim said. "Any questions?" The Frasiers shook their heads. "I'll check you again before you leave, and my nurse will confirm your appointments for Wednesday and Thursday."

She nodded at Mark. "Nice to meet you, Doctor. What department are you in?"

"Pathology," Mark said.

"So our paths may cross again. I'll watch for you." She pulled aside the curtains surrounding the cubicle.

As Mark made his way back to his office, he found himself thinking of Dr. Kim. He was certain that if he'd ever encountered her on campus, he'd have remembered it. Her beauty was stunning. There seemed no question of her professional competence. And he'd noticed that her left hand was bare. He couldn't believe she was unattached.

Like Dr. Kim, Shannon was beautiful, although she'd never admit it. Also like Dr. Kim, Shannon was an accomplished professional. So why had he even given Dr. Kim a second look, when for the past year the only woman in his life was Shannon? He decided to shove that question to the back of his mind.

Today Shannon's parents had called on him when she was unavailable, and that made him feel good. Although they apparently considered him one of the family, he couldn't help wondering if their daughter would ever come around to accepting his offer of a lifetime commitment.

STEVE ALSTON FROWNED. HE PUT ONE HAND OVER HIS EAR TO shut out the ringing phones and raised voices of the squad room, pushing the phone closer to his other ear. He wanted to be certain he was hearing correctly.

"And this is Greenwood Cemetery we're talking about?"

"Yes, sir." The voice on the other end of the phone was that of an elderly male, and it bore no hint of uncertainty. "Happened over the weekend, I guess. I found out late yesterday. When you called, I was reaching for the phone to line up some manpower to repair the damage."

"Would you please leave everything as it is for now?" Steve said. "This may give us a clue to a case we're working."

The man sounded a bit dubious when he said, "I guess I can wait a bit."

"Great. My partner and I will be there in half an hour."

Steve hung up the phone and called across the squad room to his partner, who was discussing baseball with a couple of detectives from narcotics. "Jesse, let's roll."

"Got a new case?"

"Nope." Steve shrugged into his shoulder harness and took his gun from his desk drawer. "But maybe a break in one we're working."

WHEN SHANNON PULLED INTO HER DRIVEWAY, SHE SAW MEGAN'S car at the curb, with her sister loading boxes into the trunk.

This was Tuesday. It had been eleven days since Megan called looking for a place to stay. No, change that. Since the call came after midnight, technically it was ten days. What had Megan said? In a week or so—ten days tops—she'd have a job and an apartment. Maybe her sister truly had straightened out her life.

Shannon pulled into the garage and entered the house where she found Megan lugging a suitcase toward the front door. "What's going on?" Shannon asked.

"Well, not only do I have a job now, but today I signed on to share an apartment with one of the people at work." She set down the luggage and brushed a stray lock of blond hair from her forehead. "I'm moving some of my stuff tonight, then I'm having dinner with Parker. Don't wait up."

*Dinner with Parker? Here we go again.* "Who is this Parker? You say it's someone you met at work? You've only been working there two days. How well could you get to know him in that time?" Shannon dropped onto the sofa, leaned back, and closed her eyes. "Megan, please don't repeat what's become a pattern for you, moving in with first one then another man who turns out to be a loser."

Megan stood in front of her sister with her hands on her hips. "I work with Parker, but we've known each other for over a year. Parker came to R&R Medical Supply at the same time I did, from the same pharmaceutical company where I used to work. We knew each other there and became good friends."

"So you've known him for a while. But do you want to move in with yet another man?" Shannon opened her eyes and looked up at her sister. "Believe me, I just want what's best for you."

Megan's eyes sparked. "You can't give up on being the all-knowing big sister, can you? For your information, Parker's full name is Parker Elizabeth Carrington. She's divorced from an abusive husband. She understands where I am—apparently better than you do, since she trusts me to make some decisions on my own." She turned on her heel, grabbed up her suitcase, and opened the front door. "Don't wait up for me."

The reverberation from the slamming door hadn't died before the phone rang. Shannon moved toward the phone, her gut twisting as she wondered what fresh crisis loomed on the horizon.

"Dr. Frasier, this is Steve Alston. I'm on my way to your house. I have some bad news."

# TWENTY

THE DOORBELL INTERRUPTED SHANNON AS SHE WAS RUNNING A brush through her hair. *He told me half an hour.* She grumbled her way to the front door and opened it, but instead of Steve Alston, she found Mark standing there.

"How do you always know when I need you here?" She kissed him lightly. "Come on in."

"I'm just glad to find you home and doing okay. Frankly, I was a bit worried about you."

"Why?" She followed him into the living room.

"I had some news to share, but I couldn't get hold of you. You weren't at the medical center. I tried to call your home phone, and it was busy. Then I called your cell, but you didn't answer. So I decided to swing by." He looked down at the hairbrush in her hand. "Were you getting ready to go out?"

She looked at the hairbrush as though realizing for the first time that she held it. "No, someone's coming by, and I was trying to repair the ravages of the day." She pointed to the sofa. "Have a seat. I'll only be a minute."

In a few moments, she was back and seated next to Mark on the couch. "You said you were expecting someone," he said. "What's going on?"

Shannon decided that whatever development Steve Alston wanted to discuss, it quite likely involved Mark as well. It was probably good that he was here, so she might as well let him know what was coming. "Detective Alston called to say he'd be by shortly. He said he had some bad news he needed to share."

"Shall I stay?"

"Yes, please." Shannon started to look at her watch but stopped herself. Alston would get here when he got here. She held up one finger. "Hold on. A minute ago you said I didn't answer my cell. Let me see why."

She hurried to where her purse lay on a chair by the front door. She pulled out her cell phone, flicked a switch, and stuffed the phone into her pocket. Back on the sofa, Shannon said, "For some reason, the ringer was on silent. I'm sorry for that." She tried to smile. "But it brought you here." She leaned toward him. "Now tell me your news. Why were you trying to reach me?"

"To let you know what happened to your dad today."

Shannon snatched a breath. "What's wrong? What happened?"

"Easy there," Mark said. "He got a little faint at the end of his chemotherapy session. You were in surgery, so your mother called me. He's fine now."

Shannon let out the breath she'd been holding. "Tell me about it." As Mark related the story of her father's reaction to his chemotherapy, Shannon's stomach twisted into knots. "I should have been there," she said.

"No, you shouldn't have. Your mother was with him. The doctors and nurses over there deal with this every day. I think what happened to him was what any of us might experience if we had to hold still for an hour or two, watching poison flow into our veins." He patted her shoulder. "He fainted—actually, a near-faint. Your folks just needed some reassurance. You were busy, I wasn't. And I'm glad they called me."

Shannon shook her head. "I know it wouldn't make any difference if I'd been there. It's just this feeling—"

"The same feeling you have about so much," Mark said. "You feel as though you have to make things right, all the time, for everybody. But you can't. All you can do is your best at whatever comes your way. You can't fix everything."

"I know . . . at least, I know it in my head. But my heart—"

"You have a tender heart," Mark said. "But some things you just have to turn over to God."

"I wish I could do that. I wish I had the depth of your faith."

"It will come," Mark said. "In the meantime, remember that you're not in control of everything in the world." He grinned. "That job is already filled . . . and God's doing it pretty well, I'd say."


STEVE ALSTON NOTED THE DARK BLUE CHEVROLET MALIBU PARKED at the curb in front of Shannon Frasier's house. What was Dr. Gilbert doing here? He always seemed to be around when Steve expected to be talking with Shannon alone.

Steve left his own vehicle behind the Chevy, walked up the steps, and rang the doorbell. In a moment, Shannon opened the door. She extended her hand. "Detective Alston. You didn't have to make a special trip for this."

"Actually, I thought it would be better if I shared this with you face-to-face." He grasped her hand, and was still holding it when Dr. Mark Gilbert moved into view behind Shannon.

Steve grudgingly turned loose of Shannon's hand and reached for Gilbert's. "Doctor, I didn't expect to see you here."

"Shannon asked me to stay, and since I seem to be involved in all this through my association with Shannon and Megan, I thought it was probably appropriate."

"Please sit down," Shannon said. "Would you like something to drink?"

Steve hesitated but decided this wasn't a social occasion. "No, thanks."

Shannon pointed him to a chair, then sat on the couch beside Gilbert. "Where's your partner?"

"On his way home, I'd imagine. We're both off duty, but I thought I'd swing by here and talk with you." He hoped he didn't come down too hard on the last word. If Shannon wanted Gilbert here, there wasn't much he could do about it.

"I appreciate you coming by," Shannon said. "What's the bad news you said you had?"

"There have been some new developments," Steve said. "We've found a link between Walt Crosley and Darcy Green, a small-time crook who used his last prison stint to become pretty expert with computers."

"Have you talked with Green about where Crosley might be?" Shannon asked.

"Unfortunately, no. He was on our list to be interviewed this week. When Green didn't come in for work yesterday morning, his boss was concerned and tried to call him. No answer. Then Green still didn't show up this morning, so his boss went to his apartment. When he didn't get an answer to his knocks, he convinced the landlord to let him in. They found Green dead, slumped over his computer."

"Heart attack?" Gilbert said.

"Not unless the heart attack made him fall forward onto his desk and break his neck. Medical examiner says Green had been dead since sometime this weekend. We think Crosley had Green work on the problem of the numbers. Afterward he decided to shut the man's mouth—permanently."

"So Crosley knows . . ." Shannon let the words trail off.

"We think either Crosley or Green figured out that the string of numbers represent GPS coordinates. Then when Green plugged them in, Crosley knew he'd been fed the wrong information. I'm thinking the last thing Green did was find the right numbers and give them to Crosley."

"Why do you say that?" Shannon asked.

"Because someone—and of course we think it was Crosley—someone trashed a good deal of Greenwood Cemetery this past weekend. They overturned markers, opened mausoleums, dug up a few areas. And all of this was in the area indicated by your numbers . . . the correct ones."

Gilbert frowned at this new information. "So what you're telling us is that either Crosley found what we failed to find or—"

"Or he came up empty, leaving him thinking there's more to the story. Since the people with Radick when he died were Dr. Frasier and the other doctor, Crosley will probably be coming after them next."

"And since Crosley doesn't know who the other doctor is, but he does know Shannon, she's the one in danger," Gilbert said.

At this, Shannon clenched her jaw and her face became pale, but she remained silent.

"I agree," Steve said. He looked directly at Shannon. "We'll warn the other doctor—Dr. Lee Kai, wasn't it?—but I'm pretty sure you're Crosley's next target."

"And you don't think I'll be able to get away from him this time?" Shannon said, but it wasn't really a question.

Steve shook his head. "Crosley killed Green after he'd gotten all the information he needed from him. Green cooperated, but all it got him was a quick death." He leaned forward in his chair. "I don't like to think about what Crosley might do to get information from you."

Gilbert turned to Shannon. "I told you I'd feel better if you had a gun. Now will you listen to me?"

Steve decided to join in. "I think you might want to listen to Dr. Gilbert. I can help you get a gun, arrange for a permit, take you through the instruction you need."

Shannon stood and turned first right then left, addressing both men. "I know you mean well. But, Detective, you have no idea the effect guns have had on my life. And, Mark, even though you know some of the details, I don't think you recognize the absolute terror I have of those weapons."

"But—" Mark began.

Shannon's expression hardened. "No 'but' about it. You're both asking me to do something I find impossible."

"Then what are you going to do?" Steve asked.

"I'm going to do my job. That job is saving lives, not taking them," Shannon said. She rose. "As I see it, your job is to catch Walt Crosley before he can harm me or anyone else." She took a step toward the door. "I appreciate you coming by to give me this news in person. Now don't let me keep you from doing your job."


MEGAN SHOOK THE DRESS A FEW TIMES BEFORE SHE PLACED IT ON a hanger and hung it in the closet.

"Do you think that does any good? I mean, to get the wrinkles out?" Parker asked from her seat on the edge of the bed.

"I don't really know," Megan replied, "but I've seen my mom do it a hundred times. And that's how little girls learn . . . from watching their mothers." Megan looked around at the bedroom, still getting used to the idea that this would be her new home. Soon she'd add a few personal touches, but right now she wanted to get her stuff moved.

"What did your sister think about your moving out?"

Megan paused with the last hanger halfway to the closet bar. "I thought she'd be happy. I really expected her to congratulate me on finding a job and getting a place to live so quickly." She jammed the hanger into place. "Instead, she immediately jumped to the conclusion that I was moving in with another man—I believe another 'loser' is how she put it."

"Well, we've both been down that road and learned our lesson," Parker said. "But don't be too hard on your sister. Big sisters—and, for that matter, big brothers, parents—they're all alike. They never stop caring about us. And that's sort of a good thing, when you think about it."

Megan closed her suitcase and moved it off the bed to a spot beside the door where she'd be certain not to forget it. One more trip tomorrow evening, and she'd have all her things out of Shannon's house. Then she'd be free of her interfering sister.

"Want to get something to eat, or do you have to get back to Shannon's place?" Parker asked.

Megan had visions of coming in late, of Shannon sitting in the living room waiting for her to walk through the door. It would serve her sister right for being so nosy. Then again, Shannon had been the first one Megan called when she fled from Tony. And there was no hesitation, no "What's going on?" or conditions—just an unequivocal invitation to come over, either right then, in the middle of the night, or the next day. Even when Megan had pulled a gun on her sister, there'd been no recriminations. Maybe she should . . . "I think I'd better get back to Shannon's. I guess you're right. I'm probably being too hard on her." She picked up her empty suitcases. "I'll see you tomorrow night."


ALSTON WAS HALFWAY HOME WHEN HIS CELL PHONE RANG. "Steve, this is Jesse."

"What's up? Where are you?"

"I'm back at the squad room. I want to talk over some things with you. Can you come back?"

His encounter with Shannon—and, for that matter, Mark Gilbert—had left Steve anxious to get home. Shannon's words had stung more than he was willing to admit. He wanted to put the day behind him, kick off his shoes, nuke a TV dinner, and watch a mindless sitcom on the tube.

Jesse obviously knew his partner well. "Come on, man. I know there's nobody waiting on you. I need to run this by you while it's fresh in my mind."

"Okay. I'll see you in twenty minutes."

Eighteen minutes later, the two detectives sat on either side of Callaway's desk. "I don't know about you, but I'm afraid I've gotten so caught up in looking for Walt Crosley that I've ignored Megan Frasier. I think it's time we go to a judge and ask for a warrant to arrest her," Jesse said.

Steve took a deep breath and tried to sort out the conflicting emotions he felt. "Specifically, what charges do you think we could make stick?"

"Start with her boyfriend's murder. She lived with Tony Lester. They had a fight, and she was angry. Her gun was used to kill him. Her alibi for the time of his death is shaky. Motive, means, opportunity."

"Circumstantial at best," Steve said. "What else you got?"

"The bank robbery. She admits she knew Radick in rehab. We know that Crosley came to see Radick at First Step while Megan was there—who's to say they weren't planning the robbery then, and that she wasn't the third member of the gang, the one driving the getaway car?"

"So why did Radick show up at Megan's sister's house?"

"Maybe he was looking for Megan, wanting to talk about the loot, but he was shot before he could get to the door."

"If that's so, why hasn't Crosley come after Megan?"

Jesse shook his head. "Because Dr. Frasier was the one who heard Radick's dying words. But maybe Megan's next. Anyway, I think she's knee-deep in all this. Do you agree that we ought to try for a warrant?"

Steve stood and walked to the window, his back to his partner. "I don't know."

"Listen," Jesse said. "I'll only say this once more. Are you sure you're not letting your personal feelings affect your decision?"

Steve stared out the window into the night. "Let me sleep on it." But he knew he wasn't going to get any sleep tonight.

MEGAN CHECKED HER WATCH. SHE'D LINGERED LONGER THAN SHE intended at her new apartment, talking with Parker, making plans. Still, because it was summer, it wasn't fully dark when she approached the street where Shannon lived.

Usually, Megan drove with the unconscious confidence of one who'd lived all her adult life in a particular area. Once she knew her destination, she set her internal GPS with the address and let her thoughts range far and wide. But recently she'd driven with more attention to her surroundings. Specifically, she tried to remain aware of the people and cars around her.

If Crosley could pull up next to her sister, hop into her car, and threaten her at gunpoint, Megan didn't want to give him a chance to do that and worse to her.

A glance into her rearview mirror made her frown. The late-model maroon sedan behind her had been there for quite a while. She couldn't make out the driver's features through the windshield, but she was able to tell that the vehicle had a single occupant. Should she drive on by, somehow try to lose him?

Her answer came to her as she drew within sight of Shannon's house. Mark's blue Chevrolet was parked at the curb. Megan took her cell phone from the seat beside her and punched a speed-dial number. "Mark," she said when he answered, "would you do me a favor? Come out to the curb. I think someone's following me, but I don't think they'll do anything if you're standing there waiting for me."

Before Megan could put down the phone, Shannon's front door opened and Mark emerged from the house. He walked quickly to his car, opened the door and reached inside, then waited at the end of the sidewalk as Megan pulled in. She parked her white Ford Focus behind his car and watched as the maroon sedan drove past with the driver looking straight ahead.

Megan climbed out from behind the wheel. "Thanks, Mark."

"No problem. I just wish I could convince Shannon to be this careful." He turned toward her. "I have to make her believe that this is serious."

At that moment, Megan realized that Mark's hand hung down by his right side so that his leg shielded what he held—a blued steel revolver. The hammer was back and his finger was inside the trigger guard, ready to shoot.

# TWENTY-ONE

SHANNON AND MARK WERE SITTING ON THE SOFA TALKING WHEN his cell phone rang. He answered it, listened for a second, and headed for the front door, shoving his phone back into his pocket as he went. "Back in a second," he called over his shoulder.

Shannon sat for a moment until the slam of a car door and the murmur of voices outside made her curious. She rose and walked to the open front door where she saw Megan's car at the curb. Her sister and Mark came up the front walk together, each of them carrying a suitcase. Shannon didn't know what was going on, but, for whatever reason, Megan was back home, wearing a smile on her face that was in sharp contrast to her expression as she walked out a few hours ago.

Megan dropped her suitcase and hurried toward Shannon, who ran forward to embrace her sister. "I'm sorry," they said almost simultaneously.

Mark stood by patiently until the two women separated. Then he picked up the suitcase Megan dropped and said, "Let's take this inside, shall we? I feel too much like a target out here."

Once inside the house with the door closed and locked, Megan put both hands on Shannon's shoulders. "I'm so sorry for the way I stalked out of here. I shouldn't have gone off like that. I should have explained."

Shannon shook her head. "No, I'm sorry. When you told me about your new apartment, I should have been proud, like you were. Instead, I immediately jumped to the wrong conclusion."

"I can't really blame you," Megan said. "I've made lots of bad decisions in my life, some of them involving what you called 'losers,' so it was probably a natural assumption."

Mark put the suitcases in the corner, dropped into an over-stuffed chair in the living room, and gave Shannon a puzzled look. "Will somebody please tell me what's going on? I feel like I've come into a movie that's already started."

Shannon realized that a lot had happened in the past few hours, and not everyone knew about it. Mark needed to know about Megan's leaving. Megan had to be told about their dad's episode during chemotherapy. This was going to take awhile. "I guess you're right. I need to bring everyone up to date." Shannon looked around. "Would anyone like some coffee?"

There were no takers, so Shannon sat down on the sofa, took a moment to organize her thoughts, and began. She started by telling Megan about their father's reaction to his chemotherapy session.

"Is he okay?" Megan asked, genuine concern in her voice.

Mark answered, "When I left them, your dad was fine."

"We'll call him later this evening," Shannon said to Megan. Then she turned to Mark. "Earlier Megan told me she was moving into an apartment, and I made the worst possible assumption about her new roommate. I was wrong, but it didn't keep her from storming out of here."

"But we're okay now," Megan said. "Right?"

"Right," Shannon said.

Mark reached into his pocket for his car keys. "Why don't I take you both out for dinner? We can discuss this in more detail then."

Shannon and Megan exchanged looks, and a message passed between them in a way possible only with siblings. "Sounds fine," Shannon said.

"Uh, Mark, you may want to tell Shannon what's in the glove compartment of your car first," Megan said.

Shannon had risen from the sofa, but now she sat down again, looked at Mark, and frowned. "That sounds like something I should know before we leave."

Mark gave Megan a look that could melt ice. "The reason I dashed out of here so quickly was that Megan called, wanting me to meet her at the curb. Apparently she's taking our warnings seriously and thought someone might be following her."

"So . . . ," Shannon said.

"So I reached into the glove compartment of my car and took out one of the guns I'd bought."

Shannon caught her breath and leaned back on the sofa. She thought she'd made it clear to Mark how she felt about guns. Yet here he was, running roughshod over her fear in his haste to protect her—as though she were incapable of doing it for herself. Apparently Mark didn't know her as well as she'd thought. And that hurt.

MARK COULD READ THE EMOTIONS ON SHANNON'S FACE, AND HE knew he'd made a misstep. He wasn't sure how to correct it, but he had to try.

He was in an overstuffed chair, while Shannon was on the

sofa. Mark thought about moving to sit beside her but decided against it. Right now it was probably best to keep his distance. "Shannon, it goes back to what both the detective and I told you earlier. Crosley is coming after you. That's virtually a certainty. And this time you may not be able to get away from him. You have to be prepared to defend yourself."

"So you want me to have a gun? That's your answer?" Shannon's voice hardened. "I thought a good Christian like you would be content to let God take care of me."

Mark could see from the look on her face that as soon as the words were out of her mouth, she regretted them. But she made no move to take them back. He searched his brain for arguments to rebut what she'd said, but he decided that wasn't a fight he was going to win, one he shouldn't even pursue. Not now, at least.

"I could have told you that Shannon hates guns," Megan said. "She's always been afraid of them, ever since we were kids. At first, I thought she'd get over it. But since she's seen two people's lives snuffed out by them, I can understand why she doesn't want to be around them." Megan moved to the sofa beside her sister and put her arm around her. "I should have realized that before I brought a gun into this house myself."

"I'm sorry, Shannon," Mark said. "I know what you said, and I just went right ahead anyway. I should have realized this was really a line in the sand for you."

"Thank you," Shannon said, although her tone wasn't totally forgiving.

Mark decided he should tell Shannon the whole story. "I have two guns in my glove compartment—one for each of us. I purchased them after your encounter with Crosley, when he held you at gunpoint. I know it scared you, but it scared me, too."

"Is it legal for you to keep the gun in your car before you get your concealed carry permit?" Megan asked.

"Texas law allows me to have a weapon at home or in my car—no permit necessary. I've already started the process of getting a concealed handgun license for myself." Mark looked at Shannon. "I was ready to help you do the same."

Shannon had sat with her eyes downcast while Mark talked. Now she looked up at him. Her shoulders rose and fell as she took several deep breaths. "Maybe you can't fully understand why I feel this way, but whether you understand it or not, I would ask you to respect my feelings." She paused as though measuring her words. "Mark, I know you love me, and it's in your nature to want to protect me. But no guns . . . please."

DURING THE DISCUSSION, SHANNON HAD FELT THE KNOT IN HER stomach progressively tighten. At one point, she thought she might have to rush from the room and throw up. Now that things had calmed down, she felt a bit better.

"What's the verdict on dinner?" Mark said.

Shannon looked at Megan, who shrugged. Apparently she, too, had lost her appetite. "I appreciate the offer, but I think we're going to call Mom and Dad, then forage in the kitchen for a light supper."

"I understand," Mark said. "I'm sorry I didn't ask you first about the gun. I was trying—"

"You want to protect me," Shannon said. "And I appreciate it. It's one of the things I love about you." She shivered slightly. "But you have to know how I feel about guns."

"I do, and I'll try to be more understanding." Mark stood and held Shannon for a moment. He kissed her and said, "Call me if you need anything."

As the door closed behind Mark, Shannon realized how much his presence meant to her. Now, with him gone, she felt . . .

vulnerable, exposed. She might have refused his offer of a gun, but simply having him here made her feel more secure. Would that be what marriage was like? She shrugged away the thought. Another time, maybe. Not now.

"Are you okay?" Megan asked.

"I'm fine," Shannon said. "Want me to fix something for us to eat?"

"I'm not hungry," Megan said.

"Then I think we need to talk with Mom and Dad."

Megan agreed. Shannon dialed the number and put the call on speaker. As expected, her dad made light of his "spell," as he called it, and immediately dismissed Shannon's offer to be with them at the next chemotherapy session.

The girls' mother apologized for getting upset over nothing. "I shouldn't have called," she said.

"Mom, I want you to be able to call me anytime. And if I'm tied up in surgery, call Mark again. He's already told me he was happy to be there for you today." Shannon tried to hold back her next words, but they came anyway. "It makes him feel more like one of the family."

When she ended the call, Shannon turned to Megan and raised her eyebrows. "What do you think?"

"They sound okay, I guess," Megan said. "But then I can't ever recall a time when Dad gave the slightest hint that anything was wrong." She frowned. "I don't know if he didn't want us to worry, or if he's always trusted God so completely he truly wasn't worried himself."

Shannon thought back and realized that Megan was right. And the same could be said of their mother. She'd always been in lockstep with her husband, united in anything they undertook, standing firm in the face of every crisis, as far back as Shannon could remember. What had it cost her parents to never show worry or anxiety in front of their daughters? Then again, maybe Megan was right. Maybe their faith was just that strong.

THE OCCUPANT OF THE MAROON SEDAN STRETCHED AND YAWNED.

No porch lights shone nearby, a streetlight was out of commission thanks to a well-placed rock, and traffic on this residential street was virtually nonexistent at 10:00 p.m. His car blended into the darkness, and the tinted windows hid him from curious eyes. He pushed a button on his watch and took note of the numbers. He'd give it another hour, just in case she decided to go out.

The odds that she'd leave the house, allowing him to intercept her, were slim, but it was a chance worth taking. Besides that, he had to think, and the quiet of this stakeout provided a perfect environment for that tonight.

He wished he could light up a cigarette. Then again, the flare of a match, the glowing embers in the darkness, would be a tip-off to his presence. No, he'd learned to deal with hardships worse than this. He squirmed around, seeking a more comfortable position, while his thoughts continued to focus on the problem before him.

Time passed slowly. Finally, he glanced at his watch and decided to give up his vigil. No luck tonight. Tomorrow would have to be soon enough. But the waiting hadn't been wasted time. He'd decided on a plan. And however it played out, he'd eventually get what he wanted.

SHANNON AWOKE TO NOISE FROM HER KITCHEN. SHE SAT UP IN bed, and the wonderful aroma of freshly brewed coffee brought a smile to her face. Had she added water and coffee to the coffeemaker last evening and turned on auto-brew? No, she was sure she hadn't. Despite good intentions, she neglected to use that feature at least half the time.

Shannon had burrowed under the covers once more when the answer came through the door.

Megan handed her a steaming mug. "Rise and shine, sleepyhead."

Shannon sat up and sipped the coffee. It was already sweetened, just the way she liked it. "What's the occasion?"

"This is your last day with a houseguest," Megan said. She perched on the side of the bed and drank from her own mug. "I wanted to thank you for taking me in. I know it must have been tough, getting that call at midnight from your ne'er-do-well sister, wondering what kind of trouble she'd gotten herself into this time."

Actually, that phone call and the murder on Shannon's lawn that preceded it had simply been the first events of a continuing firestorm that threatened to take over her life. She drank more coffee, then lowered her cup. "I'm glad you called. And I'm happy you seem to be getting things straightened out in your life."

"I'll try not to bug you too much," Megan said.

Shannon lowered her cup. "I wish you'd call more often—especially if you need some sisterly advice. Like don't take men at face value. Don't chase after the first man to make a move on you. Don't—"

"I get it. I'll just replay the tapes of Mom in my head, and if I have a question, I'll call you." Megan stood and took a step toward the door. She paused with her cup halfway to her mouth. "The main thing I'm worried about now is that the police seem to think I know more than I'm telling about my ex-boyfriend's murder. Since it was my gun that killed him, I can see that."

"Let our attorney worry about that," Shannon said.

"True. Maybe Ms. Waites convinced them all they had was circumstantial evidence."

"Neither of us is out of the woods yet," Shannon said. "But all we can do is keep moving ahead and leave the rest to our attorney, the police . . . and God."

ELENA WAITES CALLED UP THE STAIRS, "KIDS, BREAKFAST IS ON the table."

Her husband, Tom, had left much earlier. She looked at the kitchen clock and decided that right now he'd be scrubbing in for his first case of the day. Despite his protests, she insisted on getting up early and making sure he had a good breakfast before he left for the operating room. "It gives me some quiet time before I have to get the kids off to school," she'd told him.

She looked at the Bible, open on the kitchen table, and reflected on what she'd read that morning in her devotional. "The Spirit of the Lord God is upon me, because the Lord has anointed me to bring good news to the afflicted; He has sent me to bind up the brokenhearted, to proclaim liberty to captives and freedom to prisoners."

*That should be my life verse. That's what I do.* Elena's thoughts turned to the Frasiers. She'd argued with the two detectives that the evidence against her clients in the shooting of Tony Lester was purely circumstantial. The men apparently were willing to buy her argument, but that didn't mean the case was closed and the two women were clear. No, Elena's sources in the department told her that the investigation had hit a dead end, and in her experience, that often meant the detectives in charge of the case would circle back and take a hard look at people to whom they had given a pass earlier.

Elena reached down to the notepad that sat next to the Bible and jotted down a reminder to look into the Frasier file again. Something told her that she wasn't through with Shannon and Megan.

MARK GILBERT WAS ALREADY AT WORK, DRESSED IN SCRUBS AND WAITING for the first frozen section exam of the day. Along with other pathologists, he took his turn in the lab located near the surgical suites, reading slides prepared from tissue sent by surgeons who needed an immediate answer about the material. Most often, the question was, "Is this a malignancy?" Sometimes it was, "Are the surgical margins clear? Did I get all of it?"

Evaluation of frozen sections was one of the most difficult and critical jobs for a pathologist, and Mark was well aware of the responsibility it carried. A technician would freeze the specimen and prepare a stained microscope slide from a thinly sliced section of tissue. It was up to the pathologist to study the material and make a judgment. On occasions when the diagnosis was inconclusive, it was necessary to wait a day or even two for the more definitive permanent sections, but this might necessitate returning the patient to the operating room.

"Here's one for you," the technician said. "From Dr. Waites in OR three. Thyroid nodule. Malignant or benign?"

Mark took a moment to read the information accompanying the specimen. He breathed a silent prayer, centered the glass slide on the stage of his binocular microscope, and began scanning it. His prayer wasn't just for wisdom for himself, although he constantly asked God for that. No, he included the patient and their family, the surgical team, and everyone concerned. His answer would dictate how things might change for each of them.

As he reviewed the material, thousands of synapses in his brain fired and made connections. Mark compared the architecture of the material on the slide with hundreds of previous specimens he'd seen from thyroid masses. He recalled what he'd read about thyroid nodules, both malignant and benign. He factored in the clinical information provided. And all the while, his eyes moved across the slide.

MEGAN WHISTLED UNDER HER BREATH AS SHE SET THE TABLE. SHE consulted her watch and decided there was plenty of time before she and Shannon had to leave the house. She planned to enjoy this meal with her sister, put in a day's work, then come back here and load up her car with the remaining clothes and other items she wanted to move to her new apartment. Tomorrow would be the start of what she hoped was a new life.

"Do I smell bacon?" Shannon called from the doorway.

"Bacon, English muffins, orange juice—what you always asked for when Mom cooked breakfast for us." Megan poured juice into two glasses and retrieved two English muffins from the toaster. "Have a seat."

When the two sisters were settled at the kitchen table, Shannon said, "Shall we say grace?"

"Why don't you?" Megan replied. "I'm a little out of practice."

Before Shannon could say anything, the doorbell rang, followed almost immediately by a pounding on the door. She shoved her chair back. "I'm not sure who that could be, but it's pretty obvious they're not going away." She rose and moved toward the front door. "I'll get rid of them."

Megan sipped orange juice, hearing a murmur of voices from the front of the house but unable to make out the words. In a few moments, Shannon appeared in the doorway of the kitchen, a puzzled expression on her face. "Megan, the detectives want to have a word with you."

Detective Jesse Callaway stepped from behind Shannon and made his way into the room. Detective Steve Alston eased into the room behind his partner, his expression carefully neutral.

Callaway stopped in front of the chair where Megan sat and looked down at her. "Megan Frasier, you're under arrest for the murder of Tony Lester."

# TWENTY-TWO

FOR A MOMENT, SHANNON STOOD TRANSFIXED, UNABLE TO MOVE. She couldn't believe the scene unfolding before her. Callaway had always been a bit frightening, as much by his dominating physical presence as his demeanor. Today it was more pronounced, and she found herself pulling away as he went by.

Steve Alston leaned against the wall just inside the kitchen, keeping some distance between him and his partner, as though by doing so he could show that he had nothing to do with what was going on. His impassive gaze was fixed on the far corner of the kitchen.

Callaway took Megan's arm and pulled her to her feet. He intoned the standard Miranda warning in a flat monotone. "Do you understand these rights as I've explained them?" Before he finished speaking, he'd turned her and with practiced ease cuffed her hands behind her.

Megan looked at Shannon, who said, "I'll call Elena Waites. Don't say a word. No matter what they tell you, no matter what *anyone* may say . . ." Shannon looked purposefully at Steve Alston. "No matter what, don't say a word."

"Call my boss and make an excuse," Megan said. "Parker will know the number."

"Do you understand these rights?" Callaway said again. Receiving no reply, he shrugged and looked at his partner. "You witnessed me giving her the warning. That's good enough." He gave Megan a slight shove. "Let's go."

Shannon had her cell phone out before the detectives cleared the front door. She punched in a number she'd had the presence of mind to put on speed dial, and while it rang she thought back to what she'd just seen. If she lived another hundred years, Shannon knew she'd never forget the look Megan gave her as Callaway herded her toward the door. It said, better than any words could convey, "Help me."

ELENA FROWNED WHEN SHE HEARD THE RINGING OF HER CELL phone. A call this early was either a client in significant trouble or a wrong number. *Please don't let it be an emergency.*

"You girls finish your breakfast. We need to leave in ten minutes." She hurried to the table in the front hall where her purse lay, snatched the phone from it, and answered, "Elena Waites."

"Elena, thank goodness I caught you. This is Shannon Frasier. The police just arrested Megan. Can you—"

"Hold on," Elena said. "Take a deep breath. A minute or two won't make any difference. Tell me exactly what happened." She reached for the ever-present yellow legal pad, pulling a pen with it from the drawer of the table holding her purse.

She scribbled notes as Shannon talked, occasionally interrupting with a question. When it was clear that Shannon had finished, Elena said, "And you told her not to say a word? You're sure?"

"Positive," Shannon said. "So what happens next?"

"Just go about your business and let me get started on this. It may take awhile, though. Can I reach you on your cell?"

"Yes. I'm in clinic seeing patients all day, but I'll keep the phone with me. When—"

"The answer to every question you may want to ask is the same—I don't know. But trust me, I'll take care of things."

"So what can I do?" Shannon asked.

"Let me handle this. I'll call you as soon as I know something. And don't worry." *Like that's going to happen.*


MARK WAS TAKING A BREAK IN THE SURGEONS' LOUNGE WHILE waiting for the next scheduled frozen section. He was sipping a cup of what was probably the world's worst coffee and letting his mind wander when the intercom startled him into wakefulness. "Dr. Gilbert, please call your office for a message."

Mark picked up the phone and called his secretary.

"Dr. Frasier asked that you call her cell phone. She said it's urgent."

"Thanks." Mark broke the connection and dialed.

Shannon answered on the first ring. "Mark, I don't know what to do."

This wasn't the cool and competent surgeon Mark expected to hear. "Tell me about it. Whatever it is, together we can handle it."

Mark sat with the receiver pressed against his ear, frowning as Shannon related the details of Megan's arrest. "And you've called your attorney already?"

"That was the first call I made," Shannon said. "She said

she'd take care of things and get back to me, but I feel like I need to be doing something. What can I do?"

*Megan again. How many times . . . Never mind.* Mark took a deep breath. "Let me ask you this. When a patient of yours goes into surgery, how do you think the family feels?"

There was a momentary pause. "I think they feel helpless. For the next hour or two, their loved one's life might be in danger, but there's nothing they can do about it."

"So what can they do?"

"They have to trust the surgeon. And sometimes . . . sometimes they pray."

"Right now there's nothing you can do. You've called in the specialist. You're in the waiting room. So trust your attorney. And pray."


MEGAN HAD NEVER BEEN THROUGH ANYTHING LIKE THIS. WHEN she and Shannon were at the police station previously, she'd had her attorney on one side, her sister on the other. Their presence had been comforting, their guidance important. But right now she sat on her bunk in a holding cell, shaken by the experience of being photographed and fingerprinted. She still wore her regular clothes. She wondered when those would be replaced by prison coveralls . . . or whatever prisoners wore here.

From force of habit, Megan looked at her bare wrist. Her watch was gone, together with her belt. She was glad she was wearing flats instead of sneakers so there were no laces to give up, and that her jeans fit well enough they weren't falling off her hips in the absence of a belt.

She'd received what passed for lunch—a bologna sandwich on dry bread, tasteless pasta salad, green gelatin with a few chunks of fruit, and Kool-Aid. Megan was able to choke down a bit of food and wondered what it would be like to have this meal on a regular basis.

Megan guessed it was now early afternoon, although it seemed she'd sat here alone for an eternity. Surely Shannon would have contacted Elena Waites. Where was her attorney? For that matter, where were the detectives who'd arrested her? How long would she have to sit here before something happened? Anything!

She felt as though she'd wandered into a strange country where she didn't speak the language, couldn't read the road signs, and had no idea what was around the next bend. She was truly lost.

The rattling of the cell door made her look up.

"Megan Frasier?" a policewoman said.

It wasn't really a question, but Megan nodded.

"Let's go. Back up to the cell door, hands behind you. I have to cuff you."

Megan complied meekly. "Where am I going?"

"Interrogation room. The detectives want to question you, but first your attorney needs a few words."

The room was familiar. Either it was the same one where she'd met with Shannon, Elena, and the detectives, or all these rooms looked alike.

The officer unlocked the cuff from one of Megan's wrists and relocked it into a ring on the side of her chair, which was in turn bolted to the floor.

"Here's your attorney." The policewoman opened the door, Elena Waites walked into the room, and the officer started out.

She stopped when Elena said in a voice full of authority, "Hold on! Uncuff her!"

The policewoman's expression didn't change. "Can't. Standard procedure."

"This woman isn't dangerous," Elena said. "Talk with one of the detectives who brought her in. Until she's out of those handcuffs, I can guarantee she's not going to say a word."

The policewoman turned on her heel and walked out the door. In a couple of minutes, she returned, unlocked Megan's cuffs, shoved them into a pouch on her belt, and exited without speaking.

Elena took a seat across the table from Megan and removed a pad and pen from her briefcase. "Initially I was hired as your sister's attorney and agreed to take you on without additional charge. To clarify, and establish attorney-client privilege, do you promise to pay me a dollar when you get your purse back?"

"What? Of course."

"Then you're officially my client. If your interests and Shannon's diverge, I'll have to step away, but we'll worry about that if and when it happens. For now, everything you tell me is protected, and I can't be forced to reveal it unless it involves a crime you're planning to commit. Understand?"

Megan nodded.

"One thing is paramount—never lie to me. If you don't tell me the truth, I can't help you. Are you clear on that?"

"Yes. Yes, I'll tell the truth."

Elena leaned in and whispered, "I presume you saw the two-way mirror on the wall. Shield your mouth behind your hand to guard against lip reading. Got it?"

Megan nodded.

"Did you kill Tony Lester?"

Megan recoiled at the direct question. "No," she almost

shouted. Then her voice dropped to a low whisper. "Why would you—"

"These are questions the detectives are going to ask. Get used to them," Elena said. "We know the gun that killed Lester was at one time in your possession, but according to Shannon it disappeared from her house. Anything to add to that?"

Megan hesitated for a moment before saying, "No."

"Was Tony dealing drugs?"

Megan pursed her lips. She didn't want to get into that. But the stakes were too high for her to keep silent. "I tried to turn a blind eye to it, but I'm pretty sure he was. And I think he was using as well."

"What was involved?"

"He dealt it all—uppers, downers, narcotics, you name it. What he mainly used himself was coke."

"Did you do any drugs while you lived with him?"

Megan looked down at the tabletop, then raised her eyes to meet Elena's. "Right after I first moved in, he had some folks over for a party. He tried to get me to do a few lines with him, but I wanted to stay clean. I kept turning down his offers, and eventually he stopped asking."

"Have you used alcohol or drugs since you left rehab?"

"No!" Megan said. "It hasn't been easy, but I'm determined to stay clean and sober."

In a few moments the door opened, and Detectives Callaway and Alston walked in. Callaway took the chair next to Elena, directly across from Megan. Alston, as usual, leaned against the doorframe.

Callaway set a tape recorder in the center of the table, checked the sound level, said a few words to make it all official, then looked Megan in the eye. "Well, Ms. Frasier, are you ready to confess?"

STEVE ALSTON PASTED A DISINTERESTED LOOK ON HIS FACE AS the questioning continued. Jesse had been right, of course— Steve had let personal feelings interfere with his professional judgment. He hated to go through with this arrest, but he really had little choice in the matter.

The questioning had gone on for well over an hour when Jesse stabbed the Off button on the recorder. He rose, stretched, then walked to the doorway to stand beside Steve, his back to Megan and the attorney.

"Do you want to take a turn?" he whispered. "All I'm getting is a rehash of what she said the last time we had her in here."

"If by a rehash you mean the attorney is making you wonder why you were so anxious to arrest her client, I can see that." Steve smothered a smile. He shoved away from the doorframe and said over his shoulder, "But I'll give it a try."

Steve took the chair that was still warm from Jesse's presence. He didn't reach for the recorder. Instead, he leaned across the table and said to Megan, "Do you need a break? Would you like something to drink?"

Megan turned to her attorney with a questioning look.

Ms. Waites spoke directly to Steve. "It's refreshing to see the 'good cop' take over, but nothing's going to change. I'm waiting for you to realize you don't have any more evidence against my client than you had the last time we wasted an hour here." She dropped her pen onto her legal pad. "We've told you what I'm sure you already know—that her ex-boyfriend's death was probably drug-related. We've explained why her fingerprints were on the gun that killed Lester, and told you repeatedly that we have no idea how the gun got there. We've answered every question you've asked. So when will you admit that this arrest was pointless?"

"Sorry, Counselor. Just doing our job," Steve said.

Waites snorted. "At this point, if you release her, my client may decide not to pursue legal action against you two, the Dallas Police Department, the City of Dallas, and the judge who signed that warrant . . . which I still need to see, by the way."

"I'll take that as a no for the break," Steve said. He turned on the recorder. "Back on the record. This is Detective Steve Alston, continuing the interrogation of Ms. Megan Frasier, in the presence of her attorney, Mrs. Elena Waites." He cleared his throat. "Megan, let's take a different tack. When Walt Crosley came to visit you and Barry Radick in First Step, what did you talk about?"

"I . . . He didn't . . . I mean—"

"What does that have to do with the charges against my client?" Waites said.

"Counselor, although the arrest warrant is for the murder of her boyfriend, Ms. Frasier has previously admitted to us that she saw Walt Crosley, a known criminal, during her most recent rehab stint. We know he signed in as a visitor for Barry Radick, but we have reason to believe he made a connection with Ms. Frasier at that time. I'm simply trying to establish the facts of the matter."

Megan whispered in Waites's ear. She received an affirming nod, so she turned to Steve. "I saw Walt Crosley once, maybe twice, at First Step, but I never actually met him. I was acquainted with Barry Radick, but not Crosley."

Steve was unfazed. "So tell me—did your friend Radick tell you about the bank robbery he was planning with Crosley? Did he ask if you'd be willing to drive the car for them?" He leaned forward but kept his voice soft and calm. "Was there some disagreement about the way the loot was to be divided? Is that why Radick was killed?" He paused a beat. "Were you the one who shot him?"

Waites rose partially from her chair. "That will be enough.

My client has already stated she hardly knew Barry Radick. She had nothing to do with the bank robbery he was thought to have participated in, or with his death. And unless you have evidence that will allow you to broaden the scope of your questioning, I believe you're out-of-bounds here." She turned to Megan. "Don't say another word."

The attorney settled back into her chair and fixed Steve with a stern look. "This arrest was based on purely circumstantial evidence that we've already addressed. This new area you're pursuing is just a fishing expedition. I'm going to apply for a writ of habeas corpus immediately. In the meantime, I suggest you do some digging and find that arrest warrant you so conveniently misplaced when I asked to see it."

Steve patted the air in a calming gesture. "No need to rush off to find a judge this late in the day. We plan to arraign Ms. Frasier in the morning, and the court can decide if we continue to hold her." He stood and said, "I'll let you know when and where the hearing will be held. And I promise we'll have a copy of the warrant for you by then."

Mrs. Waites held up her hand. "Hang on. I need another few minutes with my client."

"Okay by me," Steve said. He pushed back his chair. "Just bang on the door when you're finished, and they'll take her back to her cell."

MEGAN'S HEART WAS POUNDING. HER MOUTH WAS DRY. SHE turned to her attorney. "Do I have to—"

Elena leaned in and spoke softly to Megan. "Whisper in my ear. Remember the two-way mirror."

Megan nodded. She whispered to Elena, "Do I have to stay in jail overnight?"

"Not if I have anything to do with it. The moment I walk out of here, I'm going to go to work on this. To begin with, I want to see that warrant. Meanwhile, don't worry, I'll take care of this."

Megan jerked around like a startled fawn as the door opened. Was she being taken back to her cell already? Could she tolerate a night in jail?

Steve Alston paused by Megan's chair. "Come with me."

"What . . . what's going to happen? Are you going to lock me up yourself?"

Alston smiled. "No. We're going to get your belongings." He turned to Elena. "You can stand down. Megan's free to go. I'll see that she gets home safely."

# TWENTY-THREE

SHANNON WAS IN HER OFFICE, RETURNING THE LAST OF THE phone calls that had piled up while she was seeing patients, when she felt her cell phone vibrating in her pocket. "Thanks for the referral, Dr. Mann. I'll look forward to seeing her tomorrow, and I'll be certain to keep you posted."

Shannon hung up the landline and pulled out her cell phone, hoping she was answering quickly enough to keep the call from going to voice mail. "Dr. Frasier."

"Shannon, it's me."

"Megan, where are you calling from? What happened?" Shannon got up and closed her office door. "I've been waiting to hear from Elena Waites."

"I told her I'd call you," Megan said. She sounded very tired, but otherwise there was no indication of stress in her voice.

"Where are you? What happened?" Shannon repeated.

"Let me have the phone." The male voice sounded familiar, but Shannon couldn't place it. "Dr. Frasier, this is Steve Alston."

Shannon didn't know whether to laugh, cry, or let loose a torrent of invective at the man she'd last seen putting her handcuffed sister into the back of a police vehicle. "Would you please explain to me what's going on?" She tried to make her words neutral, but there was ice in her voice.

"First, let me assure you we were only doing our job when we picked up Megan this morning. Frankly, when we arrested her we were acting on information that turned out to be flawed. We intended—well, at least it was my plan—to question Megan as soon as we got her to the station, then turn her loose if we cleared her. But we got called away to handle another case, a homicide, so it was after lunch before we could start the interview."

*Interview, my foot. More like an inquisition.* Shannon recalled how she'd felt when talking with the detectives, answering their questions, giving a statement. She couldn't fathom how her sister would respond to more of that after being arrested and hauled away in handcuffs. "So what happened?"

"My partner talked with her until he was satisfied we didn't have enough to consider her a viable suspect in Tony Lester's murder. I asked her a few questions. Then I convinced Jesse the arrest wouldn't stand up at an arraignment, and there was no need for Megan to spend the night in jail."

"What did Elena Waites say about all this?"

"She made noises about suing for false arrest, but we hear those threats all the time. I don't think Megan is going to file charges." He paused. "Are you?"

Shannon heard Megan's voice in the background, a weak, "No."

"I'm driving your sister home right now. We should arrive in about fifteen minutes. If you'd like to meet us, perhaps you could join us for dinner."

Shannon felt her temper rising. Of all the nerve . . . "I don't think that would be such a good idea, Detective. Let me speak to my sister."

"Yes?" Megan sounded subdued.

"Surely you're not seriously considering having dinner with the man who arrested you just a few hours ago."

A bit more life came into Megan's conversation. "Steve didn't arrest me. It was all his partner's idea. And he's the one responsible for my being released. I'd like to thank him."

Shannon couldn't understand it. Maybe if she could speak with Megan face-to-face . . . "Will you wait for me at my house? I want to talk with you before you leave."

"I guess so. It will take us awhile to pack and load stuff into my car so I can finish moving. Steve has volunteered to help me." Alston's voice in the background murmured something. "Got to go now. I'll see you there."

Shannon had heard of grinding one's teeth in frustration, but never experienced it—until now.


ELENA WAITES WAS IN HER CAR WHEN HER CELL PHONE RANG. SHE pulled it from the purse on the seat next to her and answered.

"Elena? Shannon Frasier. Megan just called me. She's on her way to my house, and Detective Alston is driving her there." Shannon's voice rose in both pitch and volume as she neared the end of that sentence.

"I know," Elena said. "I was going to call you, but Megan insisted she wanted to do it. How much did she tell you?"

"Not enough for me to understand what was going on. Why don't you fill me in?"

"Just a second." Elena maneuvered around a car stopped in the right-hand lane, its hood up and emergency blinkers flashing, apparently another victim of the summer heat. This was the time of year when radiators and hoses turned functioning cars into two-ton paperweights. She made a mental note to make sure everything was okay under the hood of her own vehicle.

"Okay," Elena said. "Had to pay attention to my driving. Here's the story. I hurried down to the jail, but they kept shuffling me around until after lunch. First they said Megan was in processing. Then the detectives were out on a call, and I had to speak with them before I could see Megan. It was three o'clock when I got in to see her."

"How was she doing?"

"How do you think? They kept her isolated in a cell, no idea what was happening next, and by the time I saw her she was already beaten down. I've seen it before. We talked for a bit, then the detectives came in."

Elena described the questioning from Jesse Callaway, summarizing at the end. "Pretty much the same questions they asked when we were all down there a week or so ago—and the same answers. I think Callaway thought if he softened Megan up she'd confess to something, but she held her ground."

"So then they released her?"

"No, then Alston took over. I don't know if it's his nature or the scenario they crafted, but he was a lot easier on her. First he threw her a few easy questions, then, out of the blue, he asked her about being a part of the bank robbery Crosley and Radick were thought to have pulled. She denied it, of course, and eventually the questioning lost steam and they quit."

"And . . ."

She told Shannon about Alston's offer to take Megan home. As she clicked her turn signal and wheeled onto the street leading to her house, Elena said, "Sometimes police will arrange for a ride for a witness. But a detective arresting a suspect, then driving them home—that's unheard of."

"I couldn't figure that one out either," Shannon said. "Megan sounded almost like she'd bonded with Alston."

"Stockholm syndrome," Elena said. "I've seen it before, although not as pronounced as here. Have you heard of it?"

"Yes, but I can't recall the context."

"It's named for what happened at a bank robbery in Stockholm over forty years ago. A captive—or in this case, a prisoner—mistakes lack of abuse for an act of kindness, so they bond with the person holding them prisoner. I think Megan was convinced that Steve Alston was responsible for her release, so she considered him her rescuer."

Shannon was silent.

"Look," Elena said, "I'm pulling into my driveway. I can call you later tonight, or you can feel free to call me. Otherwise, I'm going to talk with the district attorney tomorrow and get this thing settled once and for all. I'm tired of you and Megan having the constant threat of arrest hanging over you."


AS SHANNON NEARED HER HOME, SHE SAW A DARK SEDAN AT THE CURB. Alston and Megan must already be inside, packing the last of her things. Shannon was happy for her sister, but to her way of thinking, this was absolutely the worst time for Megan to be on her own. If she'd stay with Shannon, she could get the guidance . . . *Stop it. She's a grown woman, not a child.*

Shannon pulled in and lowered the garage door, but she didn't exit her car. Instead, she took out her cell and called Mark. *Please let him pick up.* On the fourth ring, he answered.

"How did things go at the police station? Is Megan still there?" he asked.

Shannon took a moment to give Mark the details of what had transpired. "I'm home and about to face Megan and

Steve Alston, but I'm frankly unsure of how to approach this."

"Let me think about that." Mark was silent for almost a minute. "How about this? First of all, don't make a big deal of it—that would only make Megan dig in her heels."

"I agree. But I don't want—"

"Thank Detective Alston for bringing her home. Tell them both you'd like to spend this last night together with your sister. Offer to load what won't fit into her car in yours, follow her to the new apartment so she can show it to you, then take her to dinner."

"What about trying to convince her the detectives aren't her friends?"

"Not tonight. Tonight, be her friend, not her big sister. Right now she doesn't need someone telling her what to do. Make sense?"

Shannon considered it. It would take some restraint on her part, but it did make sense. "That might work."

"You and Elena can nose around tomorrow to see if you can figure out what's going on with these two detectives. Tonight, just be glad your sister isn't in jail. Celebrate the fact that your prayers were answered."

Shannon put her cell phone away and opened the car door. Mark's last sentence had made her acutely aware that her prayers for her sister had stopped the moment she learned that Megan was free. Weren't prayers of thanks as appropriate as supplications for help? *Thank You, God, for delivering her. Sorry it took me awhile to get around to this.*

THE ROOM MEGAN HAD BEEN OCCUPYING LOOKED ALMOST BARREN. An open suitcase sat on the bed. The closet doors were ajar, and no clothes hung inside.

Steve Alston heard the door from the garage open and close. "Shannon must be home," he said to Megan.

Steve needed to play this carefully. His decision to take Megan home was spur of the moment, and he had to admit that he'd hoped—however unconsciously—that it would get points for him. But from the sound of the slamming door, that didn't appear to be the way it was going to go.

He paused in his efforts to close a suitcase Megan had overfilled with clothes, toiletries, and a couple of stuffed animals she'd probably hung on to since childhood. "You know, she may not be too happy to see me here. You probably should let me explain things to her."

Shannon stuck her head into Megan's bedroom, saw her sister, and hurried across the room to give her a hug. "I'm so glad to see you."

"Shannon . . . Dr. Frasier, I suppose you're wondering what's going on," Steve said.

The look Shannon gave him would have cut through steel, but he managed to ignore it. Steve had been a policeman for a long time, and he was used to those looks. Then, as though she'd flipped a switch, Shannon smiled and said, "It doesn't matter now. I just want to enjoy this evening with my sister— her last time here in my house for a while." It must have taken an effort for Shannon to get the next words out, but she did, and she managed to sound sincere. "Thank you for bringing her home."

"I was going to help her move," Steve said. "Then maybe I could buy both you ladies dinner."

Although Shannon addressed her reply to Steve, there was no doubt her words were meant for Megan. "I thought we'd load everything into two cars—Megan's and mine—and I'd help her get things settled in her new apartment. That way she could show it off to me. Then *I* wanted to take her out and have dinner with my *sister*."

Shannon bore down on the last word, and Steve saw Megan softening. He tried once more, although he felt the fight slipping away. "You know, Shannon, the arrest this morning wasn't my idea. Matter of fact, I tried to talk Jesse out of it." He indicated Megan. "I think your sister will tell you that I was pretty gentle in my questioning. This is just my way of apologizing."

"I appreciate it," Shannon said, "but I think my plan is better for tonight. If you want to apologize—and I think you owe one to both of us—we can talk about that later." She moved aside to leave the path to the door open. "We won't keep you. I'll help Megan finish packing so you can be on your way." Her mouth said the next words, but her eyes refuted them before they were fully out. "Thank you."

"But—"

"I'll tell you what, Detective Alston. How about this? If you have anything you want to tell Megan or me, just give the message to our attorney. Considering what happened earlier today, maybe that would be the best way to communicate in the future."

Steve knew when he was beaten. If anything, his gamble had made his position worse with Shannon. However, it seemed to have put him in Megan's good graces. He put on his most gracious smile, nodded to both women, and said, "No need to show me out. I know the way."

ONCE ALSTON HAD LEFT, MEGAN SAID, "WHY DID YOU DO THAT? Steve was going to help me finish my move. And then he offered to take us both out to dinner."

Shannon struggled to hold her tongue. She took a deep

breath, let it out, then another. "Don't you think it was sort of inappropriate to be going out with the detective who arrested you for murder earlier in the day?"

"That wasn't anything serious," Megan said. "Elena was there to protect my rights. And Steve got me released."

Shannon wanted to remind Megan of how she'd felt less than twelve hours earlier when she was handcuffed and hauled away to jail. She wondered what her sister's attitude was when she sat in a jail cell, not knowing what was coming next. And although Detective Steve Alston was decidedly the enemy in this confrontation, why had Megan fixed on him as her deliverer, rather than Elena Waites? But Shannon bit her tongue and said none of this. These were arguments for another time. Tonight she'd work on being a friend to Megan.

By the time they reached the new apartment, Megan showed signs of thawing. Shannon met Parker and was immediately taken with her. Megan was right—Parker was the perfect roommate for her. She was a woman who'd made mistakes in the past, learned from them, moved on, and had the fortitude to not only stay on the right track but also help someone else struggling to do the same.

Shannon ended up buying dinner for the three of them, and by the end of the evening she thought Megan was recovering nicely from the trauma of her arrest earlier in the day.

"I'll call you tomorrow night," Megan said.

"I'd like that," Shannon replied.

Megan grinned at her new roommate. "I might even cook dinner for you one evening . . . providing Parker has some pots and pans I can borrow."

Shannon climbed into her car, thinking about Megan's offer. *Better see if she has a cookbook she can loan you, too.* No matter. If it made peace with her sister, she'd even be willing to eat Megan's cooking.

SHANNON WAS IN THE SURGEONS' LOUNGE THE NEXT MORNING awaiting the start of her next case, an endoscopic hernia repair. She was looking forward to showing her resident how the operation could be done using this minimally invasive method. The surgery itself might take a few minutes longer than the old technique, but the patient's convalescence was shortened by several days.

When she heard a voice from the intercom speaker on the wall above her head, Shannon started to get up from the well-worn sofa and head to the operating rom. Maybe her case was going to start early. But instead, the female voice said, "Dr. Frasier, can you take an outside call?"

Shannon hoped this wasn't another family emergency. "Sure. Which line?"

She pulled the phone near to her and punched the button. "Dr. Frasier."

"Shannon, this is Elena. Do you have a moment to talk?"

Shannon leaned back and closed her eyes. A call from her attorney had the potential to be very good news . . . or very bad news. "Sure. Sorry I didn't have my cell with me. I'm operating this morning."

"No problem. Don't forget, I'm married to a surgeon."

Actually, Shannon *had* momentarily forgotten that. No matter.

Elena continued, "Recall I told you I was going to chat with the DA's office about yesterday's arrest. As a matter of fact, I went all the way up the chain to the district attorney himself. He agreed with me that the evidence the detectives cited to incriminate Megan—and you, for that matter—is circumstantial. Neither of you is a viable suspect in the murder of Tony Lester. Of course you're already cleared of suspicion in Radick's shooting."

Shannon noticed that Elena hadn't mentioned Megan's possible role in that shooting. Surely they didn't suspect her of Radick's death. "So why was an arrest warrant issued for Megan?"

"That's where it gets interesting. I did a lot of digging, checked with a few judges and some of the clerks, tapped a couple of other sources. Tell me, did you look very closely at the warrant Detective Callaway had?"

Shannon tried to remember. "No, actually I didn't read it at all. He waved an official-looking piece of paper in front of me, but after that I . . . I guess I was too caught up in what was happening to examine anything closely."

"Things might have gone differently if you had."

Shannon took a deep breath. She had a bad feeling about what was coming next. "Why?"

"Because no official warrant was ever issued for the arrest of Megan Frasier."

# TWENTY-FOUR

"DR. FRASIER, WE'RE READY FOR YOU IN OR TWO." AN OPERATING room nurse stood framed in the doorway of the surgeons' lounge, her mask dangling below her chin.

Shannon held up a finger and mouthed, "Be right there."

"I hear someone in the room," Elena said. "Do I need to let you go?"

"Yes, I have to get started with my next operation. Can I call you later?"

"How would this afternoon work for you? When will you be out of the OR?"

"I'll probably finish all my cases by about three," Shannon said.

"Call me after that. I hope to have more information by then."

As Shannon stood at the scrub sink, she thought about what Elena had told her. If there was no actual warrant, then the whole scenario of Megan's arrest was staged. Whoever was behind it was taking a huge chance they might be discovered, so the stakes had to be pretty high. And no matter which detective was responsible, the other had to cooperate. Who was responsible for this? And why?

Shannon left the scrub sink and, arms held in front of her, dripping hands high, bumped the swinging door and backed into the operating room. When she went through that door, as though a curtain had parted, her thoughts shifted to the patient on the table. From this point forward, she would be focused on him.

Shannon accepted the sterile towel offered by the scrub nurse. The resident, who was already gowned and gloved, said, "Shall I go ahead and drape the field?"

"Yes, please." Shannon shoved her arms into the sterile gown and spun so the circulating nurse could tie it in the back. She plunged her hands into surgical gloves, then approached the operating table.

Shannon looked down at the operative field, the familiar rectangle of skin made orange by antiseptic solution and circumscribed by green surgical drapes. It was almost like the canvas for an impressionist painting. This was the area on which she would focus her attention for the next . . . well, for as long as it took. That was another thing she wanted to teach her resident. When you're performing surgery, never look at the clock. Concentrate on the patient.

"Ready?" she said to the resident.

"Ready when you are," he replied.

Shannon checked the endoscope—no need making an incision in the abdomen, however small, if you couldn't look and work inside.

"Here we go," Shannon said and held out her hand.

ELENA WAITES GLANCED AT HER WATCH—ALMOST FOUR IN THE afternoon. Maybe Shannon had been delayed in surgery. She was familiar with that scenario. Her husband, Tom, had come home to many a cold dinner for that very reason.

Elena called through her open office door, "Helen, have we heard from Dr. Frasier?"

Helen, a spry grandmother, poked her head through the door. "Not a peep. Want me to try to get her for you?"

"No, but thanks."

Elena swiveled away from her desk to face the window behind her. She purposely kept her back to the view of downtown Dallas as she worked, but right now she needed to think. Maybe the skyline would inspire her.

"Dr. Frasier on line two," Helen called through the intercom.

Elena punched the button. "Shannon, I was guessing you'd been delayed."

"And your guess would be right," Shannon said. "Emergency cholecystectomy—I mean, gallbladder removal."

Elena swiveled her chair back to her desk and pulled her notes toward her. "I'm afraid I don't know much more than I did earlier. Since there was no warrant for Megan's arrest, both detectives must have cooperated in the charade. I did find out that one of the policemen at headquarters was asked to take Megan through the booking process—fingerprinting, mug shot—without any paperwork."

"Didn't he smell a rat?"

"Actually, that's been done before, usually with a first-time criminal the police want to put pressure on, frighten a bit. Their goal is to get names and places so they can go higher up the food chain, roll up the whole operation, that sort of thing. So this didn't particularly arouse any suspicion."

"Do we know which detective asked for the favor?"

"The policeman wouldn't say. But in any case, I think you have to be wary of both men."

There was silence on the other end of the line. "Are you there?" Elena asked.

"Yes. I was just processing this information."

"As I see it, you're definitely in danger from Walt Crosley," Elena said. "You probably can't trust either Steve Alston or Jesse Callaway. Do you agree?"

"I guess you're right. I suppose the only two people I can trust in this whole thing are you and Mark."

"How about Megan?"

Shannon's silence spoke volumes. Finally, she said, "Megan says she's turned her life around. But at this point, I think it will be safer if I don't share too much with her."

AT A BIT PAST SIX ON THIS SUMMER EVENING, THERE WAS STILL more than an hour of daylight left. Ideally, he'd be safer keeping this watch later tonight, under cover of darkness, but he wanted to catch Frasier as she got home.

The maroon sedan wasn't new, but it was a late enough model to blend in with other cars parked on the street in that upper-middle-class neighborhood. He found a spot with a good view of Frasier's driveway. It would be nice if he could park farther away, but he needed to be close in order to see and react to her arrival.

He slouched behind the wheel, hoping the darkened car windows would give him a certain amount of anonymity. The good thing about the timing was that he could smoke without fear of the glow of his cigarette giving him away.

He lit up, scooted down in the driver's seat, and turned the rearview mirror so he could see any car coming up the street behind him. Patience. He'd learned that the hard way. Put in the time. Don't get ahead of yourself. That was the key.

He needed the information Frasier had. And he'd do whatever was necessary to force her to give it up. But first he had to get her in his control.

When he glanced at the rearview mirror, he saw her car coming down the street toward him. But there was another car right behind hers. He'd wait until they went by, then make his move. Frasier's car slowed for the turn. The following car had its left turn blinker on as well. He cursed under his breath. Someone was coming home with her.

He quickly calculated the pros and cons of dealing with two people. He could do it—no question. He'd done it before. But it would be easier and cleaner with only one. He shrugged, stubbed out his cigarette in an already-full ashtray, and reached for the ignition key. There was always tomorrow.

AS SOON AS SHANNON GOT HOME, SHE LEFT MARK TO FEND FOR himself while she changed into jeans, a blue T-shirt, and sandals. Now he was in the kitchen putting together supper for the two of them, while she sat in the overstuffed chair in her living room, one leg dangling over the arm, the phone pressed to her ear.

"Megan, I'm glad you're settling into your new apartment," Shannon said. "And I know you want to have Mark and me over for dinner sometime, but we've both had a tough day. He's cooking scrambled eggs and toast for us. Then we're going to relax and watch some mindless TV. How about another night?"

"Okay," Megan said. "I guess I should have asked you ahead of time. But when Parker and I got home, she suggested we cook for you tonight."

The two women chatted for a moment more before Mark called, "It's on the table."

"Got to go if I don't want cold eggs," Shannon said.

The sisters exchanged good-byes, and Shannon arose from her chair and walked into the kitchen.

"Who was that?" Mark asked.

"Megan. She and Parker wanted to have us over for dinner."

Mark stopped with a plate in his hand. "I know she's your sister, and I'm happy she's liking her new living arrangements, but I need some time to relax tonight. How about you?"

"Yes. Unfortunately, I have some things to tell you that will probably make it tough for you to relax."

Mark dished up the food and they both sat down. "I cooked it. I guess you can bless it," he said with a smile.

At first Shannon started to say she was in no mood to pray. But then it occurred to her that was exactly what she needed to do. "Sure." They bowed their heads, and Mark eased his hand over hers.

After the amen, they sat quietly for a moment, lost in their own thoughts. Then Shannon chewed a bite, took a sip of iced tea, and said, "I talked with Elena Waites today."

"Is there more trouble about Megan's arrest?"

"You might say that. It was all faked—no arrest warrant was issued for Megan."

Mark's face mirrored his surprise. Slowly he lowered his fork, the food on his plate momentarily ignored. "So if that's the case . . ."

"Either Alston or Callaway, more likely both, had something in mind. My guess is that they wanted to soften her up and ask her some questions, but I foiled their plan by telling Megan not to say a word without Elena present."

"What sort of questions?"

"I don't know. Maybe they know something I don't know. Elena says that at the end of the interview, Alston bore down on her about being involved in the bank robbery along with Radick and Crosley. He mentioned something about her share of the loot." Shannon placed her knife and fork across her plate and wiped her mouth on a napkin. "I'm beginning to believe that there are some things about Megan I still don't know."

"Well, we certainly can't trust the detectives, can we?"

"I don't—" The ring of her phone interrupted her. She rose and hurried into the living room, with Mark trailing behind. She picked up the phone, and they both took seats on the sofa.

"Dr. Frasier."

"Doctor, it's Steve Alston."

Shannon beckoned Mark closer and punched the button to put the call on speaker. "Yes?"

"We just got some information I thought you might like to hear. Want me to drop by and give it to you in person?"

Shannon frowned and shot Mark a questioning look. He shrugged, as if to say, "Your call."

"That would be okay. Dr. Gilbert is here as well. You can tell us both. That will save me having to tell him later."

Alston's voice changed slightly, and Shannon could almost see his mind working. "Why don't you put this call on speaker and I can tell you both right now?"

"Sure." Shannon waited a second. "Now you're on speaker. What's the news?"

"Yesterday one of our patrols arrested a gangbanger who'd stolen a car. When they shook him down, he was carrying a semiautomatic pistol—unregistered, of course. The lab fired some test rounds from it and got a match to bullets from a recent crime. Want to guess which one?"

Shannon was in no mood to guess. "Which?"

"We got a perfect match with the bullets the medical examiner dug out of Barry Radick. From what the kid told us, this was a drive-by shooting, part of a gang initiation. It appears that Radick just happened to be in the wrong place at the wrong time."

Shannon wasn't sure how to take this. Not long ago she would have welcomed the news that the shooting outside her house was nothing more than a random act. Now she wasn't sure whether she could believe anything Alston said. She wasn't sure she could believe anybody.

"Anything else?" she asked.

"No. I just thought you'd want to know."

She ended the call and turned to Mark with a puzzled expression on her face. "I don't know if that makes things clearer or muddies them. I'd always thought that Radick's murder had something to do with the bank robbery. And even if his shooting was random, what was he doing at my house? He wasn't just wandering by—his car was parked down the street, and he was coming up the walk. Why?"

Mark shook his head. "We don't have the answer, do we? I mean, in medicine, sometimes the answer is clear as a bell, sometimes—"

Shannon stopped him with an upraised hand. "Wait! Clear as a bell. Let me think." Shannon closed her eyes and tried to recapture the thought that had struck her. Something was tickling at the edges of her memory, something that seemed out of the ordinary at the time. She'd shoved it into a corner of her mind, but now it was peeking out once more.

"What?"

"It was something in the cemetery. Something that was out of place."

"We scoured every inch of the area covered by those GPS

coordinates," Mark said. "And if we missed something, Crosley didn't. Remember, the police said there were mausoleums opened, gravestones tipped over, even a few holes dug. I don't know what those numbers from Radick mean, but I don't think they point to the cemetery."

"But they do," Shannon said. "I remember walking by a series of brass bells hanging from a curved metal rod. I thought it would be nice to have something like that at a gravesite, tinkling as the wind blew. But that ornament was something new, something out of the ordinary in an old cemetery like Greenwood."

"So maybe someone decided to add it to the grave of an ancestor," Mark said.

"No. There's more. I ran my hand along the bells, wanting to hear them. And one bell had a different tone, not like the others."

"So you think—"

"If we look at those bells, I'll bet we find something inside one of them—a clue that will lead to the stolen money everyone seems to be hunting."

# TWENTY-FIVE

MARK OPENED HIS MOUTH BUT CLOSED IT BEFORE THE WORDS "That's crazy" could escape. Maybe what Shannon said wasn't crazy—at least not any crazier than the other events of the past two weeks.

"Suppose there is something in there. How are we going to find where it leads us?" he asked.

Shannon was already on her feet. "One step at a time. First we go to the cemetery and find what's in that bell. Maybe there's a clue there as well."

"Why don't we just . . ." Mark let the sentence trail off. He was about to suggest they pass this information on to Alston and Callaway. But the rigged arrest of Megan had left him unwilling to trust the two detectives, and he knew Shannon shared that distrust.

She walked to the window, looked out, then turned to face Mark. "We probably have an hour or less of daylight. I don't want to go sneaking around a graveyard at night—besides which, they may lock the gates for security. I'm going. Are you with me?"

Mark sighed and bid a mental good-bye to the rest of his scrambled eggs. "Of course. I'll drive."

AS MARK'S CAR ENTERED GREENWOOD CEMETERY, SHANNON looked around and wondered if she could find the exact place where the GPS coordinates had led them before. The last time they were here, Megan directed them to the spot. But Shannon didn't have that app on her own phone, and she didn't want to include her sister in this foray. She held firm to her resolve to trust only her attorney and Mark.

"Do you have any idea where we're going?" she asked.

"Pretty much," Mark said. "Far southwest corner of the cemetery. We enter on Peace, left on Glory, right on Friendship."

"I like the names of these little streets," Shannon said.

"Well, I doubt that the names mean much to the people buried here, but the sentiment's nice."

The sun was low in the western sky, and some of the shaded areas were already darkening. Mark turned on his headlights, but they illuminated only the road, not the areas around the tombstones and monuments.

"There! There's the monument with the statue of a Confederate soldier," Shannon said. "The hanging bells are near there. I saw them when I was walking back to the car."

Mark pulled to the side of the narrow road and parked. "Check the glove compartment. There should be a flashlight in there."

Shannon opened the little door and reached in. The first thing her hand encountered wasn't the familiar cylinder of a flashlight. Rather, it was an irregularly shaped piece of cold, slightly greasy metal. She pulled back her hand as though she'd touched a snake. "Mark! The gun is still in here."

Mark leaned across, reached into the glove compartment, and pulled out first a handgun, then a flashlight. He tucked the gun into his belt on his left side, the butt forward, out of the way but ready for a cross-draw. He checked the flashlight, found that it worked, and slid it into his side pants pocket.

"Can't you leave the gun in the car?" Shannon asked.

"We're not the only ones hunting whatever Radick was talking about. What if Walt Crosley is over there somewhere hiding behind one of those monuments?" Mark reached over and laid his hand lightly on Shannon's shoulder. "I promise I won't draw the gun unless our lives are in danger."

"Can you at least put on the safety?"

"Revolvers don't have a safety. This one requires either a strong pull on the trigger or manually cocking the hammer back. It's not about to fire accidentally." He touched the handle of the gun. "Don't worry. I know how to use it, and I'll be careful."

She nodded, then opened the car door on her side and exited. "I think the bells are over that way." She headed for a spot to the left of the Confederate soldier monument.

She'd taken only a dozen or so steps when Mark called, "Right here." He was one row over from where Shannon stood. He pointed to a metal rod that extended out of the ground to almost waist height. Suspended from a curve at the top of the rod was a string of progressively larger bowl-shaped bronze bells. He reached down and started the assembly swinging. Chimes sounded, but one of the bells seemed to give off a slightly discordant note.

Shannon hurried to where Mark stood. She held out her

hand. "Let me hold the flashlight while you reach in and see what's inside that bell."

He bent down to peer inside the largest one. "Can't see anything. Let me feel." In a moment he said, "Sure enough, there seems to be something wired to the clapper." He pulled his knife from his pocket. "Let me see if I can get it free."

Shannon looked around her and marveled at how quickly darkness was falling. Maybe it got darker earlier in a cemetery. Or maybe it just seemed that way. Even the usually busy street right outside the cemetery fence was devoid of traffic at this moment. "Can you hurry?"

"Almost through," Mark said. In a moment, he pulled out a small key. "Hold the light here. I think there's a label stuck on it."

The light jerked as Shannon reacted to a noise nearby. "Did you hear that?" she said.

Mark paused. "No. What do you think you heard?"

"Just a . . . just a sound." She shivered. "Let's get in the car. I'm uncomfortable standing here in the open."

Mark looked around. "I think you're jumping at shadows, but okay."

"On second thought, let's leave. I'll feel better when I'm out of this graveyard."

A few moments later, Mark had the car in gear and moving along the cemetery road toward the exit. "There's the source of your noise," he said. He pointed to a man standing by a monument nearby, his face turned away from them, his head bowed as though in prayer. "It's probably someone who's come to the grave of a relative. Maybe this is their birthday or anniversary. Nothing to be scared of."

"I guess what I heard was his car door closing." Shannon

pointed to a dusty maroon sedan parked on the verge of the road. "You're right. I shouldn't have been frightened."

MARK GUIDED HIS CAR THROUGH THE DARKENING STREETS. Despite his having told Shannon they were in no danger at the cemetery, he glanced frequently at his rearview mirror as he drove. He even took a couple of extra turns to make sure no one was following them.

Beside him, Shannon held the flashlight like a club, apparently ready to wield it as a weapon if anyone came near them. Her other hand lay in her lap, her fingers ceaselessly turning the key from side to side, end to end. It wasn't lost on Mark that although she'd been concerned when he pulled the gun from his glove compartment, she hadn't asked him to put it back. Perhaps she was finally getting the idea—she truly was in danger.

"Can you tell what's stuck to the key?" he asked, his eyes still on the road.

Shannon shined the light onto her lap. "It's a tiny label— some sort of plastic material, like something done with a label-maker."

"What's on it?"

"I can't tell. It's too dark. Just a second." She adjusted the beam of her flashlight slightly. "It's another series of numbers." She squinted and moved the key closer. "They're so tiny I can barely read them."

Mark shook his head. "Not more GPS coordinates, I hope."

"No, it's one series: 75035299."

"What about the key? Any idea what it might open?"

The light from the flashlight began to flicker and fade.

Shannon brought the key closer to her face. "It's sort of like a house key."

"Think it could be to a safe-deposit box?" Mark asked.

"I only know about the one I have, and it's different from this key. There may be some numbers engraved on it, but if so, they're under the label. Besides, I'll need a better light to see them."

"Maybe they represent an address or something," Mark said.

The flashlight was almost useless by now. Shannon clicked it off and opened the glove compartment door just enough to shove the flashlight in. "You need new batteries for this," she said.

"I'll take care of it." He took his right hand off the wheel long enough to touch the checkered grip of the .38-caliber revolver stuck in his belt. The mate to this revolver was in the back of the glove compartment. Mark wished more than ever that Shannon would take it. Maybe he'd give that one more try.

He returned his hand to the steering wheel, and Shannon reached across to lightly touch it. He noticed that her hand was trembling slightly. *Maybe I won't mention the gun tonight.*

INSIDE SHANNON'S HOUSE, WHILE MARK MOVED FROM ROOM TO room, checking doors and windows, she went to the kitchen and pulled two Diet Cokes from the refrigerator. In a moment, Mark walked in and said, "All secure."

Shannon handed him his drink. "Want to sit down and rest a bit first?"

Mark grinned. "No more than you do."

She lifted her Diet Coke in a sort of toast. "So let's look at what we brought back."

They moved into the living room, and Shannon pointed to her desk, where a banker's lamp stood on a green blotter. "The light's good over here." She pulled the chain on the lamp, extracted the key from her pocket, and dropped it onto the desk in the center of the blotter.

Mark took his knife and teased the label off the key. He held it beneath the light and read off the numbers. "75035299. Any idea what it means?"

"No. What about the key?"

The key, when viewed in better light, still yielded no useful clues. Its faded and scratched brass surface had a two-digit number stamped along the top. "Maybe the number means something," Shannon said.

Mark was already shaking his head. "I've seen numbers like this before. I'm betting they're a designation for the key blank."

"So this is a duplicate key," Shannon said.

Mark nodded. "And that means it's not to a US Post Office box. Those carry a stamped warning not to duplicate."

"What should we do with this, now that we've found it?" Shannon asked.

"Up to you," Mark said. "I'm too tired to think about it tonight. We can decide tomorrow." He turned to face Shannon. "I'm going to head home. When I leave, lock the door behind me and don't open it for anyone. In the morning, lock your car doors before you pull out of the garage. And when you arrive at the medical center, call security to walk you into the building."

"Is all that necessary?"

"Maybe not. But it's better to be cautious." At the door, Mark kissed Shannon. "Are you sure you won't take that gun I have for you? It's easy to use. Point it, pull the trigger."

This time she paused. Then, slowly and almost regretfully, Shannon said, "No."

After he'd left, she stood for several moments staring out into the gathering darkness, wondering if she was being foolish. Time would tell.

She still wasn't hungry. And it was too early to shower and go to bed. Shannon booted up her computer, wondering what she could put into a search engine that might give her a clue to the label and key they'd found tonight.

As with most Internet searches, she found herself following rabbit trails that, while interesting, led nowhere. Eventually, Shannon looked at her wrist and discovered it was almost ten o'clock. She'd try one more search, then give it up for the night. She entered another term in the Google search box, clicked on one of the results, and there it was. The answer was right before her eyes. That was what 75035299 meant.

Now it made sense.

MEGAN FRASIER CHECKED HERSELF IN THE MIRROR IN THE HALL-way of her new apartment. She was ready to face the day and end the workweek. Her blue eyes were clear and bright behind the designer glasses she wore today, letting function triumph over vanity. Her makeup was perfect but not overdone. Megan moistened her lips and nodded with satisfaction at the effect. She patted her blond hair, then smiled when she saw how well this hairstyle flattered her face.

She turned from side to side. Her clothes fit her well. True, she carried a few more pounds on her frame than her older sister, but she'd work on that in the days to come. No more fast-food lunches. No more meeting the gang for beer and nachos after work. She was determined to turn her life around, and losing weight would be a natural offshoot.

Megan thought back to all she'd experienced. Maybe God really did have a hand in getting her through. She vowed to do better. She'd attend church, stay in touch with her parents, be more patient with her sister. Her dad had always preached that God could forgive, no matter how black our sins. Maybe he was right.

Parker walked down the hall, stopping long enough to remark, "Looking good. Want to go somewhere after work to celebrate the start of the weekend?"

Megan felt her good intentions heading out the window. She tightened her resolve. "Maybe for club soda and a few pretzels. I've got to start a diet."

Parker laughed. "You're the boss. Maybe we can find a juice bar and load up on kale chips and carrot juice." She checked her appearance in the mirror and nodded approvingly. "I'm off. See you tonight."

"Right behind you," Megan said. In the front hallway, she picked up her purse and checked the contents. She rescued her keys from the depths of the bag and went out the door.

The parking area for the apartment where she and Parker lived was behind the building at the end of a covered walkway. The parking slots were also covered, which was especially nice now that the July temperatures were climbing. Even at eight in the morning, Megan was thankful for the shade. By this evening, pulling into it would be a blessed relief.

Each apartment had two designated parking spaces, with visitor's slots interspersed here and there. Megan's little white Ford was sitting in its assigned space at the far end of the first row. When she was about half a dozen paces away, she beeped the car unlocked. She noticed a maroon sedan next to hers.

RICHARD L. MABRY, M.D.

She was pretty certain that wasn't a visitor's space, and as she recalled, the vehicle that was usually parked there was a black pickup. Oh well. Maybe a relative was visiting. Maybe someone wanted to be closer to an apartment while they did some work there. Not her problem.

Megan had the driver's door of her car halfway open when something hard prodded her back. A strong hand gripped her shoulder, preventing her from turning. At the same time, a muffled voice, harsh and raspy, sounded in her ear. "So, Megan, we meet again."

# TWENTY-SIX

DURING MULTIPLE SPELLS OF WAKEFULNESS THROUGH A TROUBLED night, Shannon wrestled with the problem of what to do now that she'd found the key. She was pretty sure she knew what it represented, what it would unlock. It might take a bit of driving, but she was certain the key and the numbers on the label could lead her to whatever Walt Crosley wanted so badly. So should she take the next step herself, or trust the detectives with the key and her thoughts on its meaning?

All during her breakfast of coffee and a muffin the next morning, while she was getting dressed and putting on makeup, as she prepared for the day she continued to turn over her options. She was hesitant to do this on her own, but neither Callaway nor Alston had her trust anymore. She might be able to go to someone else in the police department, but who would that be? What if she happened to choose one of Alston and Callaway's friends . . . or, even worse, their coconspirator? She could try another law enforcement agency—but where would she start?

As Shannon packed her briefcase, she slipped the key and label into an envelope and tucked it behind some professional journals. As she walked to her car, the answer came to her in the form of one of her father's favorite sayings: "You don't buy a dog and bark yourself." She had an attorney, one well versed in criminal law. She'd call Elena, tell her what she and Mark had found, and let the attorney take it from there.

Shannon entered her garage through the door from her house, and although she felt foolish doing so, she looked carefully into her car before climbing inside. She locked the doors, started the car engine as she raised the garage door, and backed into the driveway. This was no way to live her life.

She wondered if she'd been wise to refuse the gun Mark offered. Maybe this was a case of foolish fears overriding common sense. It wasn't as though she would be using the gun as an offensive weapon. The only way she'd pick it up, much less fire it, was for self-protection. Was it worth risking her life for the sake of a principle?

She hoped she hadn't made a potentially fatal mistake. Of course, if she had, she wouldn't know it until too late.

MEGAN'S HEART SEEMED TO STOP. SHE STOOD MOTIONLESS, transfixed not so much by the strong hand that held her shoulder as by the fear that started in the soles of her feet and radiated upward through her whole body, paralyzing her as effectively as a curare dart.

"I asked if you were glad to see me," Walt Crosley said. "What's the matter? Cat got your tongue?"

It was impossible for Megan to discern the emotion behind the words. Not only had whatever misfortune befell Crosley's vocal cords permanently rendered his speech rough and strained, it apparently made it difficult for him to convey emotion through his words. Never mind. The gun pressed against her back and the grip on her shoulder told her that he meant business.

"What . . . what do you want?" she asked.

"Get in. Crawl over to the passenger side so I can drive." The pressure was withdrawn from her back. "Leave your purse between us. And don't think about reaching into it. When I visited Barry at First Step, he told me he was going to hook you up with someone who could get you a gun."

Megan opened her mouth to say, "There's no gun in there," but decided that any edge was better than none. If Crosley was extra careful, maybe she could use that to her advantage. She scooted over until she was almost against the passenger-side door.

"Car keys?"

"I have them in my hand." She held them out in her open palm.

Crosley eased under the steering wheel and closed the door. He transferred his gun to his left hand and held out his right. She dropped the keys into it and fastened her seat belt. Megan didn't know what was coming next, but she figured she'd better be ready for it.

"Just sit there and be quiet," Crosley said. He started the car and pulled away. Megan was surprised to find he was a careful driver. As though privy to her thoughts, Crosley said out of the side of his mouth, "When you're driving stolen cars with no driver's license or papers, you don't want to get stopped."

Now that she could see him, Megan noticed several puckered scars on Crosley's neck. Maybe they had to do with the injury that affected his voice. She filed the information away in case it might be useful.

Right now she didn't know where they were going or what Crosley planned to do once they arrived. As the car gained speed, Megan did something she hadn't done in quite a while—she prayed.

MARK REACHED FOR THE RINGING PHONE ON THE CORNER OF HIS DESK, never taking his eyes off the reports in front of him. "Dr. Gilbert."

"Hard at work already?"

Mark shoved the papers aside and leaned back in his chair. "Shannon, how are you this morning?"

"Sleepy," Shannon said.

"Are you in your office?"

"I'm on my cell, trying to stay awake as I drive in. I wrestled with this key thing all night, and I think there's only one reasonable course of action. I think we should tell Elena what we've found and let her take it from there."

"I agree. We can't trust the detectives. And if the key really leads to the money Crosley is after, we don't want to contaminate the evidence, or however they say it on the TV shows."

"That's the problem," Shannon said. "All the law and the police procedure I know come from watching those shows. That's why we need to let Elena handle this. So you agree with me?"

"I think it's our only real option," Mark said. "Want me to be with you when you call her?"

"No, I can do it. Why don't I check back with you about lunchtime? Maybe we can get together then."

"Have you talked with your parents? Your dad had his last chemo treatment yesterday. Think he'll be able to preach this weekend?"

"I don't know." Shannon's deep sigh was like a strong wind in the receiver.

"It slipped your mind, didn't it?"

"I'm not sure that I didn't just bury it in my subconscious. I can't get used to thinking of Dad as anything but the rock that anchors our family. And knowing that he's being treated for a potentially fatal disease . . . well, it's hard to take."

"If you'd like to see them this evening, I'll be glad to go with you," Mark said.

"I'm pulling into the parking garage now. I'll call Elena from my office. After that I'll check with Mom and Dad."

"Don't forget to call security and let them walk you from your car to your office."

"Do you really think that's necessary?"

"Three options," Mark replied. "Take the gun I offered, get security to escort you into the building, or let Crosley ambush you—and this time, you might not get out alive."

There was a long pause. "I'm going to hang up and call security right now. Let's get together at lunch. Meanwhile, here's some news for you. I think I know what the numbers on the key mean."


ELENA WAS JUST SITTING DOWN AT HER DESK WHEN HER CELL phone rang. Had one of the girls left a book at home? Was there a permission slip Elena had to sign for a field trip today? Why could teenagers remember the words to every song the latest pop idol recorded, but never things like this?

When she looked at the caller ID, Elena felt guilty for automatically blaming her daughters. "Shannon, good morning."

"Do you have a moment to talk?" Shannon asked.

Elena checked her watch, then glanced at the schedule

centered on her blotter. "If it's not too long a conversation. What's on your mind?"

"I think we're a step closer to learning what Crosley wants." She went on to explain about finding the key at the cemetery.

Elena started to ask how Shannon and the police had missed the key the first time, but she didn't want to interrupt the narrative. "And you think the key is what Crosley wants? How do you know what it unlocks?"

"The key's pretty anonymous—small brass key, no particular markings on it. But the clue's in the label. It says 75035299. I think Barry Radick rented a private postal box in the 75035 ZIP Code, box 299, and the money is in there."

Elena doodled on a legal pad. "The robbers got away with about three-quarters of a million dollars. If Radick's share was a third, that's two hundred fifty thousand dollars. In hundred-dollar bills, that would be a package about a foot high."

"I've already done the math. Maybe it's one of the larger boxes. I don't know how it works out. But I think we've got the key to recovering Radick's share of the stolen money. The problem—"

"The problem is that you don't want to take it to the detectives working the murder case. I can see that. Let me think." Elena tapped her pen against the pad on her desk for a moment. "This really isn't about a murder case. We're talking about the money from a bank robbery. That's a federal offense. I have a contact I trust at the FBI. Let me call him."

"So I can give him the key and tell him what I think?"

"Actually, you'd better show him where you found the key at the cemetery. The chain of evidence is already compromised, but maybe we can make this work." Elena jotted another note on her pad. "Can I call you back when I have some answers?"

"I'll be free about noon."

"Great," Elena said. "I'll get back to you then. In the meantime—"

"I know," Shannon said. "Be careful."


THE CLINIC NURSE TAPPED ON THE EXAM ROOM DOOR, OPENED IT just far enough to stick her head inside, and asked, "Dr. Frasier, can you take a call from your senior resident?"

"We're almost finished here," Shannon said. "Ask him to hold." She turned back to the middle-aged lady sitting on the edge of the examination table. "Mrs. Verhuisen, my nurse will get that surgery set up and give you instructions. But do you have any questions for me?"

Two minutes later, the patient was following the nurse down the hall in one direction while Shannon walked briskly in the other. In the dictation room, she lifted the receiver and punched the phone's blinking button. "This is Dr. Frasier." *Please don't let it be an emergency. I have too much on my plate already.*

"This is Kyle. Do you recall Mrs. Molina?"

Shannon shuffled through her mental index cards. "Older woman with intestinal obstruction. No previous abdominal surgery, no mass on X-ray to suggest malignancy, probably paralytic ileus. She's getting IV fluids, nasogastric suction, conservative management because of her age and medical status. Right?"

"Right. She seems a little worse today, and I'm wondering what you want to do next."

Shannon thought for a minute. "Get a CT scan of the abdomen, and ask the radiologist to concentrate on the gallbladder area. Maybe this is a gallstone ileus."

The pause on the other end of the line confirmed that

Shannon had mentioned something the resident hadn't considered. "I'll check that out. If you're right . . ."

"If I'm right, we do an endoscopic enterolithotomy. Use a scope to get the stone out, let the patient recover, go back in after four to six weeks to remove the gallbladder and close any biliary fistula." She looked at her watch. Almost noon. "Call me when the CT's done. I'll have a look at Mrs. Molina, go over the films with you, and we'll make a decision."

After she hung up, Shannon, as she often did, rethought what she'd just sounded so confident in saying. Gallstone ileus was uncommon, but the more she thought about it, the more sure she was that her diagnosis would be correct. As for treatment, a difference of opinion existed, but she felt this was the best choice. In an older patient with numerous medical problems, do as little surgery as necessary to take care of the acute problem. Consider more definitive surgery later, after Mrs. Molina was stable.

Shannon was anxious for noon to come. Maybe Elena would have some good news for her. Meanwhile, she had another call to make. She reached for the phone and felt fear gnaw at her as she dialed her parents' number.

"WHERE ARE WE GOING?" MEGAN ASKED.

Walt Crosley kept his eyes fixed on the road. "You'll see when we get there."

"What do you want from me?"

Crosley reached into his shirt pocket and extracted a crumpled pack of Camels. He shook one out and pulled it from the pack with his lips. His eyes left the road long enough to scan the area in the middle of the dashboard. "Where's your lighter?"

"There's not one. The place where the cigarette lighter used to be is where I plug in the charger for my cell phone."

He grunted an obscenity and fumbled a pack of paper matches from the same pocket that held his cigarettes. Crosley steered the car with his knees until he managed to get his cigarette lit. He took a deep drag and blew the smoke out his nose before returning his right hand to the wheel. His left elbow rested on the open window.

Megan had a dozen more questions she wanted to ask, but she kept quiet. She knew Crosley wouldn't answer. Obviously he wanted her alive for at least a while, probably until he could get the information he needed. It didn't bear thinking about what he might do to make her talk. And if she didn't have what he wanted, the only way he'd be certain would be to torture her to the point of death.

Then it dawned on her. He'd made no effort to disguise his identity. He wasn't trying to keep her from seeing their eventual destination. The only interpretation she could put on those actions made the pit of her stomach clinch into the hardest of knots. She felt cold chills ripple down her spine as it became clear—when he'd finished, Crosley intended to kill her.

# TWENTY-SEVEN

SHANNON PERCHED ON THE EDGE OF THE DESK IN THE CLINIC DICTATING room, every nerve ending in her body tingling, each of them urging her to hurry on to her next phone call, but she knew this one was important, too. "Mom, are you sure you don't want us to come by tonight?"

"We're fine, dear. Your father had no problems with his other chemotherapy treatments. He's a little weak, but not as much as he feared. Right now he's in his study, preparing his sermon for Sunday."

*So he is going to preach on Sunday.* "How about tomorrow night? I'll call Megan, and we'll take you and Dad out for dinner on Saturday."

"I think your dad would probably rather save his strength for Sunday. Why don't I fix dinner here for all of us—you, Megan, and Mark, if he'll come? I'm sure your father would like that."

"Let me check. I'll call you tonight." She looked at her watch. "Got to go right now, though. Love you."

Shannon took in a deep breath and tapped out Elena's number. After four rings, she was about to give up. She relaxed when she heard, "Elena Waites."

"Elena, it's Shannon. Do you have any news for me?"

"I talked with my contact at the FBI. He's agreed to meet you at the cemetery this afternoon about five. I'll be there as well."

"So I show him where I found the key and label, give them to him, and he'll take it from there?"

"Exactly."

Shannon knew she should feel relief, but it hadn't come. Maybe after the actual transfer. "Can I bring Mark? He was with me when we made the discovery."

"I think that will be okay. Be sure to call me if you're going to be late, though. It took some convincing to get Seth involved—that's the special agent's name, Seth Andrews. Anyway, he's afraid you've already contaminated the chain of evidence, but he's willing to see what we've got."

"I'll meet you at Greenwood. If you arrive first, go to the far southeast corner of the cemetery and look for the monument with the statue of the Confederate soldier."

Shannon was in the process of ending the call when she heard, "Dr. Frasier?" A clinic nurse stood in the doorway. "Dr. Martin called. He's in X-ray if you want to come down and see Mrs. Molina's CAT scan."

"I'm on my way." Shannon made a conscious effort to shift mental gears. She was certain the scan would confirm a gallstone ileus, which meant she'd be taking Mrs. Molina to surgery this afternoon. She'd need to call Mark, tell him that lunch was off, and make sure he was available to go with her to the cemetery later.

As she punched the button for the elevator, Shannon

wondered if she shouldn't phone Megan to see how her sister was doing in her new apartment and new job. That would be a good idea, but for now it would have to wait.

THE WEEKS SHE'D SPENT AT FIRST STEP IN HER MOST RECENT rehab stint had done two things for Megan. First and foremost, she'd come away from the experience clean and sober, finally convinced that she was always one drink or one hit away from skidding into a fall that would most likely end in her death. But that time also brought her in close contact with a variety of people, contact that paid dividends in different ways.

For example, her acquaintance with Jeff Robiteaux had opened the door to a job with R&R Medical Supply. But she'd also met some people who weren't in the same league as Jeff. Now she hoped that might pay off, too. Because she was nice to Barry Radick despite his criminal history, he'd felt free to confide in her, including some of the things he'd done to get out of tight situations—like this one.

Megan rubbed her hands together, hoping her captor would accept it as a sign of nervousness. Once she was sure Crosley's attention was on the road, she slipped her watch off her left wrist and onto her right. Moving the watch was one of the things Radick had mentioned. Anything to get an edge.

"Here we are," Crosley said.

They were almost out of the city now. The houses here wouldn't be featured in *Architectural Digest*. The homes were small, probably one bedroom, covered by dingy siding that was barely hanging on. The yards featured rusting bicycles and discarded tires set amid weeds and patches of bare dirt. In some areas, bare foundations and piles of charred rubble marked the site of previous fires.

The house where Crosley stopped showed no signs of habitation. Megan figured that everyone who could escape this neighborhood had already done so. If she was looking to scream for help, she was in for a major disappointment.

"I'm going to unlock your door," Crosley said. "Get out slowly. And don't try to run." He pulled the gun from his waistband and waved it toward her.

She reached for her purse but withdrew her hand when Crosley lifted the gun and leveled it at her head. "Okay. Okay." Megan opened the door and stepped out of the car.

"Walk to the front door. I'm right behind you."

Megan trudged up the crumbling cement of what was once a sidewalk. When she escaped, which way would she run? She smiled to herself, realizing that there was never any question in her mind of "if she could get away," only "when . . ."

Crosley reached above the doorframe and pulled down a key that Megan thought belonged in a museum. She was used to relatively short brass keys with irregular notches cut into the bottom edge. This one was different—a two-inch metal rod with an oval head at one end and a tab at the other. Crosley put the key into the lock, gave a single turn, and pushed the door open.

"You don't see locks like this anymore." He dropped the key into his pocket.

The room they entered was bare of furniture. No curtains or drapes hung over the windows, but the panes were so dirty there was little chance for sunlight to intrude—or passersby to see in.

"In there." Crosley motioned to the next room, which turned out to be a kitchen. An empty space with a capped pipe marked the spot where a gas range once stood. Bare kitchen cabinets, their doors hanging open, flanked a chipped, dry porcelain sink with a rust stain surrounding the drain. A refrigerator stood against the wall opposite the stove, the door open wide to reveal shelves stacked on the bottom, the crisper drawer halfway out.

The kitchen table was gone, but there were two mismatched chairs in the middle of the room. Crosley motioned for her to sit in one. Megan made a feeble effort to clear a layer of dirt from the seat, then gave up and sat. Keeping her clothes neat was pretty low on her list of priorities right now.

Crosley sat in the other chair, crossed his legs, and let the gun in his hand dangle. "Here's what I want to know. When I visited Barry Radick at First Step, he pointed you out to me, said you were smart. I told him we should recruit you to drive for the bank job we were planning."

"I didn't—"

"Shut up! I got the impression you were friendly with Radick—maybe friendly enough to do him a favor."

Crosley crossed his legs in the other direction. He stuck the gun in his belt, shook another Camel out of the pack, and lit it. "So here's the deal. When he was shot, I think he was going to your sister's house, looking for you. No telling how many Frasiers he checked out before he went there."

"But—"

"He knew the cops were after him. If they caught him, someone would need money to get him a lawyer, post bail. He thought you'd do that for him. So the thing on Radick's mind was the location of his money."

"No, that's—"

The gun was back in Crosley's hand before Megan could finish. "We're not here to argue. I'll bet your sister told you about the GPS coordinates, and I think you know what they mean. Tell me where I can find the dough Radick stashed. When you do that, I'll let you go."

*Sure you will.* Megan's mind was already working at top

speed. "She already gave you the numbers, but I don't know what they mean."

Crosley snorted. "Yeah, she gave them to me . . . in the wrong order. But I figured out the right one. The only trouble was that after the numbers led me to a cemetery, I turned it upside down and didn't find any trace of the loot. So what am I missing?"

If she could only buy some time . . . "I was with my sister and her boyfriend at the cemetery. We didn't find anything either. So I don't—" The rest of the sentence was cut off by her scream as the tip of Crosley's cigarette touched her arm.

"I'll keep on doing that until you tell me what I need to know," he said. "And if that doesn't work, I can try something else." He shoved the gun into his waistband again and pulled a knife from his pocket. He snapped his wrist and a wicked-looking blade appeared. "We've got lots of time. Think hard."


HER WALK TO THE PARKING GARAGE HAD ALWAYS BEEN A TIME OF reflection for Shannon, reviewing her day, thinking of calls she'd make on the way home. Today, as she and Mark prepared to meet the FBI agents, she spent the time glancing over her shoulder, starting at every loud noise. Shannon noticed that Mark had offered his left hand for her to hold, keeping his right hand free.

"Your car or mine?" she asked.

"Mine," Mark said, and she didn't argue.

The ride to Greenwood Cemetery was a silent one. At one point, Shannon thought that perhaps this was the way journeys to this graveyard were made when it was active—mourners following a hearse, riding through the streets in silence, contemplating the solemn event in which they participated.

She knew she should feel a sense of relief at turning the key over to the FBI, but even with it out of her possession, she wasn't going to relax until Walt Crosley was safely behind bars.

Inside the cemetery gates, Mark steered his Chevrolet down the tiny roads, made the turns he'd memorized, and pulled to a stop behind a white GMC Acadia, which Shannon figured was Elena's. Beyond that, a man and woman stood by a black Ford Explorer, both talking on cell phones.

"I think this is our group," she said.

Elena exited her vehicle and stood waiting until Shannon and Mark reached her. She held out her hand to Mark. "I don't think we've met. Elena Waites."

Mark shook her hand and gave a brief nod. "Mark Gilbert."

Elena turned to Shannon. "I presume you've got the key and the label with the numbers."

Shannon patted the pocket of her dove-gray slacks. "Right here."

Elena nodded. "I see the agents headed our way."

The two people who approached were a study in contrasts. Both wore dark suits, but the similarity stopped there. The man had blond hair cut short, wore steel-rimmed glasses, and was of average build. He wore a charcoal pinstriped suit. His bow tie was navy with red polka dots. His shoes were well-shined black wing tips. Shannon reflected that five minutes after meeting him, most people would be hard-pressed to remember the man. Maybe that was an advantage for an FBI agent. His handshake was like the rest of him—unmemorable. "I'm Special Agent Seth Andrews."

His partner stepped forward and held out her hand before Andrews could introduce her. "Marlene Crowder," she said. Her voice was a rich contralto. She wore a navy blue pantsuit, but whereas Andrews was forgettable, Crowder was anything but that. She towered a good four inches above her partner. Her skin was a rich chocolate color. Her hair was jet-black and cut short, framing a beautiful face that seemed to require very little makeup.

*This is what Nefertiti must have looked like.* Shannon acknowledged the introductions and said, "I suppose you want to see what I brought."

"First, show us where you found it," Andrews said.

Shannon squared her shoulders, took a deep breath, and trudged toward the statue of the Confederate soldier.

MEGAN SLUMPED IN THE CHAIR, QUIVERING AND SPENT. SWEAT mixed with the rivulets of blood that ran between her breasts. "Okay. I'll tell you what you missed. Just don't . . . don't cut me again."

Crosley dropped his cigarette on the floor and ground it out beneath his foot. He wiped the knife blade on his pants, then stowed the weapon in his pocket. "Let's hear it."

"There's a statue of a Confederate soldier. It's at the far end of the cemetery. You must have seen it."

"I saw lots of statues, but that one . . . Yeah, I remember it."

"Start . . ." Megan tried to swallow, but her throat felt dry as dust. She closed her eyes, remembering the scene. "Start at the base of the pedestal and take thirty-three paces in the exact direction the soldier is looking. That should take you to a spot between two oak trees. Dig there. That's where Radick buried the money."

"And is it still there? Or did you already dig it up?"

"I . . . I couldn't do anything while Shannon and Mark were with me, and I haven't been able to go back." She took a faltering breath. "The money's there."

Crosley was silent, concentration written on his face. "Okay, I'm going to go have a look." He pulled a set of hand-cuffs from his hip pocket. "Move over there next to the sink."

Megan tried twice before she was able to stand. She staggered toward the sink and fell to her knees in front of it.

Crosley grasped the doors under the sink, yanked them off their hinges, and tossed them aside.

Apparently the house was built before the days of PVC pipe and flexible connection tubing. Under the sink were galvanized hot and cold water pipes and a drainpipe of similar material.

"Sit down on the floor."

Megan lowered herself the rest of the way to the floor as gently as she could and then brought her legs around so she sat cross-legged in front of the sink.

Crosley looked at Megan's arms. Then he barked, "Hold out your left hand." He grabbed it and snapped a cuff on the wrist. He fastened the other cuff around the largest of the three pipes under the sink, then gave it a tug. "That should hold you for a while."

Megan's voice trembled as she asked, "When are you coming back?"

"If I find the money, I'll be back to let you loose. If I don't find the money . . ." He pulled the knife from his pocket and made a menacing gesture. "Believe me. Eventually, you're going to tell me what I want to know."

An evil chuckle trailed behind him as he headed for the door.

Megan had two thoughts. Either he wasn't coming back, in which case she might sit here for who knows how long. Or he was going to come back to torture her some more . . . and then probably kill her.

# TWENTY-EIGHT

"SO THAT'S WHAT I THINK THIS REPRESENTS," SHANNON SAID AS she handed Agent Andrews the folded envelope containing the small brass key and the label.

Andrews tucked the envelope into the inside pocket of his suit coat. "You're telling me you think Radick went to ZIP Code 75035, which as I recall is about ten miles north of Dallas, and rented a private postal box. Then he mailed his share of the money from the bank robbery to himself there. So there's a package in box 299 somewhere that has a quarter of a million dollars in it. Right?"

Elena said, "It sort of makes sense. Radick wanted to stash the money where he could get it fairly easily, but where it would be safe. Using a safe-deposit box at a bank would leave a trail, but a postal box at someplace like a UPS store is about as anonymous as I can think of."

"It will take a little legwork to check all the private postal boxes in that ZIP Code," Crowder said. "Why don't you turn the key over to the Dallas police?"

Shannon started to open her mouth but shut it when Elena held up her hand. "I've explained that to your partner," she said with a nod toward Andrews. "And we appreciate your agreeing to look into this. After all, the money represents the proceeds from a bank robbery, which is in the FBI's jurisdiction."

"Not to mention that it would look good on our reviews if we wrap this up," Andrews said to his partner.

She shrugged. "Okay. We can expend a little gasoline and shoe leather, I guess."

"And you'll let us know what you find?" Shannon asked, directing her question to Andrews.

He inclined his head toward Elena. "I'll contact Mrs. Waites."

After the agents climbed back into their vehicle and drove off, Elena turned to Shannon. "Feel better?"

"I should, I guess, but frankly I don't think I'll relax until Walt Crosley is behind bars."

Mark cleared his throat. "We've been so engrossed with Crosley, I think we're forgetting one thing."

Shannon raised her eyebrows. Elena frowned.

"The police believe there were three bank robbers—Barry Radick, Walt Crosley, and the person who drove the get-away car." He let the statement hang in the air for a moment. "Radick apparently hid his share of the loot before he was killed. Crosley wants that money. But there's one more person who has a stake in all this. Who was the driver? And more important, where is he . . . or she now?"

MEGAN HEARD THE FRONT DOOR CREAK CLOSED—THE HINGES were probably too stiff with rust for Crosley to slam it. She listened for the click of a lock, but apparently Crosley decided he'd done enough to keep Megan there until he got back. Unfortunately, it seemed to her that he was right.

Because Crosley had handcuffed what he thought was her dominant hand, her right hand was still free. But how to use it to escape from the handcuffs remained a mystery to Megan. If she had something—a paper clip or a bobby pin—maybe she could pick the lock of the handcuffs. But she didn't have anything that might work. She tugged at the handcuffs, hoping that perhaps the pipe they were fastened to would break. No such luck.

Megan looked around her. The house had obviously stood empty for years, and if there was anything of value left behind by the last homeowner, it had been taken long ago by vandals. The only piece of furniture within her reach was the chair Crosley had sat in, but she had no idea how she could use it to get free of the cuffs.

Crosley had cuffed her to the drainpipe, which was about twice the diameter of the water pipes. But the drain also contained a U-shaped piece of pipe she recalled hearing someone call a "trap." This additional piece was held in place with rings that screwed it into place. Maybe she could turn them, disconnect the trap, and slide her handcuff off the pipe.

Turning the ring with her bare hands proved to be impossible. She removed the thin belt from her slacks and tried making a noose around the ring with it, but pull as she might, the ring didn't move. Apparently it was rusted firmly in place.

Maybe a lubricant was needed—but there was none here. What if she heated the junction—but how? Was there something she could use for leverage? She tried to picture a solution, but nothing came. Her situation appeared hopeless.

Megan's frustration mounted. She rolled, she twisted, she

bent almost double, but as much as she tugged, the pipe held firm. While still in a tucked position, she lashed out in frustration with her feet, kicking the pipe that held her fast, hitting it repeatedly with the sole of her shoe. She felt tears coming, and rather than trying to hold them back, she let them flow as she kicked the pipe again and again.

After one particularly vicious kick, she heard a noise. She peered at the area she'd been kicking and saw a small crack where the trap and the main pipe joined. Megan felt a tiny spark of hope.

IN GREENWOOD CEMETERY, SHADOWS WERE LENGTHENING AS Crosley pulled Megan's car to a spot where he could watch the group gathered near the Confederate soldier statue. It was frustrating to arrive at the cemetery and see people in the area he needed to search. But he was patient. He'd waited this long, he could wait a bit longer.

Ten minutes after the last vehicle pulled away, he started the car and rolled forward to the spot the blue Chevrolet had just left. He parked, made sure no one was around, and removed the short-handled shovel he'd bought and placed in the trunk of the car.

He figured he was going to feel foolish pacing off a marked distance like someone following a pirate map to buried treasure. But he'd feel much more foolish if he ignored an opportunity to find a quarter of a million dollars.

Crosley recalled Megan Frasier's instructions. Walk thirty-three paces in the direction the statue was looking. He moved to the base of the monument, looked up to be certain he was headed in the right direction, and began to pace.

Crosley was six feet tall, Radick about two inches shorter.

If Crosley shortened his normal stride by a couple of inches . . . He cursed under his breath. There was no way to exactly measure thirty-three of Radick's paces. But Megan said it would be between the two old oak trees that stood on the other side of the one-lane road from him. He counted off the paces and found that was approximately where they'd led him.

By now the sun was about to set. He wondered if they normally closed the gates at night. Would he be trapped inside? Or would whoever was responsible make a circuit through the graveyard to be certain there was no one here? He shrugged. He'd deal with whatever happened. For now, he had to dig.

Thirty minutes later, Crosley wiped sweat from his face with a wrinkled handkerchief. The hole he'd dug was surely wide and deep enough to find the money if it were there. Megan had lied to him.

With a curse, he snatched up the shovel and headed for his car. When he got back to the house, he'd make certain Megan told him the truth. Crosley touched the knife in his pocket.

This time he'd bring the woman with him. And after he found the money, the hole would serve as her grave . . . what was left of her.

MEGAN GAVE A YANK THAT SHE THOUGHT MIGHT FRACTURE HER wrist. The pipe cracked a bit more. She had hoped to gain an advantage when Crosley handcuffed her nondominant hand, but now all it meant was that she was pulling with her weaker arm.

She took a deep breath, drew back her foot, and slammed it once again into the drainpipe where it joined with the trap. She repeated the maneuver, sometimes hitting her mark, at others missing slightly. The arch of her foot was sore, but she'd worry about that later. Her wardrobe choice for this casual Friday had been designer jeans worn with shoes that had leather soles and mid-length heels. She was glad she hadn't gone with sandals.

Megan had fallen into a rhythm of kick, kick, kick, tug. She'd lost track of how many times she'd done this when a tug resulted in a definite *crunch* and the drainpipe parted. She reached under the cabinet with her free hand, slid the cuff through the space created, and scrambled to her feet.

There was no time to enjoy the freedom she'd gained. Crosley might return any minute, and one thing was certain. When he discovered she'd given him the wrong information, he'd ramp up the torture until she told him everything he wanted to know. And then he'd kill her.

ALTHOUGH MEGAN HAD BEEN HAPPY WITH HER CHOICE OF SHOES when it came to assaulting the drainpipe, now that she was trudging along the road looking for help she wished she were wearing athletic shoes. She grunted as she narrowly avoided twisting her ankle on the uneven road. Darkness was settling in, and so far neither of the houses she'd passed showed any light, or for that matter, any sign of habitation. A faint noise in the distance behind her made her turn, but she could see nothing. She knew Crosley could be coming back at any moment, so she hurried on.

Megan wasn't exactly sure where she was, but the words "in the country" seemed appropriate. Surely someone lived out here, and surely they'd be happy to help her—at least let her use their phone, maybe even protect her from Crosley if he came looking for her.

Were there lights in the window up ahead? She squinted. Yes. There were lights in the windows. Megan tried to hurry forward, but the fatigue from her ordeal and the pain from the cuts and burns Crosley had inflicted combined to slow her down. It seemed as though the house was like a mirage in the desert, never getting any closer no matter how many times she put one foot in front of the other to reach it. But finally, she drew close enough to make out details.

A dusty pickup truck sat in front of the house at the end of a gravel driveway. Although the porch light wasn't on, light spilling from the front windows showed white siding that looked to have been painted fairly recently. Irregularly shaped stones formed a walk of sorts, and three wooden steps led up to a small front porch.

She climbed the steps, leaned against the frame of the front door to gather her strength, and knocked. No response. She rapped once more, harder this time. Still no response. Finally, she banged with the side of her fist. *Please, God. Let there be someone here.*

Megan heard steps coming toward the door. Then she heard a sound like no other in the world, a sound that sent her heart into her throat—the *chuk-chuk* of a shell being jacked into the chamber of a shotgun.

"WOULD YOU LIKE SOMETHING TO EAT BEFORE WE PICK UP YOUR car at the medical center?" Mark asked as he steered his Chevrolet through the streets of downtown Dallas.

"It's up to you," Shannon said. "Are you hungry?"

"Actually, yes. After you called to say you'd be in surgery, I worked right through lunch."

Shannon turned in her seat to face him. "Now that you remind me, I missed lunch, too. Let's grab a quick sandwich somewhere." She reached into her purse and withdrew her cell phone. "While you find a place to eat, I need to call Megan and talk with her about tomorrow night. Are you free for dinner at my parents' house?"

"Sure, but would your folks let me take us all out?"

"No, my mom says it would be easier on Dad if we eat there. He's preparing his Sunday sermon."

Mark thought about that for a moment. "Good for him. Actually, from what I've read about the FCR regimen for leukemia, patients tolerate it better than a lot of other types of chemotherapy."

Shannon held up a hand. "Hang on. I'm calling Megan, and it's ringing."

Mark made one final turn, pulled into a parking slot, and turned off the ignition. "Café Brazil okay?" he asked.

Shannon nodded, then frowned. In a moment she said, "Megan, this is Shannon. Call me when you get this. I hope things are going okay with you." She ended the call and shoved the phone into her pocket.

"No answer?"

"No, and that's unusual. Megan almost always has her cell phone with her." Shannon consulted her watch. "She should be off work. And even if she's out with friends, I can't imagine her ignoring my call."

Mark shrugged. "I'd say we could go check on her, but we don't know—"

The ring of Shannon's cell phone stopped Mark in mid-sentence. She looked at the display. "I don't recognize this name or number." She started to let it go to voice mail, but her curiosity got the best of her. Shannon answered with, "Dr. Frasier."

An unfamiliar man's voice replied with a question that made Shannon's blood run cold. "Do you know someone named Megan?"

Shannon's heart raced. Why was this stranger asking about her sister? Had there been an accident? Was this some passerby who'd come upon the wreckage of Megan's car? Or was it a bartender, dealing with a patron who'd passed out from too much alcohol?

Shannon had to clear her throat twice before she could answer. "Yes. Yes, this is her sister."

The man's voice faded as though he was farther from the phone. "She says she knows you, so I guess it's okay."

The next voice on the phone was Megan's, weak and trembling. "Shannon?"

"Megan! What's happened? Where are you? Why didn't—"

"Please. Just come and get me. I'm going to hand the phone back to Mr. Jackson and he can give you directions. But come quickly. I'm hurt. And if Walt Crosley finds me, I'm dead."

MARK SAT IN MR. JACKSON'S FRONT ROOM WHILE SHANNON WAS in the kitchen doing a quick assessment of Megan's wounds.

"Thanks for taking Megan in," Mark said. "And for cutting off the handcuffs."

"Happy to help," the man in overalls said. Mark noted that a shotgun lay within easy reach beside Jackson's chair. "I only wish the lowlife who did that to her was here right now."

A moment later, Shannon appeared in the doorway and said, "She's okay to travel."

"What did you find?"

"Multiple burns on her arms, more burns and some superficial cuts on her chest, no active bleeding now, but dried blood everywhere." Shannon's voice caught. "Despite the way it looks, she didn't suffer much blood loss—just the shock of all she's been through."

Jackson rose. "Want some help getting her to your car?"

Guided by Shannon and supported by Mark and Jackson, Megan managed to move slowly out the front door and down the steps.

"Thanks for all you've done," Shannon said to Jackson.

Jackson helped ease Megan into the backseat of Mark's car. "Are you sure you don't want me to call the police? Maybe they can pick up the man who did this to her."

"It's complicated, but we'll take care of it," Mark said. "Meanwhile, I'd be careful. That man may come around looking for Megan."

"I hope he does. That's what the shotgun's for," Jackson said.

Mark pulled an old blanket out of the trunk of his car and gently tucked it around Megan. "We'll get you to an emergency room as quickly as possible."

"I just want to go home," Megan mumbled.

Shannon leaned inside the car and kissed her sister's forehead before closing the door. "I know," she said. "But I want someone to check you over. You have burns and cuts, and you're probably in some degree of shock."

Mark slid behind the wheel. "Don't worry," he said over his shoulder as he pulled away from the Jackson house. "You're safe. There's no way Walt Crosley is going to get you now." He felt the comforting weight of the .38-caliber revolver tucked into his belt. "Now should we call the police?"

Shannon answered that one. "No, because I don't know who to trust." She pulled her phone from her purse. "This was a kidnapping. I'll call Elena and ask her to contact those FBI agents again. They already know part of the story."

Mark kept one ear cocked to the conversation going on beside him. When Shannon ended the call, he looked at her and asked, "What did she say?"

"She's going to make the calls and get back to me. I told her we were headed for the ER at Parkland Hospital, and the agents will probably meet us there."

Night had fallen, and there were no streetlights to aid him, but Mark had paid attention to the landmarks and turns on the way here. The road was essentially empty, and he pushed a bit harder on the accelerator. If a policeman happened to see him speeding, he'd say that he had an emergency patient aboard and get an escort with siren and flashing lights. For the first time in days, he felt like he had the situation under control.

AS WALT CROSLEY WAS APPROACHING THE ABANDONED HOUSE where he'd left Megan, he saw a pair of headlights coming toward him. So far as he knew, the police weren't looking for this car, but just to be certain he decided to get out of sight. He pulled onto the side of the road and killed his lights. If he scooted down beneath the wheel, he figured his car would look like one left by a motorist who'd broken down.

A blue Chevrolet passed, and Crosley got only a glimpse of the passengers, but it was enough. He was pretty sure the blond woman in the passenger seat was Shannon Frasier. The man driving had been with Shannon at the cemetery, so he must be Shannon's boyfriend. Although he didn't get a good look at her face, he thought the blonde in the backseat, partially covered by a blanket, was Megan.

Crosley's mind was already crafting a plan as he wheeled his car in a tight U-turn to follow the Chevrolet. When there was enough distance between them, he'd turn on his lights. But even if he had to drive in total darkness, he was determined not to let the group get away. No, this was his chance.

His hand caressed the butt of the gun stuck in his belt. He had them all together now, and when he was through he'd know all he needed to about the bank loot. And he wouldn't leave any witnesses.

# TWENTY-NINE

SHANNON TURNED AS FAR AS HER SEAT BELT WOULD ALLOW AND put her arm over the seatback of the car. "Megan, how were you able to break that metal drainpipe?"

Megan's words were hesitant and faint. "I have no idea. I just kept kicking and praying."

"I think I know," Mark said. "The house was probably fifty years old—had to be galvanized plumbing. If you'd been handcuffed to the water lines, it might have been a different story. But the drainpipe was threaded to connect it to the P trap. When you thread a pipe like that, you cut away the outer galvanized part in a spiral fashion. That leaves a small surface that's vulnerable to rust. Over the years, rust and corrosion ate into the pipe and weakened the joint."

Shannon thought about that for a moment. "Still, it took some pretty strong kicks to finish the job."

Megan's voice was a bit stronger. "Must be from my soccer playing. Remember the injury that got me hooked on prescription painkillers in the first place? I kept playing amateur soccer after college—except when I was in rehab. I guess my legs are still strong."

"We'll be at the hospital in less than fifteen minutes," Mark said. "After they check you over, maybe we can get you home."

Megan huddled farther under her blanket. "All I want to do—"

"Hold on." Shannon glanced into her side mirror and noticed a set of headlights in the distance behind them. Had they been there earlier? *Don't be paranoid.* "Mark, has that car been following us all this time?"

Mark looked into the rearview mirror for a moment. "I haven't noticed headlights this close before now. Probably nothing, but maybe I'd better open up a little distance."

Shannon felt the slight surge as Mark accelerated. Then she turned toward Megan. "The hospital's not far ahead of us. It won't be long now."

WHERE WERE THEY GOING? CROSLEY GRIPPED THE STEERING WHEEL TIGHTER and wondered if he shouldn't try to overtake the car, force them off the road, and deal with the people on this relatively deserted stretch. He pressed down on the accelerator and began closing the distance between the two cars, but then he spied lights ahead. Not headlights—the neon signs, lit buildings, and billboards that signaled habitation.

He eased up on the accelerator and dropped back again. He might have missed this chance, but wherever they went, eventually he'd find a spot to confront them. And when he did, he intended to get the information about the money Radick stashed after the bank robbery.

And after that, there was one more share of the money

unaccounted for—the driver's share. Surely that money hadn't been spent. Most likely, like Radick's share, like most of what Crosley got, it was hidden safely. Now he intended to have it all. A quarter of a million dollars was good. Three-quarters of a million was even better.

Crosley felt like things were coming under control. The weight of the semiautomatic pistol in his waistband was comforting. The magazine of the Glock held fifteen hollow-point rounds. That should be more than enough.

"I CAN SEE PARKLAND AHEAD," SHANNON SAID.

Mark clicked his turn signal. "We may have a little wait in the emergency room."

"I'm on the faculty of the medical center. I'm on the staff at Parkland. I know all the surgery residents and most of the ER nurses," Shannon said. "I'll make sure Megan's taken care of."

Mark pulled into the parking area for the emergency room. He put the Chevrolet into a slot marked for unloading of emergency patients only. "Want me to let you out here and park the car somewhere else?"

Before Shannon could reply, a white Ford Focus stopped with its nose at a tangent across the rear bumper of Mark's Chevy, effectively blocking it in.

"That's my car!" Megan said. "And that's Crosley." She dove under the blanket like a kid hiding under the covers.

The car's lights went off, the driver's-side door opened, and Walt Crosley approached, a boxy-looking gun hanging from his right hand. He banged on Mark's window, pointed the gun at him, and made a downward motion.

Mark turned the key in the ignition and hit the button to lower the window. His shoulders twitched, and Shannon knew he was thinking of pulling the gun from his belt. She put her hand on his shoulder and whispered, "Don't."

Crosley leaned in until he could see Megan's form huddled in the backseat. "All three together. I seem to have hit the jackpot." He pulled back to keep his gun out of Mark's reach. "Which one of you ladies is going to tell me the truth about where Radick hid his share of the money from the bank? One of you better." He pointed the gun directly at Mark. "Or I'll take it out on your boyfriend here."

"Don't be—" Mark recoiled as the barrel of the gun crashed against his temple.

Shannon made a move toward Mark, but Crosley motioned her back with the gun. "That's just a sample. Next comes a bullet. Now start talking." He looked first to Shannon, then Megan. "You have thirty seconds to tell me what I want to know."

Shannon took a deep breath and said a silent prayer. "I'll tell." Behind her, she heard Megan draw in a sharp breath. Mark raised his head just enough to turn toward her, but she silenced him with a single shake of her head.

"Go ahead," Crosley said. "It better be good."

"The numbers Radick gave were GPS coordinates that led to a map he'd hidden—a map of where he'd buried the money. I've had it all along, but I didn't want to tell you." She stretched her hand toward the door of the glove compartment. "It's in here."

"Let's see it," Crosley said.

Shannon opened the glove compartment and reached in. She moved some papers aside until her fingers found what she wanted. This went against everything she felt, every principle she'd lived all her life. But she had to protect Mark.

As her hand closed around the handle of the gun she'd

recently refused, Shannon remembered what Mark told her. Point it and pull the trigger. And that's what she did.

Her first shot made Crosley stagger backward. His gun barked, and she heard Mark grunt.

Crosley was still upright, so Shannon kept pulling the trigger. The sounds of gunfire and the smell of gunpowder filled the car. Crosley slid below the open car window like a ship sinking from sight.

Shannon dropped the gun on the floor of the car. "Is anyone hurt?" she almost screamed.

"I'm okay," Megan said from the backseat.

"Mark? Mark?" Shannon leaned over and saw blood gushing from Mark's abdomen. *Oh, God. Not again.*

Two men in scrub suits ran up, followed closely by a police officer from the ER, his weapon in his hand. Shannon tumbled out of the car and raised her hands, palms outward. "I'm Dr. Frasier. The man on the ground is a wanted criminal. I shot him, but he shot my fiancé. Get me a gurney. We need to get Mark to surgery immediately."

Another orderly arrived, pushing a wheelchair. "The woman in the backseat's been hurt. Take her inside," Shannon told him.

About that time, a middle-aged man in scrubs covered by a white coat hurried up. He raised the ID badge clipped to his lapel and addressed the policeman. "I'm Dr. Waites, vice chairman of the surgery department here. I'll take over."

There was a brief argument, but the policeman allowed Shannon to trail Waites and the two orderlies into the hospital with Mark on a gurney.

Two nurses met the procession at the door. "Get a couple of IVs started. Cross match for six units of whole blood. I'll take him right to surgery," Waites said. "Shannon, you should wait down here."

"No!"

"Shannon, you know doctors shouldn't take care of family or . . . or close friends."

"Tom, if you want to assist, I'd be glad for some help. But it's important that I do this myself. I have to." *I'm not going to lose him like I did the others.*


IT WAS WELL AFTER MIDNIGHT WHEN SHANNON, STILL IN SWEAT-soaked scrubs, her hair tucked under a surgical cap, eased open the door of her sister's hospital room and peeked in. Megan lay still, the head of her bed elevated, an IV running into one arm. Dried blood had been washed away, revealing the pallor of her skin. Dabs of ointment covered her visible burns.

Megan was awake and talking in a low voice, hesitating periodically. The person on the other end of the conversation sat in a chair at Megan's bedside, leaning forward as though not to miss a word. Megan looked up when Shannon entered the room. "How's Mark?"

"Mark will make it, but it was a tough case. Crosley shot him with hollow-point bullets. That means they mushroomed once they hit his abdominal wall, effectively creating shrapnel inside the belly. I had to—" She saw Megan turn even more pale. "Never mind. I had to stop a lot of bleeding, repair a lot of injured areas, but I did it. We'll watch him in ICU for a couple of days, but he should recover with no long-term effects."

"Did the FBI agents—"

"Elena talked with them while I was in surgery. When I got out, I gave them the details of your kidnapping and what Crosley did to you . . . and to Mark. They're going to coordinate with the police now."

"Speaking of police." Detective Steve Alston rose from

Megan's bedside and held out his hand. "Dr. Frasier, so glad you weren't hurt. I appreciate you rescuing Megan. And I hope Mark is okay."

Shannon took the extended hand. "I suppose you'll want a statement from me about the shooting. How's Crosley?"

"We'll get your statement tomorrow." Alston looked at his watch. "Well, technically, later today. I know you're going to need some rest first." He shook his head. "As for Crosley, he's dead. You emptied the revolver—five shots—and three of them hit him in vital areas. He was DOA in the emergency room."

Shannon saw the room turning dark, felt it spinning around her. She'd killed a man—pulled the trigger of a gun and watched him die. But as the room slowly righted itself and her vision returned, she realized she'd been faced with a kill-or-be-killed situation. To protect the lives of her loved ones, to protect her own life, she'd reached for the gun she hoped Mark still had in the glove compartment of his car, the gun he'd bought for her protection.

Would she do it again? Shannon prayed she'd never again be faced with that decision. But at that time, under those circumstances, she'd done what she had to do to save the life of . . . What had she called Mark when talking with the ER staff? Her fiancé. And, yes, that's what he was. He just didn't know it yet.

"Doctor, are you all right?" Alston asked.

"I guess I will be. Tonight I took one life and saved one. It's going to take awhile for me to process all this." She squared her shoulders. "Does this mean I'm going to be arrested?"

Alston smiled. "No. We'll take your statement, but we have witnesses who'll swear you shot in self-defense. I doubt it will even go to a grand jury." His expression became more serious. "I need to apologize for the way I behaved during the investigation. You remind me so much of my late wife. I miss her terribly, and when I saw you . . . Let's just say that I let my feelings get out of hand." He took a deep breath and blew it out slowly. "I'm sorry. I know you're in a relationship, and I promise not to infringe on that."

"Apology accepted," Shannon said.

"What about Detective Callaway?" Megan asked. "It seemed as though he was ready to hang me, and supply the rope if necessary."

Before Alston could answer, there was a knock at the door. "Let me see who this is," Alston said. He admitted a woman in a Dallas Police Department uniform. "Perfect timing. Dr. Frasier, Ms. Frasier, this is Captain Locklear."

Shannon nodded but said nothing. What was going on here?

"Captain Locklear is with Internal Affairs," Alston said. "I think you need to hear what she has to say."

The captain was a middle-aged brunette with sad, brown eyes set deeply in an oval face above a straight nose and a thin mouth. Her police uniform bore an insignia that Shannon didn't recognize, undoubtedly a sign of rank and length of service. Locklear, who was a bit taller than Shannon, stepped gracefully forward, nodded to Megan, and extended her hand. "Doctor."

Shannon returned the handshake, wondering what Internal Affairs had to do with all this.

Locklear moved to stand next to Alston and addressed her remarks first to Shannon, then Megan. "IA has quietly been investigating Detective Callaway."

Shannon wasn't sure where this was going but decided it should be interesting.

"Detective Alston noticed that Callaway seemed focused on Megan, especially in the murder of her former boyfriend, Tony

Lester," Locklear said. "When Callaway wanted to bring her in and question her, Alston talked to me. I agreed that if we let Callaway do what he wanted—which was clearly going beyond the law—we could see what he was focused on." She turned to Megan. "I'm sorry you had to go through that. But Detective Alston did arrange to get you out as quickly as possible."

"So what was Callaway doing?" Shannon asked.

Locklear took a deep breath. "Callaway found out from one of his sources that Tony Lester was the driver for the bank robbery you already know about, so he decided to shake him down for some of the money. He went to Lester's, where he found the man stunned from a blow to the head. There was a gun on the floor—apparently dropped there by someone." She turned her penetrating gaze on Megan.

"I'm sorry," Megan said. "Yes, I sneaked back and retrieved the gun. I was afraid to face Tony without it, even with Mark there. As it turned out, the gun slipped out of my pocket in the fight, so I used a bottle to hit Tony. Then we got out of there."

Shannon turned to her sister. "Why didn't you—"

"It just seemed better to keep lying about it. I'm so sorry."

Locklear took up her narrative. "Callaway found the gun on the floor of the apartment and it gave him an idea. He slipped on a pair of the gloves he carried for use at a crime scene, picked up the gun, and threatened Lester with it. When Lester refused to pay, they struggled and Callaway shot him. Then he got rid of the gun. When your prints were found on it, he decided it was a perfect opportunity to frame you for the killing."

Megan's voice was a bit stronger this time. "So Radick was murdered in front of Shannon's house as part of a random drive-by. That had nothing to do with her. And after I moved out, Callaway shot Lester. It had nothing to do with me." She reached for the water at her bedside and took a sip. "My sister and I are in the clear with the police. Right?"

"There's the little matter of lying in your statement, but I imagine your attorney will handle that," Alston said. "So, yes, you're clear. Why?"

"I wanted to be certain my holding on to this wasn't going to get me in trouble," Megan said. "On the top shelf of the closet in my new apartment, you'll find a little coin purse. Inside it is a key. I took it from Tony's before I left him that night."

"And . . . ," Alston said.

"When Tony hid the key, he didn't know I was watching him. I heard him tell someone on the phone afterward that he'd just funded his retirement plan. I knew the key was important to him, so when I left, I took it."

"But why didn't you say something earlier?" Alston said.

"I've been afraid to say anything, especially after my gun turned out to be the weapon that killed Tony," Megan said. "Think how that would look. So I just tucked the key away and tried to forget about it."

"We'll check it out, but I'm guessing it's the key to a safe-deposit box—probably one that contains Tony's share of the money from the bank robbery," Alston said. "If that's the case, it means that three men thought they got away with three-quarters of a million dollars—and none of them are alive to spend a cent of it."

# THIRTY

SHANNON EMERGED SLOWLY FROM A TERRIFYING DREAM, ROUSED by the ringing of her doorbell interspersed with knocks on her door. She raised herself on one elbow and squinted at the bedside clock, which told her it was almost noon. She'd tumbled into bed, totally exhausted, six hours ago. She'd give anything for a bit more sleep, but the people at her door didn't show any inclination to give up and go away.

Wrapped in a light robe, her feet in scuffed slippers, Shannon made her way to the front door and looked through the peephole to see the two FBI agents to whom she'd talked just hours earlier. Agent Andrews was raising his hand to knock again while Agent Crowder stood patiently behind him.

"Okay, okay. I'm unlocking the door." Shannon swung the door wide, beckoned the agents inside, and headed for the kitchen. "I'm going to flip on the automatic coffeemaker. Would you like some when it's ready?"

Andrews overrode Crowder's "No, thank you" with "Yes, please. Milk and sugar."

In a moment, Shannon padded back into the living room and gestured the agents to the sofa. "It'll be ready in a few minutes. Now, how can I help you?"

"Obviously we woke you, and we're sorry for that," Andrews said. "None of us got much sleep last night. But I thought you might like a follow-up."

Shannon cocked an ear toward the kitchen. No, the coffee was still perking. "I thought I gave you what you needed last night. This morning, I mean. Anyway, just a few hours ago."

Andrews shook his head. "This is about the key and label you gave us yesterday. We figured that since we were already up, we should do some looking this morning."

"Some of us decided," Crowder said. "Others wanted to get some sleep."

Andrews glared at his partner, then continued, "Anyway, we got lucky at the third place we tried, and I thought we should stop by and let you know what we found."

Crowder smothered a yawn. "Whereas I thought—"

Andrews quickly went on. "We found a private mailbox business that had a box 299, and the key fit."

"Was it a large mailbox? Did you find the money inside?"

Crowder smiled. "Nope. It was the smallest mailbox they had, and it didn't contain money."

Shannon felt disappointment well up. "So it was a wild-goose chase?"

"Not at all," Andrews said. "Apparently Radick was afraid the bills he got in the robbery might be marked, so he used them to get something a bit more portable." The agent reached into his coat pocket and pulled out a small evidence bag, about the right size to hold a box of kitchen matches. Inside was a chamois pouch, cinched at the neck. He dropped it onto the coffee table in front of him, and Shannon heard a clink like a bag of marbles. "This is going to the evidence room just as soon as we leave here, but first I thought you might like to see how many diamonds a quarter of a million dollars will buy."

MARK KEPT DRIFTING IN AND OUT OF SLEEP. HE KNEW THE DREAMS were morphine-induced, and they left him feeling alternately euphoric and depressed. When the nurse entered his ICU room, he asked her to remove his morphine pump. He'd rather hurt than go through more of the dreams.

He had no idea how long afterward Shannon came into his room. She wore a simple red summer dress covered by a fresh lab coat. A stethoscope was draped around her neck, a symbol that attested even more convincingly than her white coat that she was a doctor and belonged in this setting.

She walked softly to his bedside, bent, and kissed him on the lips. "I did that about eighteen hours ago when you came out of surgery, but you didn't know it then. Now you do."

"What happened? The last thing I remember is Crosley firing, then feeling like I'd been kicked in the stomach by a mule."

"Crosley's dead. He shot you before I killed him with the gun from your glove compartment."

"Are you okay?" Mark asked.

"I'm having a hard time coming to grips with killing a man. I still don't like guns, but in this case I'm glad one was available."

"How about Megan?"

"She'll be fine. She's in a room on another floor. And while I was with her after your surgery, Detective Alston and a captain from the police Internal Affairs Division gave me some interesting news about Jesse Callaway."

Mark had to concentrate to follow the narrative, but when it was over he said, "I guess that explains some things."

"Why don't you rest a bit?" Shannon said. She used her stethoscope to listen for a moment to Mark's chest and abdomen. "Bowel sounds aren't back yet, but that's expected. You'll have to be on IVs for a while, but that's a small price to pay for still being alive."

"Who . . . who did my surgery?"

"I did. Tom Waites assisted."

"But . . . you told me you had to work through panic attacks when you operate on a patient with a gunshot wound. How did you—"

"I wanted to do it. It was important for me, and I didn't have any problem. I guess this was what they call getting back on the horse after you've been thrown. Besides, I had to save my fiancé."

It took Mark a few moments to process her last words. "You mean . . ."

"I'm so sorry I've kept you dangling for this long." Shannon took his hand, careful of the IV. "The past two weeks have been the most difficult of my life. But it's over now, and I'm stronger for having gone through it."

Mark started to say something, but she stilled him with a finger to his lips. "I've discovered that I love you more deeply than I ever thought possible. I can't imagine my life without you in it. If you'll still have me, I'd love to marry you."

"I've been waiting for this day," Mark said. "Of course I want to marry you."

Shannon paused. "You know, there's still the shadow of my HIV exposure hanging over us."

"As I've told you, the odds of that turning into infection are too small to even consider. We'll have our answer in just a few more weeks. Meanwhile, I have faith that God's going to get us through this, just as He has with everything else in our lives."

"I don't think my faith will ever be as strong as yours," Shannon said. "But I'm trying."

Mark smiled. "It's a long journey, but just remember that the Bible tells us two are better than one, for if one falls, the other can pick him up."

Shannon smiled. "I don't know as many scriptures as you— at least, not yet. But you can teach me."

# EPILOGUE

THINGS WERE GOING WELL FOR SHANNON. SHE'D JUST RECEIVED the results of her six-month HIV test, and there was no sign of disease. Theoretically, she had nothing further to worry about in that respect. However, as a surgeon, she knew there was always a chance she'd be exposed again. That was a risk all physicians took.

Her father's prognosis was good since he'd undergone a bone marrow transplant—with Megan as the donor. He'd had to take a leave from preaching, but he was gaining strength each day.

Megan was still clean and straight, determined to keep her life turned around while making good decisions. She'd been out on a few dates with Steve Alston. They sat together at church, but Megan had yet to ask him to come with her to Sunday dinner at their parents' home. Meanwhile, Shannon was keeping a big sister's eye on the relationship.

Mark had recovered from his gunshot wounds, although

he still had occasional pain from adhesions. They'd set a wedding date and would be married in another month. Shannon felt both nervous and hopeful as the day approached.

But there was one more thing Shannon needed to do before her marriage, something she should have done long ago, yet had been unable to carry out until now.

Shannon's stomach was turning flips as she drove down the tree-lined street. She hadn't been here in years, but she had no trouble finding the house. Put the two-story Austin stone home in the midst of West Dallas and it would stand out like the Taj Majal. But in this quiet area of Highland Park it was probably the least expensive structure in the neighborhood, sitting among others that would fetch a couple of million dollars.

She pulled her coat about her against the winter chill as she stepped from her Toyota. Shannon paused in the semicircular driveway in front of the home. What if Todd's mother didn't want to see her, didn't want to be reminded of what might have been? What if she was angry about the extended silence from Shannon since the shooting? Was it possible that the Richardsons in some way blamed Shannon for not saving their son's life?

Shannon squared her shoulders and strode purposefully toward the house. She hurried onto the porch, not stopping for fear she'd panic and turn away, and rang the doorbell. Her heart was still hammering when a white-haired woman in a sweater and slacks opened the door.

"Yes?" She dropped her head to peer over her metal-rimmed glasses, and recognition lit her face. She stepped forward and extended her arms. "Shannon. What a wonderful surprise."

After a hug that Shannon thought might fracture her

ribs, Mrs. Richardson said, "Come in. Come in." She gestured through the door. "Let's sit in the living room. There's a fire going in there. Would you like some coffee?"

Shannon eased into an armchair with a view through sliding glass doors of a beautifully manicured back lawn shaded by trees now bare of leaves. "Nothing for me, thanks," she said. "I thought—"

"It's so good to see you. How are you? I haven't seen you in . . ."

Shannon knew this wasn't going to be the quick in-and-out visit she'd hoped for. "I know—not since a few months after Todd died. I probably should have kept in touch, but . . . frankly, I couldn't face those memories."

Mrs. Richardson looked down at her hands, loosely clasped in her lap. "I understand. We still miss him. The hurt never fully goes away." She was silent a moment, then said, "But life goes on. His sister . . . you remember Alice? She's married now, and we have two wonderful grandsons."

"I know. I got the invitation to her wedding. I'm sorry I wasn't able to make it." *Get on with it. Do what you came for.* Shannon reached into her purse and pulled out a small box. "Mrs. Richardson, you sent me this ring shortly after Todd died. I appreciate that, and I've held on to it for years. But . . . but now I've met someone. We're going to be married, and I don't feel right keeping this."

The expression on Mrs. Richardson's face was hard for Shannon to read. Then she smiled. "I've thought about you a lot over the years. I know you and Todd would have been happy together. That didn't happen, but I'm glad you've found someone else. We wish you nothing but the best."

Shannon held out the box. "Do you think one of your grandsons might want to give this to his fiancée one day?"

Mrs. Richardson shook her head. "I have a better idea. I heard from a friend that your father had been ill. Leukemia, wasn't it?"

"Yes. But he's much better now."

"Do you think it would be appropriate if I took this ring to a jeweler friend of ours and sold it, then gave the money for leukemia research?"

Shannon smiled at the simplicity of the solution. "I think that would be wonderful."

They chatted for a bit longer until Shannon said, "I have to go. I'm meeting Mark for dinner. But I'll be back. I promise."

When Shannon left, she noticed the winter clouds had parted and she could see the sun shining. That was a perfect image of the way her life had turned around—for too long her soul had been mired in winter, but now she felt the warmth of the sun. For the first time in a decade she felt free of a burden she hadn't even been aware she was carrying—the burden of perceived failure, of a promise unfulfilled.

As she drove away, Shannon thought about the changes in her life since that fall evening ten years ago when she knelt helplessly at the side of the man she loved and watched him die. She remembered the vow she'd made then—to Todd and to herself. Shannon recalled the lives she'd saved since that time. Just as important was the way her life had changed.

*Todd, some battles I won, some I lost. But I wasn't helpless in the face of death. And I'll never be again. I have the talents and the training, and I'll use them. I think you'd be proud of me.*

# READING GROUP GUIDE

1. Shannon and Megan are PKs (preacher's kids). Have you known any PKs? Did they demonstrate behavior and character traits that you (or they) ascribed to growing up in a preacher's home? Do you think Shannon and/or Megan showed any evidence of such traits?

2. Mark fell away from faith when he went to college, but instead of continuing his slide while in medical school (which is often the case), he returned to a deeper relationship with God. What things might affect the faith of a physician in training? Would they be more likely to draw a believer away from God or closer to Him?

3. The name of the rehab facility where Megan met Barry Radick was First Step. The first step in the Alcoholics Anonymous twelve-step program (http://www.aa.org /en_pdfs/smf-121_en.pdf) involves recognizing that the individual is powerless in the face of their addiction. Six of the remaining eleven steps mention God. Do

you think that's important? Should addiction therapy be God-centered? Why or why not?

4. Shannon prayed that her boyfriend's life might be spared after he was gunned down, yet Todd died. This caused her to erect a wall between herself and God. What would you say to her if she voiced this anger with God to you? Do you think this is a common feeling?

5. There's a saying that there are no atheists in a foxhole. Megan admitted that she prayed when she thought she was going to die handcuffed to a drainpipe. Shannon prayed for her sister while she was in jail, but had to be reminded to thank God after Megan was released. We've all been in situations where we called on God to save us, to help us out of a jam. In your particular situation, did you have to be reminded to thank Him when He came through? If He didn't come through in the way you wanted, were you angry?

6. Shannon had problem after problem heaped on her. Do you believe that God never gives us more than we can handle? How do you think that works (or doesn't work)?

7. Through all their problems, Pastor and Mrs. Frasier seemed almost placid in their faith at times. Do you think they were hiding their anxiety, or were they really content to cast their burdens on God? Do you think a minister should have (and demonstrate) deeper faith than a layperson? What do you think are the hallmarks of faith under fire?

8. Mark resented Megan's intrusion into his and Shannon's lives. He was frustrated by Shannon's failure to commit to marriage. He seemed to hide both these things well, though. Do you think he should have been more vocal? Is freedom from outward evidence of faults the hallmark of a Christian?

# ACKNOWLEDGMENTS

THOSE FAMILIAR WITH THE CAMPUS WILL NOTE THAT I'VE TAKEN some literary license with the setup of the University of Texas Southwestern Medical Center in Dallas. This was necessary because that campus is now changing almost from month to month, and what I depicted at the time of writing might not be accurate at the time of publication. I decided it was simpler to make the description fit my needs, so I did.

My son, Allen Mabry, is an avid practitioner of geocaching, and I'm indebted to him for his advice about that activity, including furnishing the GPS coordinates for Greenwood Cemetery in downtown Dallas. I've changed the coordinates slightly from the true ones so as not to interfere with genuine geocaches in that location, but if you follow the ones listed in the book you should find a beautiful old historic cemetery that's worth a visit. However, you won't discover loot from a bank holdup there—at least, I don't think so.

I'm indebted to my agent, Rachelle Gardner, for her hard

work on my behalf, as well as her friendship. I'm grateful to all the authors who have taught, befriended, and encouraged me along my road to writing. And, as always, my thanks go to you, my readers, for your support.

A great deal of credit for this novel goes to my wife, Kay, my first reader, who suggested a number of improvements to the storyline. I continue to be grateful for the support of my children: Allen and Lynne, Brian and Catherine, Ann and Benny, David, and Shelly, as well as the patience during my writing time of my grandchildren: Cassie, Kate, Ryan, and Connor.

I'm truly blessed to work with the excellent people at Thomas Nelson. As *Critical Condition* came together, the editorial work of Amanda Bostic was outstanding—she continues to make me look better than I deserve. I appreciate the editing touch of Deborah Wiseman as the manuscript took final form. Becky Monds, Jodi Hughes, and the crew did a great job of actually putting the book together. Kristen Vasgaard designed an eye-catching cover. And, of course, no one would have heard of this novel without the efforts of Laura Dickerson and Katie Bond.

As I've said in other books, I can think of no better final acknowledgment than the one adopted by Johann Sebastian Bach and George Frideric Handel for their works: *Soli Deo gloria*. "To God alone be glory." May it always be so.

# Enjoy these other medical suspense novels from Dr. Richard Mabry.

"You are not going to want to miss
Dr. Richard Mabry's newest thrill ride!"
— USA Today (on *Stress Test*)

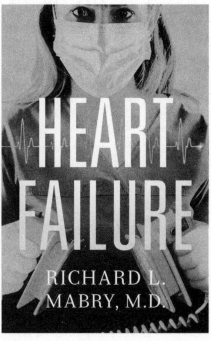

THOMAS NELSON
*Since 1798*

thomasnelson.com

**AVAILABLE IN PRINT AND EBOOK**

# ABOUT THE AUTHOR

Photo by Jodie Westfall

A RETIRED PHYSICIAN, DR. RICHARD MABRY IS THE AUTHOR OF SIX previous critically acclaimed novels of medical suspense. His previous works have been finalists for the Carol Award and Romantic Times Reader's Choice Award, and have won the Selah Award. He is a past vice president of American Christian Fiction Writers and a member of the International Thriller Writers. He and his wife live in North Texas.